AFFAIR OF THE HEART

"Frankie," he said, his lips moving to brush her cheek, his arms wrapped around her. "Do you want me as much as I want you?"

"More."

"Why the hell didn't you tell me?"

It was all so complicated that she didn't answer, so many things assumed, and she had been wrong about all of them—two people perhaps not open enough with each other.

He helped her undress then, touching her with the same gentleness he had used when she had cried in the night, then took his own clothes off while she watched.

It was all new, the way she felt about him, the way they touched each other, the way they lay together on the mattress, but when they came together, which was the newest of all, she had the sense of something very old, something immensely valuable, of having entered a venerable society she would never leave, of having arrived . . .

DON'T MISS THESE UNFORGETTABLE LOVE STORIES!

PLACES   (2004, $3.95)
by Robin St. Thomas
Diamonds. Minks. Designer originals. The finest cuisine. The most exclusive clubs. Who can resist the jet-setting world of the spectacularly wealthy? And who will be able to resist PLACES, a glittering novel about a special golden girl groomed to take her place at the top, and prepared for everything—except love.

AS SOON AS IT RAINS   (2067, $3.95)
by Kaylie Jones
Chloe was on the run, trying to outdistance the painful memories of her past with drinking, drugs, and sleeping around with various men—until she remembers the one time she was truly happy: in Paris, France, the city of lights. Compelled to return to this enchanted place, Chloe is now an adult with a purpose—to discover who she really is and find the key to her own future!

TEXAS DREAMS   (1875, $3.95)
by Micah Leigh
For Fontayne, power is an aphrodisiac. She gambles in the playground of the world's oil empire as if it were a child's sandbox; but as she nears the pinnacle of her desires, a past scandal surfaces and threatens to destroy all her carefully planned TEXAS DREAMS.

SOMEBODY PLEASE LOVE ME   (1604, $3.95)
by Aviva Hellman
Beautiful high-fashion model Cat Willingham became a vulnerable, sensuous woman in Clay Whitfield's arms. But she wondered if her independence was too great a price to pay for passion.

LOVE AFFAIR   (2181, $4.50)
by Syrell Rogovin Leahy
Young and innocent Frankie Grant is stunned at first by the frenzied glamorous world of New York City, but feels she has nothing left to loose: at twenty-one, she has already lived a lifetime of tragedy. Now all she wanted was to see the lobby of the Waldorf-Astoria. But when Henry J. MacIver, a reporter on sabbatical, discovered the beautiful woman-child, he knew he was to be the one to shelter her from the harsh truth of the big city—and that neither their lives or their hearts—would ever be quite the same again.

Available wherever paperbacks are sold, or order direct from the Publisher. Send cover price plus 50¢ per copy for mailing and handling to Zebra Books, Dept. 2181, 475 Park Avenue South, New York, N.Y. 10016. Residents of New York, New Jersey and Pennsylvania must include sales tax. DO NOT SEND CASH.

L O V E
Affair

SYRELL ROGOVIN LEAHY

ZEBRA BOOKS
KENSINGTON PUBLISHING CORP.

In memory of
Sylvan Davis

ZEBRA BOOKS

are published by

Kensington Publishing Corp.
475 Park Avenue South
New York, NY 10016

First Zebra Books printing: October 1987

The author gratefully acknowledges permission from CBS U Catalog Inc. to reproduce lyrics from "The Last Thing on My Mind" by Tom Paxton, © 1964, 1969 United Artists Music Co., Inc. Rights assigned to CBS Catalogue Partnership. All rights controlled and administered by CBS U Catalog Inc. All rights reserved. International copyright secured.

Printed in the United States of America

Are you going away with no word of farewell?
Will there be not a trace left behind?
Well I could have loved you better,
Didn't mean to be unkind,
You know that was the last thing on my mind.

—Tom Paxton

With many thanks to
Detective James L. V. Wegman

She said "Bye," when they came up to the

*Part
One*

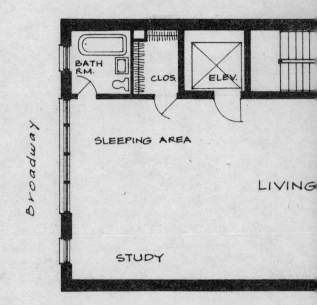

Broadway

BATH RM.

CLOS.

ELEV.

SLEEPING AREA

LIVING

STUDY

NORTH

0 2 4 6 8 10

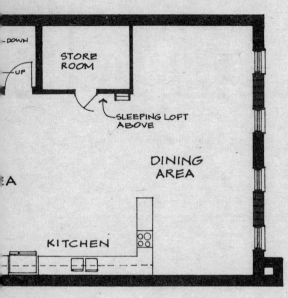

—DOWN

—UP

STORE
ROOM

SLEEPING LOFT
ABOVE

DINING
AREA

EA

KITCHEN

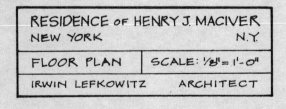

RESIDENCE OF HENRY J. MACIVER
NEW YORK   N.Y.

| FLOOR PLAN | SCALE: 1/8" = 1'-0" |
| IRWIN LEFKOWITZ | ARCHITECT |

One

Besides the Empire State Building and the Statue of Liberty, the only other place in New York that she knew anything about was the Waldorf-Astoria. She was walking toward it now, or hoped she was, assuming the directions she had been given were correct. There had been a lot of pointing and excessive verbiage in the directions. Where she came from, people spoke rather plainly, offering fewer and less-confusing alternatives. Their voices did not singsong quite so much and their hands remained still. It almost gave one the feeling of being in a foreign country.

It was cold but not nearly so cold as the place she had left only yesterday, and by comparison, there was very little snow here. She felt good, refreshed, not the least bit tired although it was dark and very likely late. She had wanted to spend the first day of the year in New York but her arrival had been delayed twelve hours and so she would have to be content to spend the first night of the year here. She was content. She was more than content. She was happy.

13

Even after the long walk the suitcase in her right hand had not grown heavy. The rest of her belongings, the heavy and unmanageable, were checked. In a day or so she would retrieve them. But first, she wanted to see the Waldorf-Astoria and then find a place to stay, perhaps a Y if she could find one in the telephone book.

But right now finding a place to stay seemed a very small problem, one she could afford to ignore. All the problems were behind her. The bad year had ended and the good one had begun.

The street she was walking on was called Lexington Avenue. (The man who had directed her had said, with much waving of his arms, "Look honey, the streets run this way, the avenooz run that way. This way's east, that way's west. Got it? Now you know the city.") No one had ever told her how simply and cleverly the city was laid out. In five minutes she had the sense of knowing her way around.

In the next block a buslike vehicle had parked beside the curb and atop a nearby car lights were flashing. There were four or five women on the street and they sounded shrilly angry. She crossed the street to get a better look.

Now that she was closer she could see that the flashing lights were on a police car. She wondered if there had been an accident, but there didn't seem to be an ambulance around. The police car was reassuring. If the police had arrived, the situation was under control.

They were strange group of women. Two of them were black. All of them were being herded into the van by two men wearing blue jeans, one in sneakers

14

and one in what looked like old army boots. Around each man's neck hung a silver badge on a chain. Beyond them, watching the scene, was a solid-looking policeman talking to a taller man in civilian clothes, one of those brown corduroy zipper jackets with a furry collar, a sport shirt showing at the neck where the zipper had not quite closed.

"Let's move it, sweetheart," one of the men wearing a badge said in a pleasant voice.

"Me?" she asked and at the same moment felt a strong hand on her arm, urging her toward the van.

"You, sweetheart. I don't have all night."

"Where am I going?" She resisted the push and the man with the badge glared at her.

"Ah, don't give me a hard time, a'right? It's late. Get in and we'll talk later."

"I'm just looking for the Waldorf-Astoria." A flurry of panic was starting to build somewhere in her midsection.

"Yeah, and I'm gonna hit the lottery for a million dollars. Move."

"No." She said it loudly and swung her body toward him so that the suitcase hit his leg.

He said, "Ow," and gripped her arm more tightly. "Get inside," he said sternly.

One of the women in the van had begun shouting angrily to leave the kid alone; couldn't he see she didn't belong there?

"Tell it to the judge," he shot back.

"I am not getting in there." She stood her ground firmly, wondering what law she could possibly have broken by walking down a street carrying a suitcase.

"What the hell is going on here?" It was the

15

uniformed policeman who had been standing on the sidelines.

"Lady's being obstreperous," the man with the badge said.

The policeman gave her a quick once-over. His eyes spent an extra second on the suitcase. "What're you doing with that bunch?" he asked gruffly.

"I'm looking for the Waldorf-Astoria."

"Well you're headed the right way." He tilted his head in the uptown direction. "You meeting someone there?"

"I just wanted to see it."

"You just come into town?"

"About an hour ago."

"Christ, Comiskey." He looked at the man with the badge hanging around his neck. "You arrest everyone walks in front of you? This is a kid in blue jeans with a suitcase. Didn't you *look* at her?"

"Sorry, Sarge."

"You know what'll happen she brings an action against you?" The sergeant turned back to her. "Come with me," he said. They walked back to where he had been standing beside the man in the brown corduroy jacket. "Look, honey, this is no place for a lady. You got somewhere to stay tonight?"

"Not yet."

"You weren't thinking of the Waldorf, were you?"

She smiled, feeling much better. "No, of course not."

"You got friends in the city?"

"No."

"You got anyone?"

"No."

"So you're just walkin' through the streets with that suitcase lookin' for a nice place to stay." The idea seemed to disgust the policeman.

"I thought . . ."

"Yeah, I know what you thought." He exhaled steamily. "Mac." He turned to the man in the brown corduroy zippered jacket. "Get her off the street, will ya? Find her a place to stay. Take her home for the night. Your wife's a good sport. OK?"

"C'mon, Tom."

"Do me a favor. You can't leave her walkin' around. She'll freeze to death if something worse don't happen first. I got a daughter her age, she's married and divorced already. Do it for me, Mac. Buy her a hamburger and give her a bed to sleep in. I'll even pay for the hamburger." He dug a chunky hand into the pocket of his uniform pants.

"Owe it to me," the man in the jacket said with an edge of irritation in his voice.

"I owe you. And you'll collect, I promise. I'm gonna call you this week like we talked about. Everything you need, you're gonna get, OK? Consider me Mr. Cooperation. You just put her back on the train to Altoona in the morning."

"Thanks, Tom." He didn't sound especially grateful. He turned away from the policeman and faced her. "Give me your bag."

"Thank you."

"Let's see if we can find a cab." He looked up the avenue.

"Are you in a hurry?"

He turned to look at her and a taxi went by, the lights on its roof lit. "I'm not in a hurry," he said

17

resignedly. "I got what I came for. And more. What can I do for you?"

"Could we walk through the Waldorf-Astoria?"

"Why not?" he said dryly, addressing neither her nor the policeman who had conveniently disappeared. He stepped off the curb. "This way."

The van pulled away, they walked farther uptown and she followed him across the street to a revolving door.

"This is the Waldorf-Astoria. Push."

Inside was an empty vestibule with escalators on the right.

"This is the back entrance," he explained. "We can go up and through and come out on Park Avenue."

"You're angry, aren't you?"

"Forget it. It's not your fault. Tom McManus and his heart of gold."

"I think he does."

"Does what?"

"Have a heart of gold."

He nodded his head toward the escalator. "Let's go."

It was a long distance up. She stepped off onto an indoor carpeted street of beautiful shops, all closed—Oriental antiques, leather goods, dresses that she could not have afforded and would not have known where to wear if she could. She walked slowly, stopping at each window. An umbrella that could make one long for rain. Crystal that shimmered with a rainbow of colors. She had heard that it was beautiful and elegant but she had not expected all this.

They went through a lobby, passed the elevators

and came out into another lobby with a huge round mosaic in the floor.

"It's called the Wheel of Life," her reluctant companion said.

"What is?"

"What you're standing on."

She looked down briefly at the mosaic, then up at the massive chandelier above it and drew her breath in a gasp. "It's wonderful, isn't it?"

"I suppose it is."

"There must be a thousand pieces."

"At least."

"Do you come here often?"

"Once in a while. Sometimes I cut through from Lexington to Park."

"It isn't the least bit disappointing." She had not taken her eyes off the glittering glass since the first moment she had seen it and the images had started to move crazily. "Everyone back home said New York would be a disappointment. They said it was a dirty city and the people were heartless. I knew they'd be wrong." She looked away, seeing lights superimposed on the man in the brown jacket.

"Ready?"

"Yes."

The walked through the rest of the lobby, down the stairs, and out onto the street. Along the divider that ran down the center, there were lighted trees as far as she could see.

"You can give me the suitcase now," she said.

"I can carry it."

"I mean, you can leave me here."

"I'm taking you home with me."

"It's OK. I won't tell the policeman. It was nice of you to—"

He opened the door of the nearest yellow taxi and said, "Get in."

She hesitated but he put the suitcase in the front seat next to the driver and she knew she couldn't go anywhere without it so she got in. He gave the driver an address that was neither an avenue nor a numbered street—in fact, it sounded like Broadway which was crazy because everyone knew people didn't live on Broadway—so that now she didn't have any idea at all where she was going. The driver drove to the corner, swung around the divider in a U, and went back down Park Avenue.

"My name's MacIver."

"How do you do. I'm Frances Louise Grant."

"Frances Louise," he echoed.

"Grant," she completed.

"I get the picture."

"I hope your wife doesn't mind the extra company."

"So do I."

When she thought about it, she was glad he had insisted that she get into the taxi. Going to someone's home meant having a cup of hot coffee or, if there were children, perhaps hot chocolate. Maybe it meant the warmth of a fire before lying down to sleep. She could remember a winter night in another year when snow had blocked the Interstate and marooned drivers had made their way to the nearest houses for shelter and sustenance. She was glad now she had been able to help.

"Your folks know you're in New York?" MacIver

asked.

"Probably."

"You come in on the train?"

"Bus."

"Bus? Where'd it leave you off?"

"At the bus station."

"You mean the Port Authority Bus Terminal?"

"I think that's what they called it."

"How did you get to Lexington?"

"I walked."

"You walked from Ninth Avenue to Lexington by yourself with a suitcase at ten o'clock at night?" He sounded incredulous.

"It was probably only nine when I started out."

"You know, it's dangerous to walk the streets of New York alone at night, Frances." He said it kindly, a friend offering friendly advice.

"I didn't bother anyone and no one bothered me."

"You were lucky. How old are you?"

She hesitated. "I'm over twenty-one."

"And you wouldn't lie to me."

She smiled. "No."

"I didn't think you would."

"That van on Lexington Avenue. Where were those women going?"

"That was a police van. The pussy posse. They were rounding up the whores."

She felt her eyes widen. "On Lexington Avenue?"

"Even Lexington. Until the police roust them."

He reached into his pants pocket, leaning slightly toward her, and pulled out a wallet. Outside the window the city had changed. The streets had narrowed, the buildings become lower, older, and more

21

deserted. Mostly they were stores closed for the New Year holiday. She could not believe anyone lived here.

"On the left," he said and the taxi moved over and slowed. "That's it." The taxi stopped.

She was on the left side and she opened the door and stepped out onto the street, looking around, wondering which of these seemingly deserted buildings he might live in.

MacIver pulled her suitcase out of the front of the taxi and joined her on the sidewalk. "This way," he said.

He stopped next to a shop called Pragmatique in fancy script. In the window were all sorts of seemingly impractical things that one might wear in the rain if one really didn't mind getting wet. It was a building like all the others, with a massive door that MacIver opened with a key. Inside on the left wall was a row of mailboxes. She read off the names: PODOLSKI, T. QUEEN, MACIVER, GEORGE F. GOLDSTEIN, SHISKIN-WRIGHT, a strange assortment.

"In here, Frances."

"In here" was an elevator. He pressed four and it lifted slowly. When it came to a stop, the door slid open to expose a second one that could have been the front door of a house in the country. MacIver used two keys and the door opened into absolute darkness.

"Careful," he said. Then he flicked a switch and a huge expanse of empty space was suddenly lighted.

She said, "Oh," in surprise and walked in, hearing the door close behind her and a lock set. Across the large room and to the left there was what seemed to be a kitchen and against the same wall, but all the way to the right, a couch with a pillow and blanket on it. Near that was a desk stacked with papers. On top of some books piled on the floor next to the desk was a telephone. At either end of the strange, enormous room was a wall of windows.

"It isn't furnished yet," he said, as though there might have been some other explanation for the emptiness. "I just moved in."

"I thought you said — I thought you had a family," she finished lamely.

"They live uptown." He unzipped the jacket and pulled it off. "Give me your coat."

She did not move. "I'm really sorry about this. I could have stayed at the Y."

"Sergeant McManus with the heart of gold would have come after me with his boys in blue. Give me your coat, Frances."

She unbuttoned it slowly and took it off. "Nobody's called me Frances since my great-aunt died."

He looked at her, waiting.

"Frankie," she said.

"Frankie is much better." MacIver smiled and hung the coat and the jacket in a closet past a door next to the elevator. "Come with me, Frankie. I've got bread, cheese, and lots of coffee. Then you can get some sleep before we decide what to do with you in the morning."

She followed him across the huge expanse of highly polished floor. "I've never seen a floor this big in my life. Where are your *rooms?*"

"This is what's called a loft in New York. This building was an old mill, then a warehouse of some sort. Now it's apartments. I'm here alone and I don't need rooms, except for the bathroom. So I'm leaving it like this. It'll look different when the furniture comes. I've put it in the hands of my"—he hesitated—"a friend of mine who's a decorator."

"And the other people on the other floors? Do they also live without rooms?"

"Some with, some without. Pretty much the way they want it."

"Isn't that wonderful." That was the New York she had come to see, where people did what they wanted. She had only been in the city for two hours and already she had found something different and wonderful. "How does someone get a name like Shiskin-Wright?" she asked, her tongue stumbling over the first syllable.

"It isn't a person, it's two people. She's Naomi Shiskin and he's Everett Wright. They live together without the benefit of holy matrimony. Are you familiar with that sort of arrangement?"

"Oh yes, and I think it's marvelous. I think it must be much more romantic to live together than to marry."

"Wright thinks so. Shiskin isn't all that sure."

"Where's the Empire State Building?" she asked.

Standing in front of the sink he thrust a thumb over his left shoulder.

"And the Statue of Liberty?"

He pointed ahead of him with his index finger, indicating the wall. The coffee had begun to scent the room and she thought for the first time in hours that she might be hungry.

"How long would it take to get to the ocean?"

24

"I wouldn't go now. I'd wait till summer. It's bitter cold out there in the winter."

"I won't be here in the summer."

"I see." He put three large wedges of cheese and a long loaf of bread on a square table made of butcher block.

"That's French bread, isn't it?"

"Or a close approximation. There's a bakery I go to."

"It's a wonderful city, isn't it?" She could feel the old excitement surging. It was all true. "Whores on Lexington Avenue, a policeman with a heart of gold, a house with no rooms. I can hardly believe I'm really here."

"And the ocean less than an hour away," MacIver said, adding to the inventory.

"An hour away. Imagine being that close to the ocean." Frankie spread a strange-looking cheese on a round of French bread and bit into it. "Oh my," she said as the taste registered sharply on her tongue. "I've never tasted anything like it."

"Gorgonzola," MacIver said. "A little strong for you, I think."

"Oh no." She swallowed it and took a sip of coffee. "It's marvelous. It's absolutely marvelous. You know, that's what I'm going to do tomorrow. I'm going to see the ocean."

She told MacIver she didn't want the couch he had been sleeping on. She would much rather sleep on the air mattress he spread on the floor because then she could stretch all night to make up for all the

25

hours she had sat on the cramped bus. The shower was steamy and relaxing and when she opened her suitcase to take out her nightclothes, she looked at the two photographs of three people with more than the usual feeling. Then she spread herself out and slept.

Two

"Where are you from?" MacIver asked. They were sitting at the same square table in the kitchen area eating toast and drinking coffee.

She used her thumb to point in the direction she assumed was west.

MacIver smiled. "Come to the big city to make your fortune?"

"Not this time. This time I just want to get to know it so that when I come back in a few years, I won't be a stranger. Three months is long enough, isn't it?"

"More than enough. You crossed most of Manhattan last night. You planning to work?"

"Maybe. I'm a very good typist."

"They don't use typewriters anymore in this city. Everybody's got a fancy machine with a screen."

"That's OK. I took a course last year. I'm good in that too."

"Sounds like you've got it made. Did you bring any money with you?"

"Oh yes. Lots. And I intend to spend it."

"You won't have any trouble doing that in New York."

"Good." She smiled. "I'll do the dishes, Mr. Mac-Iver. You've done enough already." He had stood with his own and was carrying them to the sink.

"Nobody's called me Mister since my great-aunt died," he said.

She felt herself blush.

"Mac."

"OK."

"Just don't break any," he said, setting his down in the sink and opening a door under the counter that disclosed a dishwasher. "There's a very small margin for error."

She rinsed them quickly, loaded them in the machine, and went to the bathroom with her brush and comb. Leaning against the wall was an almost full-length mirror in which she could see herself from the shoulders down. She was fairly tall, about five-six, and leggy. Without the face, she looked rather nondescript, a skinny kid in a maroon shirt and jeans that had not yet faded. The brown belt with the handmade silver buckle had been Kenny's. The belt was too long but she had poked an extra hole in it to make it fit. She bent to see her face. There was too much hair and it was too curly for today's styles but the curls were natural and the abundance had been planned. She had not cut it for months, preferring to leave that experience for New York. As soon as she could, she would find a chic salon and put herself in the hands of an expert.

When she left the bathroom, MacIver was just returning with the paper. She put the last of her things in the suitcase, closed it, and stood it up near the air mattress.

"It's a holiday today, isn't it?" she asked as he took the jacket off.

"That's right. It's just as deserted out there today as it was yesterday."

"If you wouldn't mind my leaving the suitcase, I'd like to take a quick look at the ocean and then come back and find a place to stay."

"A quick look," MacIver said.

"I can always go back another time for a longer look. It's just that I've waited so long to see it, I don't want to let another day go by."

He was still holding his jacket. "Come on, I'll take you."

"No, really."

"It's my last day of vacation too. I probably haven't seen the ocean close up for as many years as you."

"Well . . ."

He put his jacket back on. "Is that all you have to wear?"

"This and my coat."

"Not enough." He went to the invisible bedroom and rummaged around some boxes and suitcases. "Try this on." He tossed a tan shetland sweater through invisible walls and she caught it and pulled it over her head. "Good fit," he said with some amusement. It was enormous but warm. "You'll need it."

He locked the door from inside the elevator and they rode downstairs and walked to his car. It had an odd license plate, NYP on a slant after three numbers.

"Does it mean something?" she asked.

"Press," he said laconically and unlocked the door.

He drove around Washington Square Park, slowing to point things out—the archway, a statue, some buildings that were part of a university. Old and new mixed indifferently, haphazardly. Sometimes the old seemed more than old; it seemed on the point of decay.

"Is that why you were talking to the police last night, because you're working on a story?" she asked when his narrative had petered out.

"That's right."

"A story about . . . about those women getting into the van?" She did not want to use the word "whores."

"A story about something else. I need some information that Heart-of-Gold McManus is going to help me get. I rode over with him so I could talk to him."

"You must lead an exciting life."

"It probably looks that way. From the outside."

"Isn't it?"

"It's a good life. It's satisfying. Exciting means different things to different people. Maybe it means the life someone else leads that you'd like to lead yourself. I like mine the way it is, with or without excitement."

"You don't seem the kind of man who would have a full-length mirror in the bathroom," Frankie said.

MacIver smiled. He didn't smile very often, she thought. "It's for my daughter," he said. "She's twelve. She needs to look at herself every now and then for reassurance. She picked out the mirror herself. It'll get hung later this week. In a couple of years, maybe, she won't have to look quite so often. She'll know."

"You're divorced."

"Separated."

"Separated," she repeated and glanced at his profile. He was looking straight ahead at the road. "That's when you haven't made up your mind."

He looked sideways at her for a moment. "It has nothing to do with making up your mind," he said with a trace of anger. "Separating is simply the first step . . ." His voice trailed off and he pulled out of his lane and accelerated to pass the car in front of them, as if the speed of the other car had prompted the anger. Ahead of the pack, he relaxed a little and the odometer needle settled back. "You're right," he said in a more ordinary tone of voice. "It means I haven't made up my mind."

"I'm sorry."

"That tunnel"—he spoke quite naturally, nodding toward the road—"used to be the longest tunnel in the world. Till they built a longer one in Switzerland a few years ago. You ever drive through a tunnel?"

"Last night," Frankie said. "On the bus."

It reminded her of the hospital, shiny tile walls. She wondered if anyone came and scrubbed them. It wasn't "them," really. It was one continuous wall that arched. There were no corners, no comfortable demarcations. And it was very long. She was hardly aware of the tension till she saw the end and felt herself relax. "I see what they mean by the light at the end of the tunnel."

"Nervous?"

"I think so."

"I thought you were fearless."

"It only looks that way from the outside."

He moved into the right-hand lane where the view was best. "This is Brooklyn," he said and she looked out the window at the water and the island and in the distance a bridge connecting the island to Brooklyn.

"I've never been able to picture the ocean." As she spoke, she made one last futile attempt. "I've seen lakes and I've tried to stretch them out in my mind but it never works. Whatever I do, I still see the opposite shore."

"You won't this time."

Even when they were driving, on the edge of Brooklyn, she could see it would be true. She had seen land stretch out before her forever but never water and here it went on and on.

He said little else for the rest of the trip, just an occasional word about something they were passing, remarks that seemed curiously detached, as though he were really elsewhere and only the scenery and the obligation to his passenger brought him back. When he finally announced that they were almost there, she could not believe it. There was no water and the street was shabby. He parked the car and they got out and walked.

"They call this the boardwalk," MacIver said, indicating a gray weather-beaten structure set high above the street. "You can look out over the beach and ocean from up there."

She walked up the ramp, came to the top, and continued across to the other side. And there it was, the ocean she had dreamed of and not been able to see, a sandy beach stretching from left to right, empty and bleak, but surely the real thing. Nothing between the sand and the sky except water.

It was very cold and she grasped her elbows, pressing her arms against her chest. Choppy waves crested, collapsed whitely, withdrew. It was the Atlantic Ocean.

"As good as the chandelier at the Waldorf?" MacIver was beside her at the railing.

She nodded. "Better," she said but the word was lost in the roar of wind and ocean. "I'm going down," she called to him.

"You'll freeze," he called back.

She shook her head and went down the nearest flight of stairs, holding on to the splintery rail with mittened hand. On the beach she pulled a mitten off and lifted a fistful of sand, letting it trickle out as she approached the water. You could see exactly where the last wave had reached by the darker color of the wet sand. She stopped a few feet short of the dividing line and sat down. When the next wave broke, a hair closer, she could feel the icy spray. January second and Frankie Grant was sitting on the beach watching the Atlantic Ocean.

She looked back over her right shoulder and saw MacIver. He was still standing where she had left him, his forearms leaning on the railing, looking off into the distance away from her. It was the first moment she had stopped to think about him, to wonder. She did not know how old he was, but probably well past thirty. He was fairly tall, about six feet, she thought, with medium brown hair that he did not wear styled like the men in magazines. It blew freely in the wind. He was neither fat nor thin but something in between that one might think of as average, or perhaps a little sturdier than average. He did not strike her as happy but neither did he seem unhappy, merely preoccupied, as though his mind were three-quarters elsewhere and one-quarter on the visible present. He was separated from his wife and he must be considering a divorce or why would he be committing himself to an apartment full of furniture? It seemed a shame, a nice man with a twelve-year-old daughter.

He turned and she looked away so that he would not catch her watching. The beach was empty as far as she could see, the sand unruffled, perfect for running. Kenny would have loved it. Kenny would have run from here to the farthest point she could see — there he went in nothing but a black bathing suit, kicking up sand, flying. She always saw him running. Even in the most incongruous places — those fields near the road where the bus had been stopped by snow for all those hours on New Year's Eve — Kenny was running. Being older, she could remember him running at almost every stage of his life, as an unsteady two-year-old and as a spunky kid of ten who knew he could not come in first but did it anyway just for the fun of it.

She knew there were tears on her cheeks but she kept watching him, the little spot in the distance. As long as she could see him, as long as she could conjure up the image, she could believe.

A pale shadow fell across the sand and she looked up, startled. It was MacIver. She brushed at the tears quickly, resenting the intrusion of this man on her

34

beach.

"What did you run away from, Frankie?" he asked.

"I didn't run away. A friend drove me to Columbus and waited with me till the bus left."

"You're sitting here and crying."

"No." She stood and brushed sand off her coat. "I want to touch the water," she called, running.

"It's too cold," he shouted back.

She stood with her feet half on the water line and waited for the next wave. It took a moment to come. The water had been receding as she approached and she watched as a new wave formed and mounted its attack. It exploded finally in a burst of spray and she bent, extending her bare hands into its path. She cried, "Oh!" as her palm became stingingly wet. It was like liquid ice. She stepped back, nearly losing her balance, feeling MacIver's hand on her upper arm, steadying her.

"Thank you." She grinned at him and licked her frozen palm. "It's *salty*," she said in surprise. "It's really salty."

"They don't teach you that in Ohio?" He was smiling back at her.

"I didn't believe it." The teary mood had passed and she felt, again, the joy of being there. She licked her index finger. It was still salty.

MacIver was steering her back toward the boardwalk. "Put your glove on before your hand turns to ice."

"It *is* ice." She held up her hand, stretched taut.

"Let's go somewhere warm for lunch and you tell me where you've come from, what you're doing here, and what you plan to do tomorrow."

"OK," she said agreeably, feeling agreeable, feeling almost high on salt spray. He let go her arm and she mounted the stairs nimbly, pausing at the top for a last look at the ocean.

"I need a place to stay till April. Mostly, I need an address. Somewhere that I can pick up mail. But I can't live in a box number."

They had returned to Manhattan and were sitting in a rather charming little restaurant with lots of hanging plants. The coffee was served in mugs and right now she had her hands around hers, warming them. It was afternoon and she would have to get started soon if she was to find a room for tonight.

"Then you've got people who'll write to you."

"Colleges," she said.

"Colleges?"

"I'm going to college in the fall."

"You transferring from somewhere?"

"I'm starting as a freshman."

"You're over twenty-one," MacIver said.

"One of them will take me. I'm from Ohio and I did OK on the tests."

"Late decision or early mid-life crisis?"

She looked at him over the rim of the mug. "I wanted to stay home for a few years."

"You're a nice kid, Frankie." MacIver looked very earnest. He must be a good father to his little girl. Maybe she was lucky, even if he didn't come home to her every night. "A very nice kid," he was saying. "Don't let some guy muck up your life because you're too nice to say no."

"It wasn't like that," she said in a low voice.

"Where's the rest of your luggage?" he asked.

"At the bus station."

"Let's pick it up."

"But I don't know where I'm going yet."

"We'll bring it back to my place. I'll rent you a room for two weeks at a very low rate."

"You?" She was delighted. She was also surprised. "You don't even have any rooms."

"Well, that space marked 'Sleeping Area' on the floor plan, where you dropped the mattress last night. This is the last day of my last vacation for a while. Staring tomorrow early, I'll be working all day every day and a lot of nights besides. There's still a lot of carpentry that has to be done in the apartment and I don't want to hang around to let the guys in. If you don't mind waiting till nine-thirty or ten in the morning—"

"Mind! That's really all I have to do?"

"That's all."

She finished her coffee, relishing her good luck.

"Listen to me, Frankie—" The waitress came by and he said, "Check, please," and turned back to her. "I'm about to give you a lecture on New York City."

"I don't need one." She had slid out of the booth and was pulling her coat on over the bulky sweater.

"You need one more than anyone else I've ever met. To start with, in spite of your apparent success in walking from Ninth Avenue to Lexington in the middle of the night without getting mugged or worse, you do not possess a natural immunity from danger and you are never to try it again."

She repeated, "Never," but she had tuned him out.

She had a place to stay for the next two weeks, time to make some arrangements, to find a room and a job, to get a haircut, to *see the city*. She had known it would be this wonderful. She had just thought it would take longer than a day.

Beside her MacIver was ranting on about the wicked city, about the subway, about walking alone in the dark. He was still talking, and she was still not listening, when they got in the car and started uptown for the bus station.

Three

He was out by eight the next morning, having left walking and transportation instructions. They were only a short distance from Fifth Avenue — it began at the arch he had pointed out yesterday — and since two miles to reach midtown didn't sound like much of a walk, she decided to try it on foot.

The men arrived with shelves and cabinets and were at work a little after nine-thirty so she said, "It was nice to meet you," and rang for the elevator. She closed the apartment door firmly, reading the narrow plastic card at eye level: H. J. MacIver. She did not know his first name or even where he worked but she thought there would be little possibility that she would need to reach him during the day.

She set out for the arch and turned right when she reached it, sensing the miracle of planting a foot on Fifth Avenue. She walked uptown at an even pace, slowing now and then to watch a person or a dog or to look across the street. It amazed her the way the character of the avenue changed. Just as she became accustomed to the large apartment houses, they gave way to shops and then they were replaced by old, drab buildings that housed businesses that did not invite customers from the street.

She was especially careful crossing Thirteenth Street. Her mother had once refused to seat thirteen at a Thanksgiving dinner and the younger people had had to sit by themselves at a smaller table to accommodate her superstition. Where did we go wrong? Frankie asked herself, looking both ways to cross Fourteenth Street because this one had traffic in both directions. Was it fate or irony or the arbitrary slap of some evil spirit?

Kenny would have loved Fifth Avenue. Right here he would have stepped off the curb, stood on the mark in the exact center of the street, and run all the way back to that distant arch, breaking through the ribbon with his arms held high.

She got a little tangled up in the Twenties and a cabdriver yelled at her—poor harried man—but she continued undaunted. MacIver had said that at Thirty-fourth Street everything would be different.

And it was. For one thing, there was the Empire State Building. For another, there was an enormous department store with a fantastic Christmas display in its windows. She passed along the line, following mothers with small children, babies with nodding heads and wide eyes. They were round and cute and she smiled at them, forgetting to look at the display.

"He's beautiful," Frankie said to the young mother in front of her.

"Thank you." The woman beamed. "I think he finds you more interesting than the window."

"That's OK. I think he's more interesting too."

She said, "Bye," when they came to the end of the line and she continued uptown.

It was nearly eleven on Kenny's watch and she thought how nice it would be to stop and have a cup of coffee but there didn't seem to be anything like a coffee shop around. There were stores and banks . . . She turned and walked into the nearest bank and got in line.

Her savings were in her wallet, protected by a flap in the back, ten hundred-dollar bills. When her turn came, she took one of them out, handed it to the teller, and said, "Could you give me tens for this, please?"

The teller, a woman about twice her age, held the bill up and scrutinized it. "Do you have an account here?" she asked.

Frankie laughed. "I just arrived over the weekend."

"I'm afraid I can't change it for you."

"Is something wrong?"

"I can only do that for a customer of the bank. Next!"

"But —"

"See one of the officers on the platform. Next!"

Bewildered, Frankie looked to the side. A group of desks were arranged one step above the carpeted floor. Holding the hundred-dollar bill in one hand, she stepped up and found an unoccupied man at one of the desks.

"Hi," she said. "Could you change this bill for me?"

He looked up and eyed the bill without touching it. "Do you have an account at this branch?"

"I don't have an account anywhere."

"Then I'm afraid—"

"You're all kidding me, aren't you?"

"Kidding you?" he said acerbically.

"I mean, this isn't an out-of-state check. It's a greenback. Back home we think it's the best money in the world."

He snatched the bill and left without a word. She watched him go, saw him hold it under a lamp, then say a word to a teller, and a moment later he had a hand full of bills. When he returned, he counted it for her—three twenties and four tens—and handed her the lot.

"I advise you to open an account," he said.

"Oh I will."

"Or have a friend change your large notes for you."

"Thank you."

"And put it away before you go out in the street," he cautioned without a note of warmth.

"Yes. 'Bye. Nice to meet you."

There was something *wrong* with Fifth Avenue. Like the man in the bank, it took itself so seriously. She wanted a newspaper and a cup of coffee but neither seemed available. Her pace had slowed because there was now so much to see but the streets had filled and everyone else was in a hurry.

Finally, at about Fiftieth Street, she looked across the street and the sight took her breath away. Beyond an avenue of crystal and ice was the largest Christmas tree she had ever seen.

"What's that place?" she asked the woman beside her who was looking intently at a department-store window display.

The woman turned. "That's Rockefeller Center," she said. "Are you new here?"

"Very new. It looks like a fairy land."

"It does, doesn't it?" The woman sounded as though it had never occurred to her before how beautiful the scene was. "You can walk down there, you know. See the ice skaters."

"Thank you." Frankie crossed the street and walked through the fantasy land toward the tree. There really were skaters, down in a rink below street level, good ones and bad ones, gliding along, displaying a variety of skills. She watched them for a while with admiration and a small sense of longing. She had not skated for several years, was not even sure what had become of her skates. She had found Kenny's just before Christmas and had given them to one of the Harris kids.

She turned away from the rink, looking around for a place to get a cup of coffee, or maybe a hamburger because it was getting towards noon. That was when she saw what was in the window of the flower shop.

It was like nothing she had ever seen before. It was not a flower—it was indescribable. She went inside, smelling the warm dampness of the place.

"In the window," she said to the young man. "Is that real?"

"Bird of paradise," he said. "Grows in Hawaii."

"I've never seen anything like it."

"We always have them around New Year's. They're very reasonable today. Four dollars apiece."

"Yes." She said it to herself. She would give them to MacIver. More than furniture, his apartment needed color, warmth. "I'll take two, please." She

43

took a ten out of her wallet and watched as the flowers were wrapped in pretty paper. They made a large, somewhat awkward package but she had nothing to carry besides her bag and the awkwardness didn't matter; she wanted them. MacIver would be pleased.

Now that she was off Fifth Avenue, she could see that things were different. There were restaurants serving exotic foreign food, coffee shops, hamburger joints. She picked a coffee shop and sat down at the last empty table for two, laying the birds of paradise carefully over the second chair. It was a relief to sit, a pleasure to sip hot coffee and eat something.

A newspaper folded to an inside page had been left on the table and as she ate, Frankie turned it back to the beginning and started to read. On her second cup of coffee, she saw a small boxed article: "MacIver on Leave."

She refolded the paper and read it carefully. "Henry J. MacIver, city political reporter, has accepted a special assignment for the first quarter of this year and his column will not appear until its completion. Mr. MacIver joined the *Times* in 1975 and has been covering the local political scene since 1980."

There was a little more about his background. Frankie read it again. She was stunned. Henry J. MacIver. She remembered closing the door this morning as she stood in the elevator and reading: H. J. MacIver. And yesterday, the license plate. "Press," he had said as though he were some boy with a special card that allowed him to park in No Parking zones. She tore the piece from the paper and folded it

44

into her bag. It was her MacIver.

After lunch she kept off Fifth Avenue although she found herself crossing it now and then as she wove back and forth, east and west across Manhattan. She found another florist—she no longer knew exactly where she was—and went in and bought three spidery white mums while the woman wrapping them eyed her earlier purchase suspiciously. Later—it must have been on the East Side this time—she saw tulips in a window and went in and bought four, two pink and two lavender. A few blocks away there was a flower she had never seen before, something like a mum, and then again, unlike it. It came from Africa, the florist told her, folding white paper around three of them and tucking the package into her arms where she held all the others. She thought she ought to stop but there were tiger lilies she could not resist in a marvelous shade of red and then, finally, stalks of something delicate which turned out to be an unpronounceable kind of orchid.

"Enough, Frankie," she told herself as she peered over the tops of the bundles, trying to orient herself as MacIver had suggested. She looked at the number of the street and walked one block, only to find she had continued uptown. But now she knew where she was and she turned purposefully and headed toward Fifth Avenue and the bus that would take her home.

But the bus stops were very confusing. Certain buses stopped at this corner but not at that one. Others stopped at the one but not at this one. And at all the stops there were crowds of people. She waited for one of the buses MacIver had recommended, but when it came, it passed them all by and when the next one arrived, there was so much shoving that she was afraid for the flowers and she held back. Finally, she set out on foot.

She pushed the outer door open with her shoulder and back after just managing to turn the key.

"Can I help you?"

Feeling somewhat ridiculous, Frankie looked from between two of the paper-covered bouquets. The speaker was a young, beautiful, well-dressed woman who stood near the mailboxes with a small key in her gloved hand. "Thanks, I'll be fine when I get into the elevator."

"Do you know where you're going?"

"Four."

"Oh!" There was more than surprise in the syllable. "You're a friend of Mac's. He didn't tell me. How great. I'm Naomi Shiskin."

"Hi. I'm Frankie Grant. I'm just a houseguest for a while. Till I find a place to stay."

"Well come on up for a drink tonight. Sixth floor. Eight o'clock?"

"Thank you, I will."

"And bring Mac along." She opened the elevator door and held it for Frankie.

"That's awfully nice of you. I'll be there."

"See you later." Naomi Shiskin smiled and went back to the row of mailboxes with her key.

MacIver opened the upstairs door and said, "Good God."

"They're for you." She stepped onto the polished floor of the apartment. "For rescuing me." She

46

handed him one package. "For taking me to see the ocean." She handed him a second. "For giving me a place to stay." She thrust the remaining bouquets at him.

"Well I guess you're undaunted by the wicked city."

"Absolutely." She took off her coat and hung it up. "Look what they *did*," she said in admiration. At the far end of the apartment, where the dining area would be, floor-to-ceiling cabinets and shelves had been installed. "It's starting to look lived-in."

"Don't tell anyone they're all empty."

"It doesn't matter. We can put some flowers there."

"What possessed you, Frankie?" He had dropped everything on the kitchen table and was pulling the paper open so that all the colors were partly exposed. "Birds of paradise," he said with admiration. "I don't think I've ever been this close to one before. In New York girls don't bring you flowers much."

"You deserve it. Besides, I'd never seen some of them before. I was afraid to let them get away."

MacIver had opened a kitchen cabinet and was looking at its sparsely filled interior. He took out a white porcelain coffeepot, a couple of tall glasses, something that looked like a jam jar.

"They'll be fine," Frankie said. She rolled up the sleeves of her blouse and started to work on the flowers, trimming stems and arranging them in the humble vessels. "I think Fifth Avenue is the pits," she said, not looking up. "Except for the Christmas decorations. The decorations are nice but the *street* . . . There's nowhere to buy a postcard, nowhere to get a cup of coffee, nowhere to sit down. There isn't even anywhere to pee. There. How's that?" She had placed the birds of paradise in the coffeepot and the rest of the flowers in the assorted glasses and the jam jar.

"Very artistic. Especially considering the materials. Did you—were you able to find everything you needed?"

"Eventually." She pulled a chair out and sat down gratefully. "Except for the postcards."

"Frankie, you've been here two days and you haven't called anyone."

"I don't know anyone."

"I mean at home. Someone's got to be worrying about you."

"No." Softly.

"You said your parents knew where you were."

She stood up and lifted the coffeepot with the birds of paradise. "Do you mind if I put these on the floor?" she asked. "Where we can see them from everywhere?"

"Talk to me, Frankie."

She sat down again, all the flowers in front of her, a kind of shield. "They died on the Interstate almost two years ago. It was a Michigan car. Everyone in it had been drinking. It's all still in the courts."

MacIver sat on the chair to her right and turned it so that it faced her. "Were you with them?"

"I was home. Bill Hoskins—Bill was the sergeant on duty that night—he came to the house to tell us."

"Let's go out and eat something," MacIver said quietly. "No. Let's put the flowers out first."

She sat in the chair and watched him, carrying the coffeepot carefully, setting it down on the floor near the back windows, then returning for the glass of tulips and orchids, the glass of tiger lilies, and the jar with the strange African flowers. Frankie pushed the spider mums to the center of the kitchen table.

MacIver returned with her coat. "Did you find a place to pee?"

"Uh-huh."

He held her coat for her and wrapped it around her as she slid into it. She picked up her bag—she had left it on the floor near the door—and slung it over her shoulder. Then, remembering, she dug inside and pulled out the clipping.

"Is this you?" she asked.

"It's me."

"I didn't know you were somebody famous."

"I'm not."

"The J. What does that stand for?"

"James."

"You're putting me on. Henry James like the guy in Washington Square?"

"It was my mother's idea. She was a James. Claimed some distant relationship, probably apocryphal. We going to stand here all night?"

"Will it spoil your reputation to have me stay here?"

"Probably enhance it. You ever eat Chinese?"

"People or food?"

He smiled. "Come on. The elevator's here."

She let him order because she couldn't even pronounce the things on the menu and she trusted his taste. He told her no one had ever brought him flowers before, not once in his entire life. She thought that was nice. It was her first trip almost anywhere and she had given someone else a first too.

"I met the Shiskin half of Shiskin-Wright," she said, trying to handle the chopsticks. The name came out "Shishkin" both times. "She's beautiful."

"Naomi? She's a very nice girl."

"She's beautiful," Frankie repeated, giving up and taking her fork. "That dark hair and perfectly oval face. And she was dressed like a model. Is that how New York women go to work?"

"A lot of them."

"She asked us up for a drink tonight. Eight o'clock."

"Naomi's a nice girl," MacIver said again.

They detoured slightly walking back so that he could show her McDougal Alley, a street out of another time, two rows of houses lifted out of the past and planted near Washington Square Park.

"That's where I would live," Frankie said dreamily. "My own little cottage on my own little street."

"It'll cost you."

"That's OK. Everything costs. But sometimes it's worth the price."

They got back a little before eight and MacIver told her to go upstairs without him; he had some work to do and would be along in half an hour. He called Naomi and told her to expect the elevator.

The Shiskin-Wright apartment was as different from MacIver's as possible. The front door opened into a living room, dining area, and kitchen, and a hall led to a bedroom and study in the rear. It was furnished boldly, and bright contemporary paintings hung on the walls. Naomi had opened the door wearing a long loose robe patterned with gold threads.

"Wine?" she asked after Frankie had admired the apartment. "Or something stronger?"

"Wine'll be fine."

"Ev?" Naomi called. "Frankie's here."

A blurred answer came from the rear of the apartment.

"Well," Naomi said with anticipation when they had sat with their drinks, "are you going to tell me or do I have to ask?"

"Tell you what?"

"How you ended up at Mac's place."

"A policeman near Grand Central Station asked him to take me home for the night."

"And that's it?"

"Uh-huh. I'll be looking for a place to stay till April."

"Till April, till April." Naomi put her glass down. "One of the girls in my office just lost a roommate. Let me talk to her in the morning."

"Lost?"

"Nice lost. She got married."

Frankie observed Naomi with amusement. These New Yorkers were a strange lot. On the one hand they were cool to the point of absurdity, like the people this morning in the bank. And on the other, they invited you for a drink after two sentences of conversation and suddenly became part of your life. At home no one would refuse to change a greenback for you — neither would they arrange for your living quarters after a sip of wine.

"Where do you work?" Frankie asked.

"In a medium-sized bank. You've probably never heard of it."

And they all worked in banks!

"Have you met Mac's kids?" Naomi asked, thrusting deeper.

"I'm not a friend or anything. I'm just a boarder."

"No, you couldn't've," Naomi went on thoughtfully. "The bitch took them to Arizona for New Year's."

Frankie stifled a giggle. "His wife?"

"They're still married," Naomi said, answering an unasked question. "And having trouble cutting the cord."

"Maybe they'll get back together," Frankie said optimistically.

"Maybe they won't. That would be better news for Mac."

"It sounds like you know them real well."

"I met her for five minutes when she brought the kids here for Christmas week. It didn't take long to size her up. I do it at the bank every day and I have to be right a lot more than half the time. I was right about you. I could tell the minute I met you downstairs. Open but not too open. Closed but not too closed. You see that in Midwesterners. They seem nice but you're never quite sure."

"When do you get sure?"

"Oh." Naomi laughed. "I wasn't *critic*izing, Frankie. I knew you were just fine when I saw the flowers. That's what Mac needs, someone to bring him flowers. I wish I'd thought of bringing them to Everett." The thought seemed to sadden her. Then she turned toward the rear of the apartment. "Everett, honey, are you coming?"

A door opened and a tall, rather thin man sauntered into the living room. "Hello, Frankie," he said, offering his hand. "Naomi treating you OK?"

"Real fine. Hi." She liked him, liked the way he shook hands, liked the way he took the opportunity to touch Naomi's shoulder as he passed. He had a small mustache and hair almost as dark as Naomi's, but otherwise, they seemed complete opposites. He sat beside Naomi and crossed his legs. He was wearing black pants, an open shirt with a dark pattern, and a sweater obviously designed to match the shirt. It had the effect of looking elegant rather than sporty. The two of them together on the sofa, drinks in hand, looked like a picture in one of the magazines that showed how sophisticated New Yorkers lived.

They talked easily for about twenty minutes, until Everett finished his wine. Then he said, "Sorry, sweets. I've got to get back to work," and stood up. "Nice to meet you, Frankie." They shook hands again. "Come on up anytime." Then he retreated to the back of the apartment.

"Well," Naomi said, "that's Everett."

"He's awfully nice, I think."

"He's perfect." She closed her eyes and smiled. "Did you ever meet a man who's perfect?"

"I don't think so."

"Well, hold on to him when you do."

"I'll come to you for advice, Naomi."

Naomi laughed. "You can just bet I'll give it to you." She stood and brought the wine bottle over. "Another glass?"

Frankie looked down at Kenny's watch. It said nine and it had been slowing down lately. "I'd better go. I walked about ten miles today and I'm tired."

"Take the stairs." Naomi opened a door near the elevator. "It's faster."

"Thanks again."

The stairs went down to a landing, then down to a door on five, then down to another landing. As she approached MacIver's door, she heard voices.

"—just fine the way it is." That was MacIver.

"Mac, you promised." It was a woman, somewhat throaty. "You promised you'd keep it neat."

"My kids were here for a week. I have no furniture. They sacked out on the floor in sleeping bags because the damned sleeping loft wasn't built. And dammit, I have to work at that desk."

"We talked about it," the woman persisted. "If you want to live with this kind of free flowing theme, it's got to be neat. It's got to be unspoiled, no papers, no dirty clothes, no junky bric-a-brac, nothing that disturbs the harmony. You've got to take a minute every day and tidy up before you leave. It's all on view, Mac. You took an oath."

"Fuck it," MacIver said irritably.

"Fuck you." She spoke seductively, slightly stressing the *you*.

There was a pause. "Not now."

Frankie sat on a step, looked up the staircase and then down. It was possible that Shiskin-Wright had turned in for the night by now and she couldn't chance disturbing them by knocking on the door. As for below, she had no idea where these stairs went. They might end in Pragmatique or at a door to the outside and she had no coat. She hated the idea of eavesdropping, especially on lovers, but somehow,

54

knocking on the door in front of her seemed equally poor taste. Inside, the woman had resumed.

"And those flowers." There was the sound of heels on the floor. "If you want flowers, I'll tell you where—"

"I don't want flowers, Karen. I was given flowers. And if you touch a leaf on one of them—"

"I'm not touching anything. I didn't come for a scene. I came to see how the cabinets were going." The woman walked a few more steps. "They're coming nicely and we're right on schedule." A pause. "The birds are something, aren't they?" There was grudging admiration in the voice. "Even in a coffeepot. What are you drinking?"

"Scotch."

"Pour a little for me. One lump."

MacIver's heavier step passed near Frankie's door and continued away to the kitchen. A cabinet door opened and closed. Another. "I'm out of glasses, Karen." There was a touch of embarrassment in his voice. "The flowers."

Frankie smiled. Three glasses and a jam jar and MacIver was drinking Scotch. Poor lady. She would have to drink it straight—out of the bottle—or not at all.

"Well."

Frankie stood and knocked at the door. "Hello," she called, loudly enough that they would hear her.

MacIver's footsteps approached the door quickly. "Frankie," he said as he opened it. "We had a date upstairs." He looked at his watch. "I'm sorry."

"That's OK. I had a glass of wine and met Everett and Naomi thinks she can find a place for me to stay." She had got it all out in one sentence so the woman would understand.

"Great. Come and meet Karen Armstrong. Karen, Frankie Grant."

They shook hands and said polite things to each other. Karen was slim and fair-haired, over thirty and dressed in a beige wool dress with a blousy top and a silk scarf at the neck. One could hardly say she stood; rather she seemed to pose.

"Well," she said, turning to MacIver, "I apologize for the lecture. I didn't realize you had a house-guest." She looked at a small gold wristwatch. "I'd better be running along. Did you hang my coat up, Mac?"

He got it out of the closet and pushed the button for the elevator. Karen buttoned the coat, turned to Frankie with a smile, but before she said anything, the smile disappeared and she clicked across the floor to the kitchen. "They sent the wrong table," she said. "This is square."

"I changed it."

"What do you mean, you changed it? You need a rectangular shape here to continue the line of the counter. This is too wide."

"Three of us have to sit at it, Karen. We need the room."

"Well." She flashed a smile that faded rapidly. "Buzz me at the office tomorrow." She turned to Frankie and smiled again. "Very nice to meet you." She did not offer her hand.

Frankie went to the kitchen sink and rinsed her hands, not wanting to watch the good-bye kiss, feeling more of an intruder than she had ever felt before. The door closed and a key turned. She pulled

56

a sheet of paper toweling from an almost concealed roll under the cabinets and dried her hands carefully.

"I'm sorry I missed the drink upstairs."

She turned around. "I've just screwed up your life."

"Unscrewed it, more likely."

"Naomi has a friend with a room to rent. If she says it's OK, I could move out tomorrow night or the next day."

"And leave me here with the carpenters?"

"You mean it?"

"I never say anything I don't mean."

"OK."

"And if you want to drop your clothes in the middle of the damned floor, go ahead and drop them. If you don't feel like making your bed all week, don't bother. And if you want to have a party and leave the dishes in the sink, be my guest. Got it?"

"Got it."

"And, Frankie, those flowers—those flowers are the nicest thing anyone's done for me in a long time."

She took the wadded towel and dropped it in the basket under the sink. "What I'd really like," she said, feeling fatigue hit her like one of those waves at the ocean, "is to go to sleep."

"Go on," MacIver said in a gentle, fatherly way. "I shouldn't have sounded off. Will my lamp bother you?"

"Nothing'll bother me."

"Good night, Frankie."

She took a quick shower and snuggled into the makeshift bed. MacIver was at his cluttered desk, a lamp at his elbow. It brought back a lot of memories that she had to push away to get to sleep.

Four

Something woke her, a sound maybe or some ominous thought. Her breath was coming in short gasps. She saw the lamp and knew who had called her. She said, "Kenny?" and started to get up.

The man at the desk pushed his chair back and came over to where she lay. She was on the floor and the man . . .

The man squatted beside her. He was wearing jeans and the kind of gray sweatshirt that used to be the only kind before those colored jogging suits became stylish. "You OK?"

In a dizzying movement, the context straightened itself out. "Yes. You're—"

"Mac."

"Yes."

His hand touched her forehead the way her father's had touched it when she was young and feeling sick, when sick meant only having a virus or a strep throat, when sick meant missing a couple of days of school.

"Better?"

"Yes."

"Want to sleep?"

She shook her head.

He got her robe from the chair and helped her up. She put it on and tied it, a shudder passing through her.

"Sit on the couch. You can use my blanket."

She shook her head, sat, then accepted the blanket anyway when he stripped it off the couch. He turned the desk chair so that it faced her and sat.

"Bad dream?"

"I guess. I don't remember."

"Frankie, I haven't asked you anything because I think you won't want to tell me. But if you want to, go ahead. And if I can help, I will."

She thought about it for a while. She wanted something hot to drink, but she didn't want to move and she didn't want him to move. She wanted to stay just where she was and look at that ordinary gray sweatshirt. Beside him, the lamp was dimmed. He had thrown a towel over the top of the shade to diminish the glare. It seemed a thoughtful thing for him to have done.

"I'll tell you one thing that's true if you tell me one thing that's true," she said finally.

"OK."

It was a game Kenny had made up when he began to suspect how sick he was. He would start with lesser truths and work up to the big ones, the ones that said how scared he was.

"I'm twenty-two," she said, starting with a very unimportant truth that he had guessed already anyway.

"I work for the New York *Times*."

She was glad he had responded that way, not trying to match her, truth for truth.

"I'm going to college in the fall."

"I'm working on the most important story of my life."

That surprised her. It was more than a truth. It was an assertion, a belief. She remembered what Naomi had said about Midwesterners: open but not too open, closed but not too closed. MacIver was very closed. He asked nothing, but then, he said nothing. "My parents were teachers," she said.

"I have one wife, one son, and one daughter."

"I'm in New York to have a good time."

He paused and she sensed he had said all he could. She put her feet back on the floor and started to unwind the blanket.

"I'm thirty-eight years old," MacIver said.

The first thing the carpenters did in the morning was to hang the full-length mirror in the bathroom, and as soon as it was up, Frankie looked at herself in it. Something had to be done with her hair but there had been no beauty parlors on Fifth Avenue and when she saw the size of the Yellow Pages directory, she knew looking them up would be fruitless. Naomi would know where she should go, she decided as she left the apartment. She would hear from Naomi tonight anyway. Today she would walk through this part of New York and try to learn her way around it.

She looked at Kenny's watch. It had already slowed three minutes and it was only two hours since she had wound it. One day it would stop for good and she did not know what she would do then. She had already asked a watchmaker at home if it could be fixed and he had said it wasn't worth it. It wasn't the kind of watch that people kept for a long time. It was just a watch you wore until it broke down and then you went out and bought a new one. He hadn't understood, of course, that this was Kenny's watch.

MacIver had told her that this part of the city was Greenwich Village. She walked from Broadway, where his apartment was, over to Washington Square Park and cut across it. Today was the fourth of January and the winter vacation was not yet over for university students. The people in the park represented almost every other kind of person she could imagine. There were young mothers with small children in an enclosed play area. There were old men and there were old women. A few well-dressed younger people were hurrying along the crisscrossing paths as though late for appointments. There were dog walkers. Then there were the others, sad, vacant-looking men who wandered or sat or stretched out on benches, and thin quick ones who darted about faster than one's eyes could follow. MacIver had warned her about men in general and these men in particular: she was young, she was pretty (that had pleased her but she had not let on), and she was prey to the hazards of New York, the commonest ones being pickpockets and chain snatchers. He had cautioned her about wearing visible jewelry and she had told him she did not own any, or at least had not brought any with her. Her mother's things had been left with Aunt Betty for safekeeping and no one would consider Kenny's watch to be jewelry.

At the time—it was two days ago, when he had invited her to stay for two weeks—she had dismissed his admonitions as slightly hysterical; now, looking at these weird and unhappy creatures, she was not so sure.

MacIver had gone further, describing a form of hand-to-hand combat, explaining how to defend herself if she were attacked. It seemed silly, even now. These men looked like pushovers. They were zonked out on alcohol or drugs. It would take an army of them to attack one lithe young woman. Nevertheless, she remembered, with an echo of her original distaste, MacIver's advice concerning the knee to the groin. It had made her shudder. She was not without a certain amount of experience. She had had her share of boyfriends, and she knew the male groin as soft and vulnerable. She could not imagine indulging in the kind of contact MacIver had suggested.

She came out on the west side of the park, found the nearest street continuing west, Waverly Place, and kept walking. She was feeling good. All the flowers in the apartment were still fresh and beautiful. Today she would do something else; she would cook dinner. There was a marvelous stove in that long complex that MacIver called a kitchen but she had not yet seen him use much of it except for the sink and the dishwasher. She would use it this afternoon, make something hot and tasty, something that would provide leftovers for tomorrow.

She inhaled deeply and let her breath come out in a cloudy puff. It was a good plan for the day.

* * *

When MacIver returned, she was already cooking. Bookcases had been installed in the study part of the apartment, behind the couch that he slept on. Even empty, they gave a sense of warmth and completeness to the area. He saw them as he closed the door, and without taking his coat off, he opened one of the many cartons piled near his desk and took out a handful of books and put them on a middle shelf. It was the most impulsive thing she had seen him do.

"Nice," he said, standing back. He turned toward the kitchen. "And something smells good."

"Old-fashioned stew."

"You're a nice girl, Frankie." He took his coat off and hung it in the closet. He was wearing a dark vested suit, the first day he had dressed. The clothes added a dimension she had not seen before, a kind of serious, professional overlay. It was almost hard to equate this man with the one in the gray sweatshirt in the middle of last night. He unbuttoned his jacket.

"When I went to set the table," she said, "I opened this cabinet over here." She pointed. "It was full of glasses."

"I know."

"You told your friend last night that you were out of glasses. Because of the flowers."

"I lied." Something flickered in his eyes. "I wasn't in the mood to have a drink with her. I didn't have that feeling of intimacy that I like to have when I drink with someone."

"I thought — maybe you just forgot."

"It was a lie, plain and simple. OK?"

"OK with me." She went back to the stove and

lifted the lid of the stewpot.

"I think I'll change my clothes," MacIver said.

The phone rang as they were finishing dinner and MacIver went to answer it. She could tell from the conversation that the caller was Naomi.

"Looks like Naomi has your life straightened out," he said agreeably when he came back to the table.

"You mean the apartment?"

"That and moving your things over. Go on up. I'll take care of the dishes." He went to a drawer and took out a key. "For the back door," he said.

Naomi was wearing a black velvet jumpsuit with a necklace of large pink glassy beads.

"We may have you a place," she said cheerfully when Frankie got off the elevator. "Did Mac tell you?"

"Sort of."

"It's on West End Avenue and it's near everything—the IRT, the Four and Five buses, and whichever those are that go down Broadway."

"The IRT?"

Naomi smiled. "The subway."

"Sounds wonderful."

"Want to go over on Saturday? I can take you up."

"Fine. That's awfully good of you, Naomi."

"It'll be fun. I haven't been up that way for a long time. Of course . . ." Naomi paused, "if you decide to stay longer with Mac, there're no strings."

Frankie laughed. "I think he can't wait to get rid of me. My suitcases are lying around, and that mattress. I'm a lot of extra clutter."

"Forget the clutter. You're gorgeous and honest and you brought him flowers." As though that were a formula.

"I also need a haircut," Frankie said, steering the conversation firmly away.

"Well then you see Anthony," Naomi said, her tone changing.

"Is he on Fifth Avenue?"

"Good heavens no. He's right down here in the Village and he will *love* cutting your hair."

When Frankie went down the stairs a few minutes later, she had Anthony's name, address, and phone number written in Naomi's large curlicue script on Naomi's notepaper. She unlocked the door and walked inside in time to hear MacIver say, "You're right."

He was sitting at his desk and speaking into the telephone. Frankie tiptoed across the floor to the kitchen and sat on one of the chairs. There were few places to sit in the apartment besides here or on the couch that MacIver slept on and he kept that made up as a bed even during the day. He acknowledged her presence with a wave and returned to the conversation. From time to time he said, "You're right," again or "Yes," or "I agree with you." He sounded bored, then irritated. Finally, after several minutes, he hung up.

He sat for a minute at the desk, shoulders hunched. Then he came to the kitchen, opened the cabinet where all the glasses were, and took out two squat ones.

"They drink Scotch in Ohio?"

"Sure."

"How do you like yours?"

"With more water than Scotch."

"That makes two of us." He dropped ice cubes in the glasses, poured generously from a bottle that was nearly full, and added water from the tap. He sat in the chair on a side adjacent to hers and pushed one glass toward her.

"I like square tables," she said.

"So the hell do I. Cheers."

"Cheers."

"That wasn't my girlfriend, by the way. It was my wife. When all the conversations start sounding the same, I think it's time for a change." He drank from the glass and replaced it on the wet circle on the table. "How long are you staying in New York?"

"Till April. Till the colleges send out their notices."

"Naomi's place sound OK?"

"Sounds fine."

"Your watch is slow."

She glanced at Kenny's watch. He was right. It was very slow. "It doesn't matter."

He turned his wrist and looked at his own. It was metal and worn. Only the expandable strap might have been relatively new. "This was my father's. He wore it in the Pacific in the Second World War."

"This was my brother's."

There was a kind of silence after she said it and the silence must have told him what she had left unsaid.

"How old was he?" he asked in a different voice.

"Seventeen."

"When did it happen?"

"November."

"You knew it was coming."

"For a long time. Some of them are lucky and make it. Kenny wasn't one of the lucky ones."

"He was lucky enough," MacIver said. "He had you."

She felt her eyes tear and she took a sip of the stuff in the glass.

"Was that what woke you last night?"

"I guess. I don't remember. There were nights we left a lamp on. Maybe that was it."

"So after you tidied things up, you got on a bus, got off in New York, and walked over to Lexington Avenue to see the whores."

He had lightened up and she smiled. "To see the Waldorf," she corrected him.

"Right. To see the Waldorf."

"Those women—" She was relieved that they had stopped talking about Kenny. "Is it true that they're all really nice girls who had a bad break and ended up on the wrong side of Lexington Avenue?"

"It's not true," MacIver said. "It's a poetic fiction. Maybe a couple of them. Maybe a few."

"Is that the story you're working on now? Those women?"

"No. I did a piece about them in the fall. What I'm working on now is the story of an upstanding man with an unblemished record who left his office one evening and never got home."

"You mean he disappeared?"

"Into thin air, as they like to say. No one ever saw him again, dead or alive. At least, not that they'll admit to."

"It must be awful for his family, the not knowing."

"It is."

"Different from the way it was for us. We knew, we just didn't know when. But the emptiness must be the same. The morning I woke up and Kenny wasn't there anymore . . ." Seeing it as she spoke, *that morning*. "When there was no one to say 'good morning' to. It was so *quiet*."

"Let's take a walk." MacIver had stood. He went to the closet and took out his brown jacket and Frankie's coat.

It was funny how, even for a walk, you had to lock your apartment as though you were leaving for a week. On the street he put his hands in his jacket pockets and they walked side by side.

"I thought you were a kid," he said. "A kid off the bus, looking to make it big in the big city."

"That's what I am." She wanted to add, "Mac," but it didn't come out.

"A hick maybe, but not a kid. Not even the minute you got off that bus."

"What are you?"

"I used to think of myself as a reporter," he said, but he did not go on.

"This story you're writing, is it about the man's family? About what happened to them afterwards?"

"Partly. Mostly it's a profile of how the police and the papers handle these incidents, what goes on that you never hear about, the men assigned to look into the disappearance and what they do from the moment they hear that someone is missing. This wasn't a guy who had alcohol blackouts or who was high on drugs or who had a girlfriend that he'd rather spend his time with. There wasn't enough insurance to

68

make a fake death worth the trouble, and besides, you can't fake your death by disappearing and then have someone collect. There have to be credible witnesses to your demise and in this case there aren't any."

"Then what do you think happened?"

He didn't answer. They turned onto University Place and she looked across the street to see the other end of the Washington Mews. There were people around, mostly young. Broadway, where MacIver lived, had the kind of businesses that closed at five as well as record shops and clothing stores that stayed open late. The building with the five apartments was an anomaly. She could believe it had once been a mill or a warehouse. This street, too, had restaurants and bars and late-night activity.

"I think he was murdered," MacIver said and she knew he had weighed telling her.

The word made her shiver. "Do you mean robbed and killed or—?"

"I don't mean robbed and killed."

"But why would someone do that if he wasn't involved in drugs or that sort of thing?"

"He was a reporter. He was working on a story."

"And you know what story it was."

"He told me a few days before he disappeared."

"Wow."

"Right. Wow."

"Doesn't that put you in kind of a dangerous position?"

It was the second question he didn't answer right away. They crossed a street and continued uptown. There were fewer people.

"I'm not working on his story," he said finally. "I'm working on his disappearance."

"But you wouldn't mind following up on his story."

"No. I wouldn't mind."

"Then it's dangerous."

He took her arm and crossed the street and they walked toward Fifth Avenue. "Sergeant McManus will protect me. If I need protection. Meanwhile"—his voice became more matter-of-fact—"I have a lot of police records to read through, a lot of tips to follow up on. People phone in sightings in crazy places. Psychics get feelings. Bounty hunters turn handstands to make a buck. The paper and his family put up a reward."

"When did he disappear?"

"Eighteen months ago. July of the year before last. On the Fourth, as a matter of fact. Our patriotic day."

"You haven't told me what story he was working on."

"You're right," MacIver said. "I haven't. What do you say we eat out tomorrow night, uptown, somewhere fancy. Did you bring a pretty dress along?" He steered her left at Fifth Avenue and they started back downtown.

"Sure I did. I was coming to the big city."

"Good. I'll show you what the big city's like at night."

"You already did. Look at that. It's wonderful." Several blocks ahead of them was the arch, all alight.

"It's covered with grime," MacIver said.

"Not at this distance."

"Maybe that's the secret, keeping a proper distance."

"But you lose something when you're far away, detail and texture. Don't you get involved when you do a story?"

"Sometimes."

"You're not the kind of reporter who would stand by and take notes while someone was hurting." It was a question but she didn't make it sound that way.

He exhaled wintry steam. They were approaching the Washington Mews from the Fifth Avenue side. "No," he said, as though he had considered the question or reviewed his ethics in the preceding moments. "I wouldn't."

"Then what's a little grime?" Frankie asked cheerfully.

They lingered a moment at the entrance to the Mews, then went to the end of Fifth Avenue and turned left at Washington Square North. In four days the area had become familiar to her. In three months the city would be hers.

"If you ever decide you want to have your watch fixed," MacIver said, "let me know and I'll look for someone to do the job."

When the day was over, she could not decide what had been more exciting, the haircut or the dinner. The haircut made her look like someone else. When MacIver came home—he had been working on records somewhere and was wearing a sweater over a shirt and the brown jacket over all—he looked momentarily startled. She had felt that same way herself, keeping her eyes closed during the cut and

71

opening them finally to look at the stranger in the mirror. The hair fitted her head like a well-made cap, but softer. It curved instead of curling. It fell into place thickly and naturally. It flattered.

"You'll never go back," MacIver said a trifle wistfully, standing just inside the door, still wearing his jacket.

"Home? Sure I will."

"Not anymore." He watched her rather a long time. Then he unzipped his jacket and went to the closet.

"You want the shower first?" she asked gingerly.

"Go ahead," he said. "I need a little time to think."

She had heard of the Four Seasons but she could not have imagined it. They taxied uptown and the doorman opened the cab door. What impressed her most as they entered was the vast space. She had been to restaurants, even on occasion to good ones, but she had never before seen one so large and so intimately connected with its environment. Other restaurants could move to larger or smaller quarters and remain substantially the same; this one could never maintain its identity anywhere else.

They sat at the bar for twenty minutes after they arrived, sipping drinks and eating fancy nuts. MacIver chatted with the bartender about Scottish bagpipes until eight. Then they went to their table.

Ahead of them a woman in a black silk skirt and a beaded blouse walked beside a man with silvery hair. At a large round table, a group that looked like three generations of a family ate in glittery company. A woman in an evening dress, tossing long blond hair, passed them in the opposite direction, a small gold evening bag picking up the light as she moved.

They were seated at a small table at the corner of the pool. A pool! Frankie stifled a giggle.

"Something funny?"

"I've never been in a restaurant with a pool."

"This is the place everyone's heard of. When you go back, you can tell them."

"You said I wouldn't go back."

"Look in the mirror, Frankie. Some guy'll sweep you off your feet in the next few weeks."

"I'll go back," she said. "I have a reason to go back."

The menu was enormous and had no prices. One of the main courses was venison. When she was younger, a cousin had given them venison every year during the hunting season and her mother had prepared it. It was an art that had gone with her mother. There were nearly no recipes on paper among her mother's things. Cooking had been learned or intuitive and either way very successful and very hard to imitate.

"I'd like to try the venison," Frankie said, "and I'd like to switch menus."

He looked puzzled but he made the trade, glanced at the one in his hand and said, "I see."

"You didn't know."

"The last person I brought here didn't tell me."

"I won't tell the next guy."

MacIver smiled. "It was Karen. I brought her here when we—when I thought maybe I was in love with her."

"Were you?"

"I guess I wasn't."

"I'm sorry about the other night. I didn't mean to cut in on you that way."

"You heard our conversation."

"Some of it."

"It doesn't matter. None of that matters. I'm working on a story now."

The waiter took their order, MacIver pressing her to try some of this and some of that. She munched a large round of radish and watched the pool.

"Tell me about your college plans. Where have you applied?"

"A couple of big ones, a couple of small ones. In and around Ohio."

"I thought you had wider horizons."

"I admit to being intimidated by the famous and the powerful."

"So you didn't try Harvard, Yale, and Princeton."

"Huh-uh."

"Are you intimidated here?"

"I'm not alone here."

"You're only alone at college the first day. Maybe the first ten minutes."

She thought of the first ten minutes that morning when Kenny was gone. Kenny had wanted to go to a good Eastern college. He would have gotten in too. He was the brightest kid in his class. September was when he would be starting. Instead, she was going in his place.

"I don't think I'd mix with a lot of rich Eastern kids," she said finally.

"You surprise me, Frankie. It must have taken a

lot of guts to get on that bus last week. Even more to get off."

"That was different. I carried insurance. A return ticket."

"I figured you for an optimist," MacIver said.

"I wouldn't be here if I weren't, but I'm a realist too. To you I'm a kid. On a college campus I'm an old lady. I'll be four years older than everyone else."

He waited until the waiter had served the clams on their icy beds. Then he said, "You trying to convince me or convince yourself?"

"You New Yorkers are wonderful," Frankie said with genuine admiration. "You eat clams by the side of a pool and you're so *sure*."

"You want me to lay off?"

"I don't know."

"Then I'll lay off," MacIver said.

When the venison came, it was delicious, different from her mother's and with different accompaniments. She savored it, knowing she was not likely to return soon.

"Well, Mr. MacIver." The voice was an unexpected intrusion. It came from a man about MacIver's age, part of a group now walking past their table. Beside him was a slender bare-shouldered woman with hair streaked silver.

"Steve." MacIver stood, dropping his napkin beside his plate and shaking hands. "Frankie, Steven Klein from the mayor's office. Steve, Frankie Grant."

She held her hand out and felt a strong grip.

"My wife, Sissy. You've heard me talk about Mac, haven't you, Sis?"

"Often," his wife said in a low, sexy voice, "and

75

with great irritation." She smiled almost flirtatiously and shook MacIver's hand. "Hi," she said to Frankie without offering her hand.

"I hear we're going to be spared the tart MacIver tongue for the first quarter," Klein said genially.

"I'll bet you miss me already."

"That's the spirit, keep the pressure on. Good to see you, Mac." He nodded to Frankie and they moved away from the table.

Frankie watched them go, the shimmer of silver hair, the deep V at the back of Sissy Klein's dress. "The men in New York look like men anywhere," she said, her eyes still on the departing couple, "but the women are really extraordinary."

"That's what they like to think."

"How long do you know Naomi and Everett?" she asked.

"About a month. Since I moved in."

"A month." It seemed almost unbelievable. "I thought you'd known each other for years."

"That's Naomi. She had us up for dinner over Christmas when my kids were staying with me. It gave her certain insights."

"She said she met your wife."

Something in MacIver's face closed. "I think they met for a minute."

"Well," Frankie said lightly, "for Naomi that must be half a lifetime."

Five

Naomi had a roll of tokens and she paid for both their fares in the subway. The subway was loud, confusing, and at moments a little frightening. Lights flickered now and then as the train roared along and once went out altogether. At one point the train stopped, for no apparent reason and at no discernible station, and they sat in silence for several minutes before it started up again. They changed trains so many times—and Naomi moved from place to place with such sureness—that Frankie was left somewhat deflated. The system seemed so complicated, so unfriendly, the train so mutilated, apparently by human hands, that Frankie could only wonder at the kind of people who traveled with it.

When they emerged finally, she was surprised to find it was still daylight.

"This is Broadway," Naomi announced at street level.

"That was a long trip to end up where we started." It was obviously not where they had started but it was hard to believe that moving between two points on one

77

street could have required the time elapsed and the distance they had traveled.

"It's a long road," Naomi said. "It goes all the way up to Albany, about a hundred and fifty miles. Too far to walk," she cautioned quickly. Frankie had told her about her tramp up Fifth Avenue.

It was different up here, like another city. Here Broadway was wide, with an island down the center. There were stores and coffee shops and supermarkets that you might find not far from any residential neighborhood anywhere. It didn't have the chic of Fifth Avenue or the savvy of the Village. Here and there were housewives, some of them in hair curlers, pushing market baskets and dragging reluctant children. Old men stood on the street in pairs and talked at each other in loud voices. A group of three black boys walked together, knocking against each other and laughing.

"Coming?" Naomi was watching her.

"Sure."

"It's some city, isn't it? Columbia's up that way." Naomi pointed to her right as they left Broadway.

"The university?"

"Yes. Hiking distance."

"Did you go there?"

"Brooklyn College. It's all my parents could afford."

"I was in Brooklyn," Frankie said, recognizing the name. "We went to see the ocean the day after I got here."

"Cold time to see the ocean."

"But it was wonderful. I'd never seen an ocean before."

78

"Everett and I have friends who live at Belle Harbor. Maybe you'll swim there with us in the summer."

"Thank you," Frankie said, forgoing the explanation that she would not be here in the summer.

"This is West End Avenue and over there, across the street, is Sally's apartment."

Sally was closer to Frankie's age than Naomi's, perhaps twenty-four. She was dressed in jeans and a shirt tied around her waist. In spite of the cold outside, the apartment was quite hot and to Frankie's surprise, several windows were open a few inches.

Sally led them first to a large bedroom, hers, and showed off the view. "We're just high enough to see the river," she said proudly. "We get a marvelous sunset, especially in the summer. And when Macy's does the fireworks for the Fourth, this is the best seat in the city."

"The sunsets must be wonderful." Today there was only dirty snow on flat rooftops.

"But better in the summer," Sally said. "The sun's all the way downtown this time of year." She pointed to the left end of the window. "Come and look at your room. It's at the other end of the apartment."

They went down a hall, passed the living room, which was large and sparsely furnished, and came to a door.

"It used to be the maid's room," Sally explained. "It's small but it has its own bathroom."

"The maid's room." Frankie was delighted. "Is that how they build apartments in New York?"

"Used to," Naomi said. "Before the war. Also the high ceilings and the big rooms. But not anymore."

It was a narrow room with a small bed and an old

maple dresser. A faded oval rag rug covered the floor next to the bed. Someone had cleaned the room meticulously. Frankie walked to the single window on the opposite wall and looked out. In the distance slightly to the left was a bridge. She asked what it was.

"The George Washington Bridge," Sally said. "It's even prettier at night when the lights are on."

"It's real fine," Frankie said, meaning the bridge.

"It's yours if you want it," Sally said, obviously meaning the room.

"Thank you. I'll take it."

They stayed another ten minutes talking about the price — a hundred fifty dollars each plus this and that — and meeting the third roommate, who walked in just then with groceries, and then, leaving her last forty dollars in small bills, Frankie promised to arrive the following Sunday.

Back on the street, Frankie looked around with the new feeling of one who lives on this spot. My street. The entrance to my building. My subway station. The store where I do my shopping.

"I want to take you to lunch, Naomi," she said excitedly.

Naomi looked pleased. "I was just going to make the same offer."

"No, it's my treat. Everybody's been so good to me."

"OK, can you eat Chinese?"

Frankie grinned. "Only if you order for me."

"Come on."

They got bowls of noodles with lots of good things and while they ate Naomi warned Frankie about

80

coming home alone at night, how to take care of herself in the subway, what to do if she thought she was being followed.

"I'll be fine," Frankie assured her.

"By the way, do you need a job?" Naomi asked.

"I will. My money won't last as long as I will."

"Type?"

"Yes."

"Use a word processor?"

"Uh-huh."

"Good. I'll give you the name of the company we get our temps from. You can work a day, a week, a month. Anything you want."

"You know everything, Naomi."

"Not quite. There are a couple of big things I still haven't learned yet."

"You'll learn them. When you need them, they'll be right there at your fingertips."

"You're a peach, Frankie."

She felt peachy. Six days into her stay and she had an apartment, a place to go for a job, and a couple of people who had been as nice to her as anyone back home.

"Are you Jewish?" she asked, looking across the booth at Naomi's beautiful face.

"Uh-huh." There was something cagey in Naomi's voice, something guarded in her eyes.

"I thought so."

"You're not going to tell me you once knew some Jews and they were just the *nicest* people you'd ever known, are you?"

"Why would I do that?"

"Because that's what people from the South and

81

the West are always saying, as though there's something so different about us that if you knew a nice one, you ought to talk about it."

"I knew a Jewish family once," Frankie said. "In our town. I don't think I liked them very much."

"Why?"

"Their son threw snowballs at me one winter."

"What did you do?"

"About the third time, I went over and kicked him. Hard. I remember he cried."

"Sounds like you did OK," Naomi said.

Frankie smiled. "That's what my mom said."

Naomi's eyes were suddenly warm again and wide open so that you could see deep inside, as though some hurdle had been surmounted, some barrier removed. Naomi seemed so sure of herself—she knew where to have her hair cut and how to find a job and she dressed like the most beautiful of people—that it had not occurred to Frankie that she might have their own places of sensitivity, that she might withhold trust.

"Like it?" Naomi asked, using her chopsticks expertly.

"It's marvelous. Do you eat it often?"

"Chinese? Every week. I like Japanese too, especially the raw fish, but Everett won't touch it. He's not quite as adventurous as I. Yet."

"He's awfully nice, Naomi. And good to you. The way he feels about you is written all over him."

"I'm awfully happy with him."

"He's not Jewish, is he?"

"Everett? God no. He comes from one of those old, quiet, worn-at-the-elbows, politely anti-Semitic families."

"No," Frankie protested.

"Yes," Naomi assured her.

"But they like *you*."

"They've been polite the couple of times we've met, which is in character. Don't look so upset, Frankie. It's the way things are. My parents feel just the same way about him. Or worse. And it doesn't matter to either one of us. What matters is that it works."

"You New Yorkers," Frankie said with a sigh. "You are very crazy people."

MacIver had gotten up early and left before nine. It was his day to spend with his children. He had told Frankie he might be late and when she went to sleep at eleven, he had not yet returned. She awoke when she heard him and she felt that sense of relief that her mother had told her about once. He was safe. The city had not eaten him up. A day of life had passed in peace. She could sleep.

"Did I wake you when I came in?"

They were at the breakfast table and he had been very quiet until they sat down.

"Just for a second. It was late."

"I got tied up."

"Kids OK?"

He looked up. "Fine." He sipped coffee, sipped more, put the cup down. "Tan. She took them to Scottsdale for a week. They just got back Friday and they were kind of tired yesterday."

83

"Long day for tired kids."

He looked puzzled, then said, "Mm," and went back to his breakfast and it occurred to her that he hadn't spent the late hours with his children; he had spent them with someone else. He had left the apartment dressed casually, not in a way that he could have taken someone like Karen out to dinner, but in a way he might have hung around someone whom he knew well. Someone like a wife.

She got up and poured coffee but he seemed hardly to notice. When the cup was refilled, he drank from it. After a moment he pulled the glass with the white mums toward him and he touched the spidery petals, still deep in thought, still elsewhere.

"Let's go somewhere, Frankie," he said suddenly. "Want to go somewhere?"

She shrugged. "Sure."

"Then let's go." He got up from the table in a hurry and pulled his sweatshirt up over his head, baring his back.

Frankie watched in fascinated surprise. They had done all their changing in the single bathroom, politely offering each other firsts. Now he seemed almost unaware of her presence, except that he had invited her to join him when he needn't have; he could just as well have gone alone.

He tossed the shirt carelessly onto the couch, which he had not yet made up, and turned around, stopping as he saw her. His face cleared and he said, "I'm sorry. I was somewhere else."

"You're a very gorgeous man, Mr. MacIver," Frankie said with just the touch of lightness needed to make the "Mr. MacIver" sound exactly right. "If I were your wife, I'm not sure I would have let you go."

He turned and got a shirt from his makeshift dresser and started for the bathroom. "I'm not sure she did," he said as he disappeared inside.

"Tell me about the apartment." They were in the Egyptian wing of the Metropolitan Museum of Art, sitting on the raised platform with their backs to the Temple of Dendur.

"It's going to be real fine. I've got the maid's room and my own bath. It's clean and pretty and I can see the George Washington Bridge from the window."

"What about the girls?"

"They're OK. One's smiley and talks a lot and the other's kind of reserved."

"Will you get along with them?"

"Sure. I get along with you, don't I?"

"That's because I'm such an accommodating guy," he said. "Every cop in New York knows you can trust MacIver with any kid that gets off a bus."

"Every cop is right."

"But part of the deal is that I can't let you go just anywhere."

"There isn't any deal," Frankie said. She moved her coat, which was folded on her lap. She had worn MacIver's old shetland sweater again. Before she left, she would have to wash it for him. "You need to be alone and I need to get myself an address before the end of this month."

"You're starting to sound like Naomi. Did Naomi tell you I need to be alone?"

"I didn't talk to Naomi about you. I've lived in

85

your apartment for six days. It's a one-man apartment and you're writing a one-man story. You really wanted to be alone this morning and I got in your way."

"I'm sorry about this morning."

"You shouldn't be. It's your place. If you want to grouse in it, grouse."

"Get up."

"What?"

"I'm tired of being lectured to by a kid off a bus. I want to see that new apartment of yours."

"You don't have to see it." He was up and moving and she was hurrying to keep up. "Naomi gave it her seal of approval."

"That's Naomi. What would your Aunt Matilda say if I let you move into a place on the Upper West Side that I hadn't checked out personally?"

"I don't have an Aunt Matilda."

"You do now."

It was Sunday and there were parking spaces here and there. He pulled into one on West End Avenue just across the street from the apartment house and they got out.

MacIver surveyed the surroundings somberly from the curb. "Would you believe me if I told you this could be a dangerous place to come home to at night?"

Frankie grinned. "I'd probably believe anything you told me."

He took her arm and they crossed the street. "You didn't listen to me, did you? Not one word. I wore

86

myself out giving you the hard lecture and you're just as gullible as the night McManus saved your little fanny."

She began to laugh.

"You laughed last time we had a serious conversation."

"We've never had a serious conversation. And I'll laugh at the next one too."

"What am I going to do with you, Frankie?"

"Just let me do it all myself," she said as they walked into the dark, high-ceilinged lobby. "Just the way I planned it when I bought my ticket in Columbus."

There was no one home but she had the key and they went inside and she showed him around.

"Back there are the other two bedrooms. They have a sunset view and once a year some fireworks." She heard herself recapitulating the tour she had been given yesterday and it passed through her mind that if Sally or Wendy married soon, she might inherit one of the better rooms. "This one's mine." She walked in and MacIver followed and looked around. He sat on the bed and Frankie went to the window. "I have the George Washington Bridge," she said.

He didn't say anything. He was looking at the maple dresser across the narrow room from the bed. The bed, she could see, was also narrow and sagged.

"They said it's beautiful at night."

"It is."

"Do you approve?"

"We lived in a place like this when we were married."

"I guess everyone in New York must have."

"It wasn't in New York." He looked down at the faded rag rug. "I remember paint peeling and a guy downstairs who banged on his ceiling if we walked across the room with shoes on and squeezing a crib into an alcove that was an inch too small for it." He looked back up at the dresser. "I remember being happy."

She looked down at Kenny's watch. "Maybe you'll be happy again."

"Right." He stood up and came to the window. "It is a nice view, Frankie. I approve. You can sit and look at the bridge lighted up the night you celebrate your college acceptances."

"Thank you."

"Maybe I'll buy you a drink that night."

"Maybe I'll buy you one."

"Come on. I'll show you where my missing man lived."

It was an apartment house on Riverside Drive, not unlike the building she would soon be living in. MacIver pulled the car over to the park side and looked across the street.

"This is the place he never reached."

It made her feel, quite suddenly, like crying. All the places Kenny had never reached, all the places he'd been headed. "Are they still there?" she asked. "His family?"

"They're still there." MacIver sounded weary. "In

New York, when you have a good apartment, nothing gets you out, not the furnace breaking down or the elevator giving up the ghost, not even when someone you love dies or disappears off the face of the earth." He put the car in gear and pulled away from the curb.

"Anyway, that's where it didn't end."

They had driven in silence for some minutes and she could tell they were heading downtown because the numbers of the cross streets were descending. He took a sudden left in the Sixties, as though it were a last-minute decision, stopped at a light on Broadway, and turned right.

"Over there," he said, turning to his left as they glided by Sixty-fourth Street, "just down the block, there's a Statue of Liberty on top of one of the buildings."

Frankie turned and crouched to look out his window. "It's like the real thing," she said with amazement.

"Smaller. It's an insurance company. And nobody knows it's there. It's like an open secret."

"Maybe like your man who disappeared."

He drove a few blocks down Broadway. "Maybe," he said. "And maybe not."

He drove farther downtown than she had been, over to the East River, and kept driving. When he stopped, they were in front of the New York Post Building, a white building, not too tall, with 210 over the door.

"This is where it began on the Fourth of July." He eased the car a few feet forward. "He came out of that door."

"Did he drive?"

"Not that day. His wife used the car to take the baby to visit her parents."

"You think about it all the time, don't you?"

"I do now, yes." He circled around the building: Catherine Slip, Water Street, Market Slip, and back to South Street.

"What's a slip?"

"Used to be water. Boats docked here."

He began to drive south again, getting on the Drive, and she realized they were approaching the very bottom of the island. "There's the real thing," he said, slowing down so that a car behind him honked angrily.

There it was, the Statue of Liberty again from a new angle, all green and majestic.

"It's one of the places you have to visit."

"I will."

A car passed them and the irate driver shouted something that was nearly inaudible through two sets of closed windows. MacIver, ignoring him, took his foot off the brake and the car began to creep forward, then pick up speed.

"Everything's on an island," Frankie said reflectively. "I've never known island people before."

"All waiting for the next boat to come in with provisions. Or to rescue us."

"Some of you are that way, yes." She turned around but the statue had disappeared behind the towers of the World Trade Center. "Naomi and Everett. They're an island, aren't they?"

"Probably. Not by choice but by their own doing."

"It's hard to understand. I've had my feet on solid ground all my life."

"Then you're not an island."

"I hope not."

"You're not," MacIver said. He had turned away from the river and they were driving on narrow streets with names instead of numbers. "You connect easily. People like you. You'll never be alone."

"OK." She relaxed and stretched her legs. "I just stopped worrying."

Something woke her and she sat up. All the lights were off but since there were not yet any curtains, a small amount of light came in from the windows at both ends of the apartment and she could see MacIver's silhouette near the kitchen. He put a glass down in the sink and turned around.

"Frankie?" It was a half-whisper.

"Yes."

He came over and squatted next to the air mattress. "Scared?"

"No."

"I didn't mean to wake you." He was still whispering.

"You didn't."

He touched the side of her face, his fingers moving into her hair. "Feel OK?"

"Fine."

"Go to sleep, kid."

"Who's Great Jones?"

"What?" Even in a whisper he sounded confused.

"Great Jones. You know, the street just down Broadway."

He smiled and put his hand on her shoulder. "Great Jones. I don't know. Maybe he's the guy who was married to Lesser."

"Sometimes I wonder about you," she said, lying down. "You always seem to get things backwards."

He rumpled her hair and covered her and she knew she did not want to move uptown to Sally's apartment; she wanted to stay here where the dreams would go away, here where there was a need.

He was wearing only pajama bottoms and she reached out and touched his bare arm, very lightly, with a finger. He didn't move and she drew her hand back under the cover and closed her eyes.

Six

When she opened the door to the elevator on Monday morning, Everett was inside, dressed like a businessman and carrying a slim black attaché case.

"Hi," Frankie said, closing the apartment door on the noisy carpenters.

"Hello, Frankie. How's it going in the big city?"

"Real fine."

"I hear we're losing you soon."

"Sunday. I'm moving to a big old building up on the West Side." The elevator stopped at the ground floor and they got off.

"I hope you'll keep in touch with us after you move."

"Thank you, Everett."

He held the outside door, then waved and hurried on his way. A nice man, she thought, watching him hail a taxi in the distance, a man with a Midwestern kind of warmth, the kind she knew instinctively how to respond to. If she never called him again, he would not track her down to keep up an acquaintanceship, but if she called, he would welcome her. He was the exact opposite of Naomi but together they looked as though they were made for each other.

This was the day she had chosen for high places. She walked down Broadway and over to the World Trade Center and then rode up to the observation platform, then screwed up her courage and took the subway to Thirty-fourth Street and found the Empire State Building. When she was finished there, she walked uptown on one of the avenues and finally took the bus back to the Washington Square arch, marveling at her courage. It was more challenging to step onto a Fifth Avenue bus than it had been to board the one that took her to New York.

She stopped at the supermarket and bought food for dinner. The woman at the checkout gave her change from a hundred-dollar bill without a blink, another lesson learned.

The tulips had withered, the first to go, and she threw them out and started cooking, wondering if MacIver would be home for dinner. When the roast was in the oven, she went to look at the books on the new bookshelves. He had spent hours arranging them but she could see no clear system in their order. She pulled out a book of poetry and opened the cover. "To Mac, whom I will love forever. Let me count the ways. Jeannie."

Frankie looked at the title. *Sonnets from the Portuguese*. The date of the inscription was April 1967. Jeannie must be his wife. She pulled out the book next to it and opened it. It was dated shortly after the previous book and the inscription was very short: "Dear Mac, Yes. Jeannie."

She closed the book with a snap, feeling an unfamiliar pounding of her heart. She had intruded on two lives that were none of her business, but it was more than that and it took her a moment before she was willing to admit it. She was jealous, jealous of Jeannie MacIver. Jeannie aged maybe twenty had promised to love forever, had a dramatic *Yes!* — and where had it all gone to?

You're a very gorgeous man, Mr. MacIver. If I were your wife, I'm not sure I would have let you go.

I'm not sure she did.

The book in her hand was an anthology of poetry. Jeannie had given him poetry and he had kept her gifts when he had moved away. Jeannie had given him love. Had he kept that too in spite of the separation? And what had he left with Jeannie when he had come downtown? Frankie put the book away and went back to the sink to scrub the potatoes.

When the timer went off, she put them in the second oven, marveling at the luxury of having two. Then she went to his desk, passing the bookcases without a glance. A photograph was propped on the writing surface and although she had seen it from a distance, she had never looked at it closely. It was a formal portrait, one that might be used in a yearbook, although the man was clearly too old to be in school. He had a nice-looking, relaxed face and light hair that stopped short of being curly. It was the same face that was on a small poster under the word: MISSING. And beneath the picture: HAVE YOU SEEN THIS MAN?

There were other pictures of the same man on the

desk, informal ones, snapshots with a young woman and a baby, one with another man who might have been a brother. MacIver had propped the pictures up so that they formed a panorama. It was an old desk with pigeonholes and the pictures were at various levels from one side to the other.

The elevator came up and stopped and as she turned, MacIver came in the door.

"Hi," he said. "Smells good."

"Hi." She watched him take his coat off. He was wearing a sport coat today and a shirt that was off-white with a dark tie. Probably he had spoken to human beings today, not buried himself in records. Probably he would change now and become a human being himself, as he had said once last week as a joke. "He looks like a nice person," she said. "Your missing man."

"Charlie Herron? He was."

"How old was he?"

"Twenty-nine. He'd be thirty-one this year."

"You said there was a reward."

"The paper offered one. Five thousand dollars."

"I suppose it doesn't matter how much it is. If you know something, you call up and tell them."

"It matters." He loosened his tie and pulled it off. "There are people who wouldn't pick up a phone for five thousand. For fifty, they might sell their own mother. Or the guy they work for. How'd your day go?"

She smiled. "I went to the heights and the depths."

"Sounds like you must have been in New York. Still undaunted?"

"Nothing will daunt me."

"Let me change my clothes and you can tell me about it."

The coffee was his specialty. He mixed blends according to the time of day and what they had eaten and he would not let her do the brewing.

She poured when it came through the filter and sat down at the kitchen table. "I've done something awful," she said.

"I doubt it."

"No, really, I feel terrible about it."

"Frankie, if you've broken something, there isn't anything here that's worth—"

"I looked at your books."

"That's what they're there for. I look at them all the time."

"There were two with messages. Personal messages. I read them."

"The books Jeannie gave me."

"Yes."

"All hearts and flowers?"

"All love and happiness."

"It's the same thing, isn't it?"

"Is it?"

He lifted his cup and put it down without drinking from it.

"Did you give her books too?"

"Lots of books."

"It seems a nice thing to do, to give books to someone you love."

"It's what college kids do."

"What do grown-ups do?"

"You've got me. I never gave Karen anything except a hard time—which she reciprocated rather eloquently."

"Was it better than hearts and flowers?"

"You bet. Finish your coffee. We'll take a drive up the Hudson and I'll show you what that bridge of yours looks like lighted up."

The phone rang before first light and before his alarm went off and when he answered, she could hear the excitement in his voice.

"Yes, yes. What do you have for me? . . . Harry, that's terrific. . . . Uh-huh . . . And you're sure he'll see me? . . . Okay. Don't let him get away. I'll get the first plane out. . . . No, I'll do that when I get there. Hold on a minute. Frankie?"

"Yes?"

"Are you afraid to stay here alone?"

"Huh-uh."

"Thanks, kid." And he was back to phone, talking about changing planes in St. Louis.

Frankie got out of bed and brushed her teeth while he finished his conversation. She looked at her reflection appreciatively, glad again she had cut her hair, happier that she had waited to have Anthony do it in New York.

"Hot lead?" she asked, coming out of the bathroom.

"Somebody I've been looking for for a long time was just found west of Omaha. The detective who monitored the special police number they set up when Charlie Herron disappeared. He retired six months

98

ago and dissolved in thin air." He had a small suitcase open on the sofa he slept on and he was filling it rapidly. "You sure you don't mind being alone?"

"I don't mind at all. Is it . . . is what you're doing dangerous?"

"My trip? Not dangerous at all."

"OK." She smiled at him. "Then I'll let you go."

He left in a flurry of cautions, requests, and suggestions. What to say if his wife called — he would be home to see the kids on Saturday — whom to expect each morning to work on the apartment, that he would call at least once. He rang for the elevator and unlocked the door.

"Frankie," he said as the elevator reached their floor and stopped, "can I give you some money?" He had dropped his overnight bag and reached into his pocket for a wallet.

"No." The offer had come as a shock.

"I mean" — he hesitated — "do you need any money?"

"No. Thank you."

"You'll be all right?"

"I'll be fine."

"Sure?"

"Sure. Positive. Absolutely certain. Have a good trip."

He slipped his wallet back in the pocket, opened the door, and waved. A few seconds later, the elevator descended.

* * *

She let it ring three times before she answered it. If it were his wife, she would prefer not to answer at all. She said, "Hello?" tentatively and closed her eyes.

"You OK?" It was MacIver.

She had let her breath out. "Yes. You?"

"Fine."

"Get your story?"

"I'm on my way there now. I had to rent a car. It's a couple hundred miles from the airport. Still undaunted?"

"I got a job." She could not keep the triumph out of her voice.

"Hey, that's great. Doing what?"

"Typing and that sort of thing. They offered me something for tomorrow but I told them I'd call them next week. After I move in, I want to walk around my new neighborhood."

"The West Side'll never be the same."

"That's OK. I won't be either."

"Anyone call?"

"Someone from the *Times.* Said she had a bunch of messages."

"I'll check in tomorrow. Take it easy. I'll talk to you tomorrow night."

"Frankie?"

"Yes, uh-huh, it's me. I was just cleaning up the kitchen."

"How'd it go?"

"I went to the Bronx."

"You what?"

"I got on one of those subway trains—"

"Where in the Bronx?" There was a new tight sound in MacIver's voice.

"I'm not sure but it looked weird when I went outside. Like there'd been a war. Was New York ever bombed?"

There was a pause. "Not from the air. Frankie, stay on the island, will you?"

"OK."

"They shoot people in the streets up there."

"Ah," she said as though the truth had just dawned, "and I thought it was the Fourth of July."

"Where the hell have you been?"

"What do you mean?"

"I mean it's ten o'clock in New York and I've been trying you since eight."

"Oh." She looked at Kenny's watch, which was closer to nine than ten. "Everett's staying in Boston overnight and Naomi and I went out to dinner."

"I'm sorry." He sounded sorry. "I had visions of you up in the Bronx, getting shot at."

"I went to the Statue of Liberty today."

"Good. How was it?"

"It was marvelous. It was indescribable. I think I love New York."

"Don't be so generous. People will take advantage."

"You know, you're wrong about Naomi. She doesn't want to get married at all."

"There are only two people I've ever been wrong about, Frankie. I'm one of them and the other one isn't Naomi Shiskin."

"Have it your way," she said agreeably. "When are you coming home?"

"Tomorrow."

"You sound beat."

"I am." His voice was low and scratchy. "Yesterday was a loss. This guy had to take his wife to the doctor and that shot most of the day. We just finished up."

It was Thursday night. "Did you get what you went for?"

"I'm not sure."

"What time will you get here?"

"Late. It's an all-day trip counting the drive from here to Omaha."

"Well—"

"Don't wait up for me."

She stayed up waiting until she felt herself falling asleep in front of the television set and then she decided she couldn't wait any longer. When he came home, she was asleep on her mattress and he bent and patted her shoulder and said something. But all she could manage was, "Hi," and the next thing she knew it was morning.

He left early to see his children. They had tickets for a matinee and then they would go to dinner. She suggested she could move to Sally's place today but MacIver seemed disappointed.

"Don't do that," he said. "We'll have brunch together tomorrow morning."

She threw away the last of the flowers except for

the birds of paradise. The rest had died or were dying. She went out and bought more spider mums for the kitchen table, yellow ones this time, a farewell present. It was hard to believe there was someone to say farewell to. Two weeks ago today she had boarded a bus in Columbus, ridden along snowfilled fields, sat for twelve hours in some anonymous place in Ohio or Pennsylvania waiting for a snowplow to free them, and here she was, ready to say good-bye to the first person who had been kind to her, ready to move to her first apartment, ready to take her first job in New York.

She went downstairs to Pragmatique, looked in the window for a while, then went inside. She wanted something silly and playful, but something that she could use, to remind her of her two weeks in a loft on Broadway. The salesgirl was young and thin with big eyes and long hair arranged to fall over one shoulder. She wore something in a dull, unnamable color that fell irregularly, almost to her ankles, another version of the extraordinary New York woman.

Frankie bought a raincoat in clear plastic with yellow piping, more of a poncho really, with snaps down the front. The girl who waited on her suggested yellow rubber shoes and an umbrella in clear plastic with yellow trim and even a shoulder bag made to match the poncho, but she stuck with the single purchase and took it upstairs in a gaudy shopping bag with "Pragmatique" in bold rainbow letters.

MacIver returned about nine in the evening.

"How was the play?"

"Funniest thing I've ever seen. Ever been to the theater?"

"Summer stock and school plays."

"You changed the mums."

She was surprised. "A farewell present."

"Come on, Frankie. It's not farewell. It's just so long. You've got my number and I've got yours. I'll give you a call soon and we'll see a play."

She turned away, looking out the windows over Broadway. It was one of those offers like the one Everett had made. Keep in touch. Only with Everett it hadn't mattered.

She opened her suitcase and began to empty it of the little things she had never removed.

"Don't do that now," MacIver said from somewhere behind her. "There's plenty of time in the morning."

"OK." She replaced the things slowly. She had only begun her packing because she wanted to avoid looking at him, wanted to prevent him from reading her face. It was all quite silly. He was someone else's husband, separated because he had not made up his mind to divorce, sixteen years older than she, so involved in a story that he flew halfway across the country at a moment's notice. All she was to him was an air mattress spread on his polished floor, a consumer of valuable space, an occasional cry in the night.

"Want a drink?"

"Sure."

"Have another terrific day in fun city?"

She smiled. "Yes."

"Still undaunted?"

She hesitated because for a moment she wasn't sure. "Still undaunted," she said.

* * *

Naomi had said to call when she was ready to leave and they had agreed that two would be a good time. Everett had offered his car for the trip uptown since they were expected later in the afternoon in the East Eighties.

It was a marvelous brunch. They had eggs Benedict with white wine and a gallon of coffee afterward in a restaurant in a place he called SoHo, "south of Houston" Street. The talk was light and MacIver did most of it, making his trip to Nebraska a comic tale. They got back to the apartment before one and Frankie started to pack.

"Can I help?" MacIver asked.

"No thanks."

It wasn't hard because she had never completely unpacked, anticipating the eventual move. She opened the small suitcase and began rearranging things. The pictures were there and she spent half a minute looking at them. She had not put them out, partly because there was nowhere except the floor and partly because she was a transient. It was the first thing she would do at Sally's, set up the pictures on the maple dresser. Tomorrow she would buy flowers for her room. They would brighten it up and remind her of the loft — and MacIver.

He had watched her for a moment or two, then sat at the old desk. Soon there was the sound of papers moving, then a sheet going into the old manual typewriter he kept on an equally old stand next to the desk. He typed and stopped. Papers moved. He typed a few lines slowly. She had become accustomed

105

to his work sounds and they had become as comforting as the tick of an old clock or the chirp of a :ricket on a summer evening.

She gathered the last of her things together, checking the bathroom where the shetland sweater had nearly dried from its washing the previous day. With her toothbrush and toothpaste, brush and comb, gone, the bathroom had returned to its previous spareness. If Karen visited again, she would certainly approve.

And that was it. The bedding lay folded on the mattress and the suitcases were full. She closed the larger one and stood it up next to the other. Then she went to the closet, took out her coat, and folded it over the two suitcases. She looked at Kenny's watch and made an automatic mental adjustment. It was about a quarter to two but she could see no reason for delaying her departure. MacIver was still at his desk, a pen in his hand as he read over what must have been the notes he had taken in Nebraska.

Frankie walked over to the desk. "I guess I should say good-bye," she said.

MacIver turned from his work and stood and Frankie put her arms around him to give him the kind of hug and kiss that could not be taken amiss and would show him that her appreciation was deeper than a mere thank-you, more substantial than a word or a shake of the hand. As her hands touched him, he took her in his arms and kissed her lips with a surprising intensity.

"Frankie," he said, his lips moving to brush her cheek, his arms wrapped around her. "Do you want me as much as I want you?"

106

"More."

"Why the hell didn't you tell me?"

It was all so complicated that she didn't answer, so many things assumed, and she had been wrong about all of them—two people perhaps not open enough with each other.

"You've never called me Mac."

"Mac."

As though the name had a greater effect on him than the kiss.

He opened the first button of her shirt and touched what now must have been very warm skin. Then he led her, circling the boxes and suitcases that destroyed the integrity of the loft Karen Armstrong had designed for him, to the mattress which lay stripped and somehow embarrassingly bare in what would one day be an almost bedroom. He helped her undress, touching her with the same gentleness he had used when she had cried in the night, then took his own clothes off, the shirt first over his head as he had done a week earlier while she watched. *You're a gorgeous man, Mr. MacIver.* She knelt and pulled the sheet on top of the pile back over the mattress and when she stood, he was undressed.

It was all new, the way she felt about him, the way they touched each other, the way they lay together on the mattress, but when they came together, which was the newest of all, she had the sense of something very old, something immensely valuable, of having entered a venerable society that she would never leave, of having arrived.

* * *

"You OK now?"

"Just fine."

"You should have told me." He had reached over her to dislodge the blanket from under the sheets and draw it over her.

"It didn't matter anymore. Except that it was you."

"I thought you couldn't wait to move uptown."

"I thought you couldn't wait to be alone here."

He moved to accommodate the eccentricities of their bodies. "This isn't the greatest place to sleep."

"Oh but it is. I stretch my arms out one way and my legs another way and it's just super."

"Does that mean you're sending me back to the couch?"

She touched his cheek very tentatively, sampling the feeling. "Two weeks is enough stretching."

The phone rang and MacIver said, "Shit," under his breath and got up to answer it. "Hello."

It was Sunday and so quiet she could almost hear the voice at the other end, without being able to decipher the message.

"She's not going," MacIver said and she knew it was Naomi. "She's staying here."

There was a second of absolute silence and then a shriek that caused him to move the phone away from his ear and then Naomi Shiskin's reedy, filtered voice came out of the telephone and crossed the room: "Oh, Mac, I'm so *glad*."

"So am I."

Naomi said something else and he said, "Thanks, Naomi," and hung up. "Naomi's calling Sally for you." He pulled on his shirt and sat on the edge of the mattress. "Want to see an ocean."

108

"You took me to see an ocean two weeks ago."

"This time I'd like to see it with you."

"I'd love to see an ocean."

This time she recognized the route as they drove away from the apartment. They were very quiet until they reached Brooklyn and he took her hand when they were in the tunnel.

"Have you sent your address to all those colleges you applied to?" he asked when they were back in the reassuring sunlight.

"I was going to do it tomorrow."

"You'll give them my address."

"Yes."

"That's good."

"Why do I feel as if I know you better now?" Frankie asked.

"Maybe you do."

"Do you know me better?"

"I'm not sure. You may not be as easy to know better."

She rubbed her finger on the smooth surface of Kenny's watch. "Would it be all right if I kept this spot right here warm?" She laid her hand on his thigh.

"Frankie," he said, taking his right hand from the wheel and putting his arm around her shoulder, "you put anything you want anywhere at all. Got it?"

"Got it." She moved a little closer. "It's just that we're off-island now and I feel the need for a little added security. From one of the natives."

* * *

109

"Want to go down to the beach?" They were at the railing, feeling the sting of wind and salt spray.

"Yes." They went down the steps, stopping halfway because of the wind."

"Too cold for you?"

"No." They walked toward the irregular line that divided the wet sand from the dry. "It's just as big as last time."

"You cried last time."

"I was thinking of Kenny."

"Because of the ocean or because you always think of Kenny?"

"A little of both." She pulled a mitten off and bent and touched the sand. "He was a runner," she said, straightening up, thinking maybe now she could talk about it. "Whenever I see a long empty stretch of land, I see him running." He was down there, a spot on the beach, getting smaller. In a moment, she would lose him entirely. "I feel different this time," she said, turning her eyes away from the beach and toward the man who stood beside her.

"So do I. Very different."

"You look like someone I know now." She touched his cheek with her fingertips, tracing the shape of his face, assuring familiarity. "I always wondered what people said to each other after they made love for the first time."

"What did I say?"

"Nice things."

"That's because you bring out nice things in people."

"I love you, Mac." It was the easiest thing she had

ever said in her life, and the most important.

He put his arms around her and kissed her and she thought, enjoying the kiss, how pretty they must look, two people kissing on an empty beach on a winter Sunday.

"Let's go home," he said, putting his arm around her, taking her slowly back across the sand.

"It's against the rules to say that, isn't it?"

"Nothing's against the rules. There aren't any rules." He kissed her again as they walked and she fell momentarily out of step and laughed. "I like it when you laugh."

"I thought last year was the end of the world." They started across the boardwalk, empty except for a handful of diehards. "You know when I knew it wasn't? When the feelings started. For you. It was like a sign of life."

"You're very much alive," MacIver said. "Contagiously." They went down toward the street. "It's something to celebrate, don't you think?"

"Being alive? You bet. That's what sex is, isn't it? A celebration."

"With you," he said, "it's a celebration."

Feelings tingled in her body, casting off the cold. "With you too," she said as they approached the car.

She lay in the dark beside him, the day long over. Everything had changed. Even the proportions of the loft were no longer the same. His part and her part had merged, as their bodies had, removing the indefinable line that had separated the sleeping area from the study. He had not returned to his desk although

111

once, late in the day, he had stood over it, looking at the array of handwritten pages.

She knew he was still awake although they had stopped talking several minutes ago. His hand was still on her hip, moving caressingly from time to time.

"Your missing man," she said, hearing her voice break the Sunday-night quiet, "if you found him in Mexico or someplace, living with another woman, would that be a happy ending?"

"He's not in Mexico. He's not with another woman."

"But if he were."

"I'm not an expert on happy endings."

"Isn't today a happy ending?"

"No."

"No?"

"Today's a happy beginning."

"Yes." She smiled and moved against him. "That's much nicer."

"Sleep, baby." He kissed her. "Charlie's not in Mexico. Charlie's gone."

Part
Two

One

"This was a surprise." With one finger he traced a line between her breasts, being careful not to touch them. "A nice surprise. I thought you were skinny — everywhere."

"I'm not."

"You're full of nice surprises."

She moved beside him in the half-light of early morning, enjoying the pleasure of his company. "So are you." She reached out and felt the watch on the floor beside the mattress. It was just possible to make out the time but there was no connection between Kenny's time and real time.

"Still going?"

"Still."

"When did you decide to come to New York?"

"Christmas." She put the watch down carefully. It had made another day and night. It was almost like those mornings when she had woken to see if Kenny himself was still with her. "They were all so nice to me. I felt as if they'd wrapped me in a cocoon. They kept telling me to rest awhile, to take it easy. I feel better when I'm moving."

"How about moving with me today?"

"I think . . . uh, don't you think I ought to find that Margaret Sanger place?"

"They're closed Monday. You can go tomorrow."

"Closed?"

"Every Monday."

"How would you know something like that?"

"I did a piece on them last year. They told me."

"Sure discourages the kind of weekend I had."

He laughed and kissed her. "Don't be discouraged. Call them tomorrow and make an appointment. Today you'll meet me for lunch and then we'll do something."

"No work?"

"Not after lunch. Just you, me, and the big city."

"Mac." She rested her head and chest on him, appreciating the man and his body. "Yesterday was the best day of my life."

"But did the earth move?"

"Oh, Mac." He wrapped his arms around her and she lay against him. "I knew we must have read the same books. Yes it moved. Shook. Quivered. Melted. Dissolved."

"Don't," he said.

"Don't what?"

"Don't do that to me on a morning I have an early appointment."

Afterward, she did not remember what they ate. Afterward, she could not remember where they had been. She remembered eating, drinking, walking,

116

taking a taxi, being kissed on a street corner, taking another taxi, seeing so many things that what they were and where they were became a pleasant jumble, a sweet mélange, ending finally in a small dark place where a man played a piano from time to time and once she and Mac got up and danced.

"Where are we now?" she asked on the dance floor.

"I forget."

"So do I."

"On some island or other. Do you care?"

"I don't think I care about anything. Except that you're here."

"I'm here."

"I know." She closed her eyes. It was true. It didn't matter where she was—where they were. They were alive, they were together; it was neither late nor early, it was just now, a time she would like to hold forever. Here was a place she would like to stake a claim to, fly a flag from, hold the deed to. Ours.

"Tired?"

"I hadn't thought about it." Or anything else. Nor would she. Leave the thinking to someone else, along with the worrying and the remembering. "I am so happy, Mac."

"Maybe we can stay that way."

"Oh we will." Believing it because it was true.

The music stopped and he held her rather too tightly. Then they walked slowly back to the little table.

The Margaret Sanger building was on Second Avenue at Twenty-second Street, across the street from a rather pretty church, but she wasn't sure she had quite enough time to look at it before her appointment. They had said eleven and she had walked, turning down Mac's offer of a ride. An elevator took her up to the fourth floor and when she got out, the first thing she saw was the sign welcoming Visa. The second thing, as she looked around, was the Pepsi machine which a young girl was putting coins into.

She was suddenly very nervous. She had not been to a doctor for years except to accompany Kenny, and she had never had that part of her anatomy examined. It had been something of a surprise to find on Sunday that it functioned as nature had designed it to. Well, something more than a surprise.

The instructions were to pay first. It set her a little on edge. She preferred the custom of bills presented for services rendered, not for services yet to be rendered. The woman ahead of her pulled worn bills out of a change purse in which they had been folded, four tens and two fives. When Frankie handed the cashier a crisp hundred, she received two twenties and one of the curled tens as change.

Her next stop was the lab for blood and urine samples. Then there was a long wait and a form to fill out. Frances Louise Grant, care of MacIver. She spelled the words out, liking the sound of them. She was living in the care of MacIver.

On the way up this morning she had mailed the letters to all the colleges and one very long one to Aunt Betty with her new address. Yesterday, after writing them in the morning, she had forgotten all day—and half the night—to mail them.

"Sorry about that."

Frankie roused herself from her daydreaming. A girl about sixteen had taken the seat beside her, jostling Frankie with a careless elbow.

"It's OK."

"They jab you hard too for the blood?"

A conversation-maker. Frankie looked up from the form. The girl was cute and young, very, very young. Frankie said, "No," and returned to the questionnaire. Age. She wrote two twos on the line. Did she have any children? She wrote No and looked around. Surely there were women in this waiting room who had already had them and one who looked as though she might be expecting one.

"No kids?" the girl beside her asked.

Frankie swallowed and turned the sheet over. "No," she said.

"I got one. Boy. Cute. He stays with my mother."

"Excuse me." There was an empty seat next to an attractive Oriental woman who seemed intent on minding her own business. Frankie took the seat under the hurt and angry stare of the young mother and went back to the form. Did she plan to have any children?

"Do you know how pretty you are?" Mac had asked her yesterday at one of the places where they had sat facing each other.

She shook her head. Too tall for most of the years of her life, too thin even after her body had developed, a face without flaws but without the mark of great beauty, a plain face that would serve her well in later years, no small imperfections, no bumps or bends that threatened to enlarge grotesquely and

119

overwhelm with ugliness. "It's the haircut," she had said, feelings long quiescent stirring, reaching out to draw this man in, to hold him.

"I told you you'd meet some guy and never go home."

A name was called and she drifted back to the waiting room at the birth-control center. A woman left the room. On her lap, the unanswered question. *Do you plan to have children?*

There wasn't room for a long answer and she couldn't possibly explain how she felt about having children. Besides, it wasn't anyone's concern anyway. In small letters she wrote, "Not for several years." Then she finished the remaining questions and pulled a paperback out of her bag and settled back to read.

When she got to the clinic area they gave her a blue gown to change into. She was so nervous by this time that she forgot to ask about women doctors and accepted what they gave her, which wasn't so bad after all. After she changed back into her clothes, she stopped off to fill the prescription. A month's worth of pills was six dollars. She took the curled ten from her wallet and a crisper one that was just behind it and asked for three months' worth. That would hold her till the letters came in April.

There was a police car double-parked near the entrance to the building when the Sanger clinic and the officer in the driver's seat was chatting with a civilian in a casual way.

As she paused to decide where to go from here, the civilian turned from the car and said, "Frankie."

She said, "Oh," in surprise and gratitude and watched as he said good-bye to the cops and came to the sidewalk where she waited. "You know everyone in the whole city."

"Just a few people here and there. I know the cop at the window. How are you?"

"Fine."

"Everything go all right?"

"It went fine. Super. I thought you had an appointment at Missing Persons."

"The guy was tied up." But the way he was dressed, he probably hadn't even tried.

"I'm glad."

"Get your woman doctor?"

"A nurse-practitioner. Real nice."

"I thought—" He took her hand in both of his and rubbed it. She had not yet put her mittens on. "I thought we'd go back to the apartment and try it all out. I've got the car."

"Oh."

"OK?"

"Sure it's OK except—" She took a step back so that she faced him, still holding his hand. "May I speak to you frankly?"

"Frankly? To me? Anytime," he said. "Start right now."

"Well. It has to do with these pills." She dropped his hand. "I can't start taking them for another week or so and the alternative that she suggested for the interim—that's what she called it, the interim— seemed like such an unnecessary expense. I mean, we

121

could have piles of flowers for what it would have cost. So she said I should tell you—"

"I've got a pocketful."

"You *do?*"

"Mm-hm." He patted his right pocket. "Want to see them?"

"On Second Avenue?"

"Why not?"

"You are really super. You really have them? A whole pocketful?"

He put his arm around her and they started walking. "Dozens. You look better than when you came out of that place. They scare you in there?"

"Scare me? Nothing scares me. You know that." They reached the car and walked around to the passenger side. "How on earth could you get a parking space on Second Avenue in broad daylight?"

"You just hang in there and wait. I'm a master of patience."

"Oh, Mac, thank you for coming."

He kissed her cheek.

"No carpenters today?"

"None."

"Plumbers? Painters? Electricians?"

"Just you and me."

"And a pocketful of those wonderful little things that you blow up or fill with water and do terrible things to other people with."

He opened the car door. "Get in, hick."

"You didn't call Naomi, did you?" she went on as he closed the door and circled the car. "She won't call at just the wrong moment, will she?" she continued as he slid into the driver's seat.

"I'm not answering the phone this afternoon."

"Oh, Mac," she said as the car pulled away from the curb. She closed her eyes, feeling the jolt of acceleration. "If you hadn't been there when I came out, I think I would have just died."

Naomi didn't call but the agency did, late in the day, to say they had a job for her tomorrow on the Avenue of the Americas. She took it down and showed the address to Mac, who had gotten up and put some clothes on while she took the call.

"Sixth Avenue in the Fifties," he said.

"But she said—"

"That's the official name. Brainstorm of a mayor before your time. Nobody calls it that. I'll show you how to get there in the morning. It's not hard. Your hair looks nice."

"So does yours." She brushed at it with her fingers and he returned the favor by moving his face against hers. "You gave up a whole day," she said.

"Didn't give up a thing."

"You have such perfect features. Why didn't you go into television and do the six-o'clock news?"

"Because I didn't want thirty seconds for a two-column story. Because I didn't want to have my hair styled every week, brushed to a frenzy, and sprayed every night. Because I didn't want to act; I wanted to find news, write news, and comment on news. Any more questions?"

"I think I'm fresh out."

"I had an offer once," he said. "A good one. It might have amounted to something big if I'd stayed with it. I even thought about it for a while but I never regretted turning it down."

"How did your wife feel?"

"She never forgave me."

Two

He walked her to the subway and put two tokens in her hand. He always managed to buy them during an off hour when the lines weren't a mile long as they were this morning. She had a small case of nerves when she left him, compounded by the crowding. It was the first time she had ventured underground during the rush hour and it was not an endearing experience. She had thought because she was boarding so far downtown that the train might be nearly empty but she had forgotten that a Manhattan train might originate in Brooklyn. This one certainly seemed to have taken on half the population of a small Ohio city before stopping at West Fourth Street in the Village.

Mac had said to get off at Fiftieth Street and walk, and the crisp air up on street level restored her equilibrium. They had said eight-forty-five and she would be there by half-past. She got her bearings, realizing that that was indeed Radio City just up the block, and set out for her first day of work.

What was hardest to believe was that the scrambling hordes in the subway metamorphosed into pleasant coworkers in the length of time it took for them to walk from train to office. She wondered if New Yorkers did this regularly, twice a day, assuming contradictory personality traits with no ill effects. A few people in the office came in late, blaming trains that stopped in tunnels, and somehow the excuse rang truer today than it might have a month ago.

Frankie was assigned her own "work station" and found, to her relief, that the machine was the one she had trained on. The head of the word-processing section was a Mrs. Gilley and she was very tense.

"Do you know how to work the machine?"

"Yes."

"The agency said you were very good."

"Thank you."

"Our best girl went home sick yesterday. I thought I'd give you a chance at this before I ask anyone else to try. It's Mr. Benton's quarterly progress report for the last quarter of last year and it's already late. It's got to be on his desk by five."

Frankie looked at the draft. It was ten pages, originally typewritten but much altered in pencil, blue ball-point, and red felt-tip.

"I don't think there'll be any trouble," she said, looking at the first few pages.

"Just so long as it's printed out by five. That means we'll need it by—"

"You'll have it."

Mrs. Gilley looked as though she weren't sure whether to be grateful or skeptical. She looked more the latter. "If you have *any questions at all,* please come to me."

126

"I will."

Mrs. Gilley smiled what was probably her most reassuring smile and departed for her desk near the door. As Frankie turned on the machine, it struck her that ten pages—well, eleven with all that was inserted—was hardly a monumental task for a seven-hour day.

The report contained several lists of numbers which had to be lined up by decimal points and she remembered how to do that. There were numerous instructions on spacing and she followed them carefully although they didn't always strike her as consistent. There were words she had never seen before—no one had bothered to tell her the kind of business the company handled—but Mrs. Gilley was true to her word and answered questions generously. Frankie found one misspelling and one grammatical error, both of which she corrected without asking. The job ran to thirteen pages when it was spaced according to the instructions and she turned in the disk at a quarter to twelve.

Mrs. Gilley looked at her with even greater skepticism and took the disk to the printer. For some reason, this was the part Frankie liked best, watching the conversion into print.

"Is there something else you'd like me to do now?" she asked as the printer pounded away.

"No, no," Mrs. Gilley said. "Take a break. Don't leave for lunch, though. I want you here to make corrections."

There were two typos and she apologized. Mrs. Gilley's face relaxed for the first time all morning.

"Don't apologize," she said. "This is a good job,

Frances — is that what they call you?"

"Frankie."

"Frankie. We aren't used to things being done this well first time around. Mr. Benton will be very pleased."

On the way out to lunch she passed a closed door with "W. J. Benton" on a small marker to its left at eye level. Eating her sandwich she tried to imagine the man behind the door. He would be tall with silver hair and piercing eyes, a noble nose, and a deep, commanding voice. He would be the president of the company or at the very least, first vice-president. Everyone was in such awe of him — she had heard his name whispered all morning — that she wondered whether he was harsh or paternal of some subtle blend he had perfected through years of management experience.

She returned to her work station after lunch to find a new assignment on a pad. She was to do a number of letters which would be printed on company letterhead. All the letters were signed W. J. Benton. The disk she was to use and the coding for the letters were all there. Mrs. Gilley was out to lunch so she got started.

When Mrs. Gilley returned she looked over Frankie's shoulder once or twice but said nothing until two-thirty. Then she stood behind the work station until Frankie looked up. "When you finish that one, please come with me."

It was a short letter to a West Coast salesman and she wrapped it up and went to Mrs. Gilley's desk. Mrs. Gilley stood and motioned her to follow. They went to Mr. Benton's closed door and Mrs. Gilley rapped twice.

"Yo," a male voice called and Mrs. Gilley opened the door and preceded Frankie into a pleasant office with a large window and a man at the desk in front of it who could not possibly be Mr. Benton. He was years younger than Mac, with light, somewhat curly hair receding noticeably and a crooked tooth that was very visible when he opened his mouth.

"This is Frankie Grant," Mrs. Gilley said formally. "The girl from the agency." Mrs. Gilley then disappeared.

"Sit down," Mr. Benton said, indicating a chair on her side of the desk.

She sat and glanced curiously around the office. It was square with wooden furniture. The word-processing section was furnished in metal. A single bookcase stood against the left wall, filled to overflowing with unusually wide loose-leaf binders but nothing that resembled a book. Along the right wall was a very long credenza with file-size drawers. On top was a silver thermos pitcher on a tray with several mugs and color photographs of a smiling woman and three young children. The floor was carpeted in a silver gray and the chairs were covered in a dark blue wool.

"You typed the QPR?"

"I beg your pardon?"

He lifted a fire-engine-red folder that contained several sheets of paper. "The quarterly progress report."

"Oh. Yes. This morning."

"You changed something."

It had not occurred to her that he would notice it or that it might cost her her job. A verb had agreed with the nearest noun, not with the subject of the sentence, and she had fixed it up. "I thought it would read better my way," she said.

"I called those editorial people at the New York *Times* to check it," Mr. Benton said. "They told me you were right."

She nodded. She was surprised, first that he had picked up the change and second that he had checked it.

"Where are you from?"

"Ohio."

"Well. How do you like that? I was just transferred in from Illinois."

She smiled, not sure what to say.

"Mrs. Gilley and I are always looking for good people. I think you're good. How would you like to come and work for us?"

"I thought — I'm really not going to be in New York that long."

"Well" — he handed her a business card — "if you change your mind and stay, you let us know if you're available. We don't have too many girls who type this good."

"Thank you." She stood, wondering crazily if she was expected to curtsy on her way out.

"By the way, uh . . . Frankie . . ."

"Yes."

"Anytime you want to correct my grammar, you have my permission."

She smiled. "Thank you, Mr. Benton." She did not curtsy.

* * *

At three-thirty Mrs. Gilley appeared again. "You have a telephone call," she said. "At my desk."

Mrs. Gilley thoughtfully went on her rounds of the section and Frankie picked up the phone.

"I missed you," he said.

"Mac." The pleasure was unexpected.

"Yesterday was more fun."

"I know."

"You at someone's desk?"

"Yes, but she's away."

"When do you finish?"

"Five."

"I'll wait for you at the Sixth Avenue entrance. We'll eat on the West Side."

"Mac, I think my life changed today."

"Suppose I told you mine changed on Sunday."

"I'd think you were taking advantage of a kid from the sticks."

"See you at five, hick."

They ate far west in a French restaurant. Waiters moved quickly and argued with each other loudly in French but the food was good. Mac ordered a bottle of the new Beaujolais and they sipped it before the first course came.

"Your life changed."

They were sitting in a booth, close enough to touch and they were touching.

"They take it all so seriously," she said.

"I take my work seriously."

"I don't mean the work. They take the hierarchy seriously."

131

He smiled a knowing smile. "Your first taste of corporate structure."

"I thought everyone in New York would be so sophisticated. I thought the office would be full of Naomis."

"And it wasn't."

"It was like the Middle Ages computerized. I thought at the very least that women would be called women in New York. But they're not; they're still girls. What's different is that they call the boys men."

"You want me to drive you to the bus station?"

She rubbed his hand. "No, I'm not discouraged, Mac. I'm just—"

"Shaken."

"Enlightened."

"Sometimes enlightenment can be hard to take."

She nodded. "There's this young guy—he reminds me of a kid I grew up with who became a cop a couple of years ago. Benton, no first name, just two initials, W. J. He sits behind a closed door and everybody calls him Mister and flutters around doing things for him. They treat him like royalty and all he is is this young guy with a crooked smile who didn't become a cop." She took a sip of wine. "He's from Illinois."

"He told you that."

"Uh-huh."

"Behind his closed door."

"I was summoned. There were trumpets playing and a red carpet. He thinks I'm great because I know how to spell."

"It's your finest attribute. I've been meaning to tell you."

They ate leisurely and she enjoyed the wine, enjoyed listening to his account of his day. He had begun to write a section of the book dealing with Charlie Herron's background and his family, all the research for that part having been done before the first of the year. He told her small biographical anecdotes as they ate, more, she thought, for the experience of telling than to entertain. He went on for a while, then, quite suddenly, stopped.

"He sounds like a nice guy," she said in the unexpected vacuum.

"Frankie." He looked different, something emerging she had not seen before, hairline cracks in the MacIver shell. "I want to know what the hell happened to him. There are people in this city who did something to him, something terrible, and I want to know who and I want to know what." He looked at his watch. "You want to go?" he asked as though he had suddenly tired of the meal, as though he itched to move on.

"Sure."

"We'll have coffee at home." He had already signaled the waiter.

"OK."

"I've got a surprise at home. I think you'll like it."

He paid the bill and they walked outside to Ninth Avenue. It was cold and a few snowflakes fell lazily, weirdly visible only in the glare of headlights and streetlamps, as though snow could not fall in the dark.

He took her arm and held it too tightly. "You want to quit your job?"

She said, "No," and turned toward him. His face

133

was nearly as invisible as the elusive snowflakes.

"You don't have to do anything you don't want to do."

"I'm not."

"I mean working at something you don't like or around people that aren't compatible."

"The people are fine."

"You could make it a vacation, just stay in the city and have a good time."

"Mac, I didn't say I didn't like it." She looked at the dark spot that was his face. Here and there something glittered on the periphery, a snowflake lodged in his hair. He was still holding her arm.

"Let's go home," he said.

He hailed a cab which abruptly crossed four lanes of light traffic to answer his signal. He gave the address on Broadway and then said, "Go down Ninth to Forty-second and take a left."

"You wanna cross Forty-second?"

"Right."

The cabbie shrugged and started downtown, creeping up on red lights, accelerating sharply as they changed, then slowing down so as not to get caught by the next red. It seemed an oddly inconsistent way to drive. Surely some speed midway between the creep and the zoom would have had the same effect of arriving only at greens, but the driver had not learned this or preferred to make it all a game. At Forty-second Street, he turned left.

"Look out the window," Mac said. "Watch the scenery."

"Goddamn zoo," the driver muttered. "All they do is talk about cleaning it up."

"Those are kids," Frankie said, ignoring the growled invective from the front seat.

"Right," Mac said beside her. "They're kids."

The cabdriver slowed as a bus pulled in front of them without warning. On the curb a family argument exploded into shouting and tears, a woman out of control, the man beside her slapping her angrily and storming away while two small children watched in wide-eyed fear and a small crowd stood around commenting loudly.

Frankie looked away from the weeping woman. A few doors down two rather obvious prostitutes stood near each other but not quite together, one in fishnet stockings and bright red hair striking an arch pose, the other merely looking glum. There were movie theaters touting pictures with titles that left no doubt as to their sordid content.

"This is Forty-second Street?" Frankie said.

"This is it."

The taxi spurted ahead, passing the bus, braking dangerously for a pedestrian who seemed in a daze halfway across the street, and then whipped ahead, turned a corner, and Forty-second Street was gone.

"I thought it was theaters and restaurants and beautiful people," she said, turning back to the comfort of his arm.

"They're a few blocks uptown. What you saw is what it is. The story Charlie Herron was working on is one piece of what you saw."

"I see."

"You understand why I think he'd dead?"

"I understand." But there was something in his voice, something in the way he asked the question, in

135

the way he talked about Charlie Herron. He didn't believe it himself. He was only preparing himself for the worst as she had prepared herself in Kenny's last weeks. She watched the buildings on Broadway fly by as the cab zoomed downtown and wondered if he knew, as she had learned, that all the preparation in the world didn't make any difference the morning you woke up and found it had happened.

The cab stopped.

"We're home. Come on, baby. It's been a long day."

They slid out. The night-light was on at Pragmatique, flickering fluorescently so that the brightly colored rainwear seemed to move in a hypnotic psychedelic dance.

"Frankie?" It came out in the same inquiring tone she used to use to Kenny in the morning.

"Sometimes," she said, "I miss him so much I would give anything I have to have him back for one more day."

He put his arms around her, blotting out Pragmatique and the crazy dancing colors, the city with its Forty-second Street and its W. J. Bentons, its bombed-out Bronx and its bridges to everywhere else. Something icy cold nipped at her still newly shorn neck and she knew it was still snowing.

"Let's go up," he said, keeping her close as they walked to the outside door.

When the elevator stopped on four, he put the first key in the lock. "Ready?"

She had forgotten the surprise. "Sure."

He pushed the door open and flicked on the main lights.

"Oh, Mac, it's beautiful!" In the center of the loft two sofas stood opposite each other with room between them for a table. "That's why you were home today." She walked over to the nearer one, which faced the far end of the loft, the first concrete sign that a living room existed, and touched the fabric. "Nice," she said. "Elegant. I bet it's comfortable."

"Give me your coat and have a try."

She sat, stretched, relaxed. "I like it."

"Want to quit your job?"

"Nope."

He came around and stood in front of her. "Come." He offered a hand. "I'll make you some coffee."

Three

"Let me give you some tokens." He went to the desk where he left his change overnight.

"I've still got one from yesterday." She rang for the elevator, glancing at Kenny's watch somewhat nervously.

"Here's a couple more."

"OK." She looked up and he kissed her.

"As long as you live here, I keep you in tokens."

"It'll cost you."

"Keep 'em on their toes, hick." He unlocked the door to the elevator and kissed her again.

She had not slept well, the excitement of the day repeating itself in dreams and waking her several times. One of those times she opened her eyes and saw that his desk lamp was on, covered with a towel, and he was sitting in a pair of jeans and a sweatshirt, reading with a pencil in his hand.

She said, "Mac," and he turned to look at her and said apologetically, "I woke you," and she said, "No, I woke myself."

He put the pencil down and came and squatted

beside the mattress—this crazy place where people got down on the floor instead of into chairs—and he touched her hairline above her ear and said, "Part of me is a night owl."

"I know."

And the side of her breast with his fingertips. Nice brown eyes, eyes that told the truth.

"I took you away from your work."

"Did you want to?"

"Yes." Hard to believe that she could rise from sleep and feel the stirrings of desire.

"Good." He lay down next to her, still in his jeans, and touched her nipple with his tongue.

"You're nice," she said, wrapping herself around him.

When the alarm went off a long time afterwards, the desk lamp was still on and the towel over the shade was very warm.

"Give the chopsticks a try." Naomi's hand, with its beautifully manicured and polished nails, held a pair which brought a small shrimp artfully from plate to mouth.

"OK," Frankie said with determination.

It was Thursday and Everett was spending the night in Boston, while Mac was out talking to someone.

"That's it," Naomi said approvingly. "You're a natural, Frankie."

"I didn't think I'd be able to do this till I was ready to leave."

"You won't leave, Frankie. New York will work its

139

magic."

"When the letters come from the places I've applied to, I'll be ready."

"Is that Midwestern romanticism?"

"It's American realism."

"What made you a realist?"

Frankie put the chopsticks down. "I watched my brother die."

"Frankie, my God." There were suddenly tears in Naomi's eyes.

The response was so spontaneous, so heartfelt, so very generous, Frankie could feel the shell start to weaken. She had not talked to anyone about Kenny except the members of her family who had shared the grief, and there had been little discussion with them outside the reports from the doctors on the progress of the disease. She said, "Thank you," as though Naomi had offered a traditional expression of sympathy.

"I'm glad you came to New York," Naomi said.

"So am I." She worked with the chopsticks for a moment.

"You have a house back there?"

"Uh-huh. It's a nice house. Not too big but with a pretty garden out back. It's got overgrown since my mom died but I'm going to work on it this spring so there'll be flowers again. In case I decide to sell. And then, Kenny and I have our own trees."

"That you planted yourselves?"

"That my dad planted for us. Each time my mom was in the hospital having a baby, Dad went out in the woods and came back with a little tree, a sapling. Mine's a dogwood he put in the corner of the garden.

It blooms in the spring and gets those red berries in the fall and spreads way out instead of reaching very high. That's how I see myself, stretching instead of reaching."

Naomi reached for the pot of tea and poured for both of them. "And Kenny's tree?" she asked.

"Kenny got an oak," Frankie said with a touch of pride she always felt when she thought of that tree, now much taller than she after seventeen years in the back of the garden.

"Did you know that Jews have a tradition like that?" asked Naomi. "Planting a tree for a newborn baby?"

"I know very little about Jews."

"It's been lost now that we've become so urban. It's hard to plant a real tree on a windowsill overlooking an air shaft, but my parents have a summer place up in Mahopac, and they planted trees the summers after my sister and I were born."

"Then you have a tree too," Frankie said.

"The custom is," Naomi went on, "that when you marry, you use the branches of your tree to make the canopy you get married under."

"What a beautiful tradition! I really like that. It gives the tree an extra purpose."

There was something different about Naomi now. Some of the extraordinary energy had diminished and the dark eyes were merely dark; they were not luminous. "When I moved into Everett's apartment a year and a half ago, my father went up to Mahopac the next weekend and cut my tree down."

The gasp that came from Frankie was so involuntary, it surprised her. "He couldn't," she said.

"He did."

"You're their child, Naomi. They raised you and loved you and held your hand on street corners."

"And on the other side, Everett is Protestant, divorced, and not inclined to remarry. Not that that would make much difference to my parents."

"But it's so silly, Naomi."

"Silly is what you think is silly. To them what I've done is life-shattering. To them I am lost."

"When you get married," Frankie said, "—I'm making you a promise now—I'm going to give you some of Kenny's branches for your canopy. My uncle has a pickup and I can drive them in. Kenny wouldn't mind. He always shared everything. With an oak, you know, there's plenty to go around."

"Yes." Naomi fumbled for something in her purse. Her beautiful oval face was shadowed by another look, a prophecy perhaps of another Naomi at the end of a long road. "I accept the branches," she said solemnly as though they had closed a pact.

"I mean it, you know."

"I know you do, Frankie. I think you're as good as your word." She turned over the check which the waitress had left on the table a few minutes earlier, made some calculations, and put some bills on top of it. "Let's go. This meal has worn me out."

Frankie added her share to the kitty and slid out of the booth. "And here I was, scared to death that we were going to spend the whole evening talking about Mac and me."

"Oh no," Naomi said warmly. "That would be prying. Do I look like the kind of person who would pry?" Her voice had regained its natural spirit.

"Come on, let's get back so I can dream of oak branches."

The apartment was empty and the emptiness had an unfriendly quality. Light helped, but only slightly. This was Mac's place and without Mac it seemed to be nobody's place.

She hung up her coat, thinking of Naomi's tree, wondering at the kind of parents who could be so angered by their daughter's love of a man that they could be moved to commit an atrocity.

The elevator started down and a minute later returned. With it came the return of feeling, of joy. She opened the door before he had his key in the lock.

He kissed her, kicking the door shut, and with his arms still around her said, "You never learn, do you? I warned you about opening the door to strangers."

"You've warned me about everything in New York except stepping on the cracks in the sidewalk."

"I was going to talk to you about that tonight." He kissed her again. His cheek was the slightest bit scratchy.

"You smell Scotchy."

He let her go and took off his coat. "I was talking to a cop in a bar."

"About Charlie Herron?"

He nodded.

"Mac." She walked beside him to the kitchen and he put an arm comfortingly around her. "Last night when we were on Forty-second Street. What was it he was looking into, the pornography or the prostitution?"

He pulled a chair out from the kitchen table, said, "Sit," and started to make coffee. "Neither," he said, the first drops of water falling into the filter, the first pale drops of coffee into the carafe. He stood with his back against the counter, looking a little tired. "It was the kids."

"Kids?"

"Little boys. Young boys."

"Mac." She saw it now, the reason for the reticence, for the half-answers. "You're doing his story, aren't you?"

"I have to find out what happened to him." An odd note in his voice, a plea for understanding.

"You told me you were writing about his life, about his family. You said you were writing about what happened when he disappeared."

"Frankie, honey." He touched the side of her face with his fingertips. "I'm only going as far as I have to to find out the truth."

"They'll kill you." A shudder passed through her as she said it and she knew she believed it.

"I'm being very careful. Your good sergeant is taking care of me as if he were my doting mother." He took two large mugs from the cabinet and put them on the table.

"Couldn't you just stick to the story you told me you were working on?" She heard herself sound almost plaintive.

"That's only half the story. It's only a quarter. I can't write a quarter of a story."

"Mac, what do I do if you don't come home one night?"

There was suddenly one of those silences that came even in the city; no traffic, no elevator, no distant vacuum cleaner, no rustle, no whisper. Even the coffee maker had finished its cycle of hissing and dripping. She could see that his face had become a mirror of her own.

"Honey, I'm not going to get hurt."

"If you don't come home," she said firmly. "Who do I call? Whom?" she said resonantly, thinking of the New York *Times* and Mr. Benton all at once.

He sat in the chair opposite her. "Sergeant Thomas McManus. M-a-n-u-s. Seventeenth Precinct."

"Thank you." Almost no breathing.

"I thought I was the one that was taking care of you."

"Did you?" she said brightly and somewhere in the distance a fire engine wailed its siren. "I think you got everything assbackwards, Mr. MacIver."

She got up to pour the coffee but he caught her arm as she passed and held her, still sitting, his face against her breast. She had wanted to talk to him about Naomi and her tree, about how people defied comprehension, but for tonight that was gone.

"What do they use the little boys for?" she asked, her fingers messing his hair.

"Sex."

"With men?"

"With men."

"You'll call me if you're late, won't you?"

"Frankie, baby." He took a great breath and shivered slightly. "I'll call you even if I'm early."

Four

"Don't get up yet."

It was still as dark as night but the alarm had gone off and she was about to rise, dress, have breakfast, walk briskly to the subway and start her day, probably her last one at this job. Mrs. Gilley had said several times that their regular typist would be back on Monday.

"Tired?" she asked. He had slept through the night — or at least, if he had gotten up, she had not been aware of a disturbance.

"I have a confession to make."

She turned to face him, wondering and intrigued.

"I wasn't going to tell you but my kids'll probably call tonight. It's my birthday."

"Mac! I would've stayed home and baked you a cake."

"I know. With balloons and streamers. Promise me you won't."

"OK."

"I wouldn't've told you but the mailbox'll be full of cards. My daughter always sends me three or four."

146

"You're thirty-nine then."

"Hell no," he said with feeling.

"But you said—"

"I always add in the extra year at the beginning of January."

"You were the start of the baby boom, weren't you?"

"The first. I was born nine months after my father got home from the war."

"That's nice." From the far windows where someday there would be something like a dining room, a little light replaced the darkness. "That's really nice. I was born seven months after my parents married."

The admission seemed to stun him. He said nothing for a moment, as though he were waiting for her to correct the assertion. "You know that for certain?" he asked finally.

"After the accident I found their marriage certificate. They had pushed their anniversary back four months so that it looked like I'd been born when they were married eleven months."

"What did it do to you? When you found out."

"If you mean was I horrified, no, I wasn't. I thought it was a mistake at first, the date, and then I realized it was just like them to go along and do what they wanted and when the time came, to get married. They'd always known each other. Dad came home from college one vacation when Mom was a senior in high school and they started going out. They both went to Ohio State and they both came home to teach. I guess one day they started sleeping together and when Mom was pregnant they got married. It was something they were going to do anyway. They were two terrific people, Mac. I was just a little sorry they felt they had to keep it a secret."

"Not everyone accepts things like that as graciously as you have."

"But I was their love child. That's really special. No one sat down and said, 'Let's see. Finals are the third week in June. If I give birth before the Fourth of July, I won't have to miss a single day's pay.' That's how one of the girls at work talks. She's got it down to what she calls a science. One day she's probably going to ask Mrs. Gilley if she can take off from twelve to three and then she'll go home and—"

"Fuck," he completed the sentence.

"Yes. That's just what it'll be. It isn't making love anymore when you do it by the clock. How could I be angry at my mom and dad?"

"I thought you were a hick."

"That's because you're a New Yorker and anyone from off-island is a hick."

He reached out and pulled his watch over. "Move it," he ordered, reading the time by growing light. "I'll get breakfast and drive you over to the subway or you'll be late." He stood quickly and began to throw clothes on. "No birthday cake, OK? I'll pick something up at Zabar's for dinner."

"At who's?"

"Zabar's. It's uptown on the West Side. I have to see somebody around there." Jeans. A flannel shirt. Bare feet. His hair a little wild.

"Happy birthday," she called as he headed for the kitchen.

* * *

It was her last day at work and she came home to find the table covered with a colorful assortment of salads and sliced foods.

"You know," Mac said out of the blue as they were eating, "you can still apply to colleges till the end of January."

"I've done all that."

"You haven't tried NYU. It's closer than walking distance. You can practically open a window and hear a lecture. There are eleven days left to January."

"I'm a hick from Ohio, Mac. You know that. I couldn't go to school with ten thousand New Yorkers."

They looked at each other a moment and then the phone rang and he said, "My kids," and went to get it. It was a long conversation, a happy one with laughter, and Frankie wondered about Jeannie, who couldn't help but hear the other side of it.

The Monday job came through while they were having breakfast and she dressed quickly. It was in downtown New York so it wouldn't take long to get there and Mac said he would drive her because he had to move the car anyway.

Today she had something new to wear, her first New York outfit. She had gone uptown on Saturday and spent most of the previous week's earnings, but looking at herself in the bathroom mirror, she was glad she had.

It was a beige wool jumper, long and loose almost to the point of bagginess, with a brown turtleneck sweater. The bagginess was stylish and she was thin enough to carry it off but she was especially pleased by the reflection. She had capped her shopping spree with a pair of brown heels and she had the feeling of looking very New York. All that was missing was something to hang around her neck. She regretted now having left her mother's jewelry at home.

Mac turned around as she came out of the bathroom. Something on his face, the not quite smile, made her stop on her way to the closet.

"You look smashing."

He had seen the Saks box and bag when he came home Saturday night but she had refused to show him her purchases.

"Will I make it as a New Yorker?"

"You made it the day you got off the bus."

"Mac, what you said about NYU."

He took her coat out of the closet and held it but she did not move.

"College is four years," she said.

"I remember."

"It's a little scary—you know what I mean—four years in New York."

"Is that what's scary?"

She walked over to him, turned around, and slid her arms in the sleeves. He lifted the coat to her shoulders and kissed her cheek.

"Anyone ever tell you you were gorgeous, hick?"

"God, Mac, half the state of Ohio. It's why I ran away."

"Come on," he said, putting an arm around her. "If we get down there late and my car's been towed, you'll see a side of me you don't want to see."

* * *

Everybody shouted. There was so much noise from machinery the other side of the office wall that if you wanted to be heard, you had little choice but to raise your voice.

The company was called H&R Corp. and the office stretched across the front of a second floor in lower Manhattan, farther downtown than Mac's apartment. A heavyset man in shirtsleeves stood just inside the door as she entered.

"Hiya, Sugar," he said, giving her a quick once-over. "You the temp?"

"My name is Frankie and I'm from the agency. Are you Mr. Porter?"

"Yeah. You can call me Rick if I can call you Sugar. *Marilyn!*" he bellowed across the length of the office. "C'mere. Your temp's here. Marilyn'll show you what to do," he added in a more normal voice. "Put your coat on the hook over there. *Marilyn?*"

A thin middle-aged woman with pink cheeks and too much lipstick made her way between desks and tables stacked with papers. She smiled and said, "Hi. I'm Marilyn."

"I'm Frankie Grant."

C'mon. We gotta *lotta* work for you. How do you take your coffee?"

The work was setting up a mailing list for address labels. She found the instruction manual and refreshed her memory while Marilyn brought her coffee. While she worked, Marilyn's phone rang almost constantly. Once, as she put down the phone, she called to Frankie, "Anybody asks about Selma, she's sick."

Frankie nodded. "Does the noise go on all day?"

151

"What noise?"

Frankie pointed to the inside wall. "That noise."

"Oh, the presses. Yeah. All the time. Don't worry, honey, you'll get used to it."

By eleven-thirty she was feeling warm, almost faint. She opened a window and inhaled the chill outside air. It revived her but brought with it the sounds of traffic only a story below, lumbering trucks, horns, squealing brakes. She shut the window and went back to her machine.

She was about to ask Marilyn if there was a quiet place nearby to eat when the office door opened and a middle-aged graying man entered and made his way through the narrow, messy office to her desk. He looked at her accusingly.

"Where's Selma?"

"She's sick," Frankie said in absolute unison with Marilyn.

"Again?"

"Lay off," Marilyn warned.

"You her replacement, Cookie?"

"My name is Sugar and I'm from the agency."

"Sugar, huh? I like Cookie better. You wanna have lunch with me, Cookie?"

"I thought I'd have a sandwich at my desk."

"What kinda sandwich?"

"Ham and Swiss."

"On rye?"

"On white."

"White bread?" As though he couldn't have heard her right the first time.

"Yes."

"Mustard?"

"Butter, please."

"Butter?" Now there was real distaste, both in the voice and on the face. "Where are you from, Cookie?"

"Ohio."

"Figgers." He sighed. "Coffee?"

"Would it be OK if I had a Coke?"

"Sure it would be OK. I don't make the rules." He turned to Marilyn's desk. "You?" he said.

"My regulah."

"Got it." He took a quick look at Frankie. "This is a cute kid for a change. Can she do the job?"

"She's just fine, Harry."

"Our Selma," he said, addressing Frankie, "whenever there's something needs a little extra attention, her health deteriorates."

Marilyn rolled her eyes and shook her head at the departing Harry.

"See youse girls," he said without turning around.

"Selma's going through her changes," Marilyn said confidentially when he had left. "Harry's got no heart. I mean he's a good man but he thinks everybody should work eight days like him and Rick. Selma's the best typist in the world, everybody says so, it's just the new machine scares her a little. They didn't give her the proper training. You get a little older, it's hard, you know? Maybe when you're done, you could write her a little note how to add a name or get rid of one. It would help, know what I mean?"

"Sure."

"You coulda gone with him for lunch, you know. You don't have to be scared of Harry. He treats women good and he's all bark."

"Is he the H of H&R?"

"Yeah. Rick's the R." She said Ah, as if she were seeing the doctor. "Rick's his nephew," she explained. "Came into the business when his father died. That was Harry's brother. You really from Ohio?"

"Yes."

Marilyn blew smoke and then waved it away with a thin hand tipped with bright red nails. "I thought you talked funny," she said.

"They're a comedy team," Frankie said as Mac pulled away from the curb. He had been parked in a No Standing zone outside H&R Corp. "They read their lines and wait for the laughs. And the office looks like Early Depression — except for my word processor."

"Different kind of businesses down here. One-man operations, family businesses. No frills. Every penny counts for these guys. They treat you all right?"

"Terrific. Which do you like better — Sugar Louise Grant or Cookie Louise Grant?"

Mac flashed her a look of amused skepticism. "I may not let you go back tomorrow."

"That sounds very proprietary, Mr. MacIver."

"What kind of work did you do?"

"I'm setting their mailing list up on a disk. Selma's sick. Selma goes through her changes whenever she has to use the word processor."

"I see." It was definitely amusement now.

"Mac, is there something wrong with ham and cheese on white bread with butter?"

"Ask Naomi. She has a better feel for things like

154

that."

"OK."

"Cookie Louise," he said.

"What?"

"Definitely the better choice. Cookie Louise Grant."

Frankie grinned. "My very sentiment," she said.

He parked the car down the block and around the corner from the apartment on Great Jones Street.

"I'll change and we'll go out," he said, making no move to leave the car. "You wear that. I like it."

"OK."

"You going back tomorrow?"

"Sure I'm going back. But tomorrow is pants and a shirt. I'm not wasting my New York chic on that crew."

"In the glove compartment," he said, pointing with the hand that held hers. "There's something in there for you."

"For me?" She hesitated, then opened the compartment and took out a flat package several inches long and three or four wide. "Something you got today?"

"This afternoon."

She tore it open, lifting the top of the box carefully. Inside was a delicate gold chain. "Mac, it's beautiful."

"See if it's long enough."

She unbuttoned her coat. The chain went over her head easily. "It's perfect."

"My daughter let me know before Christmas that

life without a gold chain was hardly worth living."

Frankie looked at her new treasure. "When she grows up, she'll find out there are things that are even better. Thanks, Mac. Thanks awfully much."

"Button up, hick," he said. "We're going out into the cruel world."

There was an answering machine hooked up to the telephone. He had decided to have his calls switched from the *Times,* as he would be at the office less and less. Also new was a speaker-phone. He demonstrated it by calling his children and Frankie heard his son's voice booming from the little gadget, half-filling the apartment, an adolescent voice still unsure of its range.

Mac turned the volume down slightly and she sat on one of the new sofas, scarcely breathing, afraid to make her presence known, the fact of her existence in the life of this young boy's father.

"Daddy," his daughter's voice said suddenly, clear as a bell and full of excitement, "I tried out for the spring play."

"Did you make it?"

"I have to see tomorrow if I made callbacks. Will you come if I make it?"

"Of course I'll come."

"Even if Mommy is there the same night?"

"Susannah, if you're in the play, I'll be there to see it."

Susannah MacIver.

"I'll see you both on Saturday," he was saying and then, a moment later, the sound was gone.

"That's a beautiful name," Frankie said. "Susannah MacIver. What's your son's name?"

"Eric."

"Eric." She pushed her shoes off and brought her stocking feet up onto the sofa. "What marvelous names."

"They're great kids."

"It's funny hearing their voices. They were all shadowy until now. Now they have names and voices and I can sense their spirits. They're very different, aren't they?"

"Night and day."

"Do they get along? Do they fight a lot?"

"They get along," he said guardedly.

"They have you to take after. You're so terrifically even-tempered."

"You think so."

"I've watched you for three weeks."

"You want to meet them, Frankie?"

"Your kids? Sure I want to meet them."

"Saturday night," he said. "We'll all have dinner together."

The job ended on Wednesday. When the mailing list was done, she was given several "form letters" to enter on a disk. The letters were drafted in pencil and ballpoint ink, smudged with a combination of both and with other greasy marks besides. They were not easy to read but Marilyn generously made sense out of them.

"That's Rick's writing," she said. "Rick is the brains. Harry's got the business smarts."

157

Frankie did not challenge the asessments. When the letters were finished, Rick asked to see a copy of each. She called him in while the last one was printing out and he stood watching with the awe of a small boy.

"What a machine," he murmured, as though the words had gone directly from his brain to the letter-head stationery. "You got a magic touch, Sugar."

"Thanks, Rick," Frankie said, abandoning the fight to be called by her rightful name.

"Selma's coming back tomorrow," Marilyn said when Rick had returned to the noise behind the wall.

"I know."

"How do you know? Did she call when I was out?"

"I finished the job."

Marilyn smiled coyly. "You think maybe you can write out some instructions for her? So she can figure out how to work that contraption?"

"Pull your chair over, Marilyn. I'll give you a quick course and you can pass it along yourself."

Marilyn stubbed out a cigarette and pushed her chair back noisily. "You're a honey," she said and sat down beside Frankie.

She went to the library on Fifth Avenue at Forty-second Street on Friday morning and read the New York *Times* on microfilm. There was MacIver profiling the mayor, MacIver on a city-state dispute, Mac-Iver looking into the questionable practices of a Bronx councilman, MacIver in a welfare office on a hot day in August, sounding as though he were keeping his anger down to a professional low.

MacIver outside the Waldorf the night of New

Year's Day.

A whole man emerging from the white-on-black print, a man of compassion and integrity, of desire and drive, part of him not entirely known to her but not unsuspected. (She would meet his children tomorrow.) She began to imagine fanciful headlines: "Mac-Iver Saves Hick from Ohio on First Night of Year," "MacIver Cracks Case of Missing *Post* Reporter," MacIver Book Wins Pulitzer." They all lacked the controlled, low-key tone of the *Times* but they amused her and she jotted them down on the envelope her first paycheck had come in.

"MacIver Asks Hick for Hand in Marriage."

She smiled at it, then crossed it out heavily with her pencil. She had watched Kenny die and she was nothing if not a realist. There was about as much chance of Mac asking her to marry him as there was of her getting into Harvard. She had not applied to Harvard. She tore the envelope into tiny bits, realizing when it was too late that the check stub had been inside. Oh well. She had fourteen months to worry about this year's taxes and something would save her by then. Something always did. The way Mac had.

She fished in her purse for a dime and found a pay phone. The dime went in but there was no dial tone. She tried 0 with no luck. She hung up and went to another phone where someone was hanging up. In her purse were two nickels and she fed them into the slot and dialed Mac's number. As his phone began to ring she was suddenly very nervous. After the third ring his recorded voice came on with its bland message and instructions, as devoid of emotion as everything of his she had read this morning. The tone sounded and she cleared her throat.

"This is Frankie," she said, her voice wavering slightly. "I love you, Mac." She hung up, her heart pounding, feeling rather silly, wondering what other messages her own was sandwiched between.

She got a hamburger and Coke at a nearby McDonald's and took it to the park behind the library, walking in on the Fortieth Street side. A guy about her age said something as she passed and she stopped and said, "Huh?"

"Great tokes, loose smoke," he said.

Frankie shrugged and found an empty bench. She sat and pulled the hamburger out of the bag. Down the path the guy was involved in a transaction with a young executive type who pocketed something and then lit up a cigarette and walked in her direction. As he passed she got a whiff of what he was smoking, a sweetish scent that made her wrinkle her nose. She knew what the smell was. Munching on some fries she looked around the park, observing similar transactions taking place in almost every direction she looked. The buyers were young, middle-aged, well-dressed, jeaned, male, female. She sipped her Coke and watched the smokers, some nonsmokers, and the sellers. It was all very open, as though the objects for sale were hot dogs or ice-cream cones.

"Wanna buy some smoke?"

He was standing to her left, thin and young and tan-colored and she was sure he had been watching her watching everyone else.

"How much?" she asked.

He took one extra second before he answered. "Two for five," he said.

It was that extra second. "Three," she said. "Three for five."

"You drive a hard bargain, lady. Three joints."

She took them and handed him a five. He gave her a little smile and strolled off. She took two of the joints and wrapped them in her McDonald's napkin and stuffed them in her bag, feeling around to find the matches she had taken from the Four Seasons. They were thin matches in a little matchbook with a winter-black tree on one side and trees representing all four seasons on the other.

She struck a match on the edge of the matchbook and took a drag, feeling scared in spite of the openness of everyone else's smoking. She could hardly call Mac to bail her out if she was arrested. But no one else was concerned. Neither did they seem particularly high as they sat on their benches, certainly not high the way boys got after beer. Most of these people might have been enjoying an after-lunch cigarette before returning to the office.

Frankie closed her eyes, letting the feeling creep up on her. The benches were backless and once she almost fell over backward trying to lean on the support that wasn't there. She kept her bag securely under her left arm and let the right, with the lighted toke, rest on the bench. She wished Mac were beside her, sharing and ressuring. All these people sitting alone on benches surprised her, all these little islands.

She took another drag, dropped her hand, closed her eyes again, and thought of Mac. The feelings were all good: warm and sexy. Kenny skittered in and out and even Kenny seemed happy.

Something tickled her right forefinger. She lifted her hand and opened her eyes. Her hand was empty. Turning her head slowly, she saw a little boy — God, he couldn't have been more than twelve — loping away, holding something half-smoked in his hand. She started to get off the bench but the world moved too fast and she had to steady herself on the slats, dropping back, holding still. So what? she thought magnanimously. It had been a bargain anyway.

"I liked the message on the tape."

She had come home with flowers and now they were eating dinner. "I was thinking of you at the library."

"Nice place to think."

She hadn't told him about her day. He had been hard at work when she came home and a few minutes ago she had taken a steak from the boiler and put it on the table. They had just helped themselves to some of everything when the phone rang.

He put his knife and fork down. "Jeannie," he said, making a quick move to leave the table.

Frankie reached out and put her hand on his arm. "You can call her back," she said. "She'll leave a message."

He shook his head. "It's about picking up the kids." He reached the phone before the end of the third ring.

It was a typical Friday-night conversation. Whatever arrangement he had made the previous week, Jeannie changed on Friday night. He must pick the kids up either an hour earlier or an hour later. He must bring them home at a time that would not inconvenience her, regardless of his plans for them. He must see that they ate this or did not eat that because they were going to do such-and-such on Sunday.

He argued—no Friday night had passed without an argument—but in the end, Jeannie got what she wanted, and usually when he got off the phone, he seemed deflated, as if Jeannie had knocked the wind out of him.

He said, "OK, Jeannie," and hung up, remaining at the desk without moving, facing the windows on Broadway, his back to the apartment.

Frankie stood, feeling the intrusion of the other woman on her own evening—their evening—and feeling angry about it for the first time.

"I'm going out." He stood and went to the closet without facing her.

"I'll walk with you." As though she had said something earth-shaking, she felt a quickening of her heart. He had a right to be alone but perhaps she had a right too, a right to offer him company, a right earned in the accumulated days of January.

He took her coat from the closet and held it out with one hand. "It's cold out."

"It's cold in."

He put his jacket on and went to the back door, the door to the stairs, and opened it. As Frankie started down the stairs, he locked the door behind them. A weird tribe, these island folks. Even when they ran away from home, they never forgot to lock the door behind them.

On the ground floor he opened a door and they were in the lobby, on the far side of the elevator. They went out to Broadway and he turned left toward downtown. It was dark and very cold. A few students came from the direction of NYU and turned uptown, laughing, on the other side of the street. Otherwise, the street was nearly empty.

They walked side by side like strangers accidentally heading in the same direction, except it wasn't an accident and they were no longer strangers. They crossed Houston and his pace slowed slightly.

"Were you with him when he died?" he asked.

"Yes."

"What did you do?"

"I stayed with him till morning."

He put his arm around her and slowed a little more. "Call anyone?"

"No."

"You could've—"

"What?"

"I just got tangled up in time. I was going to say you could've called me."

"I wish I could've."

They reached Broome Street and he guided them across Broadway and back up the other side. Already the street names had a ring of familiarity and she knew their order: Houston, Prince, Spring, Broome.

"Sorry it got away from me tonight."

"Is it OK with the kids? I mean, will you see them tomorrow?"

"I'll see them. It's just a game I have to play on Friday nights."

"Mac, doesn't she—I mean isn't there some kind of agreement about when you see them? Like an order or something?"

"There's no order."

"I thought judges worked those things out."

"There's no judge and no court order. We have what Jeannie calls a friendly separation."

"Then you're not really separated."

"Not in the legal sense."

"So that you can go back to her."

"So that we can both make up our minds what to do," he said very deliberately, as though the sentence had been rehearsed.

"You want to go back, don't you, Mac?"

"Frankie, if I wanted to go back, I'd go. You think I want to go back?"

After Broome, Spring, and after Spring, Prince

"Why did you leave her, Mac?"

"Because our lives diverged."

Frankie laughed and he stopped and looked at her with some irritation. "What the hell's so funny?"

"People don't separate because their lives diverge They change their schedules. They hold dinner an hour. They buy a second alarm clock. They don't *separate*."

"Spare me the Ohio philosophy, hick." He put his arm around her again and they continued north.

"Mac, you and I, our lives don't even *con*verge. The only time they overlap is in the apartment and we do OK, don't we?"

"We do fine."

After Prince, Houston, and then they were nearly home.

"Maybe you'd still be married if you had a second alarm clock."

He laughed. It was the first loosening of his mood

since the phone had rung. "Let's cross here," he said, steering her toward the curb. "I don't like what I see up ahead."

Coming toward them at Great Jones Street were three young men, walking in tandem, perhaps a few happy teenagers out for a fun Friday night. Perhaps not.

"Always alert to the evils of the city," Frankie said as they reached the other side of Broadway.

"I took in a stranger, didn't I? From the wrong side of the street."

"You think that qualifies you as a hick? You got a long way to go, MacIver."

He let her go and took his keys out of his pocket. "Just don't say I didn't try."

He was so hungry they reheated the steaks and finished dinner. By the time the dishes were in the dishwasher, it was late.

"I had an adventure today," Frankie said, turning off the kitchen lights.

"It wouldn't be a day without an adventure, would it?"

"This was different." She got her bag and found the napkin with its illegal contents. "I went to that little park behind the library."

"Bryant Park? Not the nicest place in town. Lot of drug dealing."

"I dealt."

He looked faintly amused. She opened the napkin and showed him her prize.

"What did you pay?"

166

"They guy said two for five. I made him give me three."

"For five bucks?"

"Uh-huh."

"Frankie, they're a dollar apiece anywhere in town. You got taken."

"I did?"

"You did."

"Well, let's get our coats on and find him and beat him up."

He smiled and said, "Sit down. We'll beat him up tomorrow. Let me get a match and we'll see if the goods are worth the price."

They smoked in a kind of slow-motion haze. It was altogether different from the afternoon experience. Here she had a back to lean on, company she trusted, four secure walls. She reached out and touched something familiar, his shirt, buttons.

"Nice sofa," she said dreamily. "Better than a bench."

"I tried a hundred."

"Good choice," she said.

"You OK?"

"Mm." She inhaled deeply, feeling good. "I read you today. White on black."

"White on black. Microfilm."

"Mm."

"You like me?"

"Mm. I like you."

"I mean—"

"I know what you mean." Speaking slowly. "Your words. You write good words, Mac. Just no passion."

"What?"

"No passion in the words."

"Not allowed at the *Times*. We take an oath when we're hired. Lots of words but no passion."

"Too bad." She looked across at the matching sofa opposite them. The blues in the weave danced fluidly. "I like the colors," she said.

"Jeannie's black and white. I got tired of it."

"Easy to get tired of." She moved her head and now she was swimming, or maybe underwater. Jeannie was black and white. Moving slowly. A zebra. "How could you live with a black-and-white person when you write black and white all day?"

"Wasn't easy?"

So slow. "Blue's nicer. 'Specially the way it moves."

"Frankie—"

"Sitting next to you makes me feel sexy."

"Maybe it's what you're smoking."

"Huh-uh. It's you. I'm done smoking." She took a last, very long pull on the tiny butt.

"You'll burn your fingers."

"It's how we do it in Ohio."

"I see."

"Very sexy, Mac. What a sexy man you are."

"Just no passion." He put his arms around her.

"Did I say that?"

He got off the couch without letting her go and scooped her up. The motion frightened her; it was so fast. Part of her seemed left behind, but which part? She drew in her breath and held on to him. When he reached the bed, the mattress seemed so far down, she was sure she would fall endlessly, fall without ever getting anywhere, but he set her down gently and unbuttoned her shirt, then the fly front of her pants. Then he pulled her shoes off and undressed himself as she lay watching. When he was finished, he walked away and the lights went off.

She pulled her clothes off without moving too much and Mac took his place beside her.

"This what you save the passion for?" Her voice coming out in the same slow motion.

"Take me," he said.

She reached and they kissed, moved, touched, held, all slow, all very unhurried, except the feeling. She took him with both hands, stuffing him inside her, drawing him closer with legs and knees, arms and hands. He moved to accommodate, to accompany, his movements slow, flawless. No one in the world better than Mac. No one with his flawless, slow rhythm.

The telephone rang.

Oh shit, Frankie thought, not wanting to think anything. It's black-and-white Jeannie changing the plan again.

But for all she could tell, Mac didn't hear it at all. Nothing about him changed. The phone rang once— twice—three times, and then it stopped, matching the slow rhythm of their love.

Aunt Betty had said that some things were splendid. Aunt Betty never knew what splendid meant.

Five

It was five o'clock on Saturday and she was showered and nearly dressed for the early dinner up at a steak place in the West Forties. Her hair fell into place as she moved brush and hair dryer in front of the bathroom mirror. When her hair was done, she began to dress. Everything was new. In spite of Mac's assurances on the casualness of both the meeting and the dinner, she had returned to Fifth Avenue after he had left this morning and bought a black wool skirt, a black-and-white-checked double-breasted jacket with beautiful black buttons, and finally a white blouse, her first in silk. Trying on the entire outfit in a dressing room, she knew she needed a pair of black shoes. Last week's browns were out, as were the old pair she had brought with her from home. She had to go into one of her original hundreds to manage it, but the total effect was worth the price. Black and white.

Her heart sank a little as she remembered what he had said last night about Jeannie. Still, she looked good, better than good, and maybe Jeannie only favored black and white in furniture.

She got her bag and found her keys and then it dawned on her. The bag was awful. Had she really carried this old, worn, shapeless sack to the Four Seasons? It was years old, one of those large carry-everything bags that went everywhere, no discernible color and no remaining style. But it could not go with her tonight.

She stood looking at the bag, feeling helpless and pressed for time. It was time to go. If she arrived late, the kids would be hungry and irritable and they would hate her. But the bag was terrible and it was too late to go out and buy a new one.

She ran across the polished floor to Mac's desk and dialed Naomi. "The is Frankie," she said when Naomi answered. "I have a favor to ask."

A black bag? Naomi said cheerfully. *Sure* she could borrow a black bag. Come on up.

"You are *gorgeous,*" Naomi said, opening the door to the elevator. She was wearing a pale blue terry robe and looked freshly scrubbed.

"Oh, Naomi, I'm meeting Mac's kids for dinner and I'm a wreck."

"His kids. You look like you're being introduced to the Queen of England at least. Come on in. You can take your pick." She led the way to a dressing room off the bedroom and opened one of several drawers built into one wall. "Silk? Calf? Patent? Maybe a little python."

"Garter snakes are all I can handle." Her eyes ran over the assortment. "This one, I think."

It was plain, envelope style, lined in black leather and stuffed with tissue paper.

171

"It looks like you've never used it."

"Dozens of times. Take it. It's perfect."

"Thanks a million. You'll have it back tomorrow."

"Call me Sunday morning and we'll take a trip down to Orchard Street and buy you one at discount."

The elevator was still waiting. "Naomi," Frankie said, her hand on the door, "is there anything you don't know?"

"One or two things," Naomi said. "Have a good time."

In the apartment she quickly transferred wallet, keys, and tissues into Naomi's bag and dropped her own on the floor near the door. She put her coat on, noticing that there were raindrops on the windows. Damn, she thought, and went back to the closet and took out the plastic yellow-trimmed poncho she had bought two weeks before at Pragmatique. She slipped it on over her coat and went to the mirror in the bathroom for a look.

The reflection was almost grotesque. She looked like an adult who had borrowed a piece of clothing from an adolescent. She took the poncho off and looked at herself without it. The coat was not new but it was OK. The black shoes were smashing. Her legs were long and graceful. The haircut was beautiful. The face looked scared.

She stuffed the poncho in the closet, grabbed an old umbrella, and left. Mac had given her a five and ordered her to take a cab. It was so close to six now that she didn't have a choice. Going down in the elevator she did something she hadn't done in quite a while: she closed her eyes and thought, Kenny, I need you.

They were waiting inside the restaurant and as she entered, she saw Mac smile at her and then say something to the children. What she noticed was that after he said it, the boy looked directly at her but the girl turned and looked at Mac.

She had rehearsed their names in the taxi, saying them over and over, Susannah, Eric, Susannah, Eric. She had wondered more about Eric, wondered if he would remind her of Kenny. Now, sitting at a table for four, Susannah on her left and Eric on her right, she found him unfathomable.

He wasn't sullen; he was simply quiet to the point of being uncommunicative. Susannah, on the other hand, dominated the table. She asked questions, answered them, offered opinions, and told Eric what he wanted for dinner.

"I can order myself," he said, putting together his first sentence since Frankie's arrival.

"Lay off, Susie," Mac ordered.

Susannah rolled her eyes.

Mac looked across the table at Frankie. "You shopped today," he said.

"I had nothing to wear." She felt uneasy and sounded foolishly apologetic.

"See, Daddy? Everybody says it."

"I thought you'd wear the brown outfit you got last Saturday."

"It didn't feel right."

"This is very nice. Worthy of more appreciative company."

"I'm appree . . . appresha . . ." Susannah stumbled over the word. "Well, I am, aren't I?"

It made Frankie laugh. "You sure are. And it's great."

"I also appreciate your gold chain."

She could feel herself redden. "Thank you." She touched it where it showed in the V of the jacket.

Susannah turned to Mac. "That's exactly the kind of gold chain I told you about. Remember? At Christmas?"

"I remember. When I told you you were too young for gold."

"Betsy has a gold chain," Susannah said with the slightest hint of a whine.

"Good for Betsy."

"And Lisa."

"You're overdoing it," Eric said, emerging from his silence. "Can't you see no one's interested?"

Susannah turned to Frankie, ignoring her brother. "Where did you say you came from?"

"Ohio. Not too far from Columbus."

"Is it nice there?"

"Real nice."

"Do you have lots of friends there?"

"Uh-huh."

Susannah stole a quick look at her brother, then flicked her eyes to Frankie. She smiled, showing even teeth. "Do they all wear nice gold chains like yours?" she asked.

Frankie laughed. Across the table, even Mac was smiling. Eric was shaking his head.

"She never gives up," Eric said.

"Susannah," Frankie said, "you're the funniest person I've met in New York."

Susannah giggled. "Do they?" she persisted. "Do they all wear nice gold chains like yours?"

"Um." She tried to picture them. "I don't know. Does silver count?"

"Not much."

"Pearls?"

"Pearls are for old women."

"This'll daunt you," Mac said. "If nothing else has."

"How old are you?" Susannah asked.

"None of your damn business, Susie," Mac said and at the same time Frankie said, "Twenty-two."

"Twenty-two's not old. My father's thirty-eight."

"I know." She looked at Mac, realizing she had misspoken. It had not occurred to her that anything she said might be carried home to Jeannie MacIver, but she saw now that everything might. Everything would.

"Where did you meet?"

"We met the way people usually meet," Mac said. "We were in the same place at the same time."

"It isn't always that way." Susannah sounded a little deflated. "You could have met on the phone. Then you would have been in different places at the same time."

"It didn't happen that way," Mac said, his voice softening a little.

"What was the place?" Susannah persisted.

No one answered and suddenly Frankie was laughing again. "The Waldorf-Astoria," she said.

Susannah looked at her father. He looked back but didn't say anything. Observing him, Frankie could almost see the bond. Knowing he was a father and seeing him be one were quite different. It was not a relationship by agreement or blood. It was founded in affection.

"I like the Waldorf-Astoria," Susannah said finally. "It has a good ladies' room."

The coffee wasn't as good as Mac's but the apple pie a la mode was a treat. Frankie tried once or twice to talk to Eric but it was worse than difficult. He would not be drawn into the conversation and the most he would do was answer her questions with a word or two—short words. He was a nice-looking boy, resembling Mac but with the obvious influence of another person. Susannah looked nothing like either her father or her brother. Her skin and hair were light and the face was someone else's.

"Daddy," Susannah said when Mac had settled the bill, "could we see the loft again tonight?"

Mac looked at his watch.

"It's *early*, Daddy. Please?"

"Yeah," Eric said with more enthusiasm than he had shown since Frankie's arrival, "let's go. Is the furniture in yet?"

"The sofas came."

"I want to see them, Daddy," Susannah said.

"OK, let's go."

She was nervous riding up in the elevator, afraid she had left some telltale sign of her residence lying around. She had not asked him whether the kids knew, had taken it for granted they did not. The elevator stopped and Mac opened the door and turned on the master light.

"It's *nice,* Daddy." Susannah, stepping off the elevator, sounded genuinely impressed. "Did you sit on them yet?"

"Once or twice."

"I'll break 'em in for you." She plopped on the farther sofa, facing everyone, knees apart, knit argyle knee socks ending in tasseled brown shoes with thick soles. She was still wearing her coat.

Frankie took a quick look around, unbuttoning her coat. Aside from Mac's chaotic corner and a couple of cartons still to be unpacked, the apartment looked about the way it had four weeks ago.

"Did you throw away the old couch?" Susannah asked.

"Gave it to the Salvation Army."

"Mommy said you bought from them when you were married."

"We did."

"So you sleep on the floor now?"

"On the mattress."

"Did you get the sleeping loft built yet? For Eric and me?"

"Not yet. There were some complications."

"Like what?"

"It'll be done soon," Mac said.

Frankie took a step backward toward the closet. "Oh," she said, feeling her heel catch on something, sensing that something on the floor was where it shouldn't be and was tipping. There was a metallic sort of clash and then the sound and glint of something rolling across the polished floor.

"I'll get it." Susannah was up, chasing a cylindrical object headed for the far wall, for the bookcases. Anyone else might expect it to be a lipstick but Frankie knew better. Her ancient shoulder bag, which she had dropped next to the door a couple of hours earlier, had tripped her and spilled its secrets. Near her new, pretty black shoes were a mirror, a dime, the stub of a yellow pencil, a dirty tissue.

Susannah scrambled to the floor and reached around the end of the bookcase. She moved with the agility of a child and with none of the grace of a woman. It was what made the rest of her so endearing, but less endearing at this moment. Frankie could hardly breathe, waiting to see whether the little cylinder that was not a lipstick would be retrieved.

"I got it." Susannah stood and inspected the small object. "Who's Evelyn Grant?"

"My mother." As though someone else had said it, the voice came to her from a distance.

"These are her pills."

Frankie began to move toward Susannah but Mac intervened. "I'll take them," he said, and after looking briefly at the label, he dropped the vial in his pocket.

Susannah took her coat off and dropped it on the mattress. Frankie opened the closet door and shoved the offending bag inside, then doffed her own coat and hung it up. There was chatter, conversation which she heard but which did not include her. Eric asked Mac about the book and Mac showed him a folder of material on the Herron case. Eric carried the folder carefully to the sofa and sat down, looking intently at the clippings and photos inside.

"How's Karen?" Susannah asked from the bookcase.

"She's fine," Mac said.

"Do you still go out with her?"

"No."

"I thought she was pretty."

"She is."

"Mommy's out with Alex today."

"Good for Mommy."

Susannah giggled. "You mean good for Alex. He's a real jerk. And he has no hair."

"He's rich," Eric said from the sofa and went back to the folder.

"Show me how your new phone thing works, Daddy."

Frankie and Mac turned to look at each other. "The phone call," she said, remembering.

Mac went to the desk and bent over the answering device.

There was the usual introduction and then a man's voice came on, speaking in a very measured way, without haste, almost as though he were reading a prepared statement. "Listen, Mac, you know who this is. Don't try to get hold of me no more. I got my number changed after you left and I'm not calling from my phone. I told you I didn't want no part o' this and I mean it. It's a lousy business and I'm glad to be out of it. If you don't take care, you'll end up like he did. Just one thing. I shouldn't be tellin' you this, but you should listen to the tape. The notes don't say everything. They're just notes, you know what I mean? There's something on the tape. Maybe it'll mean something to you. Maybe it's nothing. Let's hope so. It's a lousy business. Did I say that before? Anyway, I'm out of it now, Mac. Leave me in peace. OK?"

There was the sound of a phone hanging up and then the start of another message. Mac shut the machine off.

"Who was that?" Susannah asked. Her eyes were wide and she sounded subdued.

"Nothing, sweetheart," Mac said. "Somebody I talked to for my book."

"He sounds weird."

"Is that the guy in Nebraska?" Eric asked.

"That's the one."

"What tape does he mean?"

"Nothing. Just a . . ." He looked at Frankie. She knew she had paled listening to the recording. She had taken off her jacket because it was so warm in here but now she wished she hadn't.

"They set up a number when someone disappears. This is the guy that took the calls. Some of the calls. If it hasn't been chucked out or used to tie a package or recorded over, maybe there's still a tape of those calls. I'll look into it on Monday. Meanwhile, how about we make some hot chocolate? You a hot-chocolate expert, babe?"

She nodded, feeling more, not less, frightened. The message had been one dire warning after another. If Mac was successful, he would destroy himself.

"Eric, how would you like to run across the street and pick us up some marshmallows?"

* * *

An hour later she sat in the car outside a large apartment house in the East Eighties. The doorman had tipped his hat as Mac and the kids went inside. They must know everything, she thought, these men in gold braid. A whole city that guarded its privacy and here were the people who knew all the secrets — who brought home lovers at odd hours, who received deliveries of strange products, who did not come home at night to sleep.

Mac came breezily out the glass door, said something to the doorman, and came around the car. "Exhausted?" he asked, shutting the door.

She shook her head. He leaned over and kissed her and she put her arms around him and held him, one more for the doorman.

"I told you they were just kids," he said.

"Mac, that phone call."

"Frankie, if you worry about every phone call, you dig yourself an early grave."

"But he sounded so . . . so ominous."

"That's the way they talk when they leave the force. All he said was there might be a tape and if there is, maybe there's something on it."

"OK."

"Did I tell you you look smashing?"

"Yes."

"Could I interest you in an adult drink with adult company in a bar I like around here?"

"No hot chocolate?"

"They throw you out if you mention it."

"I really pigged out on those marshmallows, Mac."

"Scotch'll fix it. Scotch fixes everything." He

181

turned on the motor. "Almost."

"You know me," she said. "I'll try anything."

"I'm starting to wonder." He reached over and took her hand. "If I know you at all."

Six

Naomi took her to Orchard Street while Everett and Mac remained home with their work. Orchard Street was teeming.

"Naomi, this is Sunday."

"That's why we're here."

"But everything's *closed* on Sunday. Didn't anybody ever tell them?"

"Too many times," Naomi said. "They're Jews. This isn't their sabbath."

"It was yesterday." Her voice echoed her amazement. Another layer of insularity had crumbled.

"And today's a workday. Even the parking meters work on Sundays down here."

The man who sold the black bag to her had a beard and wore a little round cap which was unpronounceable even after she tried several times. But the bag was magnificent. The leather was fine, inside and out, and the front was decorated with a single lightning stroke in black snake.

"Very in," Naomi assured her.

"I hope it wasn't one of my pals back at the pond,"

Frankie worried, thinking of summer walks over the last fifteen or so years, with boyfriends, girlfriends, or with Kenny.

They went somewhere else and she replaced the aging shoulder bag with a handsome new one.

"Would you believe I took this old thing to the Four Seasons?" Frankie said as they left the second shop. "No wonder Mac calls me a hick."

"He didn't notice."

"How do you know?"

"Mac has a different kind of eye. It only sees what's important."

"You have such a nice touch, Naomi. When you tell people they have insufficient funds, they must leave feeling wealthy."

Naomi flashed one of her winning smiles. "Come. I want you to see what kosher food tastes like."

"Raw fish?"

Naomi laughed. "More like overcooked beef."

"That sounds real fine," Frankie said with relief. "I was afraid I was the only one on this island who knew how to overlook anything."

Naomi made her try seltzer, which she didn't like, and noodle pudding, which she did.

"Good food," she said. "Is that how your mother cooks?"

"Sometimes."

"No wonder you're so healthy. Cut everything with a knife and pick it up with a fork. None of those little wooden sticks. It may even last."

"So my mother tells me."

"Naomi." Frankie put her fork down and looked across the table earnestly. "Let me talk to your mother. About you and Everett. About how right you are for each other."

Naomi sipped her seltzer, holding the glass with slender fingers tipped with a beautiful shade of pinkish red. "Thanks," she said. She shook her head.

"You got me a job. You got me a haircut, which was even more important. You lent me a great black bag when I needed one and then you got me one of my own. Let me do this for you."

Naomi looked down at the table so that her long dark lashes were set off against her fine skin. "If I thought it would work," she said, still not looking at Frankie, "I'd drive you there myself. But it won't. My mother would be polite to you for the first five or ten minutes. Then she would be rude. She's not a rude person but she would become rude if you tried to tell her what she doesn't want to hear. She doesn't want to hear that Everett and I are happy. She doesn't want to know that Everett and I will be happy. She wants me to leave him because she believes that that's right."

"Right is being honest."

"Right is living the way my mother wants me to."

The waiter put two pieces of flaky apple strudel on the table and filled the coffee cups.

"But it's a lovely offer," Naomi said.

"Will you marry him then? Anyway?"

"Marriage isn't what Everett and I want." She had shrugged off her uncertainty and become once more the woman of confidence. "You want to marry, don't you?"

"Someday."

"After Mac gets his divorce—"

"He's not getting a divorce."

Naomi looked up with sharp, curious eyes.

"They're not legally separated."

"They're not . . . I didn't know that," Naomi said. "I thought . . ." She sipped her coffee and Frankie could almost sense the wheels turning. "How long have they lived apart?"

"Since last summer."

"And no legal separation." It was a statement, a revelation. The structure on which her appraisals and advice had been founded had crumbled like the crusts of strudel on their plates. "That makes it tougher," she said thoughtfully. "He still isn't sure the marriage is over."

"Maybe it isn't."

"It should be. I told you, I met her. She's one of those beautiful, self-centered, manipulative women who always get what they want, and when she's ready, she'll manipulate him back. And he'll go because when she does it, it'll be the decent thing for him to do."

"Maybe it'll be the right thing."

"Frankie, do you want this man or don't you?"

"I don't know."

"I'm sorry," Naomi said quickly. "You're right, it's none of my business."

"I didn't say that," Frankie said with a feeling of despair.

"Only because you're too polite. Let me say something to you. You have to ask yourself that question. You've asked it already, I can tell, but you may not have answered it yet, or maybe you can't face the answer yet, or maybe it's just none of my damn business and you don't want to tell me. But *you* have to know. You have to say, Do I want this man? When the answer comes up yes, you'll see what you have to do. It's all in how you answer the question."

"Oh, Naomi." Frankie took a deep breath and let it out quickly. "All this and kosher food and two pocketbooks on a Sunday morning."

Everett smiled and patted her pinkish-red lips with the napkin. "Just remember. When Jean MacIver makes her move, fight back."

The NYP plates were parked in front of the building when they came back and upstairs Mac was finishing a sandwich. He said, "Terrific," when he saw the new bags, and watching him, she thought maybe he really hadn't noticed what she carried that night at the Four Seasons.

"Were you out?" she asked.

"I ran uptown to ask about that tape. No one with any clout is around today. I'll take care of it tomorrow."

He had been more concerned about it than he had let on.

"Do I get to hear it?" she asked.

"If they let me make a copy I'll bring it home and play it. Don't expect too much. There'll be some obscene calls, some well-wishers, some crackpots."

"But the guy who called seemed so sure."

"Frankie, he's been away from the job for six months. He took all those calls seventeen, eighteen months ago. His wife is sick. He's got things on his mind."

"But you went up on Sunday."

"Well." He smiled at her. "It's in the blood."

She put her new bags away and gathered up the sections of the *Times*, pulling her shoes off and making herself comfortable on the sofa. Mac went back to his cluttered work area and for a while there was the sound of the typewriter, first steadily, then intermittently. Finally it stopped. The Sunday silence was nearly unbroken. There was a distant siren, but there was always a distant siren in New York.

"You happy here?" Mac asked and it occurred to her that he had been watching her.

"Sure I'm happy, Mac."

"Not homesick?"

"Huh-uh." He seemed to be waiting for something further. "For my room sometimes," she said.

"What's it like?"

"Four walls, a door, and eight-foot ceilings."

"You miss that."

"Just a little."

"You think I should enclose the bedroom? Will you sleep better?"

"I sleep fine and it's your place, Mac."

"I want you to like it."

"I do."

"I mean feel comfortable here. You want your name on the mailbox?"

"No."

"Why not?"

"I'm not Naomi."

"I didn't suggest you were."

"No name on the mailbox, OK?"

"OK."

"I just want to stay in the care of Mr. MacIver."

He smiled and she realized she had added a telltale article. "You'll always be that," he said. "With or without your name on the mailbox."

When they took a walk late in the afternoon she carried her new burnished brown leather shoulder bag, appreciating its fresh, leathery smell and Naomi's choice of a hard-to-pick closing. They picked up an assortment of intriguing foods at a takeout and went home. Mac put the bag of food down on the kitchen counter and as he turned around she hit him with a wadded-up missile made from a page of the *Times*. "Good arm for a hick," he said.

"I don't really warm up till spring."

"Frankie." He pulled off his jacket. "I want to talk to you about those pills."

"Talk," she offered agreeably.

"I want to know why you were carrying them."

"I just wanted them out of the bathroom after Mom died."

"They're sleeping pills."

"I know what they are."

"You ever take any?"

"Never."

He pulled out a kitchen chair and sat facing the sofas, preserving a distance. "I believe what you tell me," he said.

"I wouldn't lie to you, Mac. To someone else, maybe, but not to you."

"They were your mother's."

"She needed them," she said, as though someone had to explain for Mom. "When Kenny got sick again, when it came back really, Mom couldn't sleep. She'd walk around the house at night. Sometimes I'd hear her crying. She changed. She looked awful. The pills helped her sleep. She looked better when she took them. Not that she was ever her real self again.

"Anyway" — she took a deep breath — "when she died, I cleaned out the bathroom and threw everything away. There wasn't much. We were a pretty healthy family." She looked at Mac. "That sounds silly, doesn't it?"

"It sounds fine."

"I found Mom's pills. There were only a couple."

"Two."

"You count good, MacIver. There were two and I put them in my bag. I don't know why. Maybe . . . maybe I didn't want anybody to find them. Maybe I didn't want anyone to know Mom had had to take pills."

"Nobody knows," he said.

"Thanks, Mac." He had stood. "Do I get them back?"

He pulled them out of his pocket. "Catch."

There was a little glitter as it came through the air but she missed it with her hands. Instead, the plastic vial struck her painlessly on her sweatered chest. She looked at it. Two pills were inside.

"You'll never make the pros with an arm like that," she warned.

"That's what they told me twenty years ago. It's why I settled for a lesser profession."

She smiled, but she could feel her hands shaking.

Seven

The numbers were money. She had been assigned to a large bank and by the middle of the week they had asked her if she wanted to stay. She said not permanently, thank you, but maybe for a week or two. She had lunch with some of the young people in the clerical pool and found they had been hired the same way, after working for a while as temps. It was a good bank to work for, they said, encouraging her to sign on. There was good medical and a savings plan and a pension . . .

She got home late—the subway broke down and she decided to walk the rest of the way although it had turned cold—and she got off the elevator to find the coat closet in shambles and a thick new mattress on the floor where the air mattress had lain for the last month.

"Taking the place apart?" she asked after the welcoming kiss.

"They got it wrong the first time." He took her coat and hung it in what was left of the closet. "The top was supposed to be a sleeping loft for the kids

191

but they didn't reinforce it so I got them back. It'll take another day." He turned and nodded at the mattress. "I couldn't move them on the bed so I took what we really needed. Give it a try."

She slipped her shoes off and padded over. It was much higher than the air mattress and far less giving. She lay down, relishing its unyielding firmness. "I may never work again," she said. "I may not even get up for dinner."

"No choice on dinner. I've gotta see a guy tonight so it's eat and run. But maybe you'll wait up for me."

She got up and padded back to her shoes, then to the kitchen, where the table was laid rather artlessly with cold cuts and a rye bread. "If you come home, I'll wait up."

"I'll come home. When have I ever failed you?"

"Hello?" It was nearly ten and she answered only because she thought it might be Mac.

"Uh—is this Frankie?"

"Yes, it is."

"This is Susannah. Is my father there?"

"Oh hi, Susannah. No, he's out right now."

"Are you there all alone?"

"I'm waiting for him."

"Oh."

"Can I give him a message?"

"When will he be home?"

"I'm not sure. He had an appointment."

"Oh."

"I can leave him a message."

"No, it's OK. I'll talk to him tomorrow. 'Bye."

" 'Bye, Susannah."

"I'll get her tomorrow after school." He kissed her again, a slightly alcoholic kiss although he was very sober.

"She doesn't know I live here, does she?"

"I haven't said anything."

"I think she suspects and I don't think she likes the idea, Mac."

"I'll see if she says anything Saturday. She's a pretty open kid." He took his shirt off as he spoke. He had not worn a tie, an indication that the meeting was with someone he knew or someone for whom he did not have to dress. "Something wrong?"

"I was thinking what it would feel like to be twelve and know that your father was living with someone."

He stopped undressing and turned to face her. "Frankie, I'm not living alone the rest of my life. And Susannah won't be twelve forever."

"But she's twelve now."

"And I'm thirty-eight now and not without a few earthy desires of my own. After Tommy McManus dumped you on me and I got over my urge to kill him, I knew I didn't want to live alone anymore. That Sunday when you didn't move uptown, when we went to bed together instead, was the first time in six months I did something without thinking about Susannah and Eric. Am I making myself clear?"

"Yes."

"Good." As though a film halted on a single frame had just restarted, he resumed undressing. "I'm taking a shower," he said very matter-of-factly. "When I get out, I don't want to talk. About anything. OK, hick?"

"Fine with me, pal."

When she awoke in the middle of the night, she realized how well she had been sleeping these last weeks. She had slept well tonight too but Mac had gotten up and now the lamp was on his desk and he was reading notes.

She turned on her stomach so she could see him and raised herself on her elbows. "Hear your tapes today?"

He said, "Oh," in surprise and turned to look at her. "Hi, sweetheart. Yeah, I heard the tapes."

"Anything interesting?"

"Some heavy breathing."

"Bring 'em home?"

"Against the rules. I listened to them at the precinct."

"So it's a dead end?"

"Pretty much."

"Great bed."

"I should've thought of it sooner. I waited till my back started giving out."

She waited a moment and then said, "Mac?"

"That was a very pregnant pause. This is going to be some question."

"Am I good in bed?"

"Very good." As though it were the most ordinary of questions.

"I mean, I couldn't have been awfully good the first time."

"I didn't think about it the first time. Besides, you were terrific."

"Do men really talk about that? Whether women are good in bed?"

"Sometimes. Yes, they talk about it."

She put her head on the pillow and moved her body back under the blanket.

"No more questions?"

"Huh-uh. I'm gong back to sleep."

Jeannie was irritable. It took only a minute of hearing Mac's side of the conversation to understand that she wanted him to forgo seeing his children this weekend.

"Forget it," he said as Frankie hung up her coat in the resurrected closet. "This is not a point of negotiation, Jeannie. I see them tomorrow. That's it."

Frankie looked around. At either end of the apartment, vertical blinds had been installed since this morning. They were drawn across both expanses of windows and were three-quarters closed. They were some light color, almost without color, a beige maybe, and textured. More than anything else in the apartment, they added a dimension of warmth.

"Fine. Then we'll talk about Sunday."

Frankie found a pair of jeans and a shirt and changed her clothes. He had acknowledged her presence when she came in. Now he bent over the old desk as though to create a small private space where he could talk to his wife without distractions or intrusions.

"I know what I gave up in January. I'm not giving anything up in February, so make up your mind: Saturday or Sunday."

In sneakers she walked quietly across the apartment to the kitchen. There was nothing on the stove or in the oven, nothing lying on the counter that might be a meal. She found some orange juice in the refrigerator and poured a glass.

"That's your problem, not mine. They can do homework tonight, they can do homework tomorrow, they can—"

She wondered how long he'd been at this and whether he was winning points.

"Don't give me shit, Jeannie."

Her mother used to go into the master bedroom and talk on the telephone to Kenny's doctor. Sometimes she didn't come out for a while but when she did, she was composed; she was Mom. It all turned on having a little privacy.

"It'll be there at ten." The telephone banged down and there was that silence.

She waited a minute, then went to the desk. "They're the best things in the apartment," she said in a careful voice.

"What are?" He was facing the blinds.

"The blinds."

"They are nice, aren't they? They were Karen's suggestion. Karen made a couple of good suggestions."

"That guy in the dorm at NYU is going to get a big disappointment tonight when I undress."

"Well." He touched the front of her shirt. "There's a way of opening them. If you have something going with the guy."

"Jeannie giving you a hard time?"

"It's what she excels at." He stood and kissed her.

196

"I'll see the kids Sunday instead of tomorrow. It'll give us a chance to do something on a Saturday night. OK?"

"Fine."

"Maybe we'll have a picnic here on Sunday."

"Now you're talkin'. Where do I build the fire?"

"Same place you always do, hick. Come on. Let's go out for a bite."

It was interesting the way Susannah did it. The three of them arrived at four, cold and very hungry. Mac had taken the kids to brunch and they had eaten nothing since. When they arrived, the table was set, several fat hot dogs and two pounds of hamburgers were ready to be grilled.

Frankie rolled her sleeves up and Susannah offered to help. Mac and Eric sat on a sofa with the *Times,* reading and talking while Susannah acted like an angel in the kitchen with Frankie.

"There's Coke," Frankie said. "Want to put it out?"

"Sure." Susannah trotted to the refrigerator and took out the large bottle. "Who's the cheese for?"

"For anyone who wants it. Your dad likes cheese."

"Don't you?"

"Some."

"My mom likes it too."

"Here's the potato salad, Susannah. Want to put it on the table?" She put the bowl in the waiting hands.

"That looks like a boy's watch."

"It is."

"Then why do you wear it?"

"It was my brother's."

197

"Why doesn't he wear it?"

"Because he died."

"Died?" It was Eric's question, from the sofa. She had not realized that the male conversation had stopped a moment earlier.

"Yes," she said.

"How old was he?"

"Seventeen."

Mac had put the paper down. Now he stood.

"What happened?" Eric asked. When she had said "Seventeen," his face had taken on a look of disbelief, a hint of fear.

"He was sick."

Mac said something to Eric and came to the kitchen, a settling influence, something you could reach out for if you really had to.

"Seventeen," Eric said like a reluctant echo.

"Those are very personal questions, kids," Mac said, standing near the refrigerator.

"That's OK, Mac. They didn't know." But it was good having him there, knowing he had the power to turn off the assault of questions with a few well-modulated words.

"I'm sorry about your brother," Susannah said. She looked sorry, her face solemn and her eyes wide.

"Thank you, Susannah. That's very nice of you."

She felt Mac's hand on her back, just below the neck—it was the first time he had touched her in front of his children—and just then the timer on the stove began to sound.

"OK," she said cheerfully. "Picnic's ready." She got everything out of the oven and on the table and they all sat down and started to eat hungrily.

198

"You look good in jeans," Susannah said.

"Thank you." It caught her by surprise. "So do you."

"Daddy says you need a small ass to look good in pants. I have one. So do you. So does my mother."

Frankie didn't look at Mac, who sat to her right, but Susannah stared straight at him across the table as though she were addressing him personally.

"Do you ever wear designer jeans?" she asked, turning to look at Frankie.

"No. I wear jeans to relax. I don't think I could relax if I paid fifty dollars for my jeans."

"You should get a pair. They'd look good on you."

"Because you have a small ass," Mac said beside her and she felt her cheeks burn.

"Everything OK, Eric?" she asked, squeezing Mac's hand, which had found its way to her knee under the table.

"Fine."

"Hamburgers done right?"

"Yeah."

"Eric likes his hamburgers mediumer than mine," Susannah volunteered.

"Is that more done or less done?" Mac asked resuming his dinner.

Susannah shrugged. "Mommy just does it right. That's all."

" 'Mediumer' isn't a word," Eric said.

"Well, Mommy understands it so it must be, right, Daddy?"

"It doesn't follow logically, but I'll accept it as part of your vernacular."

There was a silence. "My what?"

"The special language you and your mother share."

"Oh that." Susannah tossed off a big smile. "I thought you were mad at me because I said 'ass' at the table."

It was later, while they were sitting in the living room, that it happened. Mac and Eric were talking about the Herron case, quietly, as though they were in conference, and Frankie was on the floor playing checkers with Susannah.

"So what *isn't* a dead end?" she heard Eric ask.

"There're still avenues," Mac said as Susannah jumped one of Frankie's blacks. "I'm going to look into the police files on unidentified bodies from the last year and a half."

"You mean like derelicts?"

"Derelicts, runaways."

"They have pictures in those files?"

"Yes."

"Your turn," Susannah said.

Frankie surveyed the board. She had decided to lose gracefully when they started playing but found it was all she could do to stay almost even. She pushed a king and leaned back against the sofa.

"What was your brother like?" Susannah asked.

"He was the nicest person I ever knew in my whole life."

"Oh."

"Charlie Herron wasn't a derelict or a runway," Eric said. "Wouldn't they automatically match the fingerprints with all the missing people?"

"There were forty thousand missing people in New York that year."

"Wow."

"Anyway, I have to eliminate the possibility that his body surfaced and wasn't properly identified. Or was misidentified and got buried in potter's field with the derelicts."

"You're not paying attention," Susannah said grumpily. She got up off the floor and walked away toward the bedroom.

Frankie watched her. Susannah was wearing red corduroy pants and a gray, rather luminous sweater that looked handknit in a very fashionable way. She was trim and still little-girlish and she really did look good in pants. In another year or two all that girlishness would be transformed into a mixture of sex and flirtatiousness—but she would still have a good ass for jeans. Frankie smiled. Susannah was nearly to the door to the bathroom. She stopped instead at the bedroom closet, part of the built-in section between the door to the elevator and the wall of windows at the front of the apartment. She opened the closet door and peered inside. It was a large closet with many built-in drawers and shelves and a light that went on automatically when the door opened. Since her arrival, Frankie had shared the closet with Mac, hanging her things on a high rod on one side while he hung his on a low and a high on the other side. His and hers. Karen had designed the closet that way.

Susannah stood staring at the hers side. It was what she had wanted to know and she had waited till now to find out. She closed the closet door and Frankie saw the light go out. Then she went on to the bathroom.

The four of them played another game together

when Susannah came back and at seven Mac said it was time to go. Susannah put up a perfunctory protest and then got up, followed by her brother. They went to the bed, where they had dropped their heavy jackets. Frankie tidied up the pieces of the game.

"Come uptown?" Mac asked.

She shook her head. "They have a lot of things they want to ask you. Without me."

"Come anyway." He gave her a hand and she got up off the floor. "I'll get your coat."

When they got out of the car in front of Jean MacIver's apartment house, he was hit with questions from both sides. Frankie watched the three of them walk past the doorman, Mac's hand on Susannah's back, Susannah looking up at him and talking a mile a minute. They turned left inside the door and disappeared.

She looked at Kenny's watch by the light of a streetlamp. A boy's watch, slowing down. Well, you could still time things, like how long it took for Mac to get back to the car.

It was seventeen minutes.

"You were right," he said, closing the car door. "Lots of questions."

"I hope Eric sleeps well."

"He will."

"Susannah . . ." She had wanted to tell him but now she wasn't sure.

"What?"

"Susannah checked the closet. Where my clothes are hanging."

"Then she saw your clothes," Mac said.

"Right." She moved over to be close to him and he patted her thigh with his leather-gloved hand. "I like watching you be a father. It's a nice side of you."

"It's not a role I play. It's something I am, even when they're not around."

"I thought — when I first met you — I thought you were being a father to me. But you weren't. You were being something else."

"It's hard to remember," Mac said. "It was so long ago."

Five weeks. The red light on the corner turned green and he pressed the accelerator, the car rushing down an almost empty Second Avenue on this cold Sunday night. He hadn't offered her a drink or diversion when he got into the car. The presence of the kids had put a lusty edge on their closeness. He was taking her home while it was still early, no dinner to cook, the week's work wrapped up, the Sunday *Times* read and absorbed, nothing to think about except satisfying the lust.

She hoped Susannah would sleep well too.

Eight

The call on Monday morning told her to report to Mrs. Gilley. Mac got two tokens for her from the desk, where he left the contents of his pockets each night, and said, "I'll call you. When I get a minute this afternoon."

They kissed at the elevator and he unlocked the door. Inside was the man she recognized as their neighbor one flight up. She said, "Good morning," as Mac closed the door behind her and the man nodded and flicked his eyes to the front of the elevator. She shrugged, feeling carefree even if Mr. George F. Goldstein didn't. As she stepped into the lobby, Everett and Naomi appeared from the door to the stairs.

There were effusive good mornings as Mr. George F. Goldstein stonily slipped out the door.

"Frankie, we must talk but I've got to run. 'Bye, darling." Naomi turned to Everett and they kissed and then, spontaneously, kissed once again. As Naomi dashed out the door, Frankie saw the residue of a smile on Everett's face.

"Where to today?" he asked, moving briskly across the lobby.

"Up near Radio City."

"I'll give you a lift."

"Gosh, that's nice, Everett."

Up the block, Naomi's trim figure was hurrying away. Everett stepped off the curb and a cab pulled from the other side of Broadway to where he stood signaling, a kind of New York magic. He held the door for Frankie and she slid in. Everett gave an address to the driver and he pulled back across Broadway and took the first right.

"Did Naomi tell you we're going away?"

"No. How marvelous. When?"

"Friday evening. A little island-hopping. Neither one of us can take New York in February. We'll be back on Washington's birthday."

"With a suntan."

"With two suntans." He was nearly beaming.

"How super, Everett."

"We'll leave the key with you and Mac. Maybe you'll run up and douse the plants once or twice."

"Sure I will."

"We're planning to bring back a case of champagne. Maybe you and Mac will come up the night we come back and help us celebrate."

"Celebrate what?" She put her hand on the seat to steady herself as the cab went into an unexpected turn.

Everett shrugged slightly, looking mischievious. "The case of champagne," he said with a smile.

* * *

"Well, don't you look nice, Frankie," Mrs. Gilley said as she walked into the familiar room with its several word-processing stations.

"Glad to be back," she said, pulling her coat off, glad she had worn the beige jumper and the gold chain, the combined effects of living in New York and loving Mac.

"Lots of work," Mrs. Gilley was saying. "Andrea won't be in so you may as well use her station today. And Sharon's going to be late, something on the Long Island Rail Road. I nearly got caught in that myself, but I always take the earlier train."

The patter went on as Frankie hung up her coat, smiled at some familiar faces, and adjusted the chair at whoever's place she was working at. She pushed aside an ashtray that had been emptied but was still fetidly ashy.

"Here are the disks and the draft." Mrs. Gilley laid them next to the keyboard. "We thought we were finishing on Friday but Mr. Benton came in over the weekend and there we are."

The draft was marked up in blue ball-point. Frankie looked through the first few pages.

"It's for the two-o'clock presentation," Mrs. Gilley said. "The annual Eastern Division meeting." She paused. "If it's too much for you, we can ask one of the other girls to help out on the second half." It was clearly a challenge.

Frankie looked at Kenny's watch. "Let me get started," she said, rolling the chair to its most comfortable distance. "I'll let you know in a hour if I need help."

Mrs. Gilley bent to speak to her privately. "If you

need to work through lunch—"

"It's OK, Mrs. Gilley. I won't walk out till it's done."

"What I meant to say, Mr. Benton said if you work through lunch to get it done, you can have the rest of the day off."

"Mr. Benton said that?"

"Mm. But we want you tomorrow, all right?"

"Sure I'll be here tomorrow." She flicked on the word processor, found the first disk, and got started.

The last of the fourteen copies were printed and collated by five to two and Mrs. Gilley asked Frankie to deliver them to the conference room upstairs. She rode the elevator and went down a hall to the sign that said "Conference Room" and turned right. The door was open and a group of several men and two women was standing at the far end of a very long table, drinking coffee from Styrofoam cups. One of the women, a small, young, pretty woman in a black suit, pale gray blouse, and large glasses, looked at Frankie, then turned back to her conversation.

Suddenly, a familiar face looked her way, a smile showing crooked teeth. Mr. Benton put his cup down on the table and walked the length of the room to where Frankie was standing near the doorway.

"Thank you very much," he said, relieving her of the fourteen copies in their pale blue folders. "Did you check my grammar?"

"It reads fine, Mr. Benton. I didn't have time to go over every word."

"Did Mrs. Gilley tell you you've got the rest of the day off?"

"It's very kind of you."

"We will see you tomorrow, won't we?"

"Yes."

"We'll have the minutes of this meeting to be typed up. They're usually a mess but I'll give you all the help you need."

"Thank you."

"Go on and have a nice afternoon." He moved to the table and started distributing the blue folders, one in front of each chair. Frankie glanced back at the group drinking coffee. The small young woman looked at her once again and then, as though reinforcing the system which had placed them in separate and unequal castes, rather deliberately turned back to her group of men with a smile.

"You're early." Mac left his desk and came toward her.

She had not thought to ring. "I did something they defined as heroic and they gave me the rest of the day off." She handed him a large assortment of tulips, guaranteed to have been flown in from Holland, and kissed him.

"What do they define as heroic?"

"I did five hours of work in five hours."

"Sounds heroic to me. I may make you an offer."

She leaned over the flowers and kissed him again. The phone rang.

"That's my call." He tossed the flowers to her and went to answer, calling over his shoulder, "Don't giggle. I'm putting on the speaker-phone. And we have a date for dinner tonight." He pressed the button on his desk and said, "MacIver," as though he were in his office.

"Mac." The voice boomed into the room. "I got a little pink slip says you called."

"Hello, Tom. I was down at Thirty-third Street today, looking at DD-thirteens. Rossante gave me a hard time."

"He shoulda gave you a hard time. You're off your rocker. Charlie Herron isn't planted in potter's field."

"I have to check it out. I want to see the files on the unidentified bodies since the day he disappeared."

"You're talkin' fifty, sixty bodies, Mac," the sergeant's voice said with a whine. "That's a fishing expedition. Rossante's not gonna let you mess around like that in his files."

"I need to see them." Mac's voice was low and firm. "I don't want to pull strings. I don't want to get anyone sore. If you put in a word with Rossante—"

Frankie laid the flowers on one sofa and sat on the other.

Mac was half-facing the windows, visible now through the nearly open vertical blinds.

"First of all," Sergeant McManus said in a reasonable tone, "you don't need to see them all."

"All," Mac said.

"For Christ sake, Mac, half of them are little girls. You don't need to look at little girls. Right?" There was a pause and McManus said, "Am I right?"

"Right," Mac said grudgingly.

"And second, Herron was white. So we got it narrowed down to white males, and if you remind me how old Herron was, we can—"

"White males," Mac said. "I'll start with white

males."

"Gimme a coupla days," McManus said, plainly relieved. "I'm on till midnight today. If I get a chance, I'll talk to Mike tomorrow. I'll look at the file on Herron and narrow it down a little more to make him happy. You'll have plenty to start with."

"Thanks, buddy."

"Anybody ever tell you you're a royal pain?"

"Not until this minute, Tom. I think you have the honor of being the first. Let's have a drink one night. When you're back working days."

"Yeah," McManus said without enthusiasm. "I'll be talkin' to you."

Mac reached over and pressed the button that cut off the sound but remained sitting. Frankie stood and picked up the flowers, cradling them across her left arm as though they were a baby.

"What's a DD-thirteen?" she asked.

"A report on a missing person or an unidentified body. The bodies turn up around the city. They come out of the walls when an old building is torn down."

"Don't, Mac."

"Sorry, babe. I didn't think what it sounded like."

"It's so ugly and you're so . . . casual about it."

"I don't feel casual. I feel rushed and a little angry."

"Why?"

"I'm almost halfway through my leave and I still feel like I'm nowhere."

"You said you weren't going to try to find him."

"I have to find him. Finding him is the key to everything." He walked over and stood on the other side of the sofa. "Let me see the flowers," he said.

They walked a few parallel steps with the sofa between them, then together to the kitchen.

"The colors are terrific." They were half red, half yellow.

She sliced the ends of all the tulips at once with a stroke of the meat knife on the cutting board. Then she put the knife down and looked at him. "Please be careful," she said.

"I'm always careful."

She opened the cabinet. "You know what you need? A pretty vase."

"Why do you say 'you'? Why don't you say 'we'? Don't you live here?"

"You know I don't, Mac. I'm a guest."

"You're not a guest," he said. "You live here. We live here together. How does that sound?"

"It sounds very nice."

"To me too." He touched the side of her face with his fingertips. "So let's get a vase."

"OK."

"My best buddy just blew into town. First time in two years. He's on expenses and he's taking us to dinner."

"Wouldn't you rather go yourself? If it's the first time in two years?"

"I wouldn't rather. I would rather have you come with me." He looked at his watch. "It's early. I forgot you came home before sunset. Stretch out and take a nap. If I know Al, it'll be a late night."

They drove uptown and parked the car in the hotel garage. Then they rode up to a high floor on an elevator that eased to a stop so smoothly it was hard to tell when the ascent had ended. It was a long walk to the room where Al and Katie Black waited for them, down a hall lined with identical doors differing only in the number stenciled on each one at about eye level. The pattern of doors was almost unvarying: door, long space, door, short space, door, long space, door, short space. It was very quiet, only here and there the rising and falling sound of a television set in the moment it took to pass.

"Here we go."

He knocked and there were voices from within and then the door opened and Mac wrapped his arms around someone.

"Jesus, it's good to see you." It could have been either of them speaking, so equal was their enthusiasm, but the voice was not Mac's.

"Let me get a look at him," a woman's voice called from the room. "God, you're beautiful, Mac. You are *beau*tiful. Where's my Jeannie?"

She felt something happen to her heart and she reached for Mac's hand, he took hers and drew her into the room. Two very surprised people stopped in mid-breath to look at her.

"Didn't Jeannie write you?" Mac asked, still holding her hand.

"I haven't heard from her since June or July. I wrote twice and then . . ." Katie Black was a lean woman with dark hair, somewhat unkempt. She was standing near the draperies at the far end of the room, next to a table littered with folded sections of a newspaper, a glass, and a bottle of liquor. She wore an attractive straight wool skirt with shades of cream and light brown woven together and a white V-neck blouse with a collar and buttons down the front.

"We separated," Mac said. "In July."

"Jesus." Al Black exchanged a look with his wife and took a deep breath. He was fully bearded, the hair a beautiful shade of dark blond mixed with an almost red. He was ruggedly good-looking, what you could see of his face. It was hard to tell his age, but probably around Mac's.

"This is Frankie Grant," Mac went on. "Al and Katie Black."

She said, "Hello," without moving and she let Mac's hand go because one of them was sweating and she thought maybe it was she from the heat of those four eyes.

"Listen, I'm starving," Katie said, moving toward them. "I slept most of the afternoon and Al spent the day in the shower." She smiled, as though it were an in joke.

"Takes a while to get Southeast Asia out of the pores," Al said. He scratched one arm as if to show he hadn't yet accomplished the task. "Let me hide the Scotch and we'll go down to get a cab."

"See, Mac?" Katie said. "Nothing ever changes. The crown jewelry stay in full sight on the dresser"—she pointed to a large gold masculine ring—"but the Scotch gets the full treatment."

Al was down on the floor beside the bed. He laid the half-full bottle on its side and pushed it under the bed almost as far as he could reach.

"We know what's important," he said, getting up off the floor. "Come on. We'll talk over dinner."

Dinner was on the East Side, where the menu was

large and printed in French and English. Mac kept the conversation on the Blacks, asking about places, events, people Al worked with, and Al responded elaborately, his narration enhanced by Katie's intruded comments, wry and acidic barbs that enlivened her husband's journalistic descriptions.

They drank cocktails and wine and then brandy with coffee and it got late. Frankie felt absent. She could not imagine why Mac had been so adamant about her joining them. The Blacks seemed embarrassed by her presence, averting their eyes to avoid meeting hers. But the conversation was captivating. With all the complaining, the Blacks led a fascinating life. They had lived in a dozen exotic places, witnessed events that had made headlines, met people whose names were famous. There was an excitement in everything they had done.

"It was a dull place," Katie said at one point, but surely the dullness of the place was more exciting than the most thrilling moment of most people's existence.

They had been to Moscow — but that was long ago.

"I forget the year," Katie said, yawning. "Something important happened that year. Oh yes, Mac went to the *Times*."

From time to time Mac would turn to Frankie and explain some small mystery or elaborate on a detail that came up in the conversation. The day the sniper had fired, Katie hadn't been there.

"I was in Paris," Katie said in a tired voice. "A little R and R."

Each time he turned to her, she sensed a message passing between the Blacks although nothing was ever said.

Once Al looked her way and asked, "You ever been out of the country?"

"No," Frankie said, grateful that he had acknowledged her existence. "I just saw my first ocean last month."

"You've seen one ocean . . ." He shrugged.

"Not true," Katie interjected. "There are oceans and there are oceans. One of them made me cry once."

It was hard to imagine this cool, almost hard woman weeping over an ocean.

"So you've had it with Southeast Asia," Mac said while they were sipping coffee.

"Up to here."

"It's the showers," Katie said. "Al can only be happy where the showers run his way. If he could wrap one up and take it with him, he'd go to the Caucasus. Well"—she smiled—"maybe not the Caucasus."

"I'm looking forward to these two years in Washington," Al said thoughtfully. "See how it works out, how we like being home. I figure we'll get ourselves a little apartment in the Watergate—"

Katie laughed. "Albert, you're just as naive as the day I met you. You don't earn enough to tip the doorman at the Watergate."

"Let's go back to the hotel," Al said after he signed the check. "They've got one of those dark bars reeking of good leather that we used to think we'd spend our whole careers in."

"Some of us do," Mac said, taking Frankie's arm as they walked away from the table. "Minus the good

215

leather."

"Oh, Mac," Katie said dramatically, "you do lead the most enviable life."

The bar was dark and smelled faintly of leather. They slid into a booth and the men ordered drinks. After Frankie asked for coffee, Katie asked for a pot of tea.

"So you're writing a book," Al said when they had been served.

"On Charlie Herron's disappearance."

"Don't know him."

"He was working on a story."

"Figures. You got an agent?"

"An agent, a contract, and an advance."

"Sounds great. Got a story?"

"I got a story."

"See, Al?" Katie said. "New York can be fun."

"He dead, Mac?" Al asked.

Mac took a breath. "I don't know." He paused. "Yeah, he's dead. He would've surfaced by now if he were still alive."

"Killed by a story."

"Probably."

"You better watch yourself, buddy."

Mac sipped his Scotch but didn't say anything.

"So where the hell are you living?" Al asked. "The gal who picked up your phone at the *Times* gave me a number and I called it without asking."

"I've got a loft on Broadway, near NYU."

"Jesus, you've gone native."

"High-class native," Katie said.

"Someone die and leave you a million dollars?"

"Not a million," Mac said slowly. "There was

something from my father. He always said a man should own property. 'Land' is what he said but where can you find land in Manhattan?"

"Jeannie still in the apartment?"

A pause. Then, "Yeah."

"I think I need to find the ladies' room," Frankie said.

Mac dug in a pocket and pulled out some coins. "Here, honey," he said, handing her two quarters. "It'll probably cost you." He slid out of the booth and she came after him.

"Me too," Katie said, giving her husband a push with her shoulder. "If you can still move yourself."

The lounge was rectangular with makeup tables around one end, a long narrow mirror encircled with cosmetic lights in front of each one. Frankie sat in a French-provincial-style chair at the other end. It was not made for comfort but she would be comfortable enough for the time she would spend in it. The chairs and a lone settee were covered in a pink shiny fabric that might have been silk and the rug was also pink with an ivory border design.

Katie came into the lounge, saw her there, and took the adjacent chair, crossing one slender leg over the other so that the hem of her skirt lay exactly across her bent knee. She stared for a moment at the mirrors across the room.

"It's nothing personal," she said suddenly. "It's just that Jean McIver is the best friend I have in the world."

"Yes."

"And at my age, there's something more than a bit disconcerting about a man you know and care about leaving his wife for a much younger"—she paused very slightly—"woman."

"Mac didn't leave his wife for me." She was irritated that Katie Black had followed her here. She had wanted to leave Mac alone with them to explain, as she had not let him explain to her, his separation.

Katie looked back at the mirrors and touched her hair. "You're not very forthcoming, are you?"

"It's nothing personal. I'm not a very forthcoming person."

"You're not a New Yorker, are you?"

"No."

"Neither are we." She touched her hair again, her eyes across the room. "I need a haircut badly. And a dry cleaner. If I wear this skirt one more time . . ." She looked down at it and ran a slender hand across her lap. "Bloomingdale's," she said. "First thing tomorrow. When you're away for a long time, you go on shopping binges. Then you have to keep yourself from throwing out everything you got on your last binge, you're so sick of it."

"New York's a nice city to shop in."

"I'm looking forward to Washington. The weather's nice, there are people we know, we'll get to see Jeannie and Mac . . ." Her voice trailed off. "It makes it hard, you know, when your friends split up. You almost have to take sides. You go out with him and his girlfriend one week and her and her boyfriend the next week. Nothing's the same anymore. Half of them are strangers and you don't really want them to become friends. Then after a while, you stop

218

seeing one or the other socially and there goes a piece of your life. I didn't want that to happen with Mac and Jeannie."

"I expect they didn't want it either."

"Sometimes when Al and I are in one of those places that looks so exotic in pictures, when the only other people who speak our language are such lushes I can't bear to be with them, we stay home and make bets on how long our friends' marriages will last."

Frankie smiled. "Who wins?"

"Never our friends." Katie turned to her. "What was your name?"

"Frankie Grant."

"Frankie, Frankie. Even the names change. You go away for two years and everyone has a different name. Mac likes you, Frankie. He's nice to you. Of course, Mac's always nice to women."

"Mac is very good to me."

"Ah, so you can be forthcoming. Mac is very good to you. Then you're not just the first number he rang today for a last-minute date." Katie looked at her. "You're not, are you? That's why you're so quiet about it. You don't—you live with him, don't you?"

"Yes."

"God," Katie Black said. "Everyone lives together now. No more your place or mine for dinner. Everything is ours from day one. Where do you go when you want to hide?"

"Maybe Mac and I don't need to hide yet. From each other."

"It's good to hide once in a while. Stimulates the vital organs. Everyone's so together now, so chummy. I wonder if Al and I would have married if we'd lived

219

together first. Or if we would have stayed married."

"Of course you would. You've lived together for a long time."

"It's not the same. The marriage makes it different." She looked at a narrow gold band on her left hand. Her husband wore a similar one. "Marriage is more permanent than love."

"I always thought love was the most enduring thing in the world."

"Because you're young and you've never had to test endurance. The MacIvers had a good marriage, in spite of everything. We have a good marriage, maybe because of everything. When we've lived apart, it was because of Al's work. There were times early on when I couldn't tag along. I never went home to Mother, even when I probably should have. I stayed in some nearby friendly country." She put a special note on "friendly." "I lost a baby one of those years."

"I'm sorry," Frankie said, addressing Katie's profile. "I'm awfully sorry." She glanced at Kenny's watch, which didn't tell her how late it was. Then she began absently to rub her finger over the face.

"Jeannie never had trouble getting pregnant exactly when she wanted to," Katie said evenly, as though that were one sorrow she had packed up and left in the friendly country. "Maybe it's something you're born with, or maybe it was just something that was more important to her. I'll have to call her tomorrow." She said it as though it were something she would rather not do. "I'll have to tell her about you. What do you think I should say?"

"Say anything you like."

"I'm really talking too much. If I'd had less to

drink, I'd be less verbose and more circumspect."

"You mean less honest."

"That's precisely what I mean. My poor Jeannie. All she ever wanted in the world was Mac. From the day she met him. She was devastated when it looked as though he might go abroad . . ."

"That's what he wanted, wasn't it?"

"Oh they all want it. Till they get there. Abroad isn't always the place you dreamed about."

"He didn't go?"

"They got married instead. We got married too and when Al's turn came, we went together."

"It must have been disappointing for Mac."

"Lots of things in life are disappointing. Disappointments pass. Mac's not unhappy." She turned to look at Frankie. "Jeannie is."

"Jean MacIver sounds like a very manipulative woman, Mrs. Black."

Katie smiled very slightly. "Love cancels out manipulativeness and you may as well call me Katie. If you're living with Mac, we'll probably be seeing each other." She looked at her watch. "Maybe I can drag Al upstairs." She took a last look at the mirror across the room and touched her hair one more time. Then she stood.

The men had moved to the inside of the booth and the women sat on the ends of the benches. Mac gathered Frankie close with his arm and said, "More coffee?" When she nodded, he signaled the waiter and ordered it for both of them. Katie Black had nothing.

221

"Hear about Ted?" Al asked.

"Yeah. Damn shame."

"He still out of work?"

Mac nodded. "Does some free-lance."

"What a lousy deal. What about Burt?"

"Nothing."

"You'll never guess who we saw in the airport in Paris yesterday."

"Albert," Katie said, "if I can't talk you into leaving, I'm going up to bed. Jet lag and all that." Her face looked very worn.

"You got the key?" Al asked.

"It's in your pocket."

Al put both hands in his jacket pockets and pulled a hotel key out of the one on his right side. "Check the Scotch," he said, handing it to her.

"You check it. If I get down that far, I won't get up. Good night, Mac. You're still the most beautiful man I know."

"Good night, Katie."

"It was nice to meet you," she said to Frankie. "After all." Then she walked away.

"Can I put you in a cab?" Mac said, speaking quietly to Frankie. "You must be falling asleep."

"I'll stay and drive you home."

"I can drive."

"Not tonight."

The coffee came, two steamy cups. Al raised his eyebrows at the coffee and sipped his Scotch with undiminished pleasure.

"You're a nice kid, baby," Mac said. "I'll let you drive me home."

She pulled to the curb where "Pragmatique" was pinkly aglow in the window. "What time is it?"

"Almost three, Pacific War Time."

She turned off the motor and handed him the keys.

"Thanks for coming tonight."

"You say it as though I did you a favor."

"You did."

"I like a guy who needs a favor now and then."

"Nobody ever drove me home before."

"Nobody anywhere?"

"Ever."

"Not even your wife?"

"Especially not my wife."

"I think I'll sleep on that," she said.

Nine

On Friday they drove Naomi and Everett to the airport. It was a new Everett in the back seat beside Naomi, an Everett Frankie could not have imagined, expansive, laughing, more talkative than she had yet seen him. He and Naomi had put in an almost full day of work and then rushed home to finish packing. The flight left late but it was Friday, there was weekend traffic and that intense desire of both of them to get away, so there was a nearly frantic atmosphere when Frankie finally arrived home from work.

Shiskin-Wright had already locked the apartment upstairs and moved their luggage to Mac's, where Naomi sat on one of the blue sofas and Everett stood with a drink in his hand as Frankie left the elevator.

"OK," Everett said, welcoming her, "let's move."

The trip took them to Queens, a new borough for her, and highways she had not yet traveled. The mood in the car was euphoric and contagious. There was a lot of laughter. It was clear that the back-seat passengers had both left their respective rewarding,

224

life-filling, and ordinarily time-consuming jobs behind them as soon as they had crossed the river, and
as for that place they referred to as New York,
although they were still in one of the five boroughs, it
too no longer existed.

There were anecdotes and more laughter and at
one point Everett tried to sing some old song that
had come to him that morning, and Naomi could
hardly catch her breath.

"Don't forget, you guys," Everett said as they
approached signs directing them to the airport,
"champagne when we get home. I know a place
where it's so cheap you can't afford to leave it
behind. Mac, can I get you anything?"

"Thanks, Ev, I wouldn't know where to put it."

"We'll get a straw hat for Mac," Naomi said. "Isn't
that how they always show reporters in the old
movies?"

"Mac's not a reporter, honey," Everett corrected
her. "He's a journalist."

"He's getting to be a pest to a lot of people at the
moment," Mac said.

"Not our Mac." Naomi patted his shoulder. "Ev,
did you give Frankie the keys?"

Everett made a sound of surprise. He took a metal
ring out of his pocket and handed it to Frankie.
There were two keys on it.

"Plants at both ends of the apartment," Naomi
said. "Two good dousings should do it. Or three if
you have the time. And if you need any eggs, come
up and take a few. Just leave two for when we come
back."

"Don't leave anything, Frankie," Everett said.

"We'll get everything new when we come home. Right, love?" He kissed Naomi's cheek with an audible smack.

There were color-coded signs to the various airlines, half of them with names she had never heard of. Mac swung off the main road into a maze of roadway. "I'll drop you two right at the door. If no one's there to check your stuff, I'll help you get it in."

"What, and leave?" Everett sounded amazed. "Nothing doing. You'll park the car and have a drink with us, right, Frankie?"

She turned and met Mac's eyes.

"OK?" he asked softly.

She nodded, feeling suddenly part of a couple in a way she had not felt before, part also of the foursome, this warm, happy group that treated her as one, not as a poor substitute for an absent member.

He swung the car onto a ramp and stopped before a row of glass doors. "Stay with them. I'll meet you back here."

"I'll walk with you."

"It's cold."

"That'll make it nicer."

He leaned over and kissed her lips as the back door opened and Everett got out.

Mac was right about the cold. He parked as close as he could but it was still a walk. The wind was strong and after he put his arm around her, she reciprocated with hers and then she didn't think about the cold.

"They won't get there till late," he said.

"But they'll wake up in the sun. Won't that be nice."

226

"You want to take a trip somewhere warm?"

"Huh-uh. I'm taking a trip somewhere cold, remember?"

"Hear anything from your colleges yet?"

"Little postcards telling me my application is complete."

"And they've got your new address."

"Yes."

"You don't really want to go to school in Ohio, do you?"

"I need to go to school, Mac. Ohio's what I know. I'll get a good education there."

"You have other options now."

"I can't sit at a keyboard the rest of my life. The only place you can go in the kind of work I'm doing is to become a Mrs. Gilley someday. Or be assistant to someone who really does things."

"That's not true for everyone."

"Mac, if I have to spend four years working my way up to Mr. Benton's office, I'd rather spend them on a campus learning something eternal than sit behind a bunch of machines."

"I can't argue with that."

"Something happened on Monday." They were near the curb now, heading toward the walkway that would take them across streams of traffic to the terminal where all that warmth waited. "In the conference room where I delivered the fruits of my five hours of labor. There was a young, gorgeous, marvelously dressed woman talking to a bunch of men. You know, coffee at two before the next speaker. She looked at me in a certain way that emphasized our differences. She didn't exactly put me in my place;

she just acknowledged that I had one and I didn't belong where she did."

"Put cyanide in her coffee?"

Somewhere lights turned red and at least some of the traffic abated. He held her hand and they took off across the myriad of lanes.

"Just renewed my intentions," she said, feeling the cold as she inhaled deeply and more rapidly.

Naomi and Everett had a table in the little lounge and they ordered drinks and sandwiches and kept up the happy chatter. Mac seemed very relaxed, as though he had time to kill. It was Friday night, the night he usually talked to Jeannie and allowed her to rearrange the plans they had negotiated the previous weekend. Perhaps he had spoken to her earlier in the day, allowing him to enjoy an evening out. It was good to see him this way, good to share a happy occasion.

A muffled voice made an announcement on the loud-speaker and Naomi turned to Everett. "Mr. W," she said seductively, "I believe they've called our flight."

"You mean I missed it?"

"Listening too hard, Ev," Mac said, standing. "Listen, have a great time."

There were handshakes and kisses.

"You look all rosy, Naomi," Frankie said.

"I'm feeling wonderful. I think I'm happier today than I've ever been in my whole life."

"Have a super time."

She stood beside Mac and watched them go, joining a large group ambling toward the metal detectors, Everett carrying a small bag in each hand and Naomi with both coats over one arm. She turned, smiled, waved, and threw a kiss and they waved back and Mac said, "Let's go."

They went down to the ground floor and retraced their steps across the windy parking lot. It was cold in the car but it was a relief to be out of the wind. Mac started the motor and let it warm up for a minute before he pulled out of the space. By the time he was on a highway, the heat was coming up strong.

"They're getting married, aren't they?" Frankie said.

"Naomi and Everett?" He sounded surprised. "Maybe they are. You think that's what all that hysteria was about?"

"Yes. I think Everett made up his mind about a week ago. I'm so glad. They seem so right for each other."

"You told me once that living together was very romantic."

"It is."

"But for the long haul, marriage is better?"

It was a question, but she let it stand unanswered, as though it had been a statement.

"I like Naomi very much," she said.

"Better than Katie Black."

"Naomi's been very good to me." It was what she had said to Katie about Mac on Monday night.

"In a different situation Katie would be good to you too."

"She's awfully cool—as a person. Naomi's so open and warm."

"You sound like a New Yorker. I thought you were a Mid-westerner, like Katie."

229

"Maybe I was."

"You were pretty cool once yourself, back in the dark ages of January."

"When you and I used to haunt the Waldorf."

"Those dark ages. Yes."

In the night sky outside her window the lights of an airplane blinked and moved slowly toward Manhattan or some point she could not imagine. Naomi and Everett on their way, marrying, making it the real thing the way Mom and Dad had, when the time was right.

Mac checked his mirrors, put his signal on, and switched lanes. "When the Shiskin-Wrights come back," he said, accelerating, "we'll get them something nice for a wedding present."

Ten

He left so quietly the next morning she was hardly aware he was gone till the phone rang and she opened her eyes and saw that the other side of the bed was empty. She didn't like to answer the phone. It rang quite frequently when he was home, and when he remembered to check, there were always many messages on the tape. A variety of people called. People from the *Times*. His children. Now and then a policeman. People who said they were friends. People from city agencies. People responding to his queries. Jeannie. Women. She preferred not to deal with any of them. The only time she had answered the phone religiously was when he had taken the hurried trip to Nebraska, but now that seemed so long ago and their relationship so different that she was even more hesitant to intrude in his affairs by indicating that she was part of them.

If she didn't catch it by the third ring, the message would end up on the tape — or lost. She hurried.

"Hello?" Hearing the sleep still in her voice, wondering what time it was. He had left the blinds closed but light came in from between them at the other end of the room, the east end, falling in parallel rods on the floor.

"I woke you."

"It's OK."

"Did Jeannie call?"

"No one called. What's wrong?"

"She's gone. No one's home. The doorman said he hasn't seen her this morning."

"You think something's wrong?"

"I don't know." There was a pause, street noises in the background, voices. He would be at a pay phone somewhere near Jeannie's apartment. "Look, I'll hang around here for a while. Let me give you a number in case she calls." He rattled it off and she grabbed a pencil and wrote it on the margin of the nearest piece of paper. "It rings at the doorman's post."

"Are you sure she's out, Mac?"

"I had the super open the apartment for me. There's no one there. The place is in order. Beds made. They went somewhere."

"There were no messages last night." He had checked when they came home and there had been nothing on the tape except a click indicating someone had called and hung up without leaving word.

"I know." He sounded dejected.

"I'll stay here and answer the phone." She was beginning to feel cold, standing naked next to the desk.

"Frankie . . . Look, honey, this is your day off. I don't want to tie you to a telephone. Go out and do what you want today. Promise?"

She had intended to visit that odd-looking museum up on Fifth Avenue. "I wasn't planning anything, Mac. I'll be home most of the day."

He said, "OK," and they hung up.

She put her bathrobe on, washed, and made coffee. As she set the cup, saucer, and bread plate on the table, something caught her eye. Between the sofas was a low glass table with an interesting metal base. She walked over and admired, it, trying to figure out how she could have missed its arrival. But she had been in the apartment only a few minutes last evening before they left for the airport, and when they had come home, after stopping off for dessert and coffee, they had lighted only the bedroom, and not for long. There was something about walking through that door together than seemed to ignite twin fires . . .

Two glasses were on the new table, two rings left behind when she picked them up. She put them in the sink, smelling freshly made coffee. Jeannie and the kids gone. Katie Black had seen Jeannie on Tuesday and that had been it. Jeannie had packed up her kids and taken them away.

She shuddered, the tremor convulsing her shoulders and constricting her breathing. Jeannie would teach him a lesson. She would deny him his children. It wasn't very original but it would be effective. And how would he fight her? He didn't even have a lawyer.

She buttered toast and spread it with English marmalade that was almost as good as what Mom used to put up in jars. The phone rang and she hurried to answer.

"Anything?" It was Mac.

"No. Nothing since you called."

"I checked her family, a couple of friends. No one's seen her."

"Call Katie Black."

"Why?"

"Just a feeling. She was going to see Jeannie the next day after we met. She said she would have to tell Jeannie about me."

She heard him exhale. "I don't know where they are right now. Visiting probably, his family or hers. Jeannie wouldn't be there anyway. Look, I'll be home in a while."

She cleaned up the kitchen and dressed. What if Jeannie had moved somewhere and left no forwarding address? What if she had left the country?

She washed the stains from the new table and dried the surface with a paper towel. It was a beautiful table. When she found the right vase, that was where she would keep flowers.

The elevator stopped and Mac came in. He said, "Hi," and tossed a paper on a sofa. There was something in him she had not seen before and at least part of it was worry.

"Want some lunch?" It was nearly noon.

"I'll eat something later." He dropped his jacket and went to his desk.

"I just saw the table this morning."

"Nice, isn't it?"

"It's beautiful. It's so thick and I like the way the edges are beveled."

He opened the blinds so that his desk received the full effect of the sun. He looked out for a while, standing at the windows. There wasn't an awful lot to see. "Frankie." He turned around. "I won't be fit to live with this afternoon."

"Do you think there's a chance something's happened?"

"There's always a chance but I don't think so. Around four I'll go uptown and talk to the evening doorman. He was on last night and he'll remember if they left during his tour. I expect she'll be back tonight, when it's too late for me to see the kids. I'll see them tomorrow."

"I'll bring something back for dinner." She put her coat on.

"That'd be nice."

She rang for the elevator and Mac came over and put his arm around her. She turned toward him and kissed him, feeling suddenly almost teary, thoughts of his disappointment and Jeannie's willfulness mixing with that embryonic fear, that small possibility that something had happened to the children, cocky little Susannah with a small ass, a big smile, and a deep curiosity, and quiet Eric who, she realized, reminded her in small, important ways of Kenny. She had not known until this moment that she cared about them, that she liked them even, that their existence made a difference to her.

"You're not crying, are you?"

"No." She rubbed an eye.

"They'll be back tonight. And if they're not, I may need a hand to hold."

The elevator had arrived and he took out his keys and unlocked the door. She kissed him again and rode downstairs.

It was nearly six when she returned. He was at his desk and from the array of papers on the floor circling the desk at a radius of about an arm's length, either he had been working or he had made some great effort. He got up and stepped over a pile, giving it a disparaging look, as she closed the door.

"No word," he said in response to her look. "I saw the doorman. They left last night, maybe at seven. Got picked up by a car, not a taxi. They came downstairs and waited for it. That's all he remembers."

"Then they're visiting friends."

"Sounds like it. She must have called while we were out, got back on the phone and invited herself and the kids somewhere. A lesson for the old man." He said it without a smile, as though perhaps he had learned the intended lesson.

"You don't have to learn lessons, Mac. You play fair. Better than fair." She hung her coat up and closed the closet door.

"You have to understand Jeannie," Mac said.

"I don't have to understand Jeannie at all. I don't have to like her. I don't have to convince myself that there's a reason for what she does when she's unkind to you." She took a breath, surprised that she had said it all. "Because there isn't any that I would accept."

"OK." He had watched her intently as she made her statement. Now he looked wounded and she was sorry.

"I didn't say it to hurt you," she said.

"I'm not hurt. And don't apologize."

"I'm not apologizing. I'm just explaining." She smiled slightly.

"You're too damned loyal. Did it ever occur to you that I might have been the one who fucked up my marriage?"

"Never."

It made him smile.

"And even if you were, you wouldn't do this sort of thing to her, even if you wanted to."

"Let's eat dinner," he said. "I'm famished."

There were calls, but none from Jeannie. He tried her number several times but there was no answer. At about ten they drove up together and he went up-stairs and had himself let into the apartment while she stayed in the double-parked car knowing that Jeannie wasn't going to be there, understanding Jeannie in a way she did not want to understand anyone, recognizing that this was a woman who punished.

He came from the dark interior and stopped be-fore the glass doors to talk to the doorman. No wonder the police questioned doormen during inves-tigations; doormen obviously knew everything that spilled out of apartments: when, in what condition, by what means of transportation, with whom.

Finishing the conversation, the doorman pushed open the door and Mac walked into the street. It was cold. She could see him hunch up a bit. He opened the car door and sat down beside her.

"Home OK?"

"Home's fine."

He turned toward downtown. It was Saturday night in New York and long, dark stretch limousines glided by or waited, puffing exhaust, at the curbs near restaurants. Women in fur coats and high heels hung on to well-dressed men and stepped carefully to avoid patches of ice and city detritus. It was cold but everyone seemed happy. Somewhere far to the south and east, Naomi and Everett were dancing in tropical heat, perhaps on the first night of their married life.

"I'm not calling the police," Mac said as though she had questioned him about it. "And I'm not going to try to find them. She'll be back when she's ready. The kids have school on Monday. She won't keep them out of school."

She looked out the window. It was a familiar ride. She knew the way up and she knew the way back.

"You think I'm wrong in the way I'm handling it?" he asked.

"I think it's too bad the way marriages end."

"It is."

"The kids get the worst end of it, don't they? They probably didn't have much to say about where they spent the weekend."

"Probably." He cut west and then turned down Broadway. They would be home soon. "I should have called her from the airport."

"Is that what you're going to do on Friday nights for the rest of your life, Mac? Leave your friends and call your wife so she can change the arrangements she made last week?"

"It'll get sorted out," he said. "You think I shouldn't let Jeannie change the arrangements every

238

week."

Ahead on the left, Pragmatique. Slow. Look for a spot. People on the street, buying records at Tower. Laughing. A block farther a gap on the left. No hydrant. He backed in, sliding in place as easily as if it had been on the right side of the street. He turned off the motor.

"I think," she said, before he opened the door, "that an arrangement is an arrangement."

He opened the door without answering, went around to her side and helped her out. Then they went upstairs.

She awoke and he was not in bed. She was used to finding him at his desk at all hours, buried in Charlie Herron's disappearance. Tonight the desk was empty and dark. Mac was sitting on the sofa with his back to her. The small recessed lights over what was considered the living room were on, activated by living room switch 1. It was a gently light, a "conversation" light. If you wanted to read, you turned on the spots which hung from a track on the ceiling by flicking living room switch 2.

On bare feet she walked to the unoccupied end of the sofa and stood there.

Mac looked up. He seemed unsurprised to see her, as if this was the way their life together had evolved; one or the other suffered and the other came to help. "Sit down," he said.

Between them lay a stack of books. She glanced at them as she sat, and recognized the one on top. It was one of the Jeannie books. Now, in his worst moment, he was reviewing the best of his life with Jeannie, rereading her promises of undying devotion. Her heart sank.

"I'm throwing them out," he said.

"All of them?"

"It's time. Make room for new ones."

"Those are kind of special books, Mac."

"They were. Past tense."

"Maybe your kids would want them someday. Kids like to know about their parents."

"Do you know I'm ready to kill tonight?"

"I know. You're throwing books out instead."

"It's less bloody."

"Maybe you should wait a day or two."

He turned and looked at her. The spirit of Jeannie, embodied in a pile of five or six fairly slender volumes of poetic writing, hovered between them.

"You don't want to have regrets." She looked at the books. The top one had a beautiful binding and gold lettering.

"You worry about that?"

"You may go back to her someday." Very calmly because there was more between him and Jeannie than between him and Frankie, because the truth was, men often went back, especially men who had failed to leave completely, as Mac had. "And then think of how embarrassing it'll be when she finds them gone. You'll have to tell her you got rid of them that weekend she took the kids away when what you really wanted to do was wring her neck."

"I can never figure you for an optimist or a pessimist."

"An optimist, don't you think? I'm here. Isn't that

240

optimistic?"

He put his hand out and rested it on her shoulder. "If those kids aren't back by Sunday night—"

"They will be."

"I suppose they will." He worked her shoulder, rubbing it with his fingers, kneading it gently. "I've been sitting here and trying to find one thread of hope that Charlie Herron's alive."

"And?"

"And I can't."

"Maybe things'll look brighter when your kids come back."

He picked up the pile of books and put them on the new glass table. Then he slid over and put his arm around her. "Maybe," he said. "You work on it for me, OK?"

Sunday was worse. He made a try at reading the paper and then retreated to his desk. The semicircle of piles of papers had not been moved and he stepped over them carefully as he sat down. He worked in silence, or looked at his papers in silence, or stared out the window in silence, as Frankie went through the paper. When the phone rang, she felt herself jump and looked up.

"Oh hello, Ariana," he said with enormous warmth and Frankie saw him press the button for the speaker-phone.

"I'm just feeling kind of low, Mac," a clear voice said.

"It's a low day, that's all. We're all feeling that way."

"It was Charlie's birthday this week." The voice trembled.

Charlie's birthday. This was Charlie Herron's wife. Frankie laid the paper carefully on the floor.

"Need some company?"

There was a pause. "No. Thanks for offering. Just talk to me for a few minutes. I miss seeing you in the paper."

"I'll be back in April."

"Will it be done then? The book."

"Done enough that I can go back to work."

"I don't suppose there's anything new." She said it with absolute resignation.

"Pretty much the same old things but from different sources. I located the cop who monitored the special-number calls."

"He had retired, hadn't he?"

"Last summer. He didn't give me much that was new. Told me to listen to the tape myself."

"And?"

"And there wasn't much. I'll do it again one of these days. When I get a copy of the transcript, I'll let you go over it."

"I'd like to do that. I haven't been able to contribute very much."

"You've done plenty, Ariana. How's your boy?"

"Fine. Really good." There was a note of enthusiasm in the voice. "He doesn't remember Charlie, you know."

"He was kind of young."

"We were all pretty young a year and a half ago."

"I know."

"Mac, if they find Charlie—if they find him dead,

242

I'll get him back, won't I?"

It was Mac who paused this time. Then he said, "Yes," but his voice was low. "You'll get him back."

"Because I want him buried properly. You know, a place with a marker. His mother is having nightmares about it. I'm sorry to burden you with all this. It's just that it was his birthday."

"I know. I wish I could tell you I had a bunch of new leads or even a few promising ideas. I just don't think it's over yet."

"I guess that's why I like to talk to you. How's the family?" she asked in a brighter tone.

"Fine. Jeannie's taken the kids to the country for the weekend."

"How nice. Maybe a little skiing."

"Maybe."

"I hope you get back together again, Mac. I liked Jeannie. She was so good to me when Charlie disappeared."

"Thanks, Ariana. It's hard to say right now. Things are a little jumbled."

"Well. Give her my best when you talk to her. And thanks for the shoulder."

After that it was very quiet and for most of the rest of the afternoon Mac sat at his desk and looked out the window.

It was after eight when the call came. They had eaten a quiet dinner and Mac had returned to the desk and gone back to work again. The blinds were drawn and the lights were on all over the apartment. He picked up the phone on the first ring and it was clear from the start of the conversation that the doorman was reporting the return of his family. He expressed thanks and appreciation and hung up. After a minute, he turned around.

"They're back."

Frankie nodded, sharing his relief.

"Same car dropped them off." He smiled. "He got the license plate for me."

"Everybody's a detective. You feel better?"

"Yeah, I feel better." He looked at his watch. "I'll give them a chance to get settled before I call."

She guessed he was waiting for Jeannie to call, or one of the kids, but in half an hour, nothing happened. He picked up the phone and dialed and Frankie got her bag and left the apartment by the back stairs, climbing up to the Shiskin-Wrights'.

Inside everything was in order and on the counter next to the sink was a large copper watering can. She took her time watering the plants in the living room and then walked slowly back to the bedroom and took her time there too. The plants looked well taken care of and carefully chosen. Most were succulents and some were in bloom. The bedroom was a creamy white from carpet to bedspread to draperies. There was a large mirror over a dressing table with a few bottles of cologne, a hand mirror facedown, and tissues in an elegant box. It was easy to imagine Naomi there, combing her hair or coloring her lashes. In a corner was a man's wooden valet, empty now, all the jackets and shirts put away. A well-matched couple, she thought, wondering what she would buy them as a wedding present.

Finishing her task, she left the watering can and went down the stairs again. Mac was taking his jacket out of the closet as she walked in.

"I want to run up and see the kids," he said.

"Did you talk to them?"

"Just for a minute."

"I'm glad it's over."

He kissed her. "I'll be back soon."

He wasn't. It was two hours later when he returned and she had gotten into bed with a book when the elevator stopped at their door.

By the time he joined her, she had set the book aside and turned out the light. But she was not asleep. She was waiting for him.

"It was what we figured," he said, putting his arms around her, all the tension of the weekend evaporated. "She was in a snit over Friday night. She called someone and went to his apartment. Yesterday they went to the Hamptons."

"Who are they?"

"Where, not who. The Hamptons are towns on Long Island. Towns with a lot of money. Vacation homes. Beaches. Cocktail parties. Social climbers."

"You do a piece on them?"

"They're out of my beat."

"Kids have a good time?"

"They had a good time." He brushed her hair up over her forehead and she tried to think what she would do if he told her he was going back to his wife. "I think Jeannie and I came to an understanding," he said.

"That's good, huh?"

"Good for maybe a week."

"Now look at who's the pessimist."

"Realist, baby. Ever hear of realism?"

"Oh, Mac." She put her arms around him, happy to have him back for however long. "Have I heard of realism."

Eleven

Early in the week he gave her the gizmo. You dialed his number and when the recording answered, you pressed a button on the gizmo, which emitted a tone. The tone activated the answering machine to play the tape.

"So we can leave messages for each other," he said when he had showed her how to use it. "In case one of us isn't home."

"Which one of us were you thinking of that wouldn't be home?"

"Well." He seemed to be deciding what to tell her. "I might have to go somewhere."

She got a job early Monday morning at a tall building on Park Avenue. It meant taking the Lexington Avenue subway and Mac walked her to the nearest station and put two tokens in her hand. He told her to get off at Fifty-first Street and walk a block west. Then he kissed her.

"I may be late," he said. "We'll eat something out. Pay you back for the lousy weekend."

"It wasn't so lousy. It had a good ending." She

looked at Kenny's watch and then dropped her hand.

"That's because you happen to be a sweet, unselfish, patient, warm, and very sexy creature."

"All that and two tokens." She kissed him again. "See you tonight."

It was a nice job in pleasant surroundings. Certain things remained the same. The word-processing group ate together. The secretaries, who seemed to rank a notch higher, ate with each other. Everyone was talking about a sales conference and there were men running through the halls looking frantic during the first few days of the week. The typing had columns of numbers and was hard to proofread.

But it was wonderful working on the East Side. She discovered Madison Avenue, where she bought chocolate one day and a silk scarf the next, changing the look of her coat and keeping her neck luxuriously warm. On Wednesday Mac met her for lunch at a nearby restaurant, an unexpected treat he had sprung on her as she hurried through breakfast. Although she had only an hour, it was the loveliest lunch she could remember. She had a glass of cool white wine, a seafood salad, coffee, and a rich dessert that she couldn't finish. The restaurant was packed and she was sure she was the only representative of a word-processing group in the establishment. The other patrons were older, well-dressed, mostly male with some glittery women sprinkled here and there like expensive ornaments. And Frankie Grant with MacIver of the *Times*.

"You know what today is?" he asked about twenty minutes into the meal.

"February fifteenth."

"We're halfway to April first."

She touched the gold chain. "So soon? I haven't done half the things I wanted to."

"Nor have I."

They were at a small table, opposite each other, she on the banquette that lined the wall and he in a chair. From her left, at a larger table, came a man's voice talking about R and D, which, she remembered from one of her jobs, meant research and development, and to her right a group including two women were talking about buyers and the prospectus and had anyone heard what the prime rate was today.

"But you will, Mac," Frankie said. "You've got so much done and the rest is shaping up. You can go on with it after the first of April."

"I wasn't thinking about the book."

She wasn't thinking about the book either. It just made it easier to talk about it because it was something concrete, something whose progress could be measured in pages or chapters or penciled answers to questions in a notebook.

"I want you to stay on after April," he said.

She didn't say anything. The people on the left and the people on the right, who were conversing about weighty issues, dollars and cents, things that might go and things that might crash, talked with great ease and fluidity, occasionally interrupting each other, so eager were they to press their opinions on their respective groups, and here was Frankie Grant, lately of Ohio, confronted with a small decision whose influence would hardly extend beyond this small table, and she could hardly speak.

"Am I asking you to do something you don't want

to do?"

"No."

"Then where's the 'but'?"

"Well, you know, I have a house and a family and things I have to do. . . ."

"You're making up excuses as you go along."

"I have a house, Mac." He was right. None of those things was a "but."

"Aunt What's-her-name can drop in on it in the spring the way she's been doing in the winter."

"In March," she said, "I'll tell you what I'll do in April."

"You won't tell me what the 'but' is."

"The 'but' is me. I'm just indecisive."

"You're also a lousy liar."

She couldn't think of an answer so she didn't give him one.

"I'll ask you in March. When you have a longer time for lunch."

———

Saturday morning they got up early to pick up the kids. Mac had heard of an older couple upstate who were retiring to Florida and were selling off the contents of their house. Among the many pieces of furniture that were available was an old pine table that one of them had inherited years ago. Mac thought he might want the table.

As they drove uptown he said rather offhandedly. "By the way, the kids're staying over tonight."

She felt the grip of panic. "I'll have to go somewhere," she said.

"What do you mean?"

"You don't have a bedroom, Mac. I can't get into bed with you with the kids watching."

"You'll put a nightgown on. It's no big deal."

"It is."

"Because you're making it one."

"Mac, do the kids know? That I live there?"

"You know they know. You saw Susannah check the closet."

"But you haven't talked to them."

"You mean have I discussed my sex life with my twelve-year-old? No, I haven't."

"I don't mean that. You know I don't mean that."

"I told them I was seeing you exclusively. That's the word I used. No one ran for a dictionary."

"Why are you so touchy?"

"Me? Touchy? Why are you making an issue of this?"

"Because I want those kids to like me. I want to get along with them. When I put that nightgown on, Susannah's going to blame me. I don't know what Eric will think."

He turned into Jeannie's block. "No one knows what Eric thinks." Far down the block a car pulled away from the curb. He accelerated, driving past the apartment house, and backed into the newly empty space. "Frankie, they'll accept it," he said, once again in control, a voice you believed because it sounded so believable. "This is just my way of doing it. They know you, they like you, they've spent time with you. Tonight's just another step. OK?" He had his hand on the door handle, waiting for an answer.

She thought, I could give him the grin and say: OK with me, pal. But she couldn't. And it wasn't because of Susannah and Eric. It was because of Frankie Grant.

"I'll do it," she said, her voice lower than usual. "But it's not OK."

The kids came down the street carrying rolled-up sleeping bags which Mac locked into the trunk. There were cheerful hellos and then they took off. The drive was beautiful. They crossed the George Washington Bridge and then went north. Eventually they drove beside the Hudson River for a while and then Mac took a turnoff and suddenly they could have been in the heartland of the country.

"Some river," he said.

"It's wonderful."

"Bet this looks like home right here."

"It does."

"Wait till you see the place we're going."

Susannah and Eric contented themselves with games and intermittent reading. Sometimes they argued about nonsensical things. She had not argued with Kenny for years. When they were younger, he had sometimes angered her to the point that she punched him. She had always been wiry as he was but she had been stronger because she was bigger. By the time he was able to take her on, he was sick and when she knew he was sick, she stopped arguing, stopped pummeling, started caring, feeling guilty for all the times she had hurt him, unable to shake the guilt and knowing there was nothing to feel guilty about. How lucky these two in the back seat were; what a privilege it was to be able to knock your brother around.

When she saw the house, she had an attack of

homesickness or some affliction of the spirit that she had not suffered before. A pebbled drive wound up from the road to a white house hidden behind immense trees planted aeons ago for reasons of privacy. It was a house that had been born small and had grown larger. There were additions on either side, a sunporch on the right and a vastly extended kitchen on the left. There was even a weather vane atop the garage, which was set far back, a healthy walk on a cold night.

"Want it?"

She nodded.

"I can't afford it this year."

"It looks like a dollhouse," Susannah said from the back seat. It did too, a little, with its very carefully trimmed shrubs on either side of the steps.

"Be nice to have a place outside the city," Mac said.

"I never thought so till this minute."

Mr. and Mrs. Everly. Gray-haired and smiling. Come right in, Mr. MacIver, and an uncertain glance at his tallest companion.

"I'm Frankie Grant."

"She's from Ohio," Susannah said.

"Oh my, we know people in Ohio."

Plank floors, real ones, a bit uneven. A kitchen you would die for.

"Stove's a bit old," Mrs. Everly said.

"I bet it cooks real good."

"Oh my, yes."

"Have you put the house up for sale yet?"

"That's long sold. We're just emptying it out now before we go south."

Her husband didn't say much and not long after they arrived he and Eric disappeared. Looking through a doorway Frankie could see them in the living room looking at some small objects on a shelf to one side of the fireplace.

"Come and look at the table," Mac said.

It looked old enough to be real, real enough to be worthy of his loft. She wondered if Karen would approve, if he had asked her for her approval. In the center a porcelain vase filled with flowers stood on a round crocheted doily. She touched the wooden surface. It was worn and somewhat uneven, like the plank floor, but it was smooth from generations of use.

"If you don't take it, I will."

"Sold," Mac said. He took a checkbook out of one pocket and a pen out of another.

"If you just haul it away, Mr. MacIver, it's yours for the taking."

"I came to buy, Mrs. Everly. I'm sure Whit told you that."

"Whit said you'd give it a good home. That's better than money. We made an awful lot on the house, more money than we ever saw in our lives. I'm too old to be greedy."

"I can't take it without paying you."

Frankie turned and walked quietly out of the room, leaving Mac with pen and checkbook open, facing the old lady who would not be greedy in her old age. I do love that man, she thought, stepping on a worn rug in the living room.

"Mr. Everly collects lead soldiers," Eric said from across the room. "Look at these. They're handmade."

254

He was flushed with excitement.

"Been collecting 'em sixty years," Mr. Everly said.

"They're beautiful."

"These're English," Eric said, pointing to a group poised for attack. "And these over here are German." He started explaining their functions, handling them carefully.

"Smart boy," Mr. Everly said. "Learns quickly."

"Yes, he does," Frankie said, feeling pride. He was Mac's boy and some of the pleasure had rubbed off on her.

A few minutes later Mac came out of the kitchen and they all said good-bye and went out to the car. Eric's eyes were still shining.

"Those were some soldiers," he said wistfully as they drove off and Frankie knew he had wanted them, or at least one of the sets. She felt sorry for him because in that half-hour something had caught his fancy, he had learned something, and a desire had been aroused. He was such a nice boy, such an undemanding boy, she wanted to see the desire fulfilled. But he would get over it—it wasn't like wanting your brother back—and Mr. Everly would have his whole collection to take down to Florida.

During the week a ladder had been installed along the side of the closet and after Susannah and Eric had hauled their sleeping bags up to the sleeping loft on top, Susannah practiced going up and down. There was a wildness about her movements, a giddiness. It had been a wild and giddy day with much to eat, more to see, and things to do to please everyone.

Mac checked the answering machine but happily there were no messages. "Good," he said with a note of satisfaction. "They're starting to forget me." He took his jacket off and pulled a sweater over his head. "Drink?" he said.

"You promised us dessert," Susannah said, descending the ladder for the hundredth time.

"In the freezer. I got that ice cream you like. Help yourselves."

There was a race to the kitchen.

"Maybe something sweet and heavy," Frankie said, responding to the last-asked question.

"Got just the thing."

They sat on the sofa sipping different drinks while the kids ate ice cream at the kitchen table. There was a feeling of harmony, a sense of four people happy in their own ways. Eric rinsed his dish and put it in the dishwasher and a minute later Susannah followed.

"Why don't you get your showers started," Mac suggested. "So we don't all want it at the same time."

"You can be first," Eric said. He picked up a book and sat on the empty sofa to read it. Susannah walked away.

Harmony, Frankie thought dreamily. The liqueur burned pleasantly and then warmed. No fights over who showered first. No whiny little arguments. Bet it would be fun to climb up that ladder and sleep on that wide shelf with its pretty guardrail.

When she heard the sound, she thought it was a kitten at the kitchen door, except there wasn't any kitchen door here or any kittens. Eric was looking toward the bedroom and Mac got up very suddenly.

Susannah was sitting at the door to the bedroom

closet and crying, just sitting on the floor and snif-
fling, her back to the apartment.

"What's the matter, sweetheart?" Mac said, getting
down to where she was. "What's wrong?" He touched
her head and Susannah shook him off. "You feel
OK?"

"I want to go home."

"Come on, Susie. You said you like it here."

"I can't stay. I want to call and see if Mommy's
home."

"Tell me what's wrong."

"I forgot my hair dryer."

"You can live one night without your hair dryer."

"I *can't*."

Eric shrugged to show how meaningless Susannah's problem was. Frankie walked to the bedroom,
stopping a few feet from the squatting father and
sitting daughter.

"I need it," Susannah said. She rubbed her eyes
and sniffed. "I want to go home."

"You can borrow mine," Frankie said quietly, not
sure the offer would be welcomed by either father or
daughter.

Susannah looked up at her. "Where is it?"

"In the bathroom. You can use it all you want."

"How's that, Susannah?" Mac said.

Susannah sniffed a few times. "Where is *she* staying?"

"Frankie's staying here."

There was more snifling. Then, "I want to go
home."

"I'm not staying here, Susannah," Frankie said.
"It's OK. I'm leaving right now." She picked her bag

257

up off the floor and checked the contents. Susannah swiveled on her bottom, following Frankie's movements with her eyes. With the bag over her shoulder, Frankie came back to the closet, went inside, and found a nightgown, a new one Aunt Betty had given her for Christmas to take to New York. She had been saving it for her first night in the new apartment she had never moved to. Tonight she would wear it upstairs at the Shiskin-Wrights'.

"Where do you think you're going?" Mac had stood and he faced her as she came out of the closet.

"Upstairs."

"Frankie—"

"I'll see you in the morning. Good night, everybody." She opened the door to the stairs and went up to the sixth floor.

Even with the lights on she felt very alone. She didn't know where to sleep. Watering the plants, she surveyed the possibilities. The bed in the bedroom looked very inviting but it was out. There was a couch in Everett's study but it was rather hard and covered with a harsh woolen upholstery and she had neither bedding nor a pillow. That left the living-room sofa. So be it.

She took her nightgown and found the bathroom. Next to the shower there was a sauna. Perhaps that was why Naomi had such beautiful skin. Later it struck her that she had not been unduly surprised to see the sauna. Somehow it went with Naomi and Everett and their apartment.

Washed and dressed for bed, she returned to the

living room and found a magazine. She had left her book downstairs in her rush to leave and she liked to read before going to sleep. She read the magazine for about an hour and then turned the lights off.

She did not sleep. For a while she lay on the sofa covered with a blanket she had found in the closet in Everett's study, thinking about Mac and Susannah, about Mac and Jeannie, about Mac and Katie Black, about Mac. She wanted to stay with him but . . . He had to know what the "but" was. Mac didn't need things spelled out for him. Mac was the guy who spelled it out for everyone else.

She got up and walked over the plush rug to the living-room windows. The Shiskin-Wrights had reversed the apartment. Their living room overlooked Broadway and their bedroom was at the back. The view was different up here. Everything was different. She missed him. She would not return to Ohio unburdened, but she knew she would return. She would go back feeling very much alone.

The elevator rose to the sixth floor and stopped. There was the sound of a chime and in the dark she unlocked the door and opened it.

"Will you ever learn to ask who it is before you let someone in?" He sounded angry.

"I knew it was you." She closed the door and turned the bolt. "Who else could it be at this time of night?"

"Were you sleeping?"

"Looking out the window." She went back to the sofa and sat on the floor in front of it, resting her back against it, her knees, covered in the new soft flannel of the Christmas nightgown, up in front of her. It was as dark as it ever got in New York. She had not turned a light on when she opened the door but her eyes were used to the darkness. Across the width of the room, Mac sat with his back against the door, guarding the apartment. He had changed into his gray sweatshirt and jeans and something in her wished she had stayed downstairs with him. She could be lying next to him now instead of peering at his shadowy form.

"You didn't have to leave."

"Someone had to leave. I didn't want it to be Susannah."

"No one had to leave. Frankie, a lot of families go camping together. They get undressed and go to sleep in the same tent."

"I'm not your family, Mac. I'm not Susannah's family. You and your kids are a family. You and Jeannie are a family. I'm not. It's not the same thing."

"Jeannie and I aren't a family," he said.

"But you are to Susannah."

"Jeannie and I were never a family." He said it as though he were explaining something that needed to be explained. "We were lovers. We were lovers who lived together. We were lovers who had children. We were lovers who shared a checking account. When we stopped being lovers, everything else disintegrated." He had turned away from her, toward the window and the starless New York sky. He had a good profile, one the cameras could have panned on. Jeannie had wanted him to be in television. Perhaps it was a question of images, a matter of reflections. "Anyway," he said, turning back to face her, "I talked to Susannah—tonight after you left. I talking to both of them. We've straightened it out."

"What did you straighten out?"

"That you and I are living together in that apartment. That we sleep in that bed."

"That we're lovers."

"I didn't put a label on it," he said.

She could see him quite clearly now. He had his legs straight out in front of him, one hand on his lap and the other beside him on the rug.

"Will you come downstairs?" he asked.

"No."

"How's the watch?"

"Doing better, just a little better. Doesn't lose so much time anymore."

She saw him look at his own watch as though to confirm its enduring accuracy. Then he dropped his hand and leaned his head back against the wall. He sat that way for a long time. After a few minutes, he slid one foot closer to himself so that his knee was up.

"When you said I wrote without passion," he said finally.

"Mac, I didn't say it to hurt you. I was a little high and I was teasing."

"You didn't hurt me, you were right. There's no room for sentimentality in journalism, at least not the kind of journalism I practice. I was just thinking about the book. I don't want it to read like an exercise in sterility. Maybe if you have some time you can read through the first few chapters and let me know what you think."

"You want my opinion?"

"On the style. Maybe see if you pick up any errors."

"I'm not a critic, Mac."

"If I wanted a critic, I'd go and find one. I want to know what you think of it."

"I'd like very much to read it."

"Frankie." He had not moved except to bend one knee. "I want to make love to you."

She shook her head.

"You want to tell me why not?"

"Because it's not our place. Because your kids are downstairs. Because I'm feeling messed up tonight."

"So am I. About you, my kids, Charlie."

"Mac." It was the same helplessness she had felt last year. "I want so much to tell you it'll all turn out right."

"I know you do."

"But I can't."

"I don't want you to. I don't want you to say things you know aren't true. It's one of your finer qualities that you don't."

You look better today, Kenny.

No, I don't. I look the same. I know the truth, Frankie. Could you do me the biggest favor of your life and tell me you know the truth too?

He got up from the floor. "I won't be home most of next week," he said.

A touch of ice somewhere inside the rib cage. "Where will you be?"

"In the city but I won't be able to sleep at home. There are some things I have to do." He paused. "At night. But I'll keep in touch. If I can't reach you, I'll leave messages on the tape."

She rubbed the face of Kenny's watch.

"OK?" he asked, a small boy requesting permission.

She nodded.

"Something's starting to happen," he said, standing by the door. "I've stepped on some toes without meaning to. There are people who are getting fidgety."

"Please be careful." She got up off the floor. "Please."

His hand was on the doorknob. "I'll see you in the morning." He unlocked the door and opened it. The elevator was still there, all lit up. "Lock the door behind me," he said.

After she had admitted to Kenny that she knew the truth, after she had cried harder than she had ever cried before, they grew very close and very honest. She wished Mac had stayed longer. She wished she had asked him to stay. She wished she didn't feel quite so alone without him.

She worked for the telephone company on Monday in a work-processing group that was at least half temps. Mac called in the afternoon and said everything was fine and he'd see her in a couple of days. When she got home, she played the tape. There was only one call, a woman: "This is the medical examiner's office returning Mr. MacIver's call."

She played it again, feeling a second shiver. She closed the blinds at both ends of the apartment and turned all the lights on everywhere. Then she made dinner and sat down with Mac's manuscript beside her.

He began with the event and then backtracked, filling in the personal and professional biography of Charlie Herron. What was going on in the Forty-second Street area was not new when Charlie became interested. Periodically, one of the news media would pick up the story of young boys being sold like prostitutes to grown men and the illicit business would recede for a while, only to surface later when the investigative reporters were busy investigating something else. Charlie wanted to put an end to this particular enterprise. There was a hint in the manuscript that this was not the usual underworld operation, that someone important or well-known was involved. Charlie had gone undercover and learned something crucial about the man at the top in the days before his disappearance. To the world at large the unidentified man was beyond reproach and beyond suspicion. The book was tantalizing both in its suggestions and in its ultimate vagueness.

What surprised Frankie was that knowing as much as she knew before starting, the manuscript could be so gripping. She had the sense of reading a thriller, of wanting to stay with it although she had finished dinner and the dishes needed washing, of wanting to read further although it was late and she needed to shower, finally of wanting to finish although she was tired, because she could not go to sleep until she had reached the end.

There was no end, of course. There was only a point where the manuscript stopped, where the reader, breathless, wanted to know how it all turned out, when no one knew, not the writer, perhaps not even the main character. She put it down finally, having read to the end, feeling sorry for the family, for Charlie Herron, for the man who wanted even more than she to know what had become of him. Then she went into the shower.

It wasn't until she was on her way to work the next morning that she remembered that yesterday was the day the Shiskin-Wrights were coming home and she hadn't heard a word.

"I guess I'd have to say it was the best and worst vacation of my life." Naomi paused between bites of raw fish arranged in a colorful array on a raised board. In spite of its attractive arrangement, Frankie remained untempted.

They were eating together on Wednesday night, Everett on his trip to Boston and Mac still away on his mysterious mission.

"Does that mean it adds up to exactly neutral?" Frankie asked.

"I don't think it adds up to anything," Naomi said. She sipped saké from a tiny cup, then poured more for both of them. "When it was good, it was very, very good."

"You both look marvelous."

"The weather was wonderful. It was all wonderful, really."

But they had not married.

"And the plants were in great shape when we came home," she went on. "Did you import Midwestern water?"

"Just what came out of your tap. Twice they got watered because there was a crisis and I had to leave the apartment. Once I went up because I thought they needed me."

Naomi smiled. "Crises so soon?"

"Just little ones. I'm glad the plants are OK."

"We got something for you." She reached into her bag. "Ev picked it out. When he saw how great the plants looked, he said we should have gotten you two." She handed a small box across the table.

"You shouldn't have, Naomi." She looked at the box a moment before taking it. "It wasn't any trouble and you've been so good to me."

"I love to buy presents. I'm always trying to figure out what people want so I can get them the right thing. I think Everett wants one of those gorgeous old walking sticks with a silver top. Of course, he won't use it for forty years but he'll know it's his."

Frankie unwrapped the little package and opened the box. Inside was a small gold chain bracelet. "It's beautiful, Naomi."

"It's really you, isn't it?"

"Yes."

"Everett has such good taste." She said it almost wistfully.

"I think I'm going to cry."

"No, please don't. Everything's going to work out fine. Here, let me put it on you."

"Thank you." She stretched her right hand across the table and Naomi put the bracelet on. Later she thought what an odd thing Naomi had said. Everything's going to work out fine.

* * *

266

There was a message from Mac on the tape and she listened with an ache and a sense of longing. She had phoned in a message for him during the afternoon. After she had listened to his two or three times, she could erase them both.

But to her surprise, there was another beep when he finished speaking and a woman's voice came on. "Mac, it's Ariana." The voice intense, excited. It was Mrs. Herron, Charlie Herron's wife. "I got a call tonight. From a man. No one I know. Kind of a deep voice. Not very appetizing, if you know what I mean. He said"—she seemed to be trying to get herself together— "he said something like, 'Tell MacIver to lay off.' Then he made some sort of a threat. I'm not afraid, Mac. You needn't worry about me. But I'm very excited. Do you *have* something? Do you *know* something? It's a year and a half and this is the first time I have the feeling that something's happening. Am I right? Please call me first chance you have."

Frankie played the tape over, and then over again. On Monday the coroner's office, on Wednesday Ariana Herron. And last Saturday, upstairs at the Shiskin-Wrights', his admission that he was stirring things up.

She undressed and went into the shower, still wearing her new bracelet that Everett had picked out on the trip that hadn't been a honeymoon. Mac, she said to herself, please take care of yourself. Please, please.

Friday morning the rugs came, one for the dining room and one for the living room. When the men had left, she went out and scouted the city for vases.

By midafternoon she had brought two, a large crystal one for the new table and a smaller glass one for the kitchen, where they would continue to eat most of their meals.

She knew as she opened the door that he was home. Even before she heard the sound of water running in the bathroom sink or saw the shoes on the floor beside the bed, there was a sense of fullness to the apartment.

She called, "Mac?" and slammed the door behind her, moving toward the sound of occupancy, the packages still in her gloved hands.

He walked out of the bathroom, barefoot, jeaned, with no shirt and his face three-quarters covered with shaving cream. "Hi, sweetheart, I'll kiss you in three minutes."

"Oh, Mac, I can't wait three minutes." She pulled one glove off and touched his bare neck, kissed his bare shoulder, and he gave her a one-armed hug and a careful kiss on the cheek that left a smudge of shaving cream she brushed away while he resumed shaving. "You're OK?"

"I'm fine. I just had several coats of grime to wash off. I'm glad you weren't home."

"I bought us something."

"Show me."

"From the Museum of Modern Art. Did you know you could *buy* things there?"

"I heard."

She grinned, feeling light-headed. "You always say that when it's something you've known all your life."

He rinsed his face, turned off the water, and reached for a towel. "What is it?"

"Look." She pulled it out of its box and held it up. He patted his face dry. "Very nice."

"For the upstate table. And some yellow tulips."

"You look a little like a yellow tulip yourself."

"Mac, I was so scared when I heard the message from Ariana Herron."

"She's OK. Took the baby and went out of town to visit."

"And the coroner's office."

"I'm just double-checking something." He looked absolutely inscrutable. He walked over and kissed her lips very lightly. "Come and tell me how much you missed me," he said.

The lamp on the desk was on but otherwise the loft was dark. They rested lazily on the bed, neither moving to get up although it was past the dinner hour. If she raised her head just a bit she could see the vase of yellow tulips centered on the rug at the far end of the loft.

"I learned the difference between glass and crystal today," she said.

"That's almost a rite of passage. I can't call you a hick anymore."

"You haven't called me that for weeks."

"It wasn't funny anymore." He traced her hairline with one finger. "I read your note," he said and kissed her face. He had been abundantly affectionate since she walked into the apartment, and even the sexual release of their lovemaking had not abated his tenderness. "Before I started to scrub."

She had written the note after she finished the

manuscript and had clipped it to the cover page. "I was looking for something . . ." She hesitated. "I wanted to find a weakness, something where I could write a note in the margin that this was unnecessary or that was superfluous or some paragraph was unclear or just dull so you would know I had read it carefully and critically and you could count on my opinion, but there wasn't anything except that one small place when you talking about when he was young."

"I'll cut it."

"Don't cut it, Mac. Not because of me. It isn't bad. It's just that you dwelled a little."

"I know. And I don't want to dwell. It's what you said it was — unnecessary and superfluous and just plain dull."

"It wasn't dull. It's a super book and you write so cleanly. When I finished it I rummaged around your desk to see if you had something drafted so I could keep going. I yearned for an end."

"There'll be an end." He kissed her again with more than affection. "You'll be the first to hear it. You hungry?"

"No."

"I think I'm too tired to eat."

"Go to sleep," she said, kissing him back. "I'll turn off the light."

Mac and the kids went upstate to pick up the table. They got it up in the elevator by standing it on end. After it was perfectly centered on the new rug, they celebrated by eating dinner on it. It looked smaller here in the openness of the loft than it had in the Everlys' little dining room and Frankie liked that. Space was a luxury in New York and to clutter it seemed almost sinful.

The dinner went well. This time Frankie had a quart of milk on the table and she offered it around. Jeannie had complained that Susannah never drank milk when she was with Mac, that the outings had become junk-food orgies. Tonight the menu was steak, baked potato, green beans (the only green vegetable both Eric and Susannah could agree on), and a salad with a little bit of everything. The vase was beautiful and Susannah said how much she liked yellow tulips.

Monday they sent her to a large bank in downtown Manhattan. The wind howled furiously and she wrapped her scarf around her head and neck and leaned into the wind.

The work was the kind of thing she had grown used to and she fell into it with little difficulty. On her lunch hour she walked up Broadway and found Wall Street and Trinity Church. At heart she was still a tourist.

On Tuesday she called Naomi to see if she wanted to go out for dinner one night and Naomi said no, she had some things to do and it wouldn't work out this week. A little later Naomi called back.

"I didn't mean to be short with you, Frankie," she said.

271

"You weren't short. You said you couldn't make it."

"Thanks for being so understanding."

"Are you OK, Naomi?"

"Sure I'm OK," Naomi said brightly. "Just inundated. When you take a vacation they make you pay for it when you come back. We'll get together next week, OK? There's a new Hunan restaurant I want us to try."

"Fine."

Mac was cleaning in the sink. "Naomi?" he asked when she hung up.

"Something's wrong, I think."

"It wasn't a honeymoon."

"No."

"Maybe we were just wrong."

"About Naomi? We're never wrong about Naomi." She took a cloth and wiped the little table. "What's Hunan?"

"Hot Chinese."

"Good. Whatever's wrong hasn't dampened her appetite."

She came home on Thursday to a dark apartment. Mac was busy now, certain that he was on a still-warm trail, sure that he was only inches away from buried secrets. She switched lights on, needing to purge the darkness, and turned on the telephone tape.

There was a jumble of messages. Two people were returning calls. One called twice and asked to have the call returned, as soon as possible, *please*. Karen

Armstrong, in a low, seductive voice, gave a date that the living-room chairs would be delivered. Then a man's voice came on: "Mac, you better call me. I'll be in the office tonight." That was it. She played it over, recognizing the voice. It was Sergeant McManus.

When Mac came home, he smiled as he played the tape. "Old boy's getting itchy," he said with a certain degree of satisfaction.

"About what?"

"They've been sloppy with the files on the people buried in potter's field. I don't think it amounts to anything but they don't like it when a pushy reporter says, 'Show me.' "

"If it doesn't amount to anything, why are you pushing?"

"Because they shouldn't be sloppy. These are files on people, not dogs and cats in the pound. Some parents come in from halfway across the country to look for their runway daughter and the file's not in the jacket. How do you think they feel?"

She said, "Terrible," with eyes misting. "Are those the ones that don't get identified? Girls who run away from home?"

"Girls in their teens who get off buses at the Port Authority Bus Terminal and never make it out to the street because they're picked up by pimps right in the building."

"I didn't know—I didn't know that's what they were."

"They were." He erased the tape. "Anyway, there's always the slight possibility that my pushing could lead to something." He looked at his watch. "Mind if

273

I call him before we eat?"

She shook her head and sat down to listen. He always used the speaker-phone when he talked to someone about Charlie Herron and she had realized only recently that she was a witness to the conversations.

She heard the ringing sound and a man's voice said, "Seventeenth Precinct, Sergeant Schultz speaking."

"Is Tom McManus there?" Mac asked. "This is Henry MacIver."

"Hold on." A click, and a moment later, "That you, Mac?"

"Just got your message, Tom. What can I do for you?"

"What you can do for me is slow down a little. What are you doing over at the M.E.?"

"Just asking a few questions."

"You know you're making some people nervous?"

"I don't suppose you'd like to tell me which nervous person asked you to call me?"

"No, I wouldn't like to tell you. I would like you to come to your senses. Charlie Herron walked outta New York and found himself a better place to live. Guys do it every day. The only reason you know about this one is you knew him."

"He was my friend."

"Well I'm your friend too and I'm giving you good, friendly advice. Take it easy, Mac. You are making some people very unhappy."

"Thanks, Tom. I appreciate the advice."

He turned and looked at Frankie. She wondered why he didn't get himself a swivel chair; it would make things so much easier.

"Was that friendly advice or a warning?" he asked her.

"It was a warning." Her voice sounded hoarse.

"Now who do you suppose would tell Tommy McManus to issue a warning?"

"I don't even want to think about it," Frankie said.

She did some food shopping on Saturday, stopping in at one store after another and accumulating packages of both necessary and frivolous but enticing foods. She stepped out of one store with a bag full of interesting and aromatic fruits and saw Naomi just across the street. She was about to call—it was cold and it would be nice to stop in somewhere for a cup of hot coffee with good company—but something stopped her, something in Naomi's face, in the way she walked. As she passed opposite where Frankie stood, she reached into a pocket and drew out a handkerchief which she pressed to her eye as though something had irritated it—or perhaps to wipe away a tear.

Twelve

It was a fine weekend until it ended. Mac spent Sunday with Susannah and Eric and all four of them had dinner together in an Italian restaurant. After he dropped the kids off he came down to the car and said, "I have to talk to you."

It made something tumble unpleasantly inside her. "Talk," she said.

"It's about Susannah." They were parked next to a hydrant and he had left the motor running so that she would be warm. "It's her birthday next week. Saturday. Jeannie's having a party and she'll let me know in due time if my presence will be acceptable but I'll see the kids on Sunday in any case." He paused and put a hand on her shoulder. "I promised I'd take them out for a celebration and Susannah said she'd like it just to be the three of us."

She felt a flood of relief and a wave of anger. The anger embarrassed her. She should be above being angry at a little girl whose life had been torn up through no fault of her own. But she had tried and it was hard to accept the proof that she had failed. "It's

276

her birthday, Mac," she said. "She has a right to celebrate it any way she wants. And with whom."

"I know she has a right." He sounded as though he needed some convincing. "I wanted it to be the four of us."

"It's OK. It's really OK." She leaned over and kissed his cheek. "Really." She sat back. "You getting her a gold chain?"

"No, goddammit, I am not getting her a gold chain," he said with feeling. "She's thirteen years old, not twenty-three. I will not play that game. If Jeannie wants to spring for it, let her."

"Just asking, pal."

"I hate seeing Jeannie and me being played off against each other, but I suppose we have no one to blame but ourselves. We used to have a united front and it worked. Now we're always at the barricades staring each other down."

"The united front worked when Susannah was younger. She'll be thirteen now. It can't work forever."

He gave her a small smile. "Whose side are you on anyway?"

"Mine, I think."

"I am too, baby," he said. "I am too."

They sent her to the offices of a large textile company on Monday and she found herself not far from her first job with Mrs. Gilley. There was tons of work to do and for the first time since she had started, she had the sense of not getting anywhere. Every Monday morning was different and yet nothing changed. Nothing was truly new. It wasn't boredom. Rather it was the feeling of being on a treadmill. She was always busy; they were always in a hurry; but no one ever got anywhere. She wondered, setting her margins and leafing through the text, if it was the same with her relationship with Mac.

On the way home the train stopped for a long time while the riders waited restlessly for an announcement. They were at a station and the doors were open. Some people got off. Others got on, looked around, and walked out. There were whispers about a fire. Finally they were told there would be a delay because of a track fire farther down the line.

Frankie got off and went up to the street. It was cold and getting dark and the buses were still a mystery to her. She found her way to Fifth Avenue through her practiced system of trial and error and got on a bus, but she had used her second token on the train and the bus took only exact change. She had three quarters, a nickel, and a few pennies. The fare was ninety cents. The driver would not accept a dollar. Defeated, she turned to get off, squeezing past half a dozen irritable people who were boarding, when an old woman with gray hair pulled back and covered with a wool hat put a hand on her shoulder.

"How much do you need?" she asked, peering through large glasses with distinct half-moons at the bottom.

"Seven cents," Frankie said.

"Move along," the driver called and a boarding passenger elbowed her.

"Take a dime," the old woman said, pulling off her wool glove to disclose a handful of change.

"Thank you. Thanks awfully." She picked the dime carefully out of the hand.

"It's too cold to walk," the woman said, replacing her glove and giving Frankie a smile. "Next time you should try to carry a little more change."

The depth of Mac's unhappiness with Susannah's decision surprised Frankie. He brought it up as they ate dinner and he spoke more candidly than he ever had before. He wanted his children to express themselves openly, he wanted them to feel they had certain rights, but at this moment he was feeling trampled on.

"No one's trampled on your rights," Frankie said. "It's more like retaliation. For your telling her we share that bed."

"I also hate retaliation," he said. "It's childish."

"Susannah's still a child."

"And women who are always right," he persisted, but more mildly. "Especially women who are always right."

"Can't be helped. Look at who I've learned from."

A little after eight she dialed Naomi's number. It rang so many times she was about to hang up when Everett answered.

"Everett, hi, it's Frankie."

"Frankie." Sounding bewildered, as though trying to fit her into a context.

"Is Naomi there?" she asked.

There was a long silence and she began to feel

uncomfortable.

"She can't come to the phone right now," Everett said finally. "Can she give you a ring later?"

"Sure."

"Thanks, Frankie." And the phone hung up.

Mac worked late at the desk. Sometime after eleven, while Frankie lay in bed reading, the elevator rose past their apartment. There were strange sounds in the elevator shaft—the shaft carried voices sometimes although they rarely heard anything directly from the apartments above and below them—and then the elevator rushed by again, going down. She glanced over at Mac and saw him raise his head and look toward the door. Then he went back to work.

"I'm going to bake Susannah a birthday cake," she announced at breakfast. "Does she like chocolate?"

"Passionately."

"I'll bake her the best chocolate cake in the world and I'll put candles on it. And while you're out to dinner, I'll polish the rest off myself."

"The whole thing?"

"Every last crumb."

"Without leaving me a second?"

"Well." She picked up the tokens. "For you maybe a sliver."

She put her coat on and he rang for the elevator.

"I won't tell Susannah about the cake. We'll keep it a surprise."

"You just want to fill her up first so there'll be

more for you."

She rode down to the first floor and stepped out into the lobby. As she walked quickly toward the door, something registered in her peripheral vision, something on the wall where the mailboxes were, something not quite right. She stopped and turned, her eyes moving from left to right along the names as they had that first night in January, quickly past MACIVER to GEORGE F. GOLDSTEIN and then stopped. She drew in her breath so loudly that anyone listening would have thought her lungs were failing. The name on the last box had been altered—no, not altered, desecrated. Someone had cut off the first name so that the shiny white-on-black nameplate read -WRIGHT and to the left of the hyphen was the nakedly exposed brass of the mailbox.

"Oh, Naomi," she said aloud, feeling tears, feeling a tightness in her throat. She started back toward the elevator but stopped. She could not go up there. She did not know what to say or to whom to say it. When Kenny had died people had expressed their sorrow in conventional ways but this was not a bereavement. This was not conventional. It was something else, something unnameable. *My boyfriend and I stopped living together.* It sounded so—shabby. Not like *divorce, separation, terminal illness,* words and phrases that rang with legitimate despair and loss. How many people had called to tell Naomi how sorry they were that her tree had been cut down?

She left her work station at ten for a morning break and found a telephone. In her bag was Naomi's number at work and she dialed it.

"Miss Shiskin's wire," a young female voice answered, pronouncing Naomi's name effortlessly.

"I'd like to speak to her, please."

"She called in sick. I think she'll be back tomorrow."

"Did she leave a number where she can be reached? This is a personal call."

"Just a moment, I'll check." Very businesslike, as though Miss Shiskin had taken a trip for the company and might leave the conference room if the call were important enough — or from the right person. There was the sound of another telephone being lifted. "Yes, it's on her desk." She read off a number.

"Thanks very much." She hung up, thought for a minute, then dialed.

The voice sounded hoarse but the first thing Naomi said was "Frankie, it's so good to hear from you." She was staying at her cousins' — they were away in Europe and she always checked their apartment once a week when they traveled — and she would have gone to work but she looked so awful. Maybe Frankie would come around on Saturday and they would talk.

"Can I do anything for you?" Frankie asked. "Anything, Naomi."

There was a pause and when Naomi spoke, her voice shook. "I wish you could," she said. "But it's over and I've just got to get myself together and start living again."

When she got home that evening, Everett was leaving the building and he looked as though he'd just gotten out of a sickbed, his face was so pale and drawn.

"They're both miserable," she told Mac that evening.

"That's the way it goes."

"But they were happy before."

"Maybe it was all surface."

"It wasn't."

"You know that for sure. You know Naomi that well. And Everett."

"It rubbed off on me, Naomi's gift."

"Maybe they'll get back together."

"Yes. Maybe they will."

She stayed home on Thursday till the living-room chairs were delivered. Then she went out. She sampled the chairs, assuring herself that they were comfortable, made a quick sandwich for lunch, and went out. It was a perfect afternoon for the Guggenheim. She rode the bus up Madison Avenue to the Eighties and walked over to Fifth.

Across the street, beyond the sidewalk, on the land that was Central Park, there was a small enclosed park where children played and mothers and nannies sat and watched. Near the entrance, a couple stood facing each other, talking. They seemed to have no interest in the children. They looked at each other as they talked, then away, then toward each other again. It took a moment until she realized that the man was Mac.

She watched with a kind of fascinated horror. Although they did not touch, there was a familiarity between them, a sense of intimacy. The woman wore a simple straight coat that accentuated her slender, almost girlish body. She kept her hands in her pockets and did not seem to be carrying a handbag. Once she shook her head slightly.

Frankie had never experienced such jealousy before, that ache and that anguish coupled with a sense of loss. It became difficult to watch; she was facing west and the sun was lowering. The couple in the park were nearly backlighted. Two children, running, brushed the woman's coat but she did not acknowledge their existence. Her face was tilted up toward Mac's. Frankie turned and walked down Fifth Avenue.

He came in a little before five, carrying flowers. It was the first time he had ever brought flowers. He said "Hi," and started to unbutton his coat.

"Hi." She observed him as though he were a stranger, this man she loved who had met another woman in Central Park this afternoon.

"What's wrong?" His hand stopped on a button.

"Who is she?"

He looked puzzled.

"The pretty lady. The beautiful woman." Watching his face. "I went to the Guggenheim this afternoon."

He tossed the flowers on the sofa. "It was Jeannie."

"Oh."

"I had to talk to her."

Frankie nodded.

"I should have told you I was going to see her."

"You don't have to tell me, Mac. She's your wife. You don't have to clear anything with me."

There was a look of conflict on his face and she

284

had the sudden strong feeling that it was all getting to be too much—Charlie Herron, Jeannie MacIver, Frankie Grant, everyone tugging from a different direction and not enough to go around, not enough, maybe, to hold in one place.

"I brought you flowers," he said.

She started to cry and turned toward the sink. She heard his footsteps across the apartment and then his arms were around her. "Come on, kid," he said. "Nothing happened. I came home, didn't I?"

His coat was both hard and rough against her cheek, a tweedy pattern because he was a tweedy kind of man, a man she loved and didn't want to lose but was going to. She would lose him back to his wife, who was slim and girlish and fair-haired and beautiful and who had rights that went back almost two decades. She wept into the coat, feeling his arms holding her, ashamed that something as trivial as a great love would make her cry when she had stayed so calm when Kenny died.

"Frankie, do you know that I need you?" His arms so tight, so confining in such a welcome way.

Oh, Mac, she thought. I want to believe it. I really do.

Somehow it had been decided that he would attend Susannah's birthday party. There had been no phone call this week, but then, he had met Jeannie in the park and probably they had arranged it then. Over breakfast on Saturday she searched the lower part of the Manhattan map for the street Naomi was living on.

"I can't find it," she said finally. "It must be some little alley somewhere."

"What's it called?"

"Sutton Place."

"Naomi's staying on Sutton Place?"

"At her cousins'."

"You're looking in the wrong place. It's up." He reached across the table and pointed to the East Side, his finger sliding up the Fifties.

"Up there? With that kind of name? I thought only avenues went up and down." (The man that first night gesticulating about the streets and the ave-nooz.)

"Her cousins have money. That's very rich territory up there. Take the Lex and walk over or let me treat you to a cab." He reached into his pocket.

"I'll walk," she said, holding up a hand to ward off the money. "It'll give me a better chance to see how the rich live."

He left late in the morning and while the elevator was still descending, the phone rang. She walked over to the desk and answered, wondering if she could still call him back should it turn out to be important.

"Put MacIver on," a man's voice ordered after she said hello.

"I'm sorry, he's not here. Can I take a message?"

"There's no message."

"Would you like to leave your name? He can call you back later."

"Just tell him"—there was a pause—"tell him somebody called and didn't leave a message."

"That's it?" Outside, on the street three floors below, Mac was exiting the building.

"That's it, lady. Tell him somebody called and didn't leave a message." There was a click.

"Who is this?" She rapped on the window but it was too late. Mac had turned north, away from her, and was heading up the street. Besides, the line had gone dead.

She was shaking, partly with fear, partly, she realized, with anger. The man had said practically nothing but the call had been a threat. Mac was closing in on them and they were getting edgy.

She sat in the chair to catch her breath. Mac, Mac, she thought, please be careful.

She checked Kenny's watch and got ready to go. She had promised Naomi she would bring lunch and Naomi had said, please, not deli. I'm starting to feel like a pickle. The Japanese restaurant had promised to make a takeout of sushi and she had courageously ordered two.

Before leaving, she went to Mac's desk and set the answering machine. Then she looked for a pencil and some blank paper to leave him a note. There were plenty of pencils but nothing that looked like an unused sheet of notepaper. She rummaged through a pile, being careful not to change the order, but there were only letters to Mac. The top one was from a woman in New Orleans who thought she had seen Charlie Herron. Mac had spoken to her at some length the other evening and was convinced she had seen no one resembling the missing reporter. The letter underneath was . . .

She looked at it, feeling instantly remorseful and distressed. It was written by hand and began "Dear Mac." It was funny how the handwriting had not changed. Dear Mac. She felt guilty but she also felt compelled. He had encouraged her often enough to look through the Herron material. Now she had found something else. Dear Mac.

"Of course we want you at Susannah's party, me included. I don't seem able to say things right over the phone anymore. Everything sounds double-edged, or worse. Maybe in writing there will be fewer ambiguities. Please come. All of us will be disappointed if you're not there. Eleven-thirty will be fine."

It was signed, "Love, Jeannie."

Love, Jeannie. All his life there would be Love, Jeannie, all his life that connection uptown that would draw him now and then to Central Park for a meeting, that would force him out of the apartment on a cold night to regain control of his uncertain emotions.

She replaced the letter in the pile and the pile in the corner of the desk. There was typing paper in a drawer and she quickly scribbled when she expected to return. Then she went uptown to see Naomi.

You could tell that Sutton Place was rich. Entering the building as the doorman held the door, she wished she had dressed differently. At the apartment house next door a woman in a long fur cape had moved swiftly from door to waiting maroon stretch limousine, entering it as casually as Frankie got into Mac's aging car.

"Koslow," she said to the inquiry. "Miss Shiskin is expecting me." She almost had it right, now: Shiskin.

"Your name?"

"Miss Grant."

A call was made by a second operative who then nodded at the doorman. She waited to be strip-searched, or at least frisked, with the boxes of sushi submitted to a metal detector, but he showed her to the elevator where a uniformed operator took her up. It was a relief to see Naomi.

They hugged when she went inside and Naomi gave a small shriek when she opened the lunch.

"Oh, Frankie, I've been yearning for this. Come, we'll set up the good table and have a feast."

The good table was in the dining room, which, along with the living room, overlooked the East River. It was a very lavish apartment with large rooms, several bathrooms, and a knockout kitchen. They talked about it for a while as they ate, skirting what was real.

"Crazy to have English tea with Japanese sushi, isn't it?" Naomi said, setting a porcelain cup in its saucer.

"It's a nice tea. My mother used to like a cup of tea in the afternoon when it was cold."

"So do I. Everett and I had all kinds—" She stopped and looked out the window.

"I saw him, Naomi," Frankie said softly. "Tuesday night when I came home from work. He was leaving the house, going out for dinner, I guess. He looked awful. He looked the way people look at funerals."

"We had an awful scene on Monday." Naomi's eyes were glittering with tears. She reached into the pocket of the big flowered linen shirt she was wearing over her jeans and pulled out a tissue and pressed it to her eyes. "Sorry."

"You love each other, Naomi. I just know you can work everything out."

The tissue had failed to hold back the tears. With evident frustration, Naomi picked up the charming little luncheon napkin and dabbed at her eyes. "It all ended on a little island in the Caribbean on a very hot day," she said.

"You didn't get married."

Naomi looked up with surprise. "How did you know?"

"I shared a taxi with Everett before you left. He was—I don't know how else to say it—he was high with excitement." She saw Naomi smile slightly as though she could see the moment. "He said you were bringing back a case of champagne and we should come up and celebrate with you when you got back. When we took you to the airport, I guessed what the celebration was for. Only there wasn't any celebration."

Naomi closed her eyes and nodded slightly. "We talked about it before we left," she said, looking at Frankie very directly, that open, honest look that seemed able to hide nothing. "We picked a day. We planned the announcements. We joked about how surprised everyone would be. And when we got there, something happened. Or nothing happened. Or everything happened. He said wonderful things to me, all the things you want to hear from the man you love. But he stopped talking about getting married."

"He got scared, that's all."

"Maybe. He had an awful first marriage. She was

a leech and she drained him, and made his life miserable. Thank God there were no children. He told me when we met that he would never marry again and I didn't care, or thought I didn't. When he said he wanted to, I knew I had cared. I wanted that tree to be worth something. That tree was me. We grew up together. We shared birthdays." She began to cry in earnest. "I don't know how he could have cut it down." She pressed the napkin to her eyes and then brought the sleeve of the shirt up, her forehead burrowed in the crook of her elbow. "It was only a lousy sycamore," she sobbed. "They're all over Brooklyn. They grow in all kinds of filth and pollution — that's the only way you can make it in this city."

"Sycamores are beautiful trees," Frankie said. She touched Naomi's shoulder, feeling a sense of sisterhood, of eternal friendship. "They have that wonderful yellow bark that drops off and makes its own mulch. They're very practical trees."

"Practical, yes." The arm lowered. The exposed face was red and ugly with hurt. "Oh, Frankie," Naomi said, "I wanted my tree back."

She sat for a while, becoming calm. Then she excused herself and went to another part of the apartment. Frankie cleared the good table and rinsed the dishes in the enormous sink. As she finished, Naomi walked in. She had changed to a blouse and her face looked a little better, although still puffy.

"I could go now," Frankie said. "If you want to be alone."

Naomi shook her head. "I'm fine now. Please don't go. I want to know about you and Mac. I hope — I hope you'll be staying."

Frankie dried her hands on a paper towel and they walked to the living room. Outside the wall of windows the East River was almost gleaming.

"That's Roosevelt Island," Naomi said, indicating a long strip in the river. "I may live there. Someone I know is giving up an apartment."

"From one island to another."

"That one's really an island. There's a cable car that runs to Manhattan."

"And you can look across the river and see Sutton Place."

"Yes, the great dream." Something of the old Naomi in her eyes. "Tell me the truth. Was the sushi great?"

"I can't believe I ate it. I can't believe it was as good as it was. You were right, as always."

"Right, as always," Naomi echoed. "And what about you? Are you hanging in after the first of April?"

"I can't, Naomi." There was something concrete in saying it aloud, in having someone hear it.

"Frankie—"

"No, I've thought about it. I haven't thought about much else the past few weeks. Mac asked me to stay. Very specifically at a chic lunch in a gorgeous restaurant."

"But?"

It was so clear that all the distant bridges were partly visible. Mac had named them for her once but the names were long forgotten. Throg something. Throg's Neck. She had asked him what a throg was and he had laughed.

"I can't live with someone else's husband," she said.

"I see." Naomi sat in a chair with her back to the view and looked sideways at Frankie. "Have you told him how you feel?"

"No."

"Talk to him, Frankie."

She shook her head.

"Frankie, it's the age of communication."

Frankie smiled. Beneath the swollen eyes and red lids, Naomi was still Naomi. "If I talk to him about it," she said carefully, "I'll never be sure whether he left her because he wanted to or because I wanted him to. There's only one way that's right, Naomi. If Mac can't leave his wife because he wants to, I can't stay with him."

"You're not wrong. I can't say you're wrong. It's just that it's so important, I can't stand to see you stand by and do nothing. We're talking about *love*, Frankie."

Love, Jeannie.

"I know."

"There's nothing more important in the whole world. I wish I knew what was holding him. He doesn't need her anymore."

Frankie turned away from the window. "Maybe she needs him now. Maybe that's what he's always wanted."

Naomi's eyes misted. "Why do they call people from the sticks hicks?"

Frankie turned to face her. "Maybe because it rhymes."

Thirteen

The chocolate cake was perfect. She made it the centerpiece of the pine table and bought party plates for the four places. Susannah could sit in the center and blow out the candles.

They arrived at three, Susannah wearing a new suede jacket over her dress.

"It's from Grandma and Grandpa Garrett," she announced.

"It's beautiful," Frankie said admiringly. "Are you sure you're warm enough in it today?" It was more of a spring than a winter jacket.

"Oh sure," Susannah tossed off. "It'll be spring soon anyway. Grandma Garrett says after my birthday the tulips come up."

"That's real nice, to be the first sign of spring."

Eric took a deep breath and let it out in a voiceless sigh. They sat at the table and Susannah blew out the candles and cut the cake and the three of them sang.

Mac, from his end, tasted the cake and said, "It's great," and Frankie, from her end, said, "It'll be there when you come back."

"Can I take home what's left?" Susannah asked.

"No you may not take home what's left," Mac said. "What's left stays right here."

"It's good," Eric said and Frankie wished there were a way she could wrap up a slice and stick it in his pocket.

When they left the table, Susannah looked longingly at the half that was left but said nothing. It was a pleasant afternoon. If anyone was uncomfortable about Frankie's status, no one let it show. Susannah talked about the party and described her presents. Mac talked to Eric about the case, about the empty missing-persons files, about the woman in New Orleans who thought she had seen Charlie Herron but hadn't. Eric went back for a sliver of cake and Susannah said he wouldn't be able to eat dinner and then it was five-thirty and Mac said they should think about leaving.

He put his arm around Frankie while the kids got their coats on. "We won't be late," he said.

"It's OK."

"It's not OK." He kissed her lips. Their backs were to the kids but she had stopped caring. She liked being kissed. "I'll see you in a couple of hours." He kissed her again.

"I think it's raining," Eric said. He was standing at the window in the bedroom, holding one of the blinds aside. There were splashes on the glass and it was very dark out.

"No!" Susannah said with a whimper. She was wearing the new suede jacket and looked betrayed.

"Mom told you not to wear it," Eric goaded.

"It *can't* rain. I heard the weather this morning."

"Ah, they're never right," Eric said.

"But my jacket'll be ruined." She brushed a tear away before the ruin began.

"You should've listened to Mom."

"Oh shut *up*."

"I've got an umbrella, Susie." Mac went to the closet but Susannah was crying with misery.

"I've got something, Mac." Frankie slid by him and felt along the hangers until she touched the plastic. "Here it is." She hauled out the plastic poncho with its bright yellow piping. "How's that, Susannah? That should keep you dry."

Susannah's eyes widened. "I can wear it?"

"You can have it, Susannah. It's yours."

"Don't you want it anymore?" She was so pretty, her features so perfect, her skin so smooth. Jeannie must hug her all the time.

"I never even wore it once. When I bought it—I think I was a different person."

Mac put his arm around her.

"Isn't it neat, Daddy?" Susannah had snapped all the snaps. The poncho was long enough on her to cover the suede jacket completely.

"It's very nice. It suits you."

She turned back to Frankie. "Thank you very much," she said formally.

"You're welcome."

"Daddy—could Frankie have dinner with us?"

"Sure she can, honey."

Frankie shook her head. "You go."

"Please, Frankie," Susannah said. "I really want you to come. Really."

"I'd have to change my clothes," she said, weaken-

296

ing.

"Then change." He patted her back.

She gave Susannah a hug, crinkling plastic, and went to the closet to find something to wear.

She could sense Mac's excitement in the next week. A lot of people called with apologies that "things were not in order" and promised everything would be taken care of if he would just be patient. He didn't seem patient. He seemed agitated, anxious. He remained cool when he spoke on the telephone, but when he hung up he seethed.

The agency sent her to the garment district on Monday. ("It's become the apparel industry," Mac told her, "but it's still in the garment district.") She didn't care what it was called, she didn't like it. It was noisy and brusque, the streets packed as she had seen in old photographs of turn-of-the-century New York. One afternoon, returning from lunch, she saw a young man pick someone's pocket and then dart away into the anonymous crowd. It scared her more than anything else she had seen in the city. When they told her late on Tuesday that she would not be needed the next day, she was relieved that it was over.

Nothing came through on Wednesday and Mac had an early appointment. At nine-thirty Detective Mike Rossante called and asked to have Mac call back. A little while later a woman in the medical examiner's office called and said she had those names Mr. MacIver wanted but she'd like to give them to him personally. Mac came back at three and made his calls, using the speaker-phone.

"Rossante," a man answered and Frankie listened to the voice, trying to determine whether it was the man who had called Saturday morning to threaten Mac. She had not told him about it and she was quite certain this was a different voice.

"MacIver here. What've you got?" More abrupt than usual, his patience wearing thin.

"Just what you asked me for, Mac," Rossante's voice said easily. Was there a bit of a sneer in it? she wondered. Was he telling Mac that his "lead" wasn't anything at all, just an administrative glitch?

"Go on."

"Got your files right in front of me. Come down anytime and look them over."

"All of them?"

"Two of the three and the third one'll be in in a couple of days. They were just where I told you they'd be," Rossante said in a clearly patronizing tone. "The lieutenant took them to a conference and didn't hurry up to put them back."

"Got one-oh-four-two-seven?"

"I expect that one first of next week."

"I'll be in in the morning."

"I thought you were in a hurry. I thought you couldn't wait. All of a sudden tomorrow's soon enough?"

"I am in a hurry. You know who had one-oh-four-two-seven?"

"We're working on it, Mac," Rossante said with a hint of a whine. "We're not holding back on you. Nobody's withholding evidence from the holy press."

Mac was silent for half a second. "Thanks, Mike," he said with genuine warmth. "I'll see you tomorrow."

"What's one-oh-four-two-seven?" Frankie asked when he had broken the connection.

"It's the one I want. Rossante's not going to find it."

"Why not?"

"Because it doesn't exist anymore. I think someone destroyed it to save his skin."

"Mac, someone called here on Saturday. Just after you left for Susannah's party. Kind of threatening. He said to tell you someone called and didn't leave a message."

"Why didn't you tell me?" He rose from his chair as though what she had said had propelled him.

"I guess I forgot. It was kind of scary and I just put it out of my mind."

"OK," he said and he looked almost triumphant. "We're closing in, baby." He turned back to the desk. "Let me call Sheila and see what she's got for me."

Sheila was the medical examiner's office and she had three names. There was a Schneider (she spelled it), probably a patrolman, a Stokes, no rank, and a Gallagher with an FTS. Gallagher was the name associated with 10427 and Frankie saw him circle the name several times as he talked.

"One more," he said to her when he had hung up. He dialed, asked for someone, waited. "Yes," he said when the next voice came on. "This is Henry MacIver from the *Times*." The other man made sounds of recognition. "I'm looking for some members of the force in connection with some old cases."

"Shoot," the voice said.

"L. J. Schneider. First name may be Lawrence."

299

"Larry Schneider. Right." He mentioned a precinct number and a phone.

"Gary Stokes."

"Stokes, Stokes. Hang on a minute." He returned soon with precinct and telephone numbers. "Anything else?"

"Field Training Specialist John Gallagher, John G., I think."

"Ah, Jack Gallagher," the voice said fondly. "Jack retired, Mr. MacIver."

"Retired." It was more of an echo than a question. "I met him once, about a year ago. I didn't think he was near retirement."

"Well, neither did a lot of people. He just up and put in his papers one day."

"You remember when that was?"

"Yeah, I sure do. It was last August."

"August."

"Right."

"I don't suppose you know where he's living now?"

"No idea, but I guess they send his pension checks somewhere. You could check with—"

"I will. Thanks very much. You've been very helpful. I appreciate it."

"Not at all. Anytime."

Mac pressed the cutoff button and stood. "Shit," he said.

"He's the one you want."

"You know what happened last August?"

"No."

"Remember the guy I flew out to Nebraska to see? The one who told me to listen to the tape again? He retired in August."

300

She felt a shiver. "They're going to hurt you, Mac. Those men must have retired because they found out something they shouldn't have and they were afraid."

"Maybe."

"One of them went all the way to Nebraska," she said.

"It's the other one I want to find. I wonder where in hell he went."

She took the rest of the week off. Suddenly things were buzzing, Mac away day and evening, the phone ringing, messages being left.

"I have some information on FTS Gallagher but it's probably not what you're looking for." "Mr. Harrison can't meet you on Tuesday the twenty-seventh. Please call and confirm two o'clock on the twenty-sixth instead." "I'm working on one-oh-four-two-seven for you, Mac. Just hold your horses another coupla days."

She found if she wound Kenny's watch once in the morning and once in the early evening it kept better time. It was such a simple solution, she wondered that she had not thought of it sooner.

As the weekend approached, she found herself looking forward to it with happy anticipation. She had made her peace with Susannah. Giving her the poncho had been a turning point. They had had a marvelous, friendly, warm dinner together at a much more elegant restaurant than Mac usually took them to. It gave Frankie a spurt of hope. If she and Susannah could get along, if they could be friends . . .

The dining-room chairs came on Thursday and the remaining furniture for Mac's study area on Friday. Fitting neatly under the windows were filing cabinets whose drawers pulled out to expose the files sideways. Karen called to persuade him to accept the desk that would complete the room but he refused irritably. The old desk remained. The mess on his desk disappeared. He stayed up late Friday sorting and putting away. He had brought home a box of file folders and they worked together labeling and alphabetizing. The cartons that had marked the division between study and bedroom emptied and Mac collapsed them, piled them near the door, and eventually tied them into neat bundles using slip knots in the cord the way her dad had done.

He surveyed the apartment from the door. "Looks damn nice," he said. "All we need is the bed but Karen said any day. Remember what it looked like when you first saw it?"

"I remember the floor. I had never seen so much floor in my life outside a basketball court. It was so barren. And the lights."

"You were a very pretty kid."

Oh, Mac, I don't want to leave you.

"When this is over I'll be easier to live with."

"You're easy enough now."

"There are people who wouldn't agree with you."

"What do they know."

"Right." He moved the stacks of cartons with his foot so that they did not encroach on the passage to the door. "We could go out and have a bite," he said. "Or we could go to bed and see where that takes us." He put his arms around her.

"I couldn't eat a thing."

"Neither could I." He was wearing a dress shirt with the sleeves rolled up and she could feel the warmth of his skin, his life, through the fabric. "Ready for the weekend?"

"Yes." He was having the kids over for an overnight.

"Sure?"

"Very sure."

"Everything's going to be fine," he said. "For both of us."

"Real fine?" She looked up and kissed him.

"Real, real fine." His fingers hard on her back. "You'll see."

Susannah was neither more nor less friendly than she had been before. She was simply Susannah. It was as though last weekend had never happened, as though the tears had not been shed, the poncho not given, the invitation to the birthday dinner not offered. Either nothing special had happened between them or its significance had been short-lived for Susannah.

In the afternoon they drove to Connecticut to visit friends of Mac's who had a small rustic house in a woodsy area. They had a daughter in her late teens who disappeared with Eric and Susannah, leaving a relaxed foursome in front of a fire in the main room. There was no tension as there had been with Al and Katie Black. Jeannie was never mentioned and it turned out that the teenage girl was the wife's daughter while the husband had two children of his own

303

living with their mother. They were a nice couple, very comfortable with each other, and the visit was warm and pleasant.

Late in the afternoon she and Mac tramped around out-of-doors. It was still quite light after five o'clock and crisper than in the city. Frankie inhaled and blew out a puff of steamy breath.

"Will you find Charlie Herron, Mac?" she asked. They were walking cozily, each with an arm across the other's back, and if he had asked her at that moment to lie down on the hard earth and make love, she would have done so eagerly.

"I may." He brushed his lips against her forehead. "I have to find Jack Gallagher first."

"Do you know for sure that he has something to do with Herron?"

"I don't know anything for sure. All I know about him is that he was the cop who brought a body to the medical examiner's office last July and he retired unexpectedly a week or two later and can't be found. And the missing-persons file is empty."

"But if it's Charlie Herron, it means they let him live a year and then killed him."

"The body was decomposed. It had been dead a long time."

"Then you couldn't identify it for sure even if you had it now."

"We might. They can inject a mixture of glycerine and water into the fingers and get a pretty good fingerprint. And then there are dental records and X rays. Charlie broke an arm when he was twelve."

"Then why don't you just have the body exhumed?"

"I need some substantial proof. I can't ask them to exhume every male body that's five-foot-ten and had white skin. Rossante wouldn't even let me go through his files for the last eighteen months. There's no way they'll start exhuming bodies."

"Think you'll find Gallagher?"

"I hope so. He's got a post-office box out in Queens and someone told me he has a sister in New York but I haven't been able to find her married name. I've been asking around his old precinct, looking for buddies."

"Mac, when it's over, when you know what happened, what are you going to do?"

"Finish the book, go back to work, settle down. What about you?"

"I'm getting a degree."

"We haven't talked about it yet."

"We've talked about it." She kissed his cheek as they walked. "Endlessly."

"Endlessly is just a relative concept."

Frankie and Irene, their hostess, did the dishes together in the large kitchen. They fell into a good work pattern and it went quickly.

"Mac said you were living together," Irene said, her hands in soapy water in the sink.

"Since January."

"When he talked about you over the phone I thought you were older. It's nice to see him with a real person."

"Thank you."

"We met him in the city one evening last fall. He

was with a decorator."

"I've met her."

"Pretty in a way, but plastic. I wondered what they said to each other." She rinsed a dish and put it in the drainer, rinsed another and set it in front of the first. "I suppose talking wasn't high on their list of activities."

Frankie opened a cabinet and lifted a stack of dry dinner plates into it. "They look handpainted," she said.

"I made them the first summer Walter and I lived together."

"I'm very impressed."

Irene laughed. "That people over forty live together? We only married because of Jessie. Role models and that sort of thing. *We* didn't need it. Walter's marriage was over, mine was over before it started although I hung on for a dozen years. I'd have been just as happy without." She lifted her left hand out of the water, showing a plain gold band on somewhat lumpy fingers.

"I meant the dishes," Frankie said with a smile. "I'm very impressed with your talent."

"Oh, the dishes." Irene laughed again. "I'll make a set for you and Mac, just as soon as you're sure it's the real thing. I wouldn't want my dishes to get involved in a breakup."

"They won't be," Frankie said. "Thank you for the offer."

It was late when they got back to the apartment and Eric and Susannah climbed up to the sleeping loft and crawled into their sleeping bags. Mac left the bedroom light on for a while but must have felt, as Frankie did, that it spotlighted them, and soon he turned it off, leaving only the lamp on the old desk turned on. Frankie resisted all temptation to look up at the two whispering figures over the coat closet. When she crossed the floor to get to the kitchen for a glass of juice, she could hear the bags moving so that their young occupants could follow her with her eyes.

She undressed in the bathroom, lay down with a book while Mac took his turn, and closed the book when he turned off the desk lamp. He was wearing pajama bottoms which she had last seen in the early days of January. He got in bed and put his arms around her. The way they lay, the way they had arranged themselves that first Sunday afternoon, his back was to the coat closet. He kissed her and she made herself feel they were alone. She wanted him more tonight than she ever had before and she could sense his like feelings. The days of March were running out and with them the last of her hopes. He laid a hand on her breast, touching it through the nightgown, and she felt his penis harden and move against her. He said, "Good night," and she said it back, softly, a murmur, trying to keep it private. Then he took his hand away and she prepared to sleep, feeling the four eyes watching through the darkness.

Mac took the kids out on Sunday while Frankie stayed home with the paper. She liked that about him, that he always saw them alone for at least part of every weekend. Once when Susannah had complained about Jeannie, Mac had cut her off, saying they would discuss it privately. She liked that too. There was a lot she liked about him, a lot she would miss, a lot she would think about in the spring and summer and the long years ahead when she was doing what she wanted to do—but without Mac.

They came back in the afternoon and all of them had dinner at the pine table, sitting on the new chairs. Afterward, Eric went up to the sleeping loft and curled up with a history book while Mac and Susannah cleared the table and put the dishes in the dishwasher. It had been a nice weekend, even if Susannah had not shown any particular warmth to Frankie. Watching father and daughter working together in the kitchen, listening to the banter, she told herself, was warmth enough. And Eric had told her again how much he had liked the chocolate cake.

"Almost time to go," Mac said. He dried his hands on a kitchen towel and hung it to dry.

"Give me ten minutes," Eric called from his perch. "I just want to finish the chapter."

"I'm not rushing you."

"I want to read up there, too," Susannah said. She picked up a copy of *The New Yorker* and went over to the ladder.

"Come on, Susie," Mac said. "Leave him alone. He's got work to do."

"I won't bother him."

"Susie . . ."

The phone rang.

"I'll get it." Susannah dropped *The New Yorker* and dashed across the loft to the telephone. She got on the desk chair on her knees and carefully pressed the button for the speaker-phone. "Hello?" she said too loudly.

"Uh—can I talk to Mr. MacIver?" It was a man's voice, booming through the apartment. Eric closed his book and Mac went to the desk, removing Susannah from the chair and sitting.

"This is MacIver."

"Mr. MacIver, this is Sergeant Gordon Pierce at the three-oh precinct. Uh, are you the one who's working on the Charlie Herron case?"

"Yes, I am. Do you have something?"

"I sure do," the voice said. "Your man just walked in the precinct."

Fourteen

There was an air of almost total confusion. Eric said he wanted to come and Susannah said that wasn't fair and Mac said cut it out, both of you, it's time to go home. Frankie went to the closet and started handing out coats.

"You'll take them home for me."

"Sure."

"By taxi. You will absolutely go both ways by taxi."

"I promise."

"And you take them upstairs and leave them with Jeannie."

She paused briefly. "OK."

He dug in his pockets. "Shit, I've only got twenties."

"I have money."

"Take one anyway." He put a bill in her hand. "Come on, I'll get you a taxi." He had his corduroy jacket on, the keys in his hand. He pressed the elevator button.

"We'll find one ourselves. Don't wait for us."

He looked doubtful. The elevator came.

"I'll see you later, Mac."

He opened the door and kissed her. "If you're sure."

" 'Bye, Daddy."

"So long. I'll talk to you both tomorrow."

She let her breath out as the elevator descended. "Don't forget your books, Eric."

"Oh yeah." He climbed the ladder and retrieved two, jumping from the second or third rung as he came down. "I wish I could've gone with him."

"He'll tell you all about it tomorrow."

"Are you taking us home?" Susannah asked.

"I sure am. We all ready?"

"You know how to get there?"

Frankie laughed. "I get in a cab and give your address."

Susannah smiled. "That's what Mommy does."

They found a taxi on Broadway and Eric went to the curb to signal it.

"You've grown an inch since I met you," she told him as she came beside him at the curb.

He shrugged with embarrassment and they got in the cab.

"I wonder why Mr. Herron came back tonight," Susannah said.

"Maybe he escaped from wherever they were holding him," Eric said.

"I hope he's in good health," Frankie said.

"Why wouldn't he be?" Susannah asked.

"They could've beat him, you know," Eric said derisively. "You don't think they had him in the Waldorf-Astoria, do you?"

"Oh let's not think about that, Eric. Let's just hope he's OK and not in danger and he can go back to his family and forget all about this awful year and a half." She pulled her wallet out and found a five and some singles.

"Are you coming upstairs with us?" Susannah asked.

"Yes."

"Why?"

"You don't have to," Eric said.

"Your dad asked me to."

The cab turned and she recognized the street. As the taxi braked, she felt a wave of near-panic. It would be safe enough to let them go up by themselves once they were past the doorman. Or perhaps she would get off the elevator and watch down the hall until the door opened and then flee.

They stopped and Eric opened the door as the doorman approached. Frankie handed the fare through something like a mail slot, the driver's protection against the dangerous three in the back seat. Then she slid out and let the doorman close the door behind her.

She followed Eric and Susannah through the glass doors into the lobby, down the hall to the left where an elevator waited open. She could scarcely breathe. She did not want to meet Jean MacIver. Jean MacIver was their mother and his wife but nothing to Frankie, nothing but a hindrance, a pain in the neck, the only obstacle.

She was the last one in the elevator and Susannah pressed a button as soon as she was in, Frankie did not even notice which one. They went up while her stomach went in some other direction. It was really quite unnecessary to accompany these two teenagers beyond the elevator.

"Here we are." The inner door slid open and Susannah pushed the outer one and let Eric catch it.

The floor was carpeted and the halls painted some uncolor. Susannah sprinted ahead and Eric walked quickly so that several feet separated each of them. *Mac.* She could not even swallow. *Mac.* She could turn and leave, desert, pack her clothes and be at the bus station before Mac even got back, her feet moving in a steady rhythm because this was the measure of her love, that she would face Jean Mac-Iver without collapsing, that she would do what he had asked of her.

The door opened as Susannah reached it and a hand on Eric's arm drew him in. Frankie took the last few steps, preparing herself, and heard Susannah say, "This is Frankie, Mommy. Look at the nice gold chain Daddy gave her."

It fell like a blow, leaving her speechless, nearly eclipsing the sight of Jean MacIver.

"So you're Frankie." It was more an appraisal than a statement. "Why don't you come in, Frankie. I think it's time we had a little talk, don't you?"

She walked into the apartment. Jean MacIver was a waif. Passing her, Frankie could see the other woman was slightly shorter than she, as only a brief time ago she had sensed that Eric was now taller. Jean MacIver was almost girlishly thin with a face something like Susannah's and long fair hair. It was easy to see her as one of the flower children of the sixties, children Frankie had only read about since she herself had been born in sixty-one.

"I'm Jean MacIver."

"Yes."

"Take your coat off and toss it. You look pretty casual."

Frankie unbuttoned her coat and folded it over the arm of a white sofa. All the furniture was white. The rug was white. Here and there a dish or an ashtray with an art-deco look was black with a bit of gold. She sat on the sofa not far from her coat.

"Where's Max?"

"He was called away at the last minute." She was damned if she would give anything away.

Jean MacIver sat on the identical sofa across the room. She was wearing a pale lavender blouse, a rather full skirt in a lavender tweed, and flat shoes like ballerina slippers. She looked quite fragile, a stark contrast to Frankie's jeans and shirt topped with Mac's shetland sweater. "He gave you the gold chain?"

She could have killed Susannah. Susannah didn't even *know* that Mac had given it to her. "Yes, he did," she said finally.

"Generous."

"Mac is very generous."

"Yes. Excuse me." She stood and went to the hall that must have led to the bedrooms. "Eric?" she called. "Did you finish your history?"

"Yeah." From a distant room.

"Susannah, you'd better look at that space project before you go to sleep."

"I *will*."

"Anybody hungry?"

314

There was a chorus of irritable no's and Jean Mac-Iver returned to her sofa.

On the wall on either side of the doorway to the hall were built-in cabinets up to desk height and bookcases the rest of the way up. On the horizontal surface dividing them, photographs were arranged in groupings. Mac was in many of them. In one foursome, Al and Katie Black were readily recognizable. In another a young barefoot Jeannie stood beside a bearded Mac on a beach.

"That was taken on our wedding trip," Jean Mac-Iver said as she passed and Frankie turned her head away from the pictures. "You didn't know he had a beard."

"No."

"I knew. He shaved it because I asked him to."

Funny how her tension had dissolved. She looked at the slender woman across the room and said nothing.

"Why didn't Mac bring Eric and Susannah home himself?"

"Someone called him just as he was ready to leave. It was quite urgent."

"Urgent," she repeated. "He had no right to dump them on someone else and run off."

"Why don't you take it up with Mac?"

"I will." She had a clear young voice. In a few years no one would be able to tell her and her daughter apart on the telephone. "I understand you moved into that empty barn of his."

"I live with Mac, yes."

"What do you plan to do when he grows up?"

Frankie watched her quietly, a hurt woman trying

to spread the pain.

"When the mid-life crisis is over," Jean MacIver persisted. "You do know that he's thirty-eight. Do you have plans for later, for when he's over the Lolita urge?"

"My plans have nothing to do with Mac's crises or urges. They have even less to do with you."

"Don't be snotty with me, Frankie. I can give you a very hard time."

"No, you can't, Jean." She was anxious to use her first name, to establish them as equals. "You can give Mac a hard time. You can't do it to me."

"You don't know how bad things can get," Jean MacIver said.

Frankie took her coat and put it on without buttoning it. She slung her bag over her shoulder. "That's where you're wrong," she said, a finger circling Kenny's watch. She found the door and stood looking at the locks. A hand reached over and turned one one way and the other in the reverse direction.

"It's open now."

"Thank you."

"Thank you for the poncho. Susannah was very pleased."

Frankie opened the door and turned to face Jean. "I'm glad," she said. "I like Susannah very much."

"I know."

She heard the words ringing as she started down the hall. I know. I know. I know.

Downstairs the doorman asked her smoothly if she wanted a taxi and when she said yes, he went out and blew a whistle and one stopped. She said thank you and got in and they were already turning downtown when she realized she should have tipped the door-man. Damned hick, she scolded herself. You never learn. But she was glad it was over, glad she had survived, very glad to know that Jean MacIver was only human.

Fifteen

Mac wasn't home yet when she returned but she had been gone only a short while. She was surprised to see that it was only a little after eight. So much seemed to have happened, she thought the passage of time would reflect the enormity of the events.

Now that the panic of meeting Jean MacIver had subsided, she had time to become excited once more about Charlie Herron. Just on the chance that Mac had left a message, she played the tape but it was blank. What would they be doing now—sitting in a bar somewhere and catching up? Taking him to the hospital for a checkup? Had someone called Ariana with the news?

She turned on the radio and found a news station, hoping to hear an announcement, but it was all the usual blah Sunday news. Probably nothing would get out for a while, not until they finished getting Charlie Herron's story.

She showered and watched some television. After the ten-o'clock news she read till eleven, then listened to the news again. She tried to remember what the policeman had said. Had he given a precinct number? Not that she could call, but maybe she ought to go down and wait for him. Charlie Herron back after more than a year and a half. Surely it would be the biggest headline on every front page tomorrow. What a story, and it was all Mac's. She could imagine them hugging in the police station as he and Al Black had hugged that night in the hotel. "Come on, Mac," she said out loud. "You've been gone for *hours.*"

She left the kitchen light on and lay down, too tired to read. She awoke suddenly and said, "Mac?" but there was no answer and the clock beside her showed one in the morning. She sat up and listened. There were no street noises, no elevator hum. It was six hours since Mac had left.

The pain in her midsection confirmed that she was afraid. What if he had been in some accident on his way home after a long session at the police station? They would call Jeannie. Jeannie was his wife. Even now perhaps she was standing at his bedside, still wearing the lavender blouse and tweed skirt, holding his hand and telling him it was OK, he could have her back; there was nothing to forgive. Love, Jeannie.

Or maybe after he had spent several hours with Charlie Herron, after he had seen Charlie and Ariana embrace for the first time since his disappearance, Mac had decided to go back to Jeannie. Maybe something had clicked—the value of a long marriage, the sacredness of a whole family.

No. If he went back it would be because he couldn't shake loose of Jeannie. It would be for the worst of reasons, not the best. Tonight he belonged to Frankie, here in this empty barn now full and bright and warm.

"Please come back to me, Mac."

She said it aloud but who would hear it? Naomi was gone. Naomi's great love was over. To call her would be cruel, a compounding of miseries.

She lay back on the pillow and tried to sleep but she was too agitated, too frightened. She kept seeing Jeannie and Charlie Herron and Mac and even herself. I can give you a very hard time, she heard over and over. Something was wrong with Mac and she didn't know what to do, didn't know how to find out what it was or where he might be.

She had never seen time pass so slowly, never experienced such a long siege of anxiety. She thought of her mother knowing that Kenny would die. She wondered whether this was what her mother had felt for months on end, this pain. Poor Mom. She felt the urge to cry and turned her face so that the pillowcase would absorb the tears. So many urges in the human body and none of them controllable for very long—the urge to cry, the urge to urinate, the urge to have sexual satisfaction. Please let nothing happen to Mac.

It was a digital clock and it worked at passing time but it failed. Time hung like mist in tree branches on a fall morning. She wondered if Naomi's tree had held mist in its arms up in that unpronounceable place. How could a man who was her father cut that tree down? How could Kenny's body deteriorate that way when he was young and *so good?* He was *my brother.*

And only three minutes later than the last time she had looked.

When the phone rang it was a quarter to three and she was on her feet so quickly she wasn't sure whether she had actually heard the ring.

"Hello?"

A short silence. "I need you to come and get me."

"Mac." It was a half-whisper. "Are you all right?"

"No."

"Where are you?" She grabbed a pencil and moved a piece of paper nearer.

There were some sounds, voices somewhere. Then he came back. He read off a three-digit number. "Third Avenue. Got it?"

"Yes." She read it back.

"Frankie."

"Yes."

"This is Frankie, isn't it?" Slightly slow. Slightly slurred.

"Yes, Mac."

"You'll take a taxi."

"Yes. I'll be right there."

She hung up and rang for the elevator before dressing. She threw on the nearest clothes she could find, pushing her feet into shoes while she buttoned a shirt over her bare breast, her fingers shaking so that she could not get them all together. She grabbed her coat and unlocked the door, locking it reluctantly from inside the elevator, and put her coat on.

As she descended, she acknowledged to herself that she was terrified. It was three in the morning in New York City and she did not know where to find a cab. If Naomi had been home she might have telephoned to have Everett help but now she was on her own.

She walked north on Broadway, praying for a taxi to appear, keeping to the curb because Mac had warned her, among many other warnings, to stay away from buildings where hidden muggers and worse might reach out and draw a woman into a dark doorway.

Nothing. She wondered if buses ran at this time of night. Anything would be better than walking and if Mac called again and there was no answer he would know she was on her way.

A car came down the street and slowed as it passed her. She wanted to pray but she had given up prayer when Kenny's illness had returned. The driver looked her over and speeded up, beeping his horn twice in a farewell.

Her heart lifted. Two taxis were parked at the next corner. She ran to them and looked inside. Both were empty, lights out. She looked around. Just behind her an all-night coffee shop was alight and several customers, almost all men, were sitting at the counter or at small square tables. She went inside.

"I need a taxi," she announced to the patronage.

Behind the counter a man looked at her, then resumed wiping the Formica surface.

A man on a stool put his coffee cup down. "I'm off duty till three-fifteen." He took another sip of coffee, a bite of bagel.

"Please," she said.

"Go sit in the first cab. I'll be out in ten minutes."

"I need a cab now." She dug in her bag and found the twenty Mac had given her. "Here," she said.

The man looked at the twenty, looked at her, picked up a napkin and wiped his mouth, with special attention to his mustache. "Where you goin'?" he asked.

She recited the address.

"Put it away," he said. "I'll take you." He put some money on the counter, said good-bye to the counterman, and swung off the stool.

When they reached the address, it was not yet three-fifteen.

He was standing next to the door of a closed bar, his jacket open, his hands in the jacket pockets. "Hi, kid," he said.

"Hello, Mac." She was relieved to see him upright and without visible wounds. "Where's the car?"

"The car." He pulled something out of a jacket pocket and looked at it. It was a matchbook and she could see the address of the bar printed on the cover. "Around the corner," he said.

"Shall I get it and come back for you?"

"No."

He started walking, lost his footing and wavered. She took hold of his arm and held it tightly, supporting him. He looked at the hand on his arm and said, "Ouch," as though it had taken that long for the pain to reach his nerve center.

She kept her hand there, not quite so tightly, until they had walked past several doorways. "Around this corner?"

"Yes."

"Where are the keys?"

"Somewhere."

The car was wedged between two others, tight at both ends. He pulled the keys out of his pants pocket and gave them to her. She opened the door and said,

"Get in, love."

He sat heavily and pulled the door closed. While she fumbled with the key on the other side, he unlocked it for her.

She got in and closed the door. "Are you sick, Mac?" she asked.

"Sick to the soul."

She smiled. "Then I can take you home."

"Yeah. Home." He leaned back in the seat. "I called Jeannie."

She had just turned the motor on. She felt stung, pierced. "Shall I drive you to Jeannie's apartment?" she asked.

He said, "Shit," and closed his eyes. "It was the first number I thought of," he said slowly. "When she answered—Jesus, she was sore as hell. I asked her . . . Jeannie's a bitch."

"Everybody's a bitch sometimes." She started maneuvering the car back and forward, back and forward, inching it out, wondering if he had gotten it into this space or whether the drivers fore and aft had hemmed him in.

"Are you from Ohio?" he asked.

She laughed. "You know I'm from Ohio."

"You drive like a damn New Yorker. Except you don't hit 'em hard enough. I meant to call you, baby. I couldn't think of the number. What a bitch."

"You can love her even if she's a bitch, Mac."

"Who said I love her?"

The car, barely grazing the one in front, moved into the street. She took the first left and headed downtown. Mac sat with his eyes closed. Once he reached out and touched her thigh. Once he opened his eyes and said, "Careful," as a car turned into the street in front of her without looking.

She parked in front of Pragmatique and turned off the motor. He opened his eyes. "You OK?" she asked.

"I'm sick to the soul," he said again.

"Can I — can I do anything?"

"They killed him, Frankie."

"What?"

He turned and put his arms around her. As he held her, she could feel the shudder. "They killed him that night in July when they picked him up outside the Post Building and dumped his body somewhere." His voice was muffled by the collar of his jacket. "Oh shit, was I a fool."

"But you saw him tonight." She heard the shock in her voice, felt the pounding of her heart. With her hand, she stroked his hair, his cheek.

He moved away so that their faces were close but not quite touching, his hands still holding her arms. "Charlie wasn't there. Charlie was never there. They gave me a story about Charlie coming in and leaving before I got there but it was a lot of crap. I should have known. I'm the last guy in the world they'd call. They'd call Ariana or Charlie's mother if it were real. I just wanted it to be true and I lost my cool."

"Let's go upstairs."

"The whole Thirtieth Precinct's part of it."

"You're tired, Mac." She was still stroking the side of his face.

"I'm tired and I'm drunk and I'm sick and I let Charlie down."

"You didn't let anyone down." The cheek slightly

325

moist now. "He was dead before you knew he was gone."

"Someone in that precinct killed him."

"Don't say anything till you get some sleep."

"I thought I would find him alive."

"No you didn't, Mac. You just wanted it, but you never believed it."

"I wanted it," he said.

"I know. Let's go up and get some sleep."

She turned the alarm off so that it was the phone that woke her. The agency had a job.

"I can't today," she said. "I'm awfully sorry."

"Shall I put you on the list for tomorrow?"

She looked toward the mattress where Mac was still asleep. "Tomorrow'll be fine."

He had barely stirred. She adjusted the blanket and took a shower and dressed. She made a quart of coffee and found two bagels in the refrigerator. When she looked over at the bedroom, the bed was empty and she could hear the shower running.

He came out later in jeans and his gray sweatshirt. His face was pale and he took two aspirin before he said anything. His hand didn't look very steady. Then he sat down and said, "I'm sorry."

"Sorry for what?"

"For a whole list of things."

She said, "Don't enumerate," because he looked as though he was about to.

"They were trying to put me off or slow me down or maybe just finger me," he said as though there had been no hiatus between last night and this morning. "Well, the bastards got a good look. I carried on like a madman."

She poured coffee and took the bagels out of the oven.

"They knew I'd jump when they called and they were right. It's one for their side."

She put the bagels on the table and slid her arm around his shoulders.

He leaned his head against her breast for a minute. "You weren't wearing anything under your blouse last night."

"I didn't think you noticed."

"It was very sexy. You're a very sexy kid."

She kissed his head and sat down opposite him. They had changed places this morning.

"They call you for a job?"

"I told them I couldn't."

He put jam on his bagel, took a bite, and drank a lot of coffee. "I only called Jeannie because it was the first number that came into my head."

"You don't have to apologize."

"I think I do. I think I have to apologize for a lot of things."

"You don't."

"For making you take the kids home."

"It was just a quick cab ride."

"And inflicting Jeannie on you. She said something about it when I phoned."

"I wasn't very nice to her."

He smiled. He looked a little less ashen since he had come to the table. "Christ, I wanted to find him alive," he said.

She looked at Kenny's watch and felt the sting of

tears.

"I had a lead last year that he was in South America."

"Mac, you don't really believe the police were involved?"

"I'm sure of it. I have pretty good evidence there's a cop running a chicken-hawk operation, those little boys on Forty-second Street, the story Charlie was investigating. He told me he was close. I didn't realize he was right on it."

"It doesn't sound possible."

"Anything's possible. Except that Charlie's alive. That isn't possible anymore."

She got up and poured more coffee. "You think he's one of those poor people buried in potter's field?"

"I'm sure of it."

She sat down and took a sip. "Where is it, the cemetery?"

"Place called Hart Island, off Orchard Beach in the Bronx." He looked up at her. "Figures, doesn't it? Born on one island and interred on another. You have to go island-hopping to get there. Ferry leaves from City Island."

"Do they allow visitors?"

He shook his head. "It's not pretty, Frankie. No green lawns and flowers. And they use prisoners to bury the dead."

"But you and Ariana will take care of him."

"We'll take care of him. Just as soon as we can."

A little while later the phone rang. Mac answered

and almost immediately switched on the speaker-phone.

". . . sante," she heard the familiar voice say. "I been thinking about that missing file."

"Yes, Mike."

"Sometime in the fall — maybe it was September, I can't remember exactly — a captain came in and asked to see what was in that jacket."

"A captain."

"Yeah."

"You remember which one?"

"Uhh . . ."

"It's OK, Mike. I know you can't keep track of everything that goes on." Mac spoke very considerately.

"You know I would tell you if I remembered, Mac."

"I know you would. You think this captain never returned the stuff he borrowed?"

"That's what I think."

"Probably an oversight."

"Right," Rossante said. "An oversight."

"I appreciate the call, Mike."

"Don't give it a second thought. I told you, always glad to cooperate."

There was dead silence when he switched the speaker-phone off.

"That's very high up," Frankie said. "A captain."

"Very high."

"You think Rossante knows who it is?"

"Sure he knows. He's probably been trying for days or weeks to decide how much to tell me."

"What'll you do now?"

He looked at his watch. "Try to find Jack Gallagher," he said.

Sixteen

He got up first on Tuesday as though to set his life in order once again. While he was making breakfast, she dressed for work, anticipating a call. When it came, it was a surprise.

The caller read off a familiar address. "Report to Mr. Benton," she said.

"Don't you mean Mrs. Gilley?"

"No. It says right here, Mr. Benton."

"I'll be there in half an hour."

"Problem?" Mac asked.

"Just a little funny. I'm supposed to report to Mr. Benton." She shrugged. "Maybe the chain of command has changed. Are you off somewhere today?"

"I've got to find Jack Gallagher. Somebody he used to know has to know what became of him."

"Is it up at that precinct, Mac?"

"I'll talk to them on neutral territory. Don't worry. I'll leave you messages."

"And dinner?"

"Only a maybe."

He drove her to the subway since he had to move

the car anyway and she rode uptown in the thinning crowd. It was better this way, a place to sit and not quite so frantic. She rose as the train entered the Fiftieth Street station and exited easily.

She took the elevator up and unbuttoned her coat, a little unsure because she wasn't going to Mrs. Gilley. She walked down the hall of closed office doors, stopped in front of "W. J. Benton," and rapped twice.

"Yo!"

She smiled and opened the door. "Good morning," she said, hesitating in the doorway.

"Frankie. My Lord, girl, I am glad to see you. Come in, come in. Here"—he stood and came around his desk—"let me hang your coat."

"Thank you," she said warily.

He hung the coat on a hanger one hook above his, just behind the door. Then he went back to his desk and sat. "I've lost my secretary," he said gloomily.

"I'm sorry to hear it."

"Got hit by a bicycle going home from work yesterday."

"Oh dear."

"Threw her in the air. Her arm's broken. They're keeping her in the hospital a day or two for observation. These bicycles. You'd think they'd learn how to use 'em. Well, at least I got you. I told them there wasn't anybody else who could do the job."

"That's very nice of you."

He smiled, showing the crooked tooth. "Just the plain truth, Frankie. OK then, shall we get to work?"

Suddenly, everything was different. Mr. Grayson's secretary stopped by at eleven-thirty and asked if she would like to go out for lunch. Four of them—the other two secretaries stayed behind to cover the phones—ate out in a restaurant. One of them was expecting a promotion which would lift her into a new area of responsibility. Another one made a disparaging comment about the word-processing group and how her boss wouldn't send anything to them anymore because of all the mistakes they made.

In the afternoon she called home and left her number on the tape. There was no message from Mac but there was one for him: "Mr. MacIver, this is Mr. Harrison's office. We're holding two o'clock on Monday for you. Will you confirm?" That was all.

Mac called later and said he would be meeting some people and wouldn't be able to make it for dinner. After she hung up, Mr. Benton asked her if she could work late. She said sure and left another message for Mac.

He had letters he wanted her to write from notes which he dictated. She drafted them and returned for his comments. He did a lot of nodding and made a few ball-point changes. Always there was the smile with the crooked tooth.

She parried his calls, using a list his secretary had on the desk. For certain people he was never in. For others, he was in even if he had to be dragged out of the men's room. At six-thirty she was sitting in his office with the last set of drafted letters.

He looked them over, nodded, marked, smiled. "Yo," he said with a note of triumph. He looked at his watch. "Let me take you to dinner, Frankie."

She felt her cheeks color. "No thank you, Mr. Benton. I'll just run along."

"No, I insist. You make yourself pretty and I'll square it with my wife."

"I think, really, I should just—"

"Just come along and have a good dinner. See you in five."

He carried her coat and helped her on with it. They went through empty corridors to the elevator. He said, " 'Evening," to a cleaning woman who was setting up bucket and mop. The elevator was empty too and outside it was dark and the streets had cleared of the heavy evening traffic.

They went to a restaurant near Rockefeller Center and he ordered margaritas for both of them. She left hers half-drunk and turned down a second. The conversation was awkward but he seemed quite at ease and she wondered if he took his regular secretary to dinner when they worked late, if this was a perk of the job or something designed especially for her.

It was a relief to be done, a bigger relief to be in a taxi heading south on Fifth Avenue. Mac didn't come home till after ten, smelling faintly of whiskey but completely in control. She told him about Benton.

He didn't answer right away. "I'll call for you tomorrow," he said finally. "What floor are you on?"

"No, really, Mac. Everything'll be OK. He was just being nice. We had nothing to talk about. He won't ask me again."

"I don't like it."

"I won't go again. He just caught me off guard today. I'll be OK."

He pulled at her robe, baring her breasts, and kissing her skin. "You know next week is the end of

March?"

"I know."

"I want to make a date with you." He was stroking her breasts with a finger, arousing her.

"I'm available."

"Dinner," he said and touched his tongue to a nipple. "Next Monday."

"Dinner's fine." She held his shoulders hard, feeling the surge of sexual excitement.

"At the Waldorf-Astoria."

"The Waldorf. Oh, Mac."

Both hands on her breasts now, and his lips, his tongue.

"At seven. A celebration. Did you say yes?"

"Yes."

"I thought you said yes."

He lifted her and deposited her on the bed, getting down with her without even taking his clothes off. A celebration. She pulled at the robe, exposing her body, feeling his shirt against her, buttons, a belt buckle, the hard warmth of his penis finding her quickly, entering. Of course I said yes. The swiftness of her response surprising her. Oh, Mac, how could I ever say no to you.

Afterward, she felt the mark of his belt buckle on her skin. Afterward she would not let him go, even when he wanted to get ready for bed.

Mr. Benton did not ask her to dinner the next night. In fact he left early to attend to some "personal business" and she stayed until official closing and then went.

Mac got home at eight. "Gallagher's in Ireland," he announced.

"On vacation?"

"He lives there. Went there when he retired. It's one of the places these guys go—the Bahamas, Ireland. He probably has family there."

"Then you found him."

"Not yet. In the morning I'll call someone I met once on a Dublin paper and ask him for help. They probably have a record at the airport of when he arrived and maybe where he's staying."

"The last chapter."

"Looks like it, doesn't it?"

"Did that Detective Rossante ever remember who borrowed the missing file?"

"If he did, he didn't tell me."

When she left in the morning he was calling Dublin. She tried him during the day but he wasn't home and there was no message. Mr. Benton had a meeting at two and Frankie fielded his calls and finished the work he had left her. There wasn't much. She had coffee with another secretary, and Mrs. Gilley dropped by to say hello and ask how she liked her new job. Mr. Benton returned a little after four and buzzed her.

"Give me an hour?" he asked when she came into his office.

"Of course."

"I promise to be done by six tonight. Come in about four-thirty. I want to get my notes from the meeting organized."

She left a message for Mac and went in at four-thirty with a notebook and pencil. There was a report he had to write. He kept saying, "How would you say . . . ?" or "Does it sound right to say . . . ?" She offered suggestions. He played with them, dictated, changed. She thought she would die of boredom. She could not imagine spending her life worrying about the verbal expression of such unimportant facts. She wondered how this man was able to muster the interest and motivation he seemed to have.

"Well, we have done a good job," Mr. Benton said, standing and stretching his lean body slightly.

"Yes, we have. A real fine job."

"Thanks to you."

She looked at Kenny's watch. "I'd better be running along."

"How about dinner?"

"Thank you but I'm expected home." She gathered her notes and stood.

"We could have a nice dinner, Frankie." He had circled the desk and now stood before her. Suddenly, he pulled her head toward him and kissed her.

"Please," she said, pushing him away. "Mr. Benton, I just wanted to go home."

"Bill," he said hoarsely. "Call me Bill. No one's around."

"I'm not calling you anything," she said angrily, increasing the distance between them. Behind him on the credenza, his blond wife smiled bravely. There was a sharp rap on the door and then it opened. "Mac," she said.

"Well." Mr. Benton smiled, showing his crooked tooth to Mac. "I didn't know you were being called for, Frankie."

"You OK?" Mac asked.

"Just fine."

"Let's go." He stood beside the door while she passed in front of him.

She took her coat off the hook in her cubicle and they walked down the corridor to the elevator.

"Did he touch you?"

"It was nothing, Mac."

"I'll kill him," he said, stopping.

"Please don't." It was a plea. She was afraid he meant it. "He's from the Midwest," she said. "I thought that made him safe."

"You were wrong." He took her arm and started walking again. "I don't want you coming back."

"I wasn't planning to."

They reached the elevator and he pushed the button. "You were right about him," he said. "He looks like a cop."

He had not found Gallagher but he had people working on it in Ireland. She told them in the morning she couldn't work that day and that she would not return to Mr. Benton's company. It made her feel sad. It had been her first job in New York and she had liked it. She had wanted to leave on good terms with everything and everyone. It was a disappointment that it would not work out that way.

Mac left early to listen again to the tape of telephone calls and Frankie took the Madison Avenue bus uptown to the Eighties and walked over to the Metropolitan Museum of Art. Later she called

Naomi at work from a pay phone and told her briefly about Mr. Benton.

"Ever hear of sexual harassment in the market-place?" Naomi asked.

"Now and then."

"Well now and then is now. Lucky for you Mac smelled a rat. You could have ended up raped on executive broadloom."

"I would have gouged his eyes out."

"That's the spirit."

"How are you, Naomi?"

"Blue." Her voice nearly broke on the syllable.

"Have you—do you have a place to live when your cousins came back?"

"That's all fixed up," Naomi said, her voice recovering as she spoke. "I'm taking the Roosevelt Island apartment. I'll move in on the thirty-first. A week from Saturday."

"Can I help?"

"Maybe you'll come to visit."

"Of course I will."

"I'd ask you to stay over—I'd really *like* you to stay over—but I know you don't want to leave Mac."

"We'll see each other anyway."

"I hope so. I feel so—" The dime dropped. "Look, I'll talk to you. I really have to get back to work."

Blue in New York. She decided to walk home. As she tramped down the last block of Broadway to the apartment, a taxi pulled to the curb in front of Pragmatique. Everett got out and just as Frankie was about to call, a young woman stepped out behind him. He closed the car door, took her arm, and led her to the entrance of the building. She was pretty with large glasses and a lot of bouncy hair and a nice smile which she turned on Everett as they crossed the sidewalk to the door.

Oh, Everett, how could you? Frankie had stopped in her tracks as the girl got out of the cab. Now she waited until the couple were inside the lobby and enough time had passed for them to take the elevator. Naomi loves you, she cried silently. You'll never find anyone like Naomi for the rest of your life.

She was nearly in tears. Naomi was blue and Everett was inviting a woman up to his apartment. There was no fairness, but she knew that. If Kenny could die at seventeen, who could prevent relatively minor infractions of justice?

She let herself into the lobby, checked the mailbox, which was empty, and took the elevator up to four.

"I heard the tape," he said. He was sitting on a sofa with a drink and a copy of the *Wall Street Journal*.

"Find what you were looking for?"

"Yeah. Found it."

She hung her coat up and sat on the same sofa. He handed her his drink and she took a sip and gave it back.

"A woman from the *Post* called. Didn't give her name. Said she saw an unmarked police car cruising around the building several times during the day Charlie disappeared."

"Unmarked?"

"She recognized it because it was black and had an aerial that sticks out the back. They're quite distinctive. If you work on a paper it's likely you'd know what it looks like. She said if the cops were driving around, why not ask them if they saw anything. Wasn't it their job to keep their eyes open?"

"You think that's the car that picked up Charlie Herron?"

"We'll never know for sure but it's my guess that it was. The woman didn't mention any identifying numbers. The way I see it, there were at least two people in that car, the driver—who's probably the kingpin—and someone in the back seat on the other side. It was all over for Charlie the minute he got inside—or was dragged in. All the guy in the back had to do was reach over the seat, wrap something around Charlie's neck, and strangle him."

"My God."

"I'm betting that one of the guys in that car was Jack Gallagher."

"A policeman," Frankie said. "And he was part of a killing."

"At that point they had no choice. Charlie knew too much and he was about to go public."

"So it was all on that tape after all."

"In a way. I figure my guy in Nebraska may have checked out the woman's report and surmised it wasn't a car from the Chinatown precinct where the *Post* is. At which point he put two and two together."

"Why did he retire?"

"Maybe he got wind of something. Maybe he heard about the body being found. Maybe it's a coincidence. Anyway, that conversation doesn't appear on the transcript."

"He edited it out?"

"Somebody must have. He could justify it to himself pretty easily. Some irritable broad taking a swipe at the force. Who needs it?"

"Oh, Mac, I'll be glad when this is over."

Later that evening there was a stormy conversation with Jeannie. For the hundredth time Frankie wished she could avoid hearing but now she couldn't even go upstairs to visit and escape.

"She wants them back early," Mac said when he finally hung up. "No dinner."

"I should've been nicer to her."

"Things are getting a little tough. We'll all survive."

"Will we?"

"Yes," Mac said. "We will."

She stayed home on Saturday in case there was a call from Ireland. Mac called once after noon to check but there had been nothing. He had dropped off the *Times* before he left and after she finished it, she had a book to keep her occupied.

The book went quickly and she paused in her reading to make some coffee. She was just pouring her second cup at three when the phone rang. The minute she heard the static on the line and the brogue floating over, she knew she had hit the jackpot.

"He's not home now," she answered the first question, "but I can take a message for him. I know he's been waiting for your call."

"Well he'll be pleased to know we've found his John Gallagher."

"That's wonderful."

"Yes, he's living on the west coast of Ireland and entered the country on September fifteenth." She wrote furiously. "He's got a telephone now and I called him myself — on a little matter I contrived — just this afternoon. I can assure Mr. MacIver he's there." He dictated a number, including a code for the city. Frankie thanked him and he said it was nothing; if there was anything more he could do, Mr. MacIver need only call.

Mac was home before six and she showed him her notes. He wrapped an arm around her and kissed her.

"And he's there, Mac," he said. "The man who called, O'Brien or something, he called Gallagher this afternoon and talked to him."

Something in Mac's face glowed. He looked at his watch. "It's too late to call now. I don't want him hanging up on me. I'll set the alarm for four in the morning. Think you can take it?"

"Try me," she said.

"That's just what I'm thinking of doing."

She knew he hadn't really slept. The alarm sounded and he sat up, completely awake. He got a robe that he seldom wore out of the closet and put it on.

"You don't have to get up," he said. "I'll use the speaker-phone."

She turned over on her stomach and watched. He had written down the telephone codes before they went to bed and as soon as he turned on the lamp, he began to dial.

Considering the distance, the phone in Ireland began to ring in almost no time and very soon a woman answered.

"I'd like to speak to Jack," Mac said.

"Jack?" the woman called, sounding very American. "For you. Sounds like someone from home."

And a minute later, "Hello."

"Jack, this is Henry MacIver of the New York *Times*. We met about a year ago when I was doing a story up in the Thirtieth."

"Oh yes, Mac, how the hell are you? Where are you?"

"Just fine, Jack. I'm in New York. I hear you retired."

"Yeah." There was a pause. "How'd you find me?"

"Just talked to a few people. Got a couple of things I wanted to ask you. About an old case."

"Can't promise my memory's any good but go ahead."

"It's about a body you brought down to the M.E.'s office."

"Hell, I got a lotta bodies I brought down. Going way back."

"You might remember this one. It was last summer."

There was a pause. "Last summer?"

"Right."

"You know about when?"

"July," Mac said.

"Oh yeah, July. That wino down at the pumping station."

"Wino?"

"He was some kinda derelict everybody knew. Bumpy, they called him, I think. Probably got down to the pumping station when he was blind drunk and couldn't find his way out. It's pretty steep if you know where it is. By the old railroad tracks there. You could tell he'd been there awhile. Maybe he froze to death last winter."

"How'd you find him?"

"Got a call from a hysterical broad with a dog. It was the dog found the stiff. I was in a car with a rookie. Took a hell of a time just to get the car down there. That path's a bitch and we'd had a lot of rain. Muddy as hell. What's your interest in the case anyway?"

"Something I'm working on for the *Times*," Mac said. "Something a little funny about it."

"Funny how?"

"The case jacket's empty."

There was a silence and Frankie got quietly out of bed and put on her robe.

"Empty?" Gallagher said finally.

"Right."

"If the jacket's empty, how'd you know who to call?"

"Someone at the M.E. remembered you."

"Ah."

"It was your case, wasn't it?"

"Yeah. First on the scene. Pretty fucking awful if you want to know the truth."

"I would guess so. You do the paperwork on the case?"

"Uh—" He took a breath that traveled three thousand miles and stopped at Mac's desk. "Yeah, most of it."

"What do you mean, 'most'?"

"You ever been around a decomposed body in the middle of July?"

"Not so far."

"Well there are plenty of things I'd rather do. I got an ulcer. You got an ulcer, MacIver?"

"Not yet."

"Well keep it that way. I got home that night and I was sick as a dog. I had to take some time off, get myself in shape."

"So someone took over the case?"

"No one took over. A couple guys added some of the paperwork. When I did my fives, that file was complete."

"You have any idea why it's empty now?"

"Hell, they got civilians in all the precincts nowadays. They don't give a shit about what they do. Damn file probably fell behind some filing cabinet somewhere, someone was too lazy to pick it up."

"But you're sure it was complete when you left the force."

"That was my last damn case, Mac. I did my fives and I put in my papers."

"OK." Mac had been taking notes. "Did you ID the body at the M.E.'s office?"

"I couldn't. I told you. I was sick as a dog. They got someone else. Lotta people knew Bumpy."

"You have any idea who ID'd him?"

There was a silence. Frankie wrapped the robe around her and sat on the edge of the bed, waiting.

"Yeah," the voice said with sudden recollection. "Friend of the captain's. Guy in the Seventeenth. It's coming back to me now. I'll tell you who to call, Mac," Gallagher said with enthusiasm. "The guy that identified Bumpy was Sergeant Tommy McManus of the Seventeenth Precinct."

Seventeen

It was an awful stillness.

"Christ," Mac said.

"I'll make some coffee."

"I could use it."

She went to the kitchen and he went to the phone and dialed again.

"Seventeenth, Marx," a man's voice said.

"This is MacIver of the *Times*. When do you expect Tom McManus?"

"Just a minute. I'll check the roll call sheet." The sound of paper. Someone laughing in the background. A woman yelling, "Stop!" "Eight o'clock this morning."

"Thanks. Ask him to call MacIver soon as he gets in."

He came to the kitchen and sat at the table.

"Breakfast?"

"May as well. I'll never get back to sleep."

She put two plates on the table where the mugs already stood and found some croissants he had bought for Sunday breakfast. "Sergeant McManus

348

couldn't be involved," she said.

"Why? Because he smiled at you New Year's night?"

"Because he was good to me. Because he cared. People like that don't go around killing people."

"Or covering up for the ones who do? Shit." He rubbed his forehead. "Ever hear the voice of a killer before?"

"Mac, you can't know that."

He met her eyes and held them. He looked very tired. "You're right, I can't." She poured his coffee. "I shouldn't have dragged you into this, turning on the speaker. This isn't what you came to New York for."

"But I'm part of it now." A bell rang and she took the croissants out of the oven and put them on the table. The smell was wonderful.

"I'm sorry."

"I'm not. Charlie Herron's like Kenny, someone I knew for a little while and he added something to my life." She took a sip of coffee. "The way you have."

"I've added a lot of misery," he said in a low voice.

"No. And Charlie didn't either. I got to know him and I think he was honest and hardworking and an awfully good person."

"And Jack Gallagher killed him." He buttered the croissant but did not eat it. Instead, he gulped coffee.

"What are fives?" she asked.

"Forms they fill out when they complete a case. There are forms for everything. A cop'll tell you he knocked out a couple of fives. Means he finished the paperwork on a couple of cases. Makes him feel

good. It shows in black and white he did something."
He drank more coffee. "You know who might be
driving around in one of those unmarked cars? A
precinct captain. And one of his lackeys."

"Gallagher's captain?"

He nodded. "Gallagher's part of what they call the
'palace guard.' He's an FTS. Means he works directly
for the precinct commander—and he owes his alle-
giance to him. He does what he's told to do. Jesus,
I'm tired."

"Why don't we go to bed? It's only four-thirty."

He got up and tossed his robe on the sofa as he
passed. She shut off the coffee maker and turned off
the lights. About a minute after they lay down they
were both asleep.

The phone rang, waking her, and she knew with a
sinking feeling who it would be. Mac got up without
his usual alacrity and detoured to grab his robe. He
said, "Hello," and she could hear the sleep in his
voice.

"Mac, it's Tom McManus. I hear you want to talk
to me."

"It's about last summer," Mac said. "You did a
favor for someone. Who's the captain of the Thirtieth?"

"You mean Freddy Bauer? We went to the acad-
emy together. We're old friends."

"Right. Freddy Bauer. Did Captain Bauer call you
last summer to go down to the M.E.'s office and
identify a DOA?"

"Uh, yeah, a derelict they found near the railroad

tracks on the West Side."

"Did you ID him?"

"Yeah, I went down."

"Tom, did you *know* that man? Did you recognize him?"

"I musta seen him around. Bumpy something, wasn't it?"

"I'm asking you if you knew him."

"Mac, he was a derelict they wanted to close the books on. He was all decomposed. He could've been dead a year or more."

"A year or more from last July."

"Yeah. He was in terrible shape."

"You know who disappeared from the face of the earth a year ago last July?"

There was such a long silence that Frankie thought maybe Sergeant McManus had left the phone. Finally he said, "Jesus, Mary, and Joseph," as though they were a single word, an expletive.

"You got it, Tom?"

"You think that was—you think that stiff was Charlie Herron?"

"I think it could have been. What did Captain Bauer say to you?"

"Just that I should ID a derelict." His voice somewhat fainter.

"And you went down and did it. Even though you didn't know who the hell the body was."

"Mac, you gotta understand. Freddy and me go back a long ways. I *owe* him. He's been good to me. That means something."

"I know."

"I had no idea." The voice was pleading. "I

thought—"

"It's OK, Tom. No one's after you."

"But I didn't know. How could I know?"

"You couldn't."

"Jesus," McManus said. "Jesus."

"We'll have a drink soon, Tom. Don't worry about it."

"Yeah. Right. You're a good friend, Mac. You're the best. You're . . . I trust you with important things. Tell me, what happened to the little girl?"

"What?"

"The kid with all the curls. New Year's. You remember."

"I remember," Mac said, and this time his voice was husky.

"You take care of her all right?"

"I took care of her. She's home."

"You sure?"

"Yes, I'm sure. I heard from her."

"Oh that's good, Mac. She was a nice little thing. You wouldn't want anything bad to happen to her."

When he hung up, Frankie was drenched in tears.

He dressed and drove uptown to see Ariana. He was gone for most of the day and when he got back he looked beat. At eight o'clock he said he was going to bed. He showered and came out, standing naked near the blinds that covered the windows.

"You were right," he said. "The bedroom needs four walls and a door." Then he got into bed and went to sleep.

Eighteen

He was up early Monday to make breakfast.

"You sure you want to work today?" he asked.

"Sure. You said you have appointments."

"But I'll be there in plenty of time. Seven. You can meet me in the lobby near the chandelier."

"OK. Park Avenue entrance."

"Right." He was in a good mood, as though the long night's sleep had washed away the weekend's pain. "And we don't talk about Charlie tonight," he said, reading her mind. "We talk about you, me, and what's called the future."

"I'll think about it all day."

When the call came the assignment was for an address near Columbus Circle.

"D train to Fifty-ninth," Mac said. "You'll be right at the edge of the park. I'll run you over to the subway."

She calculated whether she would have time to come back and change after work before meeting him at the Waldorf, decided it would be too close and put on the black-and-white outfit she had worn the

353

first time she met Mac's kids. If she was early for dinner, and she would be, she could sit and read till he showed up. She put a paperback in her coat pocket.

"Nice," he said when she was dressed.

"The season's changing. Maybe I won't get to wear it again this year."

"We'll get you something jazzy for spring."

"My, you're in a good mood."

"It's what you do to me. Come. I've got to move the car."

It was a management consultant firm and they had twenty small jobs for her to do, including typing and answering the telephone. Today she had a sense of being able to do anything. She slipped into the job with ease and enjoyed it. A little before closing a graying man in shirtsleeves came out to her desk and looked at her.

"You're not Jennifer," he said.

"No. I'm Frankie Grant."

"No wonder things are going better. Do you think you'd have a little extra time today?" He looked harried.

A wave of something like fear passed through her, memories of Mr. Benton's unwelcome kiss. "A little," she said.

"Good. It won't take long. I need some letters typed. We've been working on them all day." He started back toward his office and she followed him. "I'll give you cab fare and we'll work out the overtime."

It wasn't much and she was finished by six. She carried the letters and envelopes into the back office for his signature. He looked up when she came in and his face lightened.

"I can't thank you enough," he said, digging into a pocket for a wallet. He took out a five and handed it to her. "Take a cab home. I hope we'll see you tomorrow."

There weren't any empty cabs so she decided to walk. After a few minutes at a brisk stride, she knew she had made a mistake. She was at the corner of Tenth Avenue, having gone west instead of east. Also she had forgotten to ask Mac exactly where the Waldorf was. Somewhere in the Fifties, or was it the Forties? At some point she would have to cross town to the East Side. Tenth Avenue was pretty shabby but she kept going, hoping to see an available taxi but the only one that approached stopped and picked someone up before it reached her.

She was in the Forties now and trying to think. Probably, she would get there faster anyway by walking. It was getting dark and Mac had said he would be there early. The sooner she got there, the more time they would have together.

Something good was going to happen tonight. She could feel it in herself as she had felt it in him. Something wonderful.

Halfway through the Forties now and still walking. Too far, she thought. She should have turned east farther back. She stopped to take stock. She was two blocks from Forty-second Street and she would absolutely not walk along that street by herself. There were theaters on Forty-fourth and that would make it safe. She quickly turned left.

It was another shabby street, plastic bags of garbage lining the curb. Just hurry, she told herself. Get there fast and let Mac wrap me up in his arms. Don't even look at the garbage piled at the curb. Keep moving.

It happened so quickly, so suddenly, that afterward she could not remember the sequence of events. Something hard and unyielding around her neck, choking her, some person who had emerged from the shadowy front of one of the unremitting old brownstones that lined the street. He was grabbing for her bag with the arm that wasn't strangling her.

She lurched against him and then away from him, using the strength that had supported Mac when he was drunk, the strength that had lifted Kenny in his last days on earth. Something aided her, a patch of ice, maybe, that caused the man to lose his footing long enough for her to free herself, to turn and face him, to look him in the eye as he came toward her again, hand out for the black bag with the stroke of lightning on the front in snakeskin. And because Mac had told her, because she was now so angry at this—not even a man—this boy who would destroy her celebration, she lifted her foot as he came at her and thrust it heel-first at his softest part, thrust it so hard that it sent her falling backwards and the last thing she heard before she struck her head painfully on the stone front of the building behind her was the wail of pain from the injury she had inflicted.

When she saw where she was and understood what had happened, she could not stop crying. She could remember little things—a policeman saying they

356

should get a bus, an ambulance ride, mumbling, "I have to go somewhere," and a black woman riding beside her saying, "You gonna be fine, honey." Her head hurt badly and she was frightened. Her watch was gone and she had no idea what time it was.

There were beds on either side of hers and voices. It was the smell that told her she was in a hospital. There was nothing near, nothing she could see, that belonged to her.

He came in like a roll of thunder. She heard him before she saw him. He was angry, furious. Someone tried to shush him but he would not be quiet. He stopped in the middle of the ward and she saw him. He turned, saw her, came to the bed, and held her. Nothing had ever felt quite so good in her life.

He sat up and brushed the hair back from her face. His fingertips wiped away the tears. He didn't say anything.

"I'm daunted, Mac."

"I know." He looked injured himself. "You see him?"

She nodded.

"Can you identify him?"

She nodded again.

"I'll kill him."

"No."

"Fucking little bastard."

"Don't, Mac."

"They got him."

"Good."

"Got a record up to here."

She took his hand and rubbed the back of it on her cheek.

"What did he do to you?"

"I did it to myself. I kicked him so hard" — she stopped to take a breath — "I fell backwards."

He leaned over and pressed his cheek against hers. "I'll stay here tonight," he said, sitting up again. "I'm not going to leave you."

"Don't." She had seen a nurse stop near the foot of her bed and look askance at the visitor. "They won't like it."

"I don't give a shit what they like."

"Mac, I don't have Kenny's watch. I don't know where it is."

"I'll get it for you."

He left and she saw him talking to a nurse, who nodded and led him away. When he came back, he had the watch.

"Here you go, babe," he said. "Give me your hand." He fastened the strap and she smiled and rubbed the familiar smooth surface.

"I need another favor."

"Go on."

"When you come back tomorrow, if you would bring me a pair of jeans and a shirt. And shoes and socks. I can't wear that outfit anymore. I want to throw it out."

"You don't have to throw anything out."

"I do. I don't even want to touch it."

"I'll bring you something to wear tomorrow. The nurse said she thinks they'll let you go."

"What time is it?"

"After eleven. I've been looking for you since seven-oh-one."

She smiled but there were more tears. "I knew I

could count on you."

"You can. I promise. For as long as you want." It had the sound of a declaration. "I found out about the chandelier."

"The chandelier?" She looked around at the lights, feeling confused.

"At the Waldorf. There are forty thousand pieces. I was going to tell you tonight."

"Forty thousand." She started to shake her head but it hurt. "I can't even think forty thousand. It's like trying to see the ocean in your head. You didn't count them, did you?"

"I found the guys who sold it to the Waldorf."

"Oh, Mac." She touched his cheek, loving him enormously. "You always know everything."

"Not everything. And not soon enough." He looked suddenly different, as though the energy that had propelled him this far had just this moment run its course.

"Go home, Mac," she said. "Before they tow your car and get you in real trouble."

"I'll stay till you fall asleep."

"OK."

He kissed her and she turned and closed her eyes, holding his hand, feeling the comfort of what he had said, his declaration. They had shut off the main lights and it was dark enough to fall asleep. She drifted off eventually but she felt his hand move when he got up to go. It was enough that he had found her. It was more than enough that he had stayed. It was everything that she wanted that he had said she could count on him forever. After he was gone she slept.

* * *

She dressed when he arrived and she checked herself out. The doctor had said to take it easy but that there was nothing to worry about. It felt very good to walk outside. It felt better to step into the apartment, to see it light and bright and beautifully furnished.

"I called the agency this morning," Mac said, closing the door to the elevator and locking it. "I told them you wouldn't work for the rest of the week."

"Fine."

"Then some guy named Hecker called about ten minutes later, very upset. Said he'd kept you late and given you five dollars to take a cab."

"He did. I couldn't find one so I walked. He was awfully nice, Mac. He called me Miss. Can you believe it?" She brushed away tears. There seemed to be nothing that didn't get them started this morning.

"Want to lie down?"

She shook her head carefully. "Just sit for a while."

He took her to the sofa and sat beside her, his arm holding her. It was a warm, safe feeling. She could sense a measure of calm return.

"I'm sorry I messed up our dinner last night," she said.

"You didn't mess up anything."

"I was just stupid."

"You weren't stupid. You should be able to walk anywhere you want."

"I picked Forty-fourth because there are theaters there. I thought that would make it safe."

"So do the people who go to the theater."

"You have anywhere to go today?"

"No. I had thought we might take a trip somewhere for the rest of the week. I was going to ask you last night. Now —"

"I'd rather stay here."

"Maybe in the summer."

The summer, the future, a time that extended forward without end. "The summer would be really great."

By evening she was feeling better. She wound Kenny's watch and reset it, showered and got ready for bed. The clothes she had worn yesterday lay in a shopping bag near the closet. She could not bear to look at them. The beautiful black handbag had a scuff mark on it but otherwise it was intact. He had never gotten it away from her. It would have been a prize. She had nearly as many hundreds as the day she arrived in New York.

She slept well, feeling Mac beside her.

Nineteen

That morning, on a day that she would not forget, she had awakened surprised that she had slept. She was still in the chair beside Kenny's bed, still holding his hand. The hand was the only part of him that was still warm, warm from Frankie's transmitted warmth. His cheek was cool to the touch, but he looked at peace. She had cried only a little, more like a sniffle and a few tears. She let the warm hand rest beside him and stood, aching from a night in the chair. "I'll be back," she told him and walked out the front door.

It had been damp and fresh that morning, one of those mornings that once would have made her very happy to be alive. She wasn't sure why she had come out the front door. Walking through wet grass, she went to the back of the house and kept going. She was still wearing the jeans and sneakers she had put on last night when the evening became cool. Her feet became wet as she walked but she felt no discomfort. She kept going, back to the places she had played and hidden as a child, all the ups and downs of the earth, the hills and valleys of her youth, so familiar she could have charted them, could have steered a ship through them like a river pilot.

She must have cried, she must have thought thoughts, but she remembered only walking and finally standing beneath the tree, the tree that was Kenny, young, strong, tall, and healthy. She patted the trunk with her hand, put her arm around it as though it were a brother, spoke to it. Then she went back in the house, took Kenny's watch from him, and strapped it to her own wrist. After that, she picked up the telephone.

Mac had not set the alarm. Daylight woke her. He was already awake, watching her.

"How do you feel?"

"Better."

"Good. Eat some breakfast?"

"Sure." She reached out and pulled Kenny's watch over, looked at it, drew in her breath, and whispered, "Oh, Mac."

He put his hand on her shoulder. "What is it, baby?"

She could not speak for a moment. She handed him the watch, trying to control the emotions. "It stopped, Mac." She was crying. "Kenny's watch."

He took it from her and looked at it, reached beyond the other side of the bed, and handed her his own. "Take this."

"No."

"Please. I want you to have it."

She slipped the watch over her hand, stretching the

expansion band slightly. "Kenny's dead," she said.

"I'll have it fixed. I know someone who'll fix it."

"It can't be fixed."

"Let me try."

"No." She wiped her face with her wrist, pushing the tears to one side. "He's gone. It's too late to fix anything. Trying will only make it harder."

"Frankie, I'll do whatever you want me to."

"Give it back to me and let me put it away."

He was holding it in his hand. "I still think it could be fixed."

She took it from him and rubbed her thumb over the face, a nice, smooth face, young and clear, free of blemishes. "You have to know when it's over, Mac. You can't prolong the agony forever."

He wrapped his arms around her and held her but all she could think about was Kenny, that the time had come to lay Kenny to rest.

He took her out for lunch to the Japanese restaurant she had gone to with Naomi. She ordered sushi and he watched her eat it, letting her know he was surprised. She lifted the pickled vegetables with a sure hand, not hurrying to carry them to her mouth. He told her she was a pro. She said Naomi had taught her. Then she told him she had seen Everett on Friday night with another woman.

He opened his mouth to say something, but didn't. He watched her. Maybe he sensed the fragility of her calm. Finally, he said, "They split up, Frankie."

"I know."

"We don't really know what happened."

"No."

"Maybe it was only a limited partnership."

"Maybe. I just felt so bad for Naomi, maybe because I love her so much."

"I love her myself. She's been very good to my kids and to you."

"He could have waited a little longer. He didn't have to bring her home." She looked down at Mac's watch and touched the crystal. It was slightly rounded and slightly scarred, a watch that had seen action when her own father was still a small child. "I wanted to believe," she said and stopped.

"We all wanted to believe," Mac said. "We were all honest and hopeful at the beginning."

"Yes." She picked up her chopsticks and went back to her sushi.

On the way back to the apartment they stopped in a drugstore and Mac bought himself a Timex. Frankie protested, saying she could wear the new one, but he insisted, setting it and putting it on his wrist without another word.

They went to the supermarket and stocked up on enough to keep them fed for a few days. When they got back to the apartment, she was exhausted. She pulled off her shoes and lay down on the bed. In no time at all she was asleep.

It was a little after three when she awoke and Mac made some coffee and cut slices of a cake they had bought in the supermarket. The coffee and the sweet seemed to revive her. They started to talk.

He told her about his early jobs, how he came to

the *Times*, how he met Al Black, how they had done some crazy things together. He filled in the details of his life like a man wanting to present a complete package, nothing missing, no holes, no questionable gaps. He asked her once if she had any questions about him and she smiled and shook her head. The package suited her just fine. What suited her even better was the offering, the sense that he had finally done it; he had made a choice. It gave her a feeling of comfort she had not experienced before, comfort that stretched out in front of her without end.

The phone rang and Mac answered. It was Mr. Hecker, he told her when he got off, the man from the Monday job, inquiring after her. She heard Mac say, "I'm a friend."

"He's really worried about you," Mac said when he hung up.

"He's a nice person. It was a good job. There was a good feeling there. I think maybe they did something interesting. It started out with these two men who quit their jobs and went into business for themselves. I liked that."

"That makes all the boring jobs worth it."

"Yes, it does."

He cleaned up the dishes and they sat on the sofa and kept talking. It was calming to talk about things that had happened long ago, that had already been resolved. From time to time her index finger would wander over to the watch crystal and she would remember, as she had remembered so many times and so painfully in the days after Kenny died, that he was gone. This time was different. This time she did not feel alone.

At ten after four the phone rang again and Mac went to answer it. When she heard him say, "Yeah, hi," she knew it was Jeannie and she prepared herself for the inevitable clash. It was Wednesday, early in the week for Jeannie to demand a change in schedule. He said, "Oh Christ," and she thought, It's something else, and felt the beginnings of discomfort.

"Did you call Fletcher?" he asked. And then, "Well what did he say? . . . Okay. yeah. OK. . . ." And then, "Jeannie, I can't." There was a silence and he said it again, very firmly: "I can't." Frankie picked up the *Times* and started to turn pages without reading. Behind her, Mac said into the phone, "You know I do but I just can't do it now. Let me see what I can — Yeah. OK." He took an audible breath. "Just let me think."

He hung up and Frankie put the paper down.

"Nothing to worry about," he said, sitting beside her.

She did not worry. Jeannie would learn to handle her problems the way everyone else did, without saddling her former husband with them. Former husband. She said it to herself, liking the sound of it. Jean MacIver's former husband. The phrase added to her feeling of security, her growing well-being.

Mac got up and walked around restlessly. He was a man who needed to move, who could not tolerate the confines of walls, of small spaces. In a day or two she would be ready to move with him, to set these events aside. She rubbed the watch crystal, familiarizing herself with it, learning the new shape.

"Jeannie wrenched her back." He was standing at

the dining-room windows, looking out through open blinds.

She lowered her book, feeling a small spark of compassion for Jeannie, who at last had something real to complain about. "Is that what she called about?"

"Yes. It's very painful." He sat on one of the chairs at the dining table.

"It must be."

"It's something that happens to her sometimes."

There was a note in his voice that sounded oddly out of tune. She closed the book and put it down next to her.

"If I brought the kids down here, there'd be no one to help her. She'll have to stay in bed for a few days. At least."

The new note was unmistakable. She struggled to believe that she was hearing it. Mac stood, looked out the window again, sat.

"I'd call her mother," he said, "but Jeannie and her mother . . ." He shrugged, making the meaning clear.

Her body, which had been on the mend, now felt invaded. Something cold down the center, an attack she could not ward off. Naomi warning her that day they had lunch on the Lower East Side: *Just remember. When Jean MacIver makes her move* . . . This was the move and Mac was about to respond predictably.

"I would be back tomorrow."

He had been speaking but she had not heard what had preceded the last statement. She said, "Yes," not in agreement but because she realized she had said nothing for a long time. Where had it all gone, the sense of comfort and security, the feeling of being on the mend? Gone along with the phrase, "Jeannie's former husband."

He went to the large closet and pulled out a small suitcase, about the size of an overnight bag. He opened it on the bed and began filling it. She watched him moving and could not believe it was happening. Once he looked up and said, "I know I shouldn't be doing this," but he didn't stop packing. She pulled the watch off her wrist, trying to control emotions that she knew, finally, she had no power over.

The clasps on the suitcase clicked shut, closing the suitcase and sealing their respective fates. She walked over.

"You'd better take this," she said, handing him the watch.

"Frankie, I gave that to you."

"I'll trade."

"No. Put it back on."

She put it on because there was no sense in arguing. There was no sense in anything anymore. Jeannie had called and there was no one in the world who could answer the call but Mac.

He put his arms around her. "I don't want to go," he said.

"I know."

"I'll call you tonight and I'll see you tonight."

"OK."

"If you need me, the number's by the phone."

She lifted her face and accepted his kiss. He kissed her again before the elevator arrived.

"You'll be OK, won't you?" he said.

"I'll be fine."

"Lock the door."

"I will."

"So long."

As the elevator started down, she found herself wondering what time the next bus left for Columbus.

Part
Three

One

He had really gone. Jeannie had called and Mac had packed a bag and gone to her. Mac had left Frankie to be with his wife.

She turned to face the apartment, her back to the locked door to the elevator shaft. It was hardly the same place she had seen that first night in January, only now, filled with furniture, rugs, and blinds, it looked emptier than it had then.

Mac was gone.

I will not cry, she told herself as she rummaged in the closet for her suitcases, pausing to wipe tears from her face. She backed out of the closet, holding a suitcase in each hand, and looked again at the loft. Jean MacIver had been right. It was an empty barn. Twenty minutes ago it had been light and bright and full and exactly where the right people lived, but all that had changed. Mac was gone.

She knew only that she had to leave. She could not stay here alone. Mac was gone and without him the loft was unlivable. She packed haphazardly, swiftly, her hands moving without her mind consciously directing them. All her thoughts were on Mac, who had left her.

When the suitcases were full, she closed them and looked at the watch. Nearly five. It was Mac's watch, she observed again. She pulled it off and laid it on the desk. Then she wrote a short note to Mac, stuck it under the watch, and rang for the elevator.

In the lobby, she put the suitcases down near the door and looked around, a silent farewell. Something had changed on the mailbox at the right. She went over to take a better look. The -Wright that Naomi had left three weeks ago had been removed. In its place was a shiny new nameplate that said "E. V. Wright." She swallowed hard and went out to find a taxi.

Kids walked by, kids younger than she and kids older. Two girls came out of Pragmatique loaded down with brightly lettered shopping bags bulging with purchases. They crossed Broadway and walked down Washington Place toward NYU and the park. Three boys, one a redhead, came from the direction of Tower Records, all of them holding flat, rectangular bags, two of them talking at once, kids having a good time, kids with money in their pockets and nothing to worry about.

A taxi with its overhead light on came down the street and she lifted her hand halfheartedly. The taxi stopped in front of her and she went back to the door to get her suitcases. "Good-bye, Great Jones," she said out loud and got into the cab.

"Where to?" the driver asked, his hand ready to flip the meter lever. His voice was soft and Spanish.

She was embarrassed that she did not know where

374

she was going. She was running away but she had no idea where she was running to. The bus station was out. If the last bus to Columbus had already left, she could not spend the night in that terminal. There was nowhere, really. Jeannie's? Naomi's? Not without an invitation.

"You wanna go somewhere?" the Spanish voice asked, prodding.

"The Waldorf-Astoria," she said, sitting back. The cab took off.

It was the way she had always imagined it. The doorman opened the door of the taxi and helped her out. Someone else carried her luggage in. She walked up the stairs and glanced at the noble chandelier as she passed beneath it, all forty thousand pieces. The clerk said yes, they had a single room for a hundred thirty dollars and how would she be paying?

"Cash," she said and signed her name, wondering if that labeled her a lesser person because she did not sport a gold card that entitled her to instant credit and instant status.

The room was quite beautiful with a bed large enough for two and all the desirable amenities. She hung her coat up, took her clothes off, and showered. She hadn't been hungry when she arrived but she was after the shower. It seemed like half her life ago and in some other hemisphere since she and Mac had had coffee and cake in the loft. She did not want to dress again, wanted even less to dine in some opulent restaurant where only she would be alone at a table.

Room service provided her with a Bloody Mary and a shrimp cocktail. It arrived the way it did in movies and when the man had left, she sat in a comfortable chair and ate. When she finished she sat for a while, just thinking, wondering if there had been mistakes and if so, who had made them. It had happened so quickly—falling in love, the three months, the call from Jeannie, Mac leaving. There had been no time to correct mistakes and now it was too late. Mac was gone.

She went to the window and looked out but all she could see was the reflection of the light interior of her room. She turned the lights off and went back to the window. Far below were a street and streetlights. Traffic moved from left to right. It was Lexington Avenue with only a handful of pedestrians, an occasional taxi, one stretch limousine of indeterminate color traveling too fast. There were no whores, no police rounding them up, no man in a brown corduroy jacket zipped almost to the collar, a man willing to be coerced into taking home a kid from Columbus. It had started here and it was ending here, her love affair with Henry James MacIver who had gone home to be with his wife.

She tried not to cry because tears were reserved for death, for Mom and Dad and Kenny, but there it was, Lexington Avenue and without Mac it was empty. That morning last fall she had thought that after Kenny nothing would touch her, nothing would eat away pieces of her, nothing would make her feel despair. But now Mac was gone and everything was empty, everything in pieces, most of all she. The street was empty, the loft was empty, and she was alone. She cried.

* * *

The Waldorf said she could have the room for another night and even with the prospect of greatly depleted resources, she decided to stay. It would be her last night there and tomorrow she would have to move, either to a less expensive place or back to Ohio.

The Do Not Disturb sign she had hung on the door last night gave her the best night's sleep of the week. By the time she had finished a large breakfast and looked at all the shops, it was nearly twelve and the room had been made up. She thought she would relax and read the paper but after a few attempts, she knew she had to call Mac's number to see if he had left a message for her. She was nervous and her mouth was suddenly dry, but she dialed and listened to the ring. But instead of Mac's recorded voice, there was only one ring after another. It took a minute to register; in her haste to leave she had forgotten to set the machine. Her oversight had cost her their only means of communication.

She lay back on the propped pillows, missing him, missing knowing that later on today he would come home to her. The bus ride back to Columbus seemed bleak when she thought of it. There was even something bleak about the thought of returning to the cozy little house with all its warm memories. "I don't believe in bleak," she said out loud but the voice failed to convince her.

After a while she went to the window. The scene surprised her. Thick flakes of snow were flurrying past the window and way below, even the sidewalk was showing a white cover. March twenty-ninth and the weather had finally decided to become winter.

She pulled her boots on and her coat, wound her scarf around her head, and took the elevator down to the lobby. Outside, it was almost glorious. This was the winter she had missed, the winter that never came east to New York. If only Mac were here, she thought as she crossed Park Avenue and walked toward Madison. What a good time we could have together in the snow.

The snow changed the character of the city. People became giddy and laughed. They extended supporting hands at street corners. When two cars collided because of a skid up on Madison, both drivers got out and said they were sorry.

It fell and accumulated. Men's hat brims were heavy with it. Car roofs were coated with it. Taxis became unavailable and after a while it didn't matter. Traffic stopped moving. The lanes from one side of Madison to the other were uncountable. Cars inched northward in a haphazard arrangement, if they moved at all. She longed for Mac to be beside her. He would have something memorable to say about it all, about the snow, the traffic, the people, the accidents. Or maybe he would have nothing to say. Maybe he would just walk beside her with his arm around her, enjoying it.

She circled around and came down the west side of Park. A small yellow car with New Jersey plates had just made the difficult turn into the southbound lane. Halfway down the block it passed her. She walked by it and when she got to the corner, it had not yet arrived. She never saw it again.

At Fiftieth she crossed to the Waldorf side of Park.

She had to make her way between cars that filled the intersection so chaotically that it was hard to tell whether they were heading south or east on one side or north or east on the other. Under the Waldorf marquee groups of travelers stood unhappily, surrounded by luggage. Among them was Mac.

They saw each other at the same moment. She stopped in her tracks and he pulled his hands out of the pockets of the brown jacket and sprinted toward her. When he put his arms around her, she knew that what she wanted most was to be with him.

"Don't cry," he said, easing them out of the line of pedestrian traffic to stand beside the building.

"I can't help it."

"Can we go somewhere and talk?"

"No."

"Why not?"

"Because I haven't thought what to say."

"Will it help if I say I'm sorry?"

"Some."

"Can we go up to your room?"

"No."

"Then inside."

"OK."

"Got a Kleenex?"

She pulled one out of her bag and blotted her face.

Inside and up the stairs they passed under forty thousand pieces of chandelier and stopped on the rim of the Wheel of Life mosaic. Every visible chair was occupied. People in clusters and by themselves took up every space that might be private.

Mac unzipped the jacket but left it on. Frankie pulled the scarf off her head, spraying droplets of water. She brushed her hand over her hair, which was wet in front.

"Better?" he asked.

"A little." She felt the enormous comfort of his presence. What she wanted was to take him upstairs to her room and just hold him. What she wanted was to forget that Jeannie existed, to go home with Mac for the simplest of reasons, that she wanted to.

"Will you come home with me?"

"I can't." And let it last or not last but have it now because now was what counted.

"You scared hell out of me last night."

"I couldn't stay there without you."

"Everett went down to check. He found your note. When the phone didn't answer—"

"I left in a hurry. I forgot the phone."

They could go upstairs and be alone in her room, work everything out and come to an understanding. It might last a week or a month but it would alleviate this great pain which was now. Beneath her wet boots the Wheel of Life went on and on, one step after another, without end, without beginning. She wondered if there was a spoke on the wheel for falling in love or if that was such a small part of life that it was left unrepresented.

She reached a hand over to touch him, her fingers brushing the velvety surface of the corduroy.

He took her hand. "I can't talk to you here."

"I know."

"What do you want to do?"

"I just want to think. I want you to go away and let me -think."

"OK." Reluctantly. He took her arm and they

380

walked to the elevators. "Will you let me know where you are?"

"When I figure out where I am, I'll call you."

It was the worst snowstorm of the year and one of the latest in the season ever to hit New York. She tried Naomi in the evening but no one answered. Tomorrow at checkout time she would have to leave but she could not think where to go or how to get there. In a city this large it seemed strange to have so few options.

It was nine o'clock when she thought of Sally. The telephone number was on a crumpled piece of paper in her bag. She dialed it with fading hope.

Sally was home and the little room was available — for a hundred and sixty a month, in advance, slightly more than a night at the Waldorf. She said she'd be up tomorrow.

"I ought to tell you . . ." Sally said, hesitating. "Uh, my boyfriend lives here with me now. Is that OK?"

It wasn't OK but it didn't matter. She wouldn't be staying long, one way or another. "It's fine," she said agreeably, wondering how the boyfriend would feel about it, how any couple could share an apartment with another person. Kids, she thought charitably. Grown-ups like Mac and me need to be alone.

The north-south streets were clear enough for the taxi to make the trip uptown with comparative ease but negotiating the block from Broadway to West

End Avenue was hazardous. Whole families were digging out their cars in the after-storm sunshine, tossing shovelfuls of snow into the center of the street, which had not yet been plowed. But they got through and the cabbie carried her luggage into the lobby.

Sally and her boyfriend were both home—"Too much snow to go to work"—and in a few minutes Frankie was in the little room, trying to think how to improve its appearance. It had lost a lot of its charm since the first time she had seen it early in January but it didn't matter; there was plenty of heat and the view of the bridge was still striking. She opened the smaller suitcase and took out the photographs, looking at each with tenderness. Then she set them on the old maple dresser, in front of the mirror. It occurred to her that she had no picture of Mac, nothing besides a memory. She wondered how long it would be until she forgot what he looked like.

The thinking got nowhere. Everything added up to Jeannie. She went out into the snow on Saturday, looking for something but not sure what. Snow was still everywhere, on curbs, in piles on street corners, even packed down on the sidewalks, making passage risky. Dogs had a good time, and children, but something was missing. What she was looking for was Mac and he wasn't there. Without him the city was empty.

She tramped from Riverside Drive to Broadway and hailed a taxi. Closing the door she asked for the street in the Sixties where the miniature Statue of

Liberty was.

"The Statue of Liberty's all the way downtown," the taxi driver said with that skepticism that indicated he knew he was dealing with some kind of weirdo.

"The Sixties," she affirmed. "Take Broadway and slow down when you see Lincoln Center."

The man shrugged. "You're the boss," he said, telling her plainly he doubted her mental capacity but a fare was a fare.

They took off and she watched the streets. "Slow down now," she ordered when she saw a familiar triangle where Broadway cut across Columbus Avenue.

He slowed.

Just beyond Sixty-fourth she said, "Stop." She had the money ready. "Look to your left," she said, handing him the fare.

"How do you like that!" the cabbie said with astonishment. "It's the goddamn Statue of Liberty. Wait'll I tell my wife."

Frankie smiled and opened the door.

"Hey, lady," he called after her. "Thanks."

"You're welcome," she called back. She crossed Broadway and went down Sixty-fourth. There it was, perched on top of an old building, an open secret like Charlie Herron's death. They had buried his body in their own precinct so that if it was ever uncovered, they could cope. Bumpy the wino. The Statue of Liberty hiding in broad daylight. Mac, how am I ever going to make things come out right without you?

On Sunday she took the subway to Brooklyn. It was a long ride out to Coney Island but she wanted to see the ocean again, wanted to visit a place she had shared with Mac. It was snowy and icy when she left the station and she had never experienced a wind like this one. How calm, by comparison, it had been on those wonderful days she had been here with Mac.

She made her way up to the boardwalk with difficulty. It felt like war, the wind pelting her with steel spray. She stood at the railing looking out at the blue-black ocean that once she had not been able to imagine and which now she would never forget. Mac had taken her here on her first full day in New York. Mac had taken her here after they had made love the Sunday she didn't go uptown to Sally's.

She went down the stairs to the beach. Snow covered the sand except where the tide had washed it away. She looked along the beach, searching for Kenny, for the little dot running, but she could see nothing except sand and snow and almost hideous waves. Kenny was gone. Kenny had stopped running.

She wept, missing Mac. Without Mac the beach was empty, the ocean threatening, the weather assaulting. Mac had been the difference; Mac always would be.

She called, "Good-bye," to the ocean but was unable to hear her own voice. Then she took the long train ride back to Manhattan.

Monday the apartment was blissfully empty, the other two occupants back at their respective jobs — or whatever it was that they did all day. It was four days since she had seen Mac at the Waldorf and she knew she could not put off talking to him much longer.

She went out, feeling physically better than she had in a week. She walked south on Broadway, into the Nineties, then the Eighties, finally arriving at a triangle of space formed by the intersection of Broadway and Amsterdam Avenue, that crazy Broadway that started in the northwest of the island and went down to the southeast. The triangle was called Needle Park by the locals. Sally had warned her about it. Drugs and unsavory characters. It looked quite innocuous from across the street.

She darted into a bank—a place she still considered a haven of safety—counted out some change, and put it in her mitten. Then she crossed the street to the infamous park.

A young black boy in his teens, wearing a sheepskin jacket, watched her approach. She met his eyes and saw him move toward her.

"Wanna buy some smoke?" he asked.

"One."

He looked at her, the familiar sizing up.

"I have ninety cents," she informed him.

"Hey, lady, a dollar apiece."

"Ninety cents."

"That's my whole profit," he whined.

"Ninety cents," she said firmly.

He uttered an obscenity, then another. She pulled the mitten off and showed him the change. For a minute he looked as though he were about to spit at her, but he flung some more invective and made the swap, tossing the joint so that she had to move to catch it.

She put it in her pocket and walked north, warmed

by her triumph.

The apartment was still empty. She hung her coat in the hall closet, locked the door, found matches, and sat in the living room on a sofa that had seen better days a long time ago. From here the George Washington Bridge was clearly visible as well as snow-covered roofs, chimneys, a section of the Hudson River.

She lit the joint and leaned back to savor the experience, remembering her first in Bryant Park and her second in the loft. Mostly she remembered the one with Mac, the strong sexual desire that had accompanied the smoke, the moving patterns, the exquisite sense of safety, knowing Mac was beside her. Out the window snow lay immobile on roofs, the bridge did not sway visibly, and on the floor the faded, thinning Oriental-style rug lay stationary in its decline. She felt nothing apart from the heat of the smoke. She sucked twice at the joint, waiting for the dope to take hold, to give her the expected high. Nothing happened. It had all been Mac, the highs and the lows, the good times and the better times, the ocean and the flowers and the fragrant muffins at breakfast, the tastes, the smells, the tokens on the table given with affection and tenderness, the deep, searing feelings that usurped her body and exploded in pleasure. It had all been Mac.

She pressed the lighted end of what was left of the joint in a glass ashtray, opened the window to air out the room, and emptied the ashtray in the toilet. Then she left the apartment to get something for lunch.

* * *

She called Naomi and they met for lunch the next day at a restaurant on the East Side.

"It happened," Frankie said. "Just the way you predicted it."

"Shit."

"Yes."

"What are you going to do?"

"I keep telling myself I have to think but I can't think."

"Maybe it's too soon."

"Maybe it's too late."

"No," Naomi said firmly. "That doesn't sound like our Frankie. How would it be—I'm just throwing this out so don't react too strongly—how would it be if you went back and gave it another try? Since he's asked you to."

"And wait for Jeannie to wrench her back again. Or worse."

"You love him, Frankie. Is it a waste of time to live with a man you love?"

"I wasn't thinking of time."

"He can't go back to that woman."

"He already has."

"A quirk," Naomi said quickly. "A misjudgment. An accident. Frankie, I believe in that relationship."

"Thank you. Believe it or not, it helps."

"Listen, I know I'm being very selfish but I don't want you to leave New York. We hardly know each other but you've made a difference. In my life."

"Well." She swallowed, not looking at Naomi. "Then the trip's been worth it, hasn't it?"

* * *

She was back at the apartment a little after two, the lunch having been curtailed by the demands of Naomi's bank. When, sometime around three, the doorbell rang, it startled her. No one came during the day. With a certain apprehension, she opened the peephole and saw Mac.

He was standing directly in front of the door holding several white business envelopes spread like a hand of cards. He dropped his hand after she had opened the door and seen them and said, "Hi."

She said, "Come in," a voice that was less than steady and watched him enter. She could not describe her feelings, could not even identify them, but seeing him was the best and most disturbing thing that had happened to her since she had left the Waldorf.

"Naomi told me where you were," he said. "Looks like you made it." He handed her the envelopes.

She felt confused and looked from him to them and back to him.

"It's April," he said. "Did you forget?"

"Oh my God!" April. "Oh, Mac. Yes, I did forget." She took the envelopes and felt them, three thick and one thin, a healthy choice. "Oh, Mac," she said again. "It's *April*." Her heart suddenly pounding.

"You didn't apply to NYU."

"No."

He unbuttoned his coat. "Can I stay awhile?"

"Oh yes, here, let me—"

"It's OK." He walked into the living room and tossed it on a chair. "I thought you were going to apply to NYU so we could spend the next four years together."

"It was too soon in January."

"And now it's too late."

"Now everything's changed."

"Has it?"

"I think it has."

He had a copy of the *Times* folded long and narrow. "See the *Times* today?" he asked.

"Not yet. Sally brings it home later."

"You can read this one." He sat on the sofa. He was holding a brown paper bag in his hand. "This is for you."

It was soft. She pulled out a T-shirt, opened it and saw the lettering on the front, PUSSY POSSE. She smiled and held it to her. "Those men on New Year's."

"All you need is the badge."

She held it lovingly and took a chair near the windows. "How's the book?"

"There is no book."

She looked at him with shock. "What do you mean?"

"I mean if I tell the whole story, and it's not worth doing if the story is incomplete, Tommy McManus will lose his job and maybe get into much worse trouble. He identified a body he had never seen before. He did it as a favor to a friend but that doesn't count for much in court. I want to get that bastard Bauer up in the Thirtieth, and Gallagher too if I can, but I want to keep Tom out of trouble if that's at all possible."

"Thank you, Mac."

He looked down at his hands. "You asked me once if I was the kind of reporter who would take notes

389

while someone was hurting. Well I can't. I wanted this book. I wanted it as much as I've wanted anything in a long time. I just can't do that to Tom. It may all come out sometime, maybe in court, but it won't come from me. When that happens, I'll think about publishing."

"Have they—did they exhume the body yet?"

"Late last week. They did the autopsy yesterday. The fingerprints match Charlie's. He was strangled. Probably in that unmarked car that picked him up outside the *Post*. I've turned over everything I have on Captain Bauer to the district attorney. It's only a matter of time now before they charge Bauer with a number of crimes—murder included. He was running the chicken-hawk business around Times Square. That's what Charlie found out just before they killed him. I guess there're people who've known for a long time Bauer was a homosexual but no one suspected he was involved in anything like this. McManus didn't. They just happened to be old friends. I saw Ariana this morning. I gave her the two hundred it cost to have the body exhumed. They're your hundreds, by the way. I changed them for you in January and stuck them in the back of my wallet. I thought it might please you to know."

"It does. I just wish it hadn't turned out that way."

"I wish a lot of things. I wish you hadn't left that watch on the desk."

"It's your dad's, Mac. I couldn't take something that was part of your family."

"I want you back, Frankie." His voice was low. There was a quality to it she had not heard before. "I know I've been a disappointment to you."

"You haven't. You've never disappointed me. You've been more than anyone else I've ever known."

"I shouldn't have gone to Jeannie."

"You did what you thought was right."

"Come home with me and let's see what we can do right together."

"I can't."

"I thought we loved each other."

The sentence hung in the air, the echo of a declaration he had never made.

"We do," she said, her own voice failing her.

"Then what else do we need?"

To Mac, whom I will love forever. Jeannie.

She could still hear the ring of his last statement. "I need to think about some things. There are things I haven't told you." She looked around the room. "I lied to you once."

"I know and it isn't important."

"You don't know and it is important."

"It's about the pills," he said. "I know about the pills and it doesn't matter."

The little plastic vial rolled across the floor and Susannah running after it. Something tightened in her chest. "How do you know?" she asked, her voice in a half-whisper.

"I called your local newspaper in Ohio and checked on the date of your parents' accident. Your mother had the prescription filled a few days before she died. It must have been nearly full when you took it out of the bathroom. I figured you put it away in case . . . someone needed them."

She nodded, scarcely able to speak. "I put them away so they wouldn't be there if anyone looked.

Then, a long time afterward, Kenny asked me if I had them. I said I did. I knew he must be thinking about . . . what was coming. We would talk about it sometimes as though it were a classroom discussion. What if a person felt a certain way or what if a person did a certain thing. Then one day he said he was thinking about taking them. He was afraid the doctor would put him in the hospital and I wouldn't be with him when he . . . when he died."

"You don't have to tell me."

"Yes, I do. I have to tell someone and there's only you now." This time she had a tissue in her pocket and she used it on her face. "I knew he was thinking about it. I knew if he asked me I had to give them to him. He was in pain and his life was—it was almost over. There wasn't much left to it. One night he asked me for the pills. I gave them to him. That was it. I sat next to his bed and held his hand while he fell asleep."

She saw a shudder go through Mac's body. He stood but he didn't go anywhere. "What you did was right," he said.

Frankie smiled. "Oh I know that."

"Show me your room."

She stood and walked by him. They had not touched, not kissed since his arrival, but something else had happened, something that had not happened in the three months they had lived together. She opened the door of the little bedroom between the living room and the kitchen and walked in. When he was inside, she closed the door.

"It's kind of small."

"I like it."

"Nothing else available?"

"One of the big rooms at the other end but it's next door to Sally's and she's living with her boyfriend now. They're at it all the time and I'd rather put some distance between us to dull the sound."

"The New York singles scene," Mac said.

Frankie put the shirt and the four envelopes on the dresser top. There would be time tonight to look them over, to think about which she would take.

"That your family?"

"Yes." She stood aside so he could look at them.

"Why didn't you take them out in our place?"

"There wasn't any room. I didn't want to put them on the floor."

"I would have made room."

"It didn't matter, Mac. I had them."

"This you with all the hair?"

"That's me."

"You look like a nice kid."

"I was."

"Your father was tall."

"Lanky. Look at those jeans. Everything he had was too big on him."

He stood looking another minute, then went to the window. "Kind of cramped," he said.

"It's what I needed."

"Four walls and a door."

"Yes."

"I talked to a carpenter. About enclosing the bedroom."

"Don't do it for me, Mac. I know how much you want your light."

"I'll still have it in the study." He looked out the

window. It had turned suddenly warmer and snow was melting everywhere. "I don't like this place."

"Last time you were here you said it reminded you of when you were very happy."

"I said that?"

"You did."

"I remember being very happy in January, February, and March of this year. I thought you were too."

"I was."

"Don't you think we could do it again?"

"I don't know." But she did know. Funny how the room came to life once Mac was in it. *Is it a waste of time to live with a man you love?* Is it a waste of time to live without him?

"Frankie." He was still at the window, standing, looking out of place in this narrow, high-ceilinged room with its furniture salvaged from a lost generation. "I want to talk to you about Jeannie and me."

"No." She was next to the dresser, near the comfort of her family.

"I have to talk to you about my marriage," he said.

"I don't want to hear. Jeannie is your wife. She's part of your life, not mine. Whatever goes on — or went on — between you is yours. I don't want to know about it."

"Don't you think you should know?"

"I know too much already." He moved uncomfortably. "What are you doing now? I mean, without the book."

"It's April. I'm back at work. At the *Times*."

"April. I really missed the new month."

"Your head better?"

"Much."

"Your check came today." He pulled an envelope out of a pocket, something else she had forgotten along with the agency when she left the loft.

"Want me to cash it?"

"That would be very nice." She got a pen and signed her name on the back. He took out his wallet and counted out the bills, reached into his pocket and found the coins. "Thank you." She put it all on the dresser.

"Will you let me take you out somewhere?"

"Not today."

"But I can call you."

She nodded.

He opened the bedroom door and got his coat from the living room. He put it on without buttoning it and stood near the door.

"I gave Susannah your number here," he said. "She said she might want to talk to you."

"Fine."

"She said—she told me she said something to hurt you when you brought the kids home two weeks ago. She said she's sorry."

Look at the nice gold chain Daddy gave her.

"It didn't hurt. How's your wife?"

"Jeannie's a little better. Her mother came on Sunday."

"That should help."

"You will let me see you."

"In a few days."

He looked undecided, as though maybe he wanted to touch her but he wasn't sure. Finally he said, "So long," and walked out.

Something like a sob shook her body. *I thought we*

loved each other. Mac, if I could only tell you how much.

She went to the living room to find the paper he had brought. It was on the sofa, folded the way the men on the subway folded them, so that you turned and twisted the paper, folding and unfolding it, as you read from column to column.

She looked at the heavy print on the visible surface. It was a piece by Henry J. MacIver. She untangled the paper so that she could see it all clearly.

"I have been accused of writing without passion," she read, and her eyes filled. "My friend and fellow journalist Charles Herron, who was murdered nearly two years ago, is soon to be laid to rest in a manner befitting a decent man. He deserves a eulogy and it is hard to write a eulogy for a friend without passion."

She read it through tears. There was nothing she didn't know in the article, except the message. The message was that it was dedicated to her.

Two

She spent the next morning writing a letter to Mac. For all the time it took, it should have been long but it wasn't. In the end there was very little to say, just that she loved him and hoped that someday they would see each other again, that the trip to New York had been more than she had hoped, that she was fine now and looked forward to being home again.

The last wasn't entirely untrue but there was more truth in the rest of the letter. She sent her best to Susannah and Eric, told him she loved him, realized she had said it before but let it stand. There was more truth in that than anything else she had ever said in her life.

She wrote a quick second letter to Naomi at her new address on Roosevelt Island. Then she called Trailways and asked about buses to Columbus. There was one at night that she could make easily. It arrived before noon the next day and she could hang around the bus station till someone was able to drive in and get her. Much better than arriving at night.

On the way to the bus station she would mail the letters.

The phone rang at ten and she answered it.

"Is this Miss Grant?" It was a man.

"Yes, it is."

"This is Jonathan Hecker of Hecker Associates. I talked to your . . . friend and he gave me this number. I can't forgive myself for what happened to you last week."

"It wasn't your fault, Mr. Hecker. I walked where I shouldn't have."

"No. I should've gone downstairs and put you in a cab. This is a tough town. How are you feeling?"

"Much better, thank you."

"I hope this . . . this whole thing hasn't broken up your romance."

"No, it hasn't."

"He sounded very sympathetic, the little I've talked to him."

"He is."

"What I wanted to say . . . I really appreciated your being there last Monday. The girl whose place you took is out more than she's in and it looks like she's probably going to be out for good pretty soon. There's always a place for a smart young person in our company. A smart old person for that matter. We don't discriminate." He chuckled. "If I did, I'd have to get rid of myself first. And there's nowhere to go but up. We teach, you learn, you can go out and help with the seminars."

"That's really very nice of you. I'm only a high school graduate, you know."

"Who cares?"

"I was planning to start college in the fall."

"That's six months from now. You give it some thought. Call anytime and ask for me."

"Thank you."

"And don't let this awful business ruin your love life."

"I won't."

She looked him up in the phone book and took down the address. When she was back in Ohio she would write and thank him, let him know she appreciated the offer and say she considered herself solely responsible for the incident.

After lunch she packed. There was no use staying around anymore. Mac would never divorce Jeannie and seeing him again would not ease the pain. Only distance would do that, if anything could.

She put the photographs away last and closed the little suitcase. There was still something of hers in the refrigerator so she thought she would have dinner here and then take a taxi down to the bus station. She would have plenty of time. She lay down on her narrow bed, hoping to make up for the sleep she was likely to miss on the bus. She had just fallen asleep when the phone rang.

The clock in the kitchen said three when she picked up the phone.

"Hello?" Hearing the grogginess in her voice and hoping it wasn't Mac because she couldn't see him again.

"Is this Frankie?"

"Yes." It was a young voice but she couldn't place it.

"Hi. This is Eric."

"Eric." The grogginess gave way to pleasure. "Hi, how are you?"

"OK. Dave gave Susannah your number but it took me all week to get it from her. I had to bribe her."

Frankie laughed. "You must be a brother and sister."

"Yeah. Uh—could I talk to you?"

"Sure, Eric."

"I mean over here. I'm at this place on the East Side where I come sometimes after school."

"I'll take a taxi."

"Gee thanks." He gave her the address.

"I'll be there in twenty minutes."

"How about hot fudge?" she said. They were at a table for two and the place was half empty, not the teenage hangout she had feared.

"Yeah sure."

"Two," she said to the waitress. "Big ones."

"You got it," the waitress said with a smile.

"Gosh I love hot fudge," Frankie said to Eric.

"Me too."

"And it's good to see you. Your dad told you about Charlie Herron, didn't he?"

"Yeah. Last week, before it got in the papers. He also said you got hurt."

"I was dumb. I acted like a hick and walked where I shouldn't've. I'm fine now. I just look over my shoulder more than I used to."

"I wanted to ask you something."

"OK."

He fiddled with the spoon, then put it down. "Are

you going to marry my father?"

"No, I'm not, Eric."

Her response brought a flush to his face. "I thought you were," he said.

"No. I really care about him—you must know that. But I don't think he's ready to marry anyone right now."

"Is he coming home?"

"I can't tell you that. I don't know."

The sundaes came and he looked at his for a while before he started to eat it. "Back in January I thought he would," he said after a few bites. "When we came back from our Christmas vacation with Mom, Dad took us out and when he brought us back, he stayed with her. They went in the bedroom together and they stayed a long time."

She remembered the night, the first weekend she had been in the loft, when she was sleeping on the air mattress and not calling him by his first name. She had known when he came back that he had slept with his wife.

"I thought he'd come back then," Eric said. "Now I don't think he will."

"Why?" Frankie eyed him across the little table.

Eric shrugged. "They never really wanted to get married," he said.

"I think they did. I think there was a lot of love there when they got married."

Eric shook his head in an absent kind of way. His ice cream had started dripping over one edge of the glass sundae dish and he scooped it up and licked the spoon off. "They only married because of me."

"Because of you." She said it quietly.

"My mother was"—he shrugged again—"you know, pregnant when they got married. It's the only reason they ever got married."

"It's not the only reason, Eric." She put her spoon down and patted her mouth with the napkin. "Are you sure about your mother?"

"I saw some papers once. They don't know. I was in their room. I was looking for something else."

Dear Mac, Yes. Love, Jeannie.

She had thought it was a response to a proposal but it might have been an answer to a question: Do you? Would you?

"They were in love with each other," she said.

"Yeah, I guess. But Dad had a job somewhere, in Europe, I think, and he gave it up because Mom couldn't go with him."

Katie Black in the pink ladies' lounge telling her that Jeannie could always get pregnant exactly when she wanted to.

"If he'd wanted to go, Eric, he would have found a way."

"You don't know my dad."

It was a beautiful answer. She smiled, not because she didn't know Mac, but because Eric did.

"When my parents died," she said, "I had to do a lot of poking around for papers for the lawyer. I found the same thing you did, that they'd only been married a few months when I was born."

"Really?"

"Yes. I told your dad that when I met him in January and he asked me how I felt about it. I told him the truth. I was disappointed that they'd never told me but it made me feel very special. I was their

402

love child. I was the one that came along just because they loved each other, not because they sat down and figured out, gee, wouldn't it be nice to have a baby next year."

There was a sort of a smile on Eric's face. He saw her looking at him and went back to his sundae.

"It's something that only happens to people once. It'll never happen to me; I'm much too practical. But my parents were the kind of people that just went on, having a nice life and taking everything as it came. They would have married anyway. So would yours."

"How did they die?"

"In a car accident."

"Oh. What did your father do?"

"He was a history teacher and basketball coach."

Eric grinned. "That sounds crazy."

"Well you're a New Yorker. Lots of things sound crazy to New Yorkers. Back home a lot of teachers do two things. He was very good at both. He was tall and skinny and he never worked at being athletic but he was. And he thought American history was the greatest thing in the world. He could read it night and day."

"And you had a brother."

"Yes, I had a brother."

"Not a . . . love child."

"No. That was just me. Kenny came about four years later. He was a great kid, lots smarter than I was, and he liked to run."

"Did he compete?"

"I think he would've if he'd lived. He only had seventeen years and he was sick at the end. He wasn't a great runner, he was just pretty good, but he really tried. My dad used to coach him."

"Where'd he run?"

"Oh, back of the house we had a path. Dad would clock him with an old stopwatch. And then a few years ago he had his great moment in a football game."

"Carrying the ball?"

"Uh-huh. He was only second string but we were losing so bad the coach put him in in the last quarter. Dad went down to the field and stood on the sidelines. The other team kicked and Kenny caught it on about the thirty-yard line and he started to go. And there was my dad running right beside him across the boundary line. My mom and I were up in the stands, screaming our heads off, and we could hear Dad shouting, 'Come on, Kenny. You can do it. Come on, Kenny.' " She stopped. Eric was watching her, expectant. "They just went down that field, the two of them — everybody was screaming — and when they got to the end zone, they hugged each other." She cleared her throat. "I get hoarse just telling the story."

"It's a great story."

"Yes. That's the way he was, my dad."

"I thought you were telling about your brother."

She drank half the water in her glass. "I was. It was all Kenny's story."

They both ate quietly for a few minutes, finishing their ice cream at about the same time. There was a reservoir of hot fudge in the bottom. Nothing had ever tasted quite so good to Frankie. She saw Eric licking his lips. He had a small line of fudge on them. When she used her napkin, he took his off the table and wiped it inelegantly across his lips.

404

"I don't feel that way about my sister," he said. "She's really a pain."

"I know." Frankie laughed. "I don't mean I know she's a pain. I mean I know how you feel. You won't feel that way forever. I only had seventeen years with my brother. I couldn't waste any of it. It really wasn't the best way to learn to get along with someone. There were times I just wanted to punch him."

Eric grinned. He had Mac's way of smiling, she could see now. The eyes were his mother's but the rest of his face was Mac's.

"But I didn't," she went on. "I used a lot of self-control."

"Maybe you got it from being a love child." There was a twinkle in his eyes.

"I told you it was very special."

"You know what time it is?"

"No. I don't have a watch anymore."

"I better get home. Will we see you on Saturday?"

"No, I don't think so, Eric."

"You're not going out with Dad anymore?"

"No, I'm not. I'm going home."

"You are? When?"

"Maybe tonight. Maybe tomorrow night."

"Will you come back?"

"I don't know. I don't think so. But I'm real glad we got to talk." She looked at the bill the waitress had left facedown on the table. In New York two sundaes cost as much as dinner at Harvey's back home. It would take some getting used to, the lower prices. Of course, no one would pay her what she had been earning using a word processor.

They stood and put their coats on. At the next

table an old woman had just sat down and was looking at the dinner menu. It must be early for dinner, Frankie thought, but if the woman ate early, she would get home before dark, a lesson she had probably learned a long time ago.

"That was a great story," Eric said when they were outside. "About your brother's touchdown."

She nodded.

"You know my father isn't publishing the book."

"He told me."

"My mom's mad."

"We're all disappointed. It's because your dad is so decent that he isn't publishing it."

"Well, I better get going."

She put a hand on his arm. She wanted desperately to kiss him but she knew better. "Good-bye, Eric."

" 'Bye. Thanks for coming."

"Thanks for asking."

He turned and started down the avenue. She watched him for a minute, then went to the curb. A cab was coming toward her, its light on. She hailed it, heard the screech of brakes as it slowed, watched it cross several lanes of traffic and stop in front of her. Shaking her head she got in and gave the driver Sally's address.

Three

The bus left from the lower level. Even after cooking a meal and cleaning up the dishes she had plenty of time. She had gotten a cab on West End Avenue, saving her the difficult walk over to Broadway with two suitcases. She had showered before leaving and put on clean jeans and a shirt and a warm sweater in case the bus was not well-heated. On the way into the terminal, she had bought some magazines and a copy of tomorrow's *Times*. She wondered if Mac would have something in it. He had not told her his schedule—if he had one. The last article, the eulogy to Charlie Herron, was pressed carefully at the bottom of her suitcase. She wondered if she would ever know anyone—the way she knew Naomi—well enough to say, I lived with him for three months. We loved each other but it didn't work out because he had a wife.

A handful of people had gathered beside the bus to Columbus. The storage compartments were open and a man in uniform was taking some heavy suitcases from a woman with a little boy and stowing them.

Frankie watched with detachment. They were an ambiguous group, people going home, people going away from home, no easy way to tell them apart. She thought of herself as one of the homeward-bound but she wasn't quite sure. When Mac was there, the loft had been as much of a home as the little house she was now returning to.

The couple ahead of her pushed their suitcases toward the storage compartment, scraping them on the concrete surface. She lifted her own two and moved three small steps forward. She was in no hurry. She would check her luggage when the time came, board, read, sleep, wake, see Columbus. It would all happen and New York would be a memory. On the ride down, she had asked the cabbie to slow at Sixty-fourth Street so that she could see the little Statue of Liberty and he had. He had won a bet once, he had told her, from someone who thought he was nuts to imagine there was a statue on that block.

Someone bumped her from behind and she turned to look. It was a woman with a sleeping baby. "Go ahead," she said, standing aside. "I'm not in a hurry."

The woman thanked her and moved ahead. The line moved. Frankie inched forward.

"Frankie!"

She turned and saw him, the man of all her dreams, the last person she wanted to see tonight.

"Where the hell are you going?" He was dressed in business clothes, his topcoat unbuttoned, and he smelled faintly of alcohol.

"Ohio," she said. She could not bring herself to say

408

home. "How did you know?"

"Eric left a message on the tape."

"Eric. *Eric*."

"He said he'd seen you this afternoon."

"I saw him, yes."

"Will you tell me what this is all about?"

"I'm leaving New York."

"You mean you're leaving me."

"Yes. I'm leaving you."

"Frankie—"

"Listen to me, Mac." She moved away from the line so that others could check their bags, so that their conversation might be a little more private. "You know that I love you. I didn't really know it until you came to see me the other day. But I know it now. There won't ever be anything like this for me again. It just didn't work out." She felt tears on her cheeks and was embarrassed. People always cried in bus stations but after all she'd lived through, she thought she carried some immunity.

"What makes you think it didn't work out?" His voice had that quality again, that uncertainty.

"You're married, Mac." She said it reluctantly. She had told Naomi she would not say it and now she had.

He reached inside his jacket and pulled out a thick envelope, carelessly torn open. She took it and looked at the return address. There were several names in heavy print, one of them Harrison. Harrison meant something but she couldn't think what. She pulled the many-paged document out and unfolded it. It was dated March 26. It was a separation agreement. Her lips were trembling. She looked up at him without saying anything.

"I saw the lawyer the day we were supposed to meet at the Waldorf. That's what the celebration was all about."

"Harrison," she said. "That woman who kept calling to change the appointment."

"That's his secretary. I told Jeannie I was doing it and she asked if we could meet. That was the day you saw us in the park. She wanted us to give it another try. I said no."

She pulled a tissue out of her bag and wiped her face so she wouldn't look like all those hicks who cried in bus stations.

"I tried to tell you the other day," Mac said. "But you wouldn't let me. You said you didn't want to hear."

"I thought you wanted to talk to me about . . . other things."

"I do." He touched the side of her face, brushing her hair back. "At home. I think Jeannie knew it was all over last Wednesday night when I made thirty-seven calls trying to find you."

"Thirty-seven. Did you actually count?"

"Jeannie did." He took the agreement from her, folded it back into its envelope, and stashed it inside his jacket. "These things take a couple of years. I don't know what your staying power is."

"Fair to moderate." She smiled.

"Sounds like a weather forecast."

"I thought Eric wanted me far away."

"He may but he's a very fair kid. I told them last Saturday that Jeannie and I had separated."

"He never said a word."

"That guy Hecker called to offer you a job. Sounds like a decent sort. And the *Times* let me know they're considering a transfer for me."

"To where?"

"Can't say. Maybe Europe."

"But you love New York, Mac."

"I love a lot of places. Think you could stand a couple of years in a foreign country?"

"Try me."

He picked up the larger suitcase.

"Let me take the other one," she said. "So we can walk closer."

He kissed her and put his free arm around her. "The bed came today," he said.

"The bed. I forgot about the bed."

"How could you forget the most important thing in the apartment?"

"Can I put my pictures out somewhere?"

"Right next to where you sleep."

"That's nice."

"And I think it's time you had a watch that's all yours, not mine or your brother's."

"Long as it tells time." They went up to the main level. "Where are you parked?"

"In a place where it says no anything ever."

"That sounds like you. I went out to the ocean, Mac. All by myself last Sunday. It wasn't the same. I even smoked pot and couldn't get high. I think you were the high."

He put the suitcase down and kissed her. Through the roar of the crowd she could hear Dad shouting, *Come on, Kenny. You can do it.*

Mac looked at his watch. He was wearing his

411

father's watch again. "I think you just missed your bus."

"Fine with me, pal. Can you take me home?"